I0561918

The Calling Buds Remix

The Calling Buds Remix

B. COYNE DAVIES

IGUANA

Copyright @ 2021 B. Coyne Davies
Published by Iguana Books
720 Bathurst Street, Suite 303
Toronto, ON M5S 2R4

All rights reserved. No part of this publication may be reproduced, stored in a retrieval system or transmitted, in any form or by any means, electronic, mechanical, recording or otherwise (except brief passages for purposes of review) without the prior permission of the author.

The Calling Buds Remix is a work of fiction. Names, places, events, occurrences and incidents are either products of the author's imagination and/or used in a fictitious manner. Any resemblances to actual persons, living or dead, or to actual events is strictly coincidental.

Publisher: Meghan Behse
Editor: Paula Chiarcos
Front cover design: TinyFleaArt

ISBN 978-1-77180-486-8 (paperback)
ISBN 978-1-77180-487-5 (ebook)

This is an original print edition of *The Calling Buds Remix*.

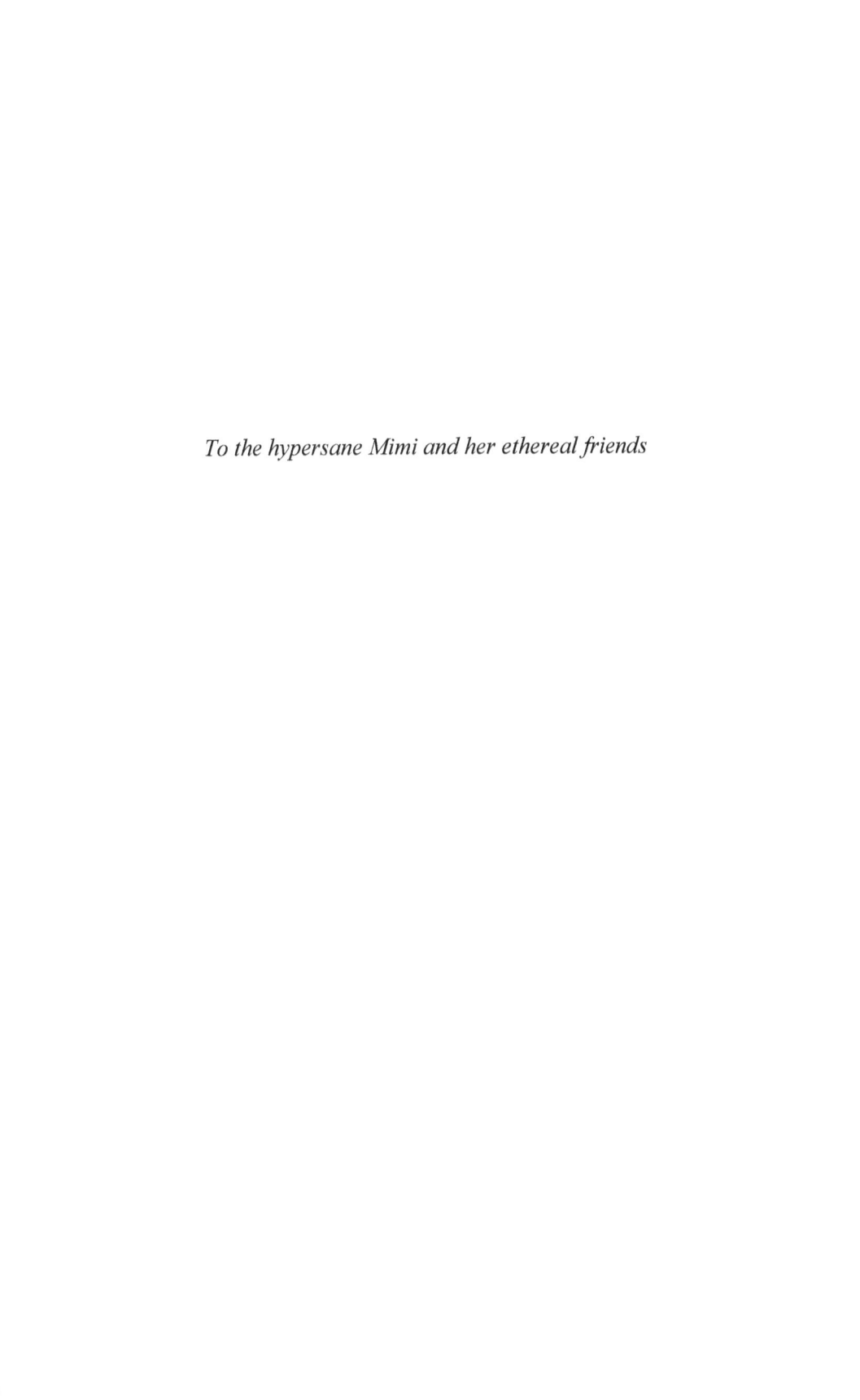

To the hypersane Mimi and her ethereal friends

Author's Note

So many people can be involved in a legal medical marijuana start-up that sometimes the most interesting characters might pass unnoticed. So it was with *The Buds Are Calling*. This book is not a sequel, though it does take the story a little further and it begins as the cultivation facility becomes operational. As the title suggests, it's a remix, perhaps a more humble perspective on the commercial endeavors of the state-sanctioned marijuana industry. But more than anything, it's about one young man's experience, and yes, there is music here too.

~ B. Coyne Davies

PART ONE

Pieces

You thought this speck was the war in your eye. You thought you saw reluctance, the balk at forever, the prime of resistance. Some righteous poisoned splinter advanced itself, pierced deep, behind the sweat on your brow. But it's always something out there. Something unbidden. The night of calamity that took all your pacing, that rifled the landscapes and ransacked your smile. You forgot the sound of blood in your veins, the bell that is your breath and now a touch only rings in the silence. You whisper you've lost. Your heart's in a thousand pieces. You are lost. Whispering ceaselessly.

from Cannto IV, *Cannabidadas*

Chapter 1

Ray considered the slope of the field. They couldn't have grown much here. Too steep. Must have been just pasture or used for hay crops. There were a few poplars and wild plum trees at the bottom of the hill. A creek meandered by, just past the trees, but this time of year it was quick and deep, more like a river. Rocks along the creek bed created eddies and ripples on the surface. In summer, the water level would likely drop by half, leaving the rocks visible and useful for heron on the hunt for frogs. The next field over, the creek widened out into a swath of bulrushes and then gathered and headed to the main river basin through the neighboring valleys. Ray saw about a half dozen red-winged blackbirds descend into the bulrushes, and a warbling chorus quickly ensued. Must be plenty of bugs. Early midges probably.

"I like this view," Ray said.

"Yup. Sure. You could build right here." The real estate agent looked back over his shoulder. "You know there must be an old well somewhere. Over there, closer to the barn I bet."

The two men climbed over the rubble that had been a stone fence and wandered along the crest of the hill toward the battered gray buildings. "That's where the house was." The agent pointed out a slight mound. "Burned down about sixty years ago, I heard say. You can see that bit of the foundation still there, and that hollow over to the right likely shows the extent of the old basement. Probably just a dirt floor. Common enough around here."

"Huh," Ray murmured, and then thinking out loud more than trying to make conversation, he added, "If it wasn't, you know, not a dirt floor, but cement or something, I could use it for a root cellar. Maybe I could use it for a root cellar anyway."

"Yup," said the agent. "Yupper. You surely could, I bet."

A few seconds later they spotted a round concrete slab sticking up about half a foot from the ground. Another month or so and they likely wouldn't have seen it in all the grass. It was about four feet in diameter with a square cement plate set into the middle of it with rusty rings sticking up. The real estate agent crouched down and pulled on the rings. The plate didn't budge.

Ray gestured he'd give it a try, and the real estate agent stood back. He watched Ray grab the rings with both hands. Ray had only the first two fingers and a thumb on his right hand. The agent was curious but couldn't quite get up the nerve to ask what happened to the other fingers. Ray leaned back with the weight of his whole body then gave the plate a sudden yank straight up. The plate dislodged a little. Another yank and it was out. He dragged it over to the side.

The agent fumbled in his pocket and pulled out a small LED flashlight and shone it into the pit. "Well, how about that! Those fittings look almost new."

They were staring at a cluster of four valves with pipes going off in three directions. The valves still had the original red enamel. "Don't know about the pump, though."

He handed Ray the flashlight. About eight feet down and a foot or so below the valves was the pump. It was half submerged in soil. There was a crack and a big chip out of the pit wall. Sediment had piled up over the years.

Won't be much chance of anything working, Ray thought. "Least it's not all sitting in three feet of water. Must be a hole in the bottom of the pit." He moved the flashlight beam up the pit wall, following the metal pipe that would hold the wiring. The control box was only a foot or so below the cap he was squatting on. He could open it from the surface. He lay down flat and reached into the hole, pulled the cover open and grabbed the flashlight again. "Looks like the electrical stayed pretty dry anyway." He got to his feet. "Could still be a good water source there. Fix the cracks, re-grout the pit. New pump. Might still be okay."

"Yupper," the agent said. "Still might." As the agent dragged the cement plate back onto the well, he noticed Ray looking out at the view again. He got a sense this might finally be the place for Ray. Over the last month he'd shown him several properties around Hullbrooke. Most were just land, because Ray said he wanted to build. It was cheaper, he said, because he could do most of the work himself and he wouldn't have to deal with someone else's old building problems. The agent didn't totally agree with the reasoning but he didn't say anything. He just tried to show Ray a mix. He knew Ray, who couldn't have been more than thirty, didn't have a whole lot of money, and if you were looking for cheap land, properties with rundown buildings were often a better deal. At least around Hullbrooke.

The agent figured the more space he gave Ray the more luck he might have with a sale. "I got to be on my way," he said, "but you can stay. Keep the flashlight. Probably wouldn't hurt to have a good look at that barn and the drive shed."

"Good idea. Thanks." Ray held up the flashlight. "I'll give you a call tomorrow."

Ray watched the agent walk back to his car. The sun was low in the sky and the light would be gone within the hour. He headed down to the creek where frogs and all kinds of insects and birds were ratcheting up for the evening. These days he couldn't take a lot of noise. There was often an unbidden roaring in his head, and external sounds would exacerbate it, but this was more amusing than irritating. It was even a little mesmerizing. He stood for a while, closed his eyes and let the chirping and buzzing permeate his brain and the rest of him. All his other senses were obliterated. It was a well-practiced and familiar kind of surrender. He hadn't been able to do it for ages and it made him feel almost weightless. Just like the view from the hill had made him feel better, given him a sense of space he hadn't had since he was a child.

As the sun began to dip into the horizon Ray made his way back up to the barn. The old building was nestled right in the hill so a farmer could drive a tractor into the loft. It probably wouldn't support a tractor now. The barn must have been there for a century or more and the west corner of it had slumped. There were boards missing, so the loft was largely open to the air at the front. Depending on the state of rot in the beams, a person might just want to just tear the whole thing down. The metal on the gambrel roof still looked good though. Ray walked up and around the back to the loft level and found a rickety door that abutted the huge sliding door. The moving parts on the sliding door looked to be nothing but rust. He pulled open the rickety one and stepped inside.

Given all the missing boards from the exterior walls, the view was even better from the barn. But the advanced ventilation hadn't diminished the smell of old hay, mice, bats and bird shit. Pigeons and swallows had taken up residence undisturbed for countless generations. White residue from their droppings stained the rafters. Ray stood in the center section. It would have been used for threshing a century ago and the floor still felt solid. He took out his pocketknife, snapped open the blade and jabbed it into the beam in front of him. He was expecting the resistance of something like sponge taffy and was surprised when the wood held its own and he had to give a good tug to get the knife back out. He tried the same thing with the floorboards, and where he was standing was not bad at all.

Ray moved around the loft systematically, checking for rot. The vertical beams were good as far as he could reach. He did find rot in the floor though, especially in the corner where the slump was. He figured the rafters there were probably toast too.

He spotted the ladder to the lower level where the animals would have been kept. The daylight was completely gone now, and he held the lit flashlight between his teeth as he descended. When he got to the bottom, he shone the light all around. The outside walls of mortar and stone had to be almost three feet thick. And the lower level must have been built for shorter people. It looked like there had been a granary to his left, with a couple of sectioned-off areas to his right. One had pipes and tubing, a huge sink and a cracked and ancient rusted water heater. Next door were two more sectioned-off areas that looked to be empty — storage and maybe an office — and several small pens. In the few windows along the sides, all the glass was gone apart from one small pane, so dusty that it barely reflected the glow from the flashlight. Ahead and to either side were two rows of stanchions, metal and all rusted. The owners had been dairy farmers. Nothing big though, no more than thirty head of cattle. All in the days before free stalls and automated milking parlors. They'd have manually moved the hydra-like contraption from one cow to the next as the animals munched and stared at each other across the mangers.

Ray was picturing all this when he heard a *thwap* and a *buzz*. Something had smacked into his flashlight. He shone the light on the floor. A beetle — fat, dark brown and an inch or more long — staggered around between his feet. Ray didn't recognize the bug, and it was early in the season. It looked bigger and darker than a May bug. There'd be plenty of those around soon enough, stupid and bashing into porch lights everywhere.

He bent down and picked the bug up to get a closer look. It struggled to right itself in the palm of his hand. He noted the hairy tufts along the abdomen while the chunky segmented legs with their tarsal spurs flailed in groggy irritation. Ray nudged it over with the flashlight. "Holy shit!" he said. A shiny curved horn grew right out of the top of the beetle's head. He'd never seen a rhinoceros beetle before, at least not a live one and nothing like this since he was a kid. He stared at it while the bug sat passively, basking in the flashlight beam and the warmth of Ray's hand. Eventually Ray walked to one of the blown-out windows and gently gave his hand a shake. He felt the beetle drop immediately and thought he heard it buzz away.

He went back to the ladder and climbed up into the loft again, taking a last glance around. All in all, the barn would probably stand for several more years and give him lots of time to figure out how much work he'd want to put into it, if any.

On the way back to his truck, Ray took a quick look at the drive shed. He wandered right into the upper level because it was built into the hill, same as the barn. It looked to be a younger building but not by much. The couple of windows were still intact. At some point, half of the upper level had been divided into rooms with a ceiling, rather than being open to the rafters. Maybe that part had been used as extra sleeping quarters for farm help. Who knew? It was pretty crude. Old wallpaper was peeling off chipboard and in the few places where plasterboard had been used, it was stained and bowed out with water damage. Mostly everything was full of junk: wood scraps, wire, grimy barrels, dried-up paint cans and broken machinery, like an old lawn mower and chain saw. There were drooping shelves too, with metal boxes and tins full of rusty bolts, screws and nails. The lower level was completely open, facing out from the hill. It was easily wide enough for three modern vehicles. It had the same thick stone walls as the barn and tucked in at the back was more derelict equipment. An ancient manure spreader lay on its side with one wheel remaining, and next to that was a harrow with a rusted-out disc somehow lodged on top of it.

Ray thought about the property long into the night as he tossed in his bed at Gina and Jiggy's house. He wasn't a hundred percent sure. Then again, he wasn't sure about much these days. Not with his recurring backaches, the constant thudding pain in his arms, the roaring and crashing in his head that must be rearranging his brain. He needed to make a move though, and that land was pretty much the perfect distance from Hullbrooke. A half hour drive, maybe more in winter. It was far enough away from Gina and Jiggy too. He could get out of their day-to-day lives but be close enough to still help on the farm when needed. Gina and Jiggy kept telling him he could stay as long as he wanted. He knew they'd never say otherwise, even if they desperately wished him gone. He also knew that wasn't the case either, but he did think moving out sooner rather than later was the best idea, even if the rent was discounted. He'd been with them six months already.

The real estate agent didn't seem surprised when Ray called him back the next day and told him to make an offer on the place. "Yupper! Sure thing! It's been sitting there for a long time," the agent said. "We could come in pretty low and see what happens. Worth it if they bite. That way you'll have more left for building."

#

"You got a problem with me?" The electrician was glaring at Ray.

"I'm just sayin' I think that's backward."

"Oh and you're an expert and you got a piss load of time to just stand around and watch me. Guess I don't give you enough to do. Is that it?"

"No. I'm just saying it's an easy mistake and if it's backward well . . . you know . . . might not ground properly."

"What the fuck! You arrogant piece of shit!"

The electrician Ray was apprenticing with must have had something more than his usual quart and a half of beer with lunch. This time he was screwing up the simple outlet installation closest to the kitchen sink. Ray had been noticing the guy screwed up more and more. And the plans he'd shown Ray were usually cryptic and messy. Ray was beginning to wonder if it was the alcohol or just incompetence. A couple of times Ray had watched the guy nick wires or damage conductors and just proceed anyway. One time they'd had to spend several hours troubleshooting because an arc-fault circuit interrupter kept tripping and shutting down the power. All because of a nick!

"What's goin' on?" The contractor, Ray's actual boss who signed the paycheck, stood in the doorway.

"Oh, the big man here is tellin' me how to do my job."

"I just said the wires got mixed up. That's all."

"Did you mix the wires up?" The contractor was not oblivious to the electrician's drinking habits, and given the callbacks on a couple of jobs recently, he was not altogether surprised by Ray's observation.

"I don't have to take this shit," the electrician snarled.

Somewhat emboldened, Ray then said, "Maybe you could finish work first, then hit the bar and—"

"You fucker!" The electrician picked up a wrench that was lying handy beside him and raised it like he was going to throw it.

"Shut it down! Both a yas!" the contractor yelled.

Ray backed away with his hands up. "Meant no offense. Just trying to do my job."

The electrician lowered the wrench and kept staring at Ray. "Yeah well. You got a lot to learn. Like mindin' your own goddamn business."

"It is my business if there's a mistake."

"Who the fuck do you think you are? Soldier boy savin' the day again?"

"Down the road somebody finds the mess, you blame me. Right?"

"Fuck you!"

Ray stood at the doorway to the kitchen and suddenly it all made him furious. He looked up at the ceiling momentarily and then he glared at the electrician. "Assholes like you" — he held up his right hand with the missing fingers — "is just how this happened!"

Ray left and got into his truck. He thought he'd just sit there for a minute until the anger simmered down. Then he thought to hell with it. He started up the truck and drove about ten minutes to an old unused side road that he'd noticed the day before. He made his way very slowly, weaving around the potholes until he came to a battered, hand-painted sign a few hundred yards in: Lusteadt 3886 mi. It broke the spell. Ray stopped the truck and got out. He leaned against the vehicle for a while looking at the woods that bordered the road and he started to feel calmer. Some of the trees were starting to turn yellow, and a few plants, vines and creepers mostly ran little riots here and there with brilliant red. Good thing he'd discovered the countryside was an antidote to frustration. He looked at the sign again and pulled out his phone. He tried to Google *Lusteadt* but the signal was too weak. He put his phone back in his pocket.

Ray was surprised at the rage he'd felt toward the electrician. He hardly ever got angry, but when he did these days, it was a fierce, uncompromising sensation. He had to get out of there fast. He didn't want to be tempted to lob wrenches himself or something worse. Ray knew right then he couldn't work with the guy anymore. There was so much wrong he couldn't pinpoint any one thing. The guy was a drunk and a jerk. So what? Wouldn't be the first asshole Ray had dealt with in his life or the first one he'd had to answer to. Maybe it was the expectation, the assumption of respect the man was supposedly due from an apprentice that got up Ray's nose. He'd pretty much lost all respect for the guy after about the second week. The notion that Ray's progress could depend on that man's good opinion really rankled.

And Ray couldn't remember exactly when it occurred to him, but he liked doing a good job. The job didn't matter. There was a satisfaction that came from doing something well, even sweeping a goddamn floor. And this guy was definitely getting in the way of that.

Ray looked up at the sky. It was a sunny day and the clouds were speeding along quickly. He was breathing easier now but he still wasn't ready to go back to work. He'd just go back to the farm. It was only about a fifteen-minute drive. Gina and Jiggy had gone to the city for the day. It would be really quiet. He could take a walk. Maybe have a beer.

When Ray checked his phone again he saw his boss had tried calling him twice. When Ray called back the boss wanted to smooth things over. He'd already started looking around for another electrician. Meanwhile Ray could just work with the carpenters if he wanted. And he could take the rest of the day off too if he liked. When Ray hung up, he wondered at the wisdom of sticking around

Hullbrooke at all. Maybe he should just take off for good. Try his luck on the West Coast for a change. Forget about that property too.

Idyllic and desirable as that piece of land seemed to Ray at times, it was all beside the point. Nobody had been able to locate the current owner. He'd disappeared to some place halfway across the globe on a mining project. No one had heard from him in months. All sorts of people besides real estate agents were trying to get in touch with him.

"What happens if the guy never makes it back? Or dies?" Ray had asked.

"Well," the real estate agent said, "if he dies, I guess it depends on the will. If he's got one. If he doesn't come back, I don't know. Never had to deal with it before."

"Well then I guess I'd better be looking for another place."

"I don't know about that. I'd say it's worth sitting tight for a while. He might show up any day!"

So Ray waited. And waited. Soon it would be too late to start building anthing anyway. It was almost as if the mining firm the fellow worked for had lost interest in finding him. "Who knows what kind of corruption goes on in friggin' Gabon?" Jiggy had pointed out. "They might talk the socialist talk in passin', but a tale of twists an' turns always follows. People bein' people that is. You should brush off your French an' check it out, Little Cousin." Ray didn't speak French and he figured Jiggy had already checked it out in some way via the deep web or some library somewhere. Ray didn't want to be reminded of the world. All he wanted was a quiet little piece of property. And some space.

#

About a month later, after Ray had landed yet another apprenticeship that had him working not on the West Coast but in Lyston, a mere thirty miles from Hullbrooke, he got a call from his lawyer. Initially the man was just supposed to handle the purchase, but being a small-town lawyer, he had his ear to the ground. Rumors and allegations had been swirling about the property owner's family for years and the disappeared grandson was keeping up the tradition.

"They found your boy!" the lawyer said.

"That's great!" Ray said. "You know if he's seen the offer yet?"

"I doubt that. Regardless, I don't think he's in much shape to make any decisions about anything."

"Oh?"

"Turned up in some little Congolese hospital."

"I thought he was in Gabon."

"Yeah, that's where he went for the job. But Congo's right across the border."

"So he was sick all that time?"

"Nobody knows yet. Head injury maybe. Some black SUV dumped him off in the middle of the road outside this village. A missionary found him about two months ago. Yup. Orthodox! I didn't know anybody still had missions in the Congo."

"So the guy, he's all right?"

"Nope. Nope. He definitely is not. Doesn't even know his own name. Right out of it apparently. Like a zombie."

"Jesus! Is he going to get better?"

"Anybody's guess. But it doesn't look good."

"Huh."

"So just letting you know. The deal's probably going to be seen through by the girlfriend. She's got power of attorney. Lives in Manhattan. He set it all up before he left."

"Maybe he was psychic."

"Maybe. At least he's not dead. Take you another year to wait for everything to go through probate. By the end of that, no telling who might own it and what they'd do with it. Trouble most likely. Lord knows with that family," the lawyer said and paused. "They sure never had a reputation for making friends. Anyway, my money is on the girlfriend wanting to unload the land pretty fast. They might need the money for his care. I should hear something in the next few days and your agent is already on it too by the way."

"Sounds good," Ray said. "I mean . . . terrible for the guy. But I guess we can finally go ahead with the purchase."

Chapter 2

If there was one thing Jiggy knew about, it was ordnance, and explosives in particular. That, computers and IT generally. Nowadays, minus his foot and his unblinking loyalty, he'd rather forget about his history. If anybody asked or even if they didn't, he only ever mentioned he was in communications. That included Gina. Nobody apart from his former superior officers, and even they weren't always given the full story depending on where he'd been sent, ever knew he'd majored in big kabooms, with or without incendiaries. In a space of ten years he'd set up and monitored more devices to blow sky high than most career army men saw in a lifetime. And he'd never found a device or an account he couldn't hack so nobody who didn't need to know could ever figure out where the orders came from. And he'd done that sort of thing here, there and everywhere. The US has many interests globally, and he'd been a good soldier for the empire.

It had been a very strange day years before when Jiggy's sergeant had screamed at him to meet at fourteen hundred hours in the lieutenant colonel's office. Sergeant Graves, or "Rippy" as he was known among the unit because of his slight speech impediment, was more red-faced and agitated than usual as he barked out the order at lunch. Jiggy simply assumed he was in shit again for some smart-assed thing he'd done and tried to recall any recent incidents that might have gone unnoticed up to that point. He came up with nothing. In fact by his own estimation, he'd been low-key for six weeks, either angelic or comatose depending on how you looked at it.

Jiggy was often in trouble and it was usually for some minor insubordination, but that sort of thing hadn't ever led to a lieutenant colonel's office, let alone one he hadn't even heard of before. Perhaps the army was downsizing. Maybe Jiggy had pointed out flaws in the protocols just one too many times. Maybe this new CO was checking the records and cleaning house.

Jiggy was prone to obsessing when he couldn't figure out something right away and so finally, at five minutes to fourteen hundred hours, as he stood outside the CO's door, he concluded it must be about paperwork. He'd probably fucked up the numbers. There was a word for that. He just couldn't remember it. And maybe it cost big money. That thought made Jiggy smile. He could reasonably claim mild dyslexia and it would be legitimate, and he'd never have to fill out another purchase order again. He'd even suggest Specialist Jasper Smiles do it in future. If ever there was a guy to pick nits and bitch about details, it was Jasper. So Jiggy pulled himself up straight and knocked at the lieutenant colonel's door.

"Yup. Come in."

Jiggy saluted. "Private Stitz reporting s—"

"Sure, I know . . . sit . . . sit down . . ."

Jiggy looked around for a chair suitable for a lowly subordinate in the presence of a very superior CO.

"There, Stitz." The CO motioned to the big comfy leather armchair opposite him. In fact the chair looked more like a recliner than anything you'd see in a military office. Even the CO's chair was spartan by comparison. So Jiggy very cautiously sat down and did not lean back.

"Nice, isn't it?"

"Sir?" Jiggy responded somewhat breathlessly.

"The chair, Stitz. It's nice, isn't it?"

"Sir. Yes, sir. The chair's really nice, sir!" Jiggy barked back.

"Jesus. At ease, Stitz." Lieutenant Colonel Pinsky sighed and shook his head. He was an electrical engineer from MIT rather than West Point, known for his digital wizardry. He spoke six languages. And he'd probably forgotten more programming languages than most people learn. He'd moved up through the ranks quietly with one stroke of genius after another. Of course he'd never much taken to routine military formalities and he'd been on enough special ops where his input was vital, game-changing even, that he was rarely held accountable for the lesser things. Initially he rationalized joining up as the best alternative to taking over his uncle's basement when the tech sector took its first nosedive in the eighties. "Be all you can be" actually struck a chord with him at the time, though in retrospect, he wondered if it hadn't been because of the all the acid and weed. And now here he was sixteen years later, still a military man and still mostly sitting at a desk playing with computers, programs and the latest gizmos, and even playing with lives as it turned out. Lieutenant Colonel Pinsky didn't like to think about that last bit. He gratefully ingested all notions of duty to flag and country and moved along accordingly. And besides, a part of him years ago had rather enjoyed the special-ops training. It was kinda cool to be so special. Still, formalities were tiresome.

"Stitz, let's just talk here. No shit."

Jiggy started getting that itchy feeling. Maybe this was going to be something completely unpleasant given the army's normal rejoicing in shit. Like maybe if he wasn't already in the army reporting to this CO, he should get up and leave.

"The thing is, Stitz," the CO continued, "you're a smart guy."

Jiggy's face showed a degree of skepticism.

"It's true. And we really need smart guys like you. Smart young men I should say . . . and young women too," he apparently needed to add as an afterthought. "Know how we know you're so smart?"

Jiggy shook his head. Best to play stupid. It was clear now he'd have been better off never pointing out the flaws in the instrument manuals or sloppy rules and procedures over the past three years. And he'd have been way better off not flaunting he was learning Russian and Farsi in his spare time just to piss off Rippy Graves.

"This, Stitz. All this." And the CO picked up the big file sitting on the desk like he was weighing it. Must have been Jiggy's file, made thick by all the shit he'd gotten himself into since he'd finished basic training. "This," the CO continued, "would indicate to me that you are somewhat bored. Routinely bored in fact. A little like a zoo animal, maybe. And you know what they do in the best zoos, Stitz?"

"No, sir." Jiggy's voice dropped. A CO making reference to him and a zoo animal in the same breath was not promising.

"Well, Stitz, they keep the animals busy. Hide their food. Give them challenging tasks that they can truly invest in."

Jiggy stared straight ahead.

"It keeps the animals healthier, Stitz, in just about every respect. And we want to keep you healthy!"

And so with that Jiggy had been given another choice, just like when he was eighteen and the local sheriff told him he could either face serious mischief charges or cross the street and avail himself of the US Army recruiting office. Now he was being given the choice to apply for Special Forces. Somehow the paperwork was expedited and the whirlwind began two weeks later. The training was horrible, physically torturous, with stresses of every kind manufactured to take Jiggy past his breaking point to a state of exhaustion he'd never thought possible. But the CO or somebody propelled the process along. Jiggy made it through and then the army got really interesting for him. The CO had been right — he could be a happy zoo animal. Jiggy thought he'd make a career of it too just like the lieutenant colonel himself. But then that didn't work out quite so well. Shit happens. And a lot of shit happens in the military. Then again, shit happens everywhere and the nice thing about it is, eventually it rots and you can grow stuff in it.

Jiggy's career plans took a one-eighty after the totally fucked-up 2006 what-the-fuck-just-happened actually happened in Pakistan. The one nobody really wanted to talk about. The one where the madrassa got blown up along with sixty-nine kids and not the bad dude who was supposed to have the date with the drone. In fact the bad dude was nowhere around. The Pakistani military took the PR hit and told the villagers they were very, very sorry. Nice try but the drone was still American. And who showed the Pakistanis? Afterward they decided they'd hit a quasi-bad dude so it hadn't been all in vain. And maybe it was really just a school for little extremist jihadis. Gotta nip 'em in the bud. There's the spirit! Or maybe this was just the best thing since AK-47s to motivate thousands more jihadis to keep the War on Terror hale and hearty.

At the time, Jiggy's unit was getting downsized. Personnel with "special" skills were being shifted over to go play with the CIA full time because the drones were supposedly that much more efficient. It didn't really matter who sent the one off to school in Pakistan, Jiggy saw his future in the kids' body parts. And he wanted none of it. Jiggy knew he'd never have targeted a school during the day, not even at gunpoint. He'd have actually been to the building and known the schedule too. There was no way he'd be sitting at a computer for the rest of his life playing Oops, the videogame where every time you took out civilian bystanders you lost points but still advanced. He was pretty sure he'd end up with zero Joy, zero Pride, zero Confidence, and if he bought into the I'll Take Hell option, which everybody did, there'd be zero Accountability. But then the whole game would blow up, wouldn't it? Maybe not soon enough.

He was already close to the end of his game and figured he'd be too warped to live in a peaceful part of the world if he didn't get out soon. So Jiggy was getting out. He'd leave at fifteen years on the nose. To hell with a pension. He'd finish his tour, go back to North Carolina for another ten months and then he'd be done. He'd officially be a veteran. No one could ever say he hadn't done his duty. The last week on tour he was having second thoughts though. If he stayed for another five years he'd get a nice pension . . . or at least a pension. Pensions are good. Every little bit helps.

But then his foot got blown off. Some high-level UN diamond-between-cheeks NGO hoity-toit was setting up house in the sunny suburbs of Kabul. The private security firm attached to the guy was supposed to have cleared the new pretty pink building and the compound. But they never got around to it, like they never fuckin' do! So politics being politics, Jiggy's little unit had to pick up the slack. They were supposed to be having some R and R. Jesus! Poor Fred Kim, most cheerful guy in the goddamn War on Terror you'd ever meet. He was standing right beside Jiggy and he was the one to open the dumpster. And big fucking boom! There went Fred along with Jiggy's foot.

Jiggy saw it as a cosmic command. Possibly even a gift, if he could ever get that last image of Fred out of his mind. The minus-one-foot tax-free financial compensation was a pension of sorts. And Jiggy did not want to die. Not there in Afghanistan. Or anywhere the US wasn't very popular, which was taking up more and more terrestrial surface area. Losing his right foot put Jiggy's own mortality into urgent perspective. He wanted to go home and live with Gina, raise cattle and grow vegetables in the country.

So that's just what he did. After rehab and some very easy deskwork, followed by his official discharge, he and Gina bought seventy acres, ten miles outside of Hullbrooke. It was one state over from where they'd both gone to high school. Gina got a part-time job as a bookkeeper. They raised beef and grew vegetables in the summer.

Jiggy found he liked digging in the gardens and the smell of tomatoes as they grew. He also liked the feel of dirt between his remaining toes. And Jiggy kept a little greenhouse where he could grow his state-sanctioned quota of six medical marijuana plants — the main reason for the one-state-over location. Since losing his foot, he'd found smoking the old ganja was the only thing that would stop the pain in the nonexistent appendage and maybe give him a good night's sleep from time to time. The foot's ghost, that's all Jiggy could think it must be, was a mean one and routinely raised a ruckus. Occasionally it even made him nauseous. That and the recurring nightmares, a different breed of ghosts, would deprive him of sleep or make him avoid it altogether.

So the weed tamed the ghosts. And the farm tamed Jiggy.

#

Jiggy was now pushing forty, happy to still be alive and out in his little greenhouse harvesting the Borealis Raj. They weren't tall. Just bushy and flowered early, Jiggy thought — but he wasn't complaining. He and Harold, who'd given him the seeds, spent hours arguing the benefits of sativa cannabis when a person was up against nerve damage. Harold swore the terpenes had to be good and stinky for it to work properly so he liked the skunky stuff, and Jiggy was convinced the opposite was true and that it had to be another of the c's that made it all work: the CBD, CBG, CBN or whatever. At any rate both of them agreed it wasn't just the THC.

The Borealis Raj were supposedly Northern Lights hybrids crossed with some indica hybrid. Jiggy figured the parentage might provide a less offensive aroma and quite a varied cocktail of cannabinoids. It was the first time he'd grown them and he had three really good plants. If he harvested two completely and chopped off just a good chunk of the third, he could maybe get it to revegetate. By the time it re-established itself, he'd know if the harvested weed was any good for him. If it was, he could overwinter the plant in the house and take clones in the spring. Alternatively, under the stress of it all, the plant might start sprouting male parts if it was that way inclined, so maybe he'd get self-fertilized seeds. They just might grow true enough.

Jiggy wished he could grow more than six plants and really experiment. No one from the Department of Health had ever been around to check up on him after the first year, but Jiggy didn't want to push his luck. He loosely interpreted the rules already.

Gina came through the door with a couple of coffees and handed a mug to Jiggy. Today her bandana was blue with turquoise splotches. She often wore one, especially when she came into the greenhouse. The humidity made her strawberry-blonde mane frizzier than she could tolerate. Jiggy always looked as if he'd stuck his hand in a socket anyway, and hair was the last thing he cared about. If Gina didn't bug him to get it cut every six months or so, it would probably be down around his knees and encroaching on the neighbor's property.

"Nice looking weed," she said. "Compared to those anyway." She looked at the two rangy plants that were as tall as Jiggy. Their biodegradable pots had been lowered into the ground so they were growing right out of the greenhouse floor. They weren't even close to flowering. Jiggy was hoping this would be imminent. They were purportedly a Congolese landrace breed, another gift from Harold, and Jiggy had grown them from seed too. Congoliaths, he called them.

"For all we know, they could be male. Still can't tell. Waste a time." Jiggy set his coffee down and began wiping off the shears.

"Kinda cool, when you think of it though. The Congo connection. I wonder what life is like for a marijuana plant in the Congo?"

"They're probably refugees."

"Maybe you got a male and a female. One's a little smaller!"

"Yeah, then we could have a population explosion. I could sell seeds to that fuckin' commercial place up the road."

"You still pissed about that?"

"Jesus, Gina," Jiggy said mournfully. "It just never fuckin' stops. Every goddamn greedy prick finds some way to wreck it for everybody else."

"But there's no big multinationals there."

"Give it time. The multinationals are just bidin' theirs. You watch. Big Pharma's gonna take it all down one way or another. Fuckin' in bed with the FDA anyway. All that goddamn pharmaceutical global harmonization! *We the fuckin' people* don't exactly figure ya know. In fact *we the fuckin' people* are just a bunch of fuckin' lab rats. The sicker they make us the healthier their bank accounts get." Jiggy paused and snorted. "All those boomers an' agin' populations — a fuckin' wet dream for 'em. Fuckin' wet dream!"

"But maybe they won't bother." Gina took a sip of coffee and closed her eyes. "Big Pharma needs patents. They can't patent what nature already gives everybody."

"Exactly! So they'll genetically modify it. History repeats itself, ya know. And the drugs now! Feedin' 'em to kids just so they stand in line quietly, half lobotomized! All of it dumbin' people down, along with all the fuckin' media, social and otherwise comin' out of every goddamn orifice of civilization! We're just like a bunch of stupid chickens on the way to the slaughterhouse. Still worried about peckin' orders an' not a fuckin' clue about what finally happens when the truck stops."

"Well maybe you and me will be dead anyway by the time the truck finally stops."

Jiggy raised his coffee cup to her. "Good point." And then he added, "You know, maybe I should join forces with the Guardians on this."

They both started to snicker. The Guardians of Jude and Ezekiel were an eccentric and strict cult. They owned several hundred acres of land, holdings that dated back more than a century and a half. Inbreeding and insanity were considered inevitable and this in turn led to a measure of compassionate interest, especially by social workers, when they weren't driven off the compound at gunpoint. They had a reputation for digging tunnels in their compound — some practice connected with either Jude or Ezekiel — and for hoarding vehicles and perhaps guns, though no one was sure about the latter. They stretched the First Amendment and were very demonstrative in their disapprovals when they felt society was going astray. They'd been spectacularly against the commercial medical marijuana company with a blood-red school bus set aflame and fireworks bursting out of it right in front of the Hullbrooke town hall at midnight.

"Jiggy, they'd probably be the ones driving the truck."

"True enough, but then you'd go out with a flare at least. Wouldn't have to leave the truck for the slaughterhouse. They'd roast you right in it."

There was silence for a while as they sat on the greenhouse bench and drank their coffee. When Jiggy was finished, he got up and began harvesting the branches off the second plant and putting them gently into the big pan. He and Gina would hang the branches upside down to dry on clotheslines set up in the garage. While he was working, the sun came out and the Congoliaths intercepted the light, creating a lace of shade that dappled the greenhouse. It made Gina smile.

"It's really nice in here, Jiggy. We should do weekend mornings in the greenhouse more often."

"Peaceful, isn't it!" He turned and studied his Congoliaths for a second before resuming his cutting. "We don't see much of Little Cousin these days, do we? I barely heard him come in last night."

"He's busy, that's for sure."

"He's still a wreck."

"I know."

"Sure set himself up a big fuckin' project. I wouldn't be buildin' a house."

"No. You're a better man. You'd go find yourself a cave."

"Actually, I think I'd find myself a trailer. He told me he's still got a little left from the trust."

"Yeah, and he's spending it the way he wants to."

"I'm not criticizin' him, Gina. It's just it's a hell of a lot of work an' he's strugglin' as it is. He could be easier on himself is all I'm sayin'."

"He's never been easy on himself."

"Oh, I know. He picks the high road. All the fuckin' nobility that best kills him."

"You still blame yourself."

"As a matter of fact, I do. Sure as shit, Alvin had nothin' to do with it."

"I suppose I should blame myself too then. If we hadn't visited, he'd never have met you."

"Knock yourself out on that. How motherhoodly guiltish of you, Gina."

"I pitched in when I was needed. Anybody would have done as much."

"An' you still do. You're a stellar mother hen you know. No wonder the chickens lay like crazy. Constantly inspired."

"Screw you, Jiggy." Gina stood up half laughing. She grabbed the coffee cups and headed for the door. He always teased about her fussing over Ray along with her fussing over most of the animals on the farm.

"I'm ready when you are," he smiled.

She let the door slam behind her.

Gina was Ray's cousin by blood. She was eleven years older than he was and she'd spent a lot of time with him as a child. She'd called him Sprout, and the name stuck for a while. That was when they all lived in California, before Gina's family moved out east. Gina missed California so much that during high school she took every little odd job she could to save money to go visit for the summers. Her aunt and uncle would pay half the fare and then some. She worked in the fields sometimes and ran errands once she learned to drive. But mostly she looked after Ray. He was her little Sprout and always would be.

But now Gina saw the same things Jiggy did and it worried her. Ray looked exhausted all the time. A year ago he'd been in really good shape. He'd been working for an old contractor friend on the Jersey Shore and the job had suited him. Physically it wasn't demanding. He'd been on the phone mostly rather than the construction floor. But it was a one-time deal. Ray couldn't cope with cities anymore and all his friend's new contracts were in downtown Jersey City and Newark. So Ray had come north for rural living and to finish getting his electrician's license.

Apprenticeships seemed like indentured servitude to Gina. She didn't like the sounds of his new boss any more than she'd liked the sounds of the old one. Why was it guys just had to suck it all up, buttercup, and pretend be so tough? It was stupid. How could anybody do well, Gina'd like to know, when the boss hurled insults and assumed the worst about everything? Men could be such shits to each other. Mind you so could women. Gina had an ongoing war of her own with one of the women at work.

Unlike Gina, Tammy was a delicate type, always getting sick or so she said. So on top of doing her own job, Gina was asked to fill in for her. It meant extra hours but no overtime pay, no time-and-a-half or anything like that to sweeten the load. Gina invariably found mistakes or omissions in the woman's work that she'd correct but she never mentioned the problems to the boss. Instead she'd point them out to Tammy upon her return. It was the generous thing to do, Gina thought. Women have a hard enough time in the workplace and they need to have each other's backs.

One day some of Tammy's shoddy work caught the notice of the boss, but who did she turn around and point the finger at? Oh, not outright, not directly, but bruisingly enough — "Well I do see it's a problem and I'm sorry, but it's not like I have sole access to the books. I'm not sure when those records were filed." Jesus Almighty! The ungrateful little bitch. And the boss, ever charmed by the woman's little girl voice and big bobbly boobs started looking askance at Gina. So after that, Gina refused the extra work. She didn't have the time. She was needed on the farm. Tammy was furious. She had to stay late herself to catch up. And my, my, but the office got frosty.

Gina was betting with herself, counting the days until the woman was found out and fired. Gina had written a date down — February 5th — and if the termination was within a month of the actual day, that meant she'd won a treat for herself, a night out. Even if she had to rope Jiggy and drag him to the restaurant or the movie or both, they'd make a party of it. She'd order lobster and her favorite dry cider.

Chapter 3

Ray shifted in the wooden chair. He never would have guessed he'd be applying to work at a place like this. Not in a million years. And Jiggy, well if he knew he'd probably have a coronary. Ray looked around the room. The wall, ceiling, doors — everything that was finished was shiny and white. There were a couple of utility sinks stacked in the corner, unattached pipes and tubing coming out from one wall and a lot of loose wiring. All of it waiting to be hooked up for some purpose or another. The big guy, Greg, would be back in a minute to conduct the interview. *They must really be desperate to hire at this marijuana outfit*, Ray thought. When he'd filled out the application four days before, they'd called him back two hours later.

Ray had applied as a joke, but everybody said this was the only place with anything happening these days. Unless you were a professional, like a lawyer or doctor or teacher maybe, or happy to work in a grocery store or coffee shop. Or maybe you were involved with renovations and doing electrical work like Ray. He still hadn't completed his apprenticeship hours but wasn't having any good days, and the roaring in his head was becoming unbearable again. His shoulder was a mess too and he wasn't sure he was all that determined to be an electrician anymore. Also he had his own property now and a house to build. It wasn't going well because Ray was so tired.

He figured if he could work at something really quiet or maybe not work at all, he could make some headway on the property. Then he could try going back to the electrical stuff. He'd sorted things out with the current boss, who begrudgingly recognized Ray was struggling. The guy didn't want him around anyway if he was going to screw something up. "Sure, take the whole year," he told Ray. "If you're lucky I might have the time of day for you when you get back." Ray had one more week with the contractor, then he'd be done.

When Ray mentioned to one of the guys he worked with that he'd put in an application to CannRose-Medi, the guy had cracked right up. So had Gina. Likely everybody would see it as hilarious. Except Jiggy. He'd never mention it to Jiggy even if he got the job. Gina'd keep it quiet too.

Greg entered the room and Ray stopped thinking about Jiggy.

"Well, isn't this great. Can I call you Ray?" Greg asked.

"Sure." Ray started to stand but with a big smile, Greg motioned him to stay seated. Greg looked to be well over six feet and probably close to three hundred pounds. Not fat but beefy. He was redheaded with curly hair and a full beard. He reminded Ray of a Viking.

"Well, Ray, your timing is pretty terrific." Greg took a seat in the chair opposite. "We really need someone like you right now. Responsible. Proven track record. And I gotta tell you Ray, I got a lotta respect for you ex-military."

Ray nodded.

"You vets all been through shit. I know," Greg continued. "I got a couple of inlaws ex-military. Both been to Afghanistan and one even to the fuckin' Congo or . . . or Darfoo or somethin', wherever the hell that was, you know in Africa somewhere. But anyway, I've been on police forces one way or another all my life since high school, even when I was going to college so I know the crap you deal with around people every day. But hey it's not fuckin' war zones. So yeah, my hat's off to you."

Ray just sat there. He hadn't a clue what to say to this. There was no point in telling Greg he'd mostly worked in the quiet places: storerooms and offices, housing units and buildings away from the action. "Fobbits don't fucking count, asshole!" a marine had screamed at him one day, though he couldn't remember why. The two lost fingers had been the result not of some stray ordnance but faulty wiring in one of the CHUs, the housing units. A few extra volts had changed his life for sure that day but not in the way Greg meant. Ray looked down at his hands. *Greg should be talking to Jiggy maybe, but then Jiggy wouldn't be caught dead here.*

"So you know we're not looking for security at this point, right?" Greg smiled broadly again. "But hell, we're always looking for *security-cleared*." And Greg lowered his fist, solidly pounding the desk. Ray had been assigned low-level security clearance in the

military, so that would speed the background checks and satisfy the
state. "And I see you've got all this work under your belt with
electrical stuff. Hell, looks like you've got construction, shipping and
receiving too, inventory and even janitorial experience, and Ray,
we're looking for all of those right now. Would that be a good fit for
you?" Greg laughed at his own joke.

Ray hesitated. He didn't exactly have his heart set on a security
job, although that was what he had applied for because that was what
had been listed in the local paper. Anything would do though for the
next few months as long as it wasn't too noisy or strenuous. "Would
I be working all those jobs or just mostly one?" he asked.

Greg cleared his throat. "Yup," he said, still chuckling.

"So, how . . . how would that work . . . I'd be cleaning and . . ."

"Ray, let me be straight with you here. We're still a start-up
company" — Greg was lightly tapping the table — "and pretty much
everybody does a lot of everything. We've still got finishing
construction going on. Details, details. Basically it's a crazy fuckin'
job but it can be a lotta fun." Greg looked Ray in the eye at this point
to gauge his appreciation of the situation. Ray smiled, so Greg
continued, "We'll get you looking after shipping and receiving, doing
a little custodial work too maybe. Like I said we're looking for
somebody just like you. Somebody responsible."

"And inventory?" Ray ventured.

"Oh yeah, general inventory for sure." Greg sighed deeply. "See
I have enough to do tryin' to keep track of every little gram of plant
material, and the QA Officer, well as far as I can tell, he doesn't really
know shit. He's a boyfriend of one of the bosses' daughters."

The mention of *bosses* made Ray ask the obvious. "So who would
be my boss? Would I report to you or someone else?"

"Well, there's the executives, see, and they are bosses but I don't
think they really believe in bosses. Or chains of command, like you'd
experience in the military. Or how we did things in the force . . . They
have this kind of lateral-approach thing going on, I'd say. Though I guess
Caldwell does figure prominently." Greg cocked his head and gazed
thoughtfully at the mess of unfinished wiring on the sidewall. "Maybe a
little difficult to understand until you start working here . . . yeah." He
looked back at Ray, "So what do you think?" And without waiting for
any answer, Greg then went on to outline the pay, benefits, share

options, vacation and possibilities for advancement at CannRose. Ray could rest assured that advancement would be swift. And then in all probability, especially in his case, this would result in a managerial position for one section of the operation. "Instead of havin' to spread yourself all over hell's half acre, like everybody has to right now." And then Greg waxed on about the future at such a pace that Ray only really caught bits of it like "achieves profitability" and "the inevitable success is just a matter of time," and "burgeoning breakaway industry." And then finally he said, tapping the table harder at that point for effect, "This position currently on the table could represent the opportunity of a lifetime." He took a breath. "Course, you gotta have some time to think about it, I'd guess."

There was a pause and Ray looked out the window. A cloud of starlings swarmed up from the field next to the facility where last year's sumac berries were providing a spring feast. It gave Ray a peaceful feeling but also made him acutely aware of his own weariness. Part of him wished he could escape into the sky too. Greg noticed the change in Ray's expression and began nodding to himself.

"So I gotta ask you," said Greg wrapping up the interview. "You use the stuff? Bein' a vet and all. And hey, it doesn't make a bit a difference to me if you do or don't. Just curious. We gotta do drug tests here for everyone but if you're registered for medical, it's not a problem. As long as it's just marijuana traces they're finding and not Snow White and the seven or so dwarfs if you get my drift." He chuckled again.

Ray considered this question. "No, I don't . . . I don't use it." He replied as if it was almost a surprise to himself. He'd only ever tried marijuana a few times as a teenager and gave up. Didn't seem to affect him right. Not like it did his buddies. Didn't make him laugh or anything. He'd never really liked the experience. Just made him feel heavy, like he weighed six hundred pounds. And then he'd fall asleep. Classic couch lock. "But I do know vets who use it," Ray said, "and they swear by it." Ray was thinking of Jiggy again.

"Guess it helps with the PTSD and all that."

"Well, I guess. Pain too though. Nerve stuff."

"Yeah?"

"Yeah. I know a guy. Actually, he's my cousin's husband. I'm living with them right now, 'til I get my own place sorted."

"Well, that won't take long. Rents around here're real cheap."

"I bought some property. I'm gonna start building once I get things organized."

"Oh yeah? That's great," said Greg raising his eyebrows. "Lotta work though."

Ray nodded. "Anyway, this guy, my cousin's husband, he lost his foot in Afghanistan."

"Oh jeez."

"And he can still feel it like it's there. Same as the day when it got blown off. Drives him crazy. Wakes him up at night."

"And the weed helps?"

"Yup. He grows his own. Out in a little greenhouse in the backyard."

Greg considered this. "So you're familiar with growing too then. Ray, this is just great. I'm tellin' ya right now. You want this job, you got it! Course you take all the time you want to think about it."

Ray really didn't have to think much about the offer. The work sounded simple enough and Greg's enthusiastic presentation had pretty much sold him. The newness of the industry made no difference to Ray: that it was a start-up or he was getting in on the ground floor or all the stuff about share options. He didn't quite follow it anyway. Greg was a nice enough guy and the pay was only a couple of bucks less an hour than what he'd been making. It was temporary either way. He figured working there would be more pleasant than his job with the Lyston contractor who'd been a grouch from the get-go. In fact when he told his boss the next day he was going to take a quiet job for a while at the new medical marijuana grow facility in Hullbrooke, the man snorted. "Jesus! You sure pick 'em don't ya! Place'll prob'ly fall down around your ears, Lazlo Porter has anything to do with it. Hear he's got himself an executive position there. Good thing. One less goof in the industry to give everybody else a bad name."

One of the carpenters on site nodded toward the door after Ray's boss left the room. "He's pissed he never even got to make a bid on that job."

"Oh yeah?"

"Lotta money. Mind you I have heard Lazlo Porter's old outfit was a bit dicey. There's a couple of things in the courts. Probably why he shut the business down. Nice enough guy to work for though. My girlfriend's brother worked for him for a few years. Still, might want to watch your back depending on what he's doing up there."

"I don't think I'll be dealing with executives much," Ray said. "More'n likely I'll be mopping floors."

"Whatever floats your boat."

"I like a challenge," Ray panned. "Like to soar with the eagles."

"So call me if they're givin' away free samples. You know if they need tasters for the brownies."

"Sure."

"You take care of yourself now."

"That's the plan," Ray said.

Ray called Greg the next day and told him he would take the crazy start-up job.

"This is just great!" Greg boomed. "Welcome to CannRose, Ray. You're gonna get along great here. I just know it."

#

Three weeks after his interview, Ray arrived at CannRose for work. He had forms to fill and papers to sign, a confidentiality agreement being among them: What went on at CannRose stayed at CannRose. The worry was that exclusive processes might be leaked to competitors. When Ray asked what kind of processes might be proprietary, Greg shrugged and told him they probably didn't have any yet. "Yeah. Might have to wait for that," he said.

Greg introduced Ray to several people in the administration section of the building. It was all something of a blur, but a few of them did stick out. Among the executives, there was Lazlo of course; he was the vice president. Ray noted the man's bulging froggy eyes and low gravelly voice, which sounded more like a whisper. Lily, blonde, very pretty and pregnant, who worked as the facility receptionist, smiled welcomingly and made Ray think he might like this new job more than he'd expected. Then there was Lydia, a tall dramatic-looking woman who wore large jewelry and high-heeled boots and spoke with a Southern drawl. In fact she reminded Ray of an opera singer from the Met he'd been introduced to once when he was out with some friends in New York. She was the president and the reason the whole place existed. Greg told him he'd have to wait to meet Caldwell because he was in California wooing some seed king. Greg explained the facility was Caldwell's concept and that "whatever Caldwell says pretty much goes."

Ray was to be given the full tour of the cultivation area by Damian, the master grower. Damian's history was said to be very colorful, though Greg mentioned much later, the coloring was mostly Caldwell's doing. Damian had a lot of unpaid parking tickets, not big victories in court for cannabis. But Greg said Caldwell preferred an impressive story. Damian had been imported from Colorado with much fanfare. Caldwell had insisted that the best indoor growers would come from there, not California. "The Emerald Triangle rose to distinction outdoors not indoors," Caldwell said.

Damian was tall, about the same height as Ray, and in his midforties. He was possibly the skinniest, palest man Ray had ever seen. He had a lot of hair too, blond dreadlocks tied into a ponytail that reached down to the middle of his back. When he was introduced to Ray, he shook his hand slowly, for a long time and finally said, "Bro', okay." And then after a pause, "Cool." Then he turned in kind of a swoop, boney arms stretched into the air and said, "Follow me, Ray."

Damian's tour was surprisingly detailed given his few words of greeting. He began with the electrical room full of door-sized power panels. Ray heard them hum. "For the lighting in the grow rooms. And the HVACs," Damian said. "Everything's controlled by computers in the cultivation office. And right here, outside the building" — he rapped on the wall — "are the backup generators. They're the size of effin' school buses, man! But hey, lose your lights, lose your crop!" There were also large CO_2 tanks outside, and Damian showed Ray the gauges where the gas lines came in.

The next room, larger but quieter, contained the water control for the building and had several huge tanks, numerous canisters, cylinders and a dizzying array of valves, pressure gauges and switches. Damian pointed to the biggest tank. "That's your RO. Well water, you know, with the ions cleaned out by reverse osmosis. It's the starting place you could say." The other tanks held reconditioned water and nutrient solutions that all fed into the automated fertigation system. The solutions were checked and tested daily. "At least if somebody remembers."

At that point a somber heavyset man about the same age as Ray walked in shaking his head. "Why do you have to say things like that Damian? Everybody is doing overtime for this place. You know that."

"Gus! My man!" Damian turned back to Ray. "Gus here bears a great load. He's the production manager. It's a serious job. He's eternally plagued by responsibility."

As it turned out, Gus was Lazlo's son but Ray couldn't see much resemblance. He was such a big guy for starters, hulking in his gray sweat suit. The racing stripes only accentuated his girth.

Gus joined them as Damian continued the tour, and while they were in the various rooms, especially the potting room and nursery, Damian gave voluminous accounts about growing stages. At one point they all went through an air shower and Ray liked the wind-tunnel feel of it. When they came out the other side they ran into a couple. "Cassie and Joe here are local folks," Damian said. "They're our horticultural specialists," and he emphasized the last two words. "Used to run a garden center. Isn't that right?"

"Yes," said Joe quietly.

Ray sensed tension. The woman was focused on a touchscreen pad she was carrying. She looked up briefly, smiled politely and shook Ray's hand. Then she went back to the screen and immediately walked down the hallway to their left. Joe mentioned something about fertilizer and went on through the air shower.

In one of the flower rooms, Ray was introduced to Ernie, who was crazy tall. He had a toothy smile, a patch over one eye and was about the same age as Damian. He cleaned mostly but occasionally worked with the plants. Pretty much everybody worked with the plants when a hand was needed. As Damian talked on about the Jambalaya Kush they were staring at, Ray thought he heard Ernie humming to himself but then turned around to see that Ernie was no longer in the room. *Must be an overtone created by all the fans and the air handlers*, Ray thought. As the noise continued, Ray found its odd pulsing a little disorienting. It stopped as soon as they made their way to the room next door.

There Ray met three men who still looked like teenagers, all with shoulder-length sandy-brown hair. Ray could barely tell them apart let alone remember their names. Damian referred to them as "the lads," and said they were so keen it restored his faith in the future of humanity. "They're excellent banana hunters too. Bananas are the male flowers," Damian explained, "not what you want to see in a crop. Means the plants are going hermie on you." It took Ray a second or two to catch on that *hermie* meant hermaphrodite.

When they got to the processing rooms, Ray realized there was way more to growing weed on an industrial scale than he'd imagined. The section had trimming rooms, drying chambers, curing rooms, bottling rooms and the unfinished extraction room where Ray had his interview. Damian elaborated in great detail about mechanical trimmers and the drying process, the burping throughout the curing, the care needed in bottling. Then he mentioned rather gloomily that they hadn't actually got anything ready for packaging yet and were months away from extractions. So this part wasn't finished. There were more air showers that weren't working yet, and Damian pointed to a large area left vacant for a kitchen, to make edibles if and when the state ever allowed them. "The state," Damian announced, "amends the regs every other effin' day."

"Yeah! And you never know what could happen if the wrong government gets elected," Gus chimed in.

"The feds, man!" Damian said, shaking his head. "They could go all Nixon on us in a heartbeat. Shut everybody down!"

The remainder of the tour included the production offices — one of which was for the cultivation staff and housed the computers — and the vault, which had more security locks and cameras than surely even a bank would need. "The state is effin' psycho about diversion," Damian said, and Gus heartily agreed.

As they walked back to the loading dock, Damian pointed to a large room that was set aside for a lab. "Caldwell wants to hire some scientist. Beats me why that would be at all useful."

"Hard to know where he's going with that," Gus added drearily.

Ray's head was spinning by that point and he figured he wouldn't remember anything.

"It's an art, man," Damian announced. "I've been at this since I was a teenager. Just gets more interesting." Damian said he could recommend a couple of books. "You new to all this?"

"Pretty much," Ray admitted. "When I was a kid we grew everything in fields, no greenhouses, no fancy tech. Lot of irrigation. Though mostly it was more like spread the manure and hope for the best."

"So was your dad into organic?"

"Not really. My grandmother told me Dad was cheap though and he figured he'd hang on to more money by farming like my great granddad."

"Cool. We're taking this place organic you know."

#

On the Friday of Ray's first week at CannRose, he got up very early to pick up supplies in Lyston. In spite of Greg indicating to Ray he would be doing anything and everything, Gus had looked puzzled when Ray mentioned this. "But we just needed somebody for general inventory and purchasing. I told Greg that."

"That'll be fine," Ray said. "I can do that." Then he asked if they had inventory and purchasing procedures. The army had them after all.

At this request Gus had looked puzzled again. "I don't think those things have been organized yet."

Ray looked at him and Gus blinked back. It became clear to Ray that he could make it up as he went along. Maybe that's what Greg had meant about doing everything.

When Ray got back from Lyston a little before ten o'clock, he found the grow facility in an uproar. Half the cultivation rooms had flooded overnight. "It's biblical, man! Effin' biblical," Damian said as Ray came in through the back entrance. Ernie came by smiling and handed Ray rubber gloves, a bucket and a mop. All the Shop-Vacs were working overtime and Lily had been sent to the local Rent-All to see if they had any more.

Right from the air shower the catastrophe was evident. There was water seeping under the door. When Ray stepped through to the other side, which was lower, he stepped into about two inches of water or liquid of some sort. Hard to tell. There were so many different solutions in the place. Vats and vats of them. Ray surmised the problem was tricky to locate or stop. He peered into the grow room closest to him. Somebody scurried past dragging a full Shop-Vac. The floor was wet, but only one corner of it was flooded. It occurred to Ray the floors were not level and that would make perfect sense because you'd need that for draining. Except where were the drains? He spotted Ernie in the hallway pouring a bucket of water into one of the big sinks so he asked him.

Ernie laughed. "Well some of 'em got drains. Maybe not in the right place. Or they're not working. We gotta lotta plugged drains. Specially here in the hallway." Ernie pointed to a grate in the floor that was about four feet from where they stood. Ray hadn't noticed it before but then he saw a single bubble welling up very slowly.

"This place's just full of surprises," Ernie said.

"Where's the leak?" Ray asked him, and Ernie glanced back at the flower rooms.

"The West Mother Pod backs onto one of them," Ernie added. "That got hit too."

Ray headed down the hallway to Flower Room I. He figured he should start mopping up in the hallway but he was curious. As he got near the flower room door, it burst open. One of the horticulture specialists, Cassie, came tearing out, the tails of her a lab coat flaring behind her.

"Exactly how many assholes does it take to run this place?" Her face was flushed as she sped by. Ray doubted she'd noticed him. "Where in God's name is Lazlo?" she muttered.

When Ray looked inside the room, he saw Gus standing on one of the tables and someone else up a ladder. There was water or something still spurting from a pipe that was close to the ceiling. Ray figured it must have been part of the fire sprinkler system. The fertigation pipes were much lower but one of them was gushing too. The fertigation system was passive: water or fertilizer solution periodically flooded the grooves in the tables or the trough tubes so the plants would uptake water and nutrients as needed. It didn't look very passive now.

The fellow on the ladder was saying, "I still can't see anything. Better shut it off again."

"Whatever. Still doesn't explain the solenoids though." Gus wandered over to the wall with the main valves and shut off one of them. The fertigation water stopped spurting. Then he headed out, presumably to shut off the valve for the sprinkler system.

People had managed to move all the troughs and plants away from the spurting pipes. Many of the troughs had lost most of their grow media. In some cases the plants were tilted as if they were ready to topple over. Greg told him later that when he first saw the flood, it looked like Niagara. "Water was spillin' off the tables in sheets. The plants were floating, I tell you. Coconut coir was everywhere!"

The three lads, the ones Ray thought still looked like teenagers, were busy cleaning, scraping up the loose media from the floor and tables. Cassie's husband, Joe, the other horticultural specialist, was standing over a drain holding a plumber's snake.

"I've gone as far as I can. Probably plugged to Timbuktu."

"Plumber's coming after lunch," Gus said as he came back into the flower room.

"Roto-rooter man, I love you," sang the guy on the ladder.

"How come we don't rate their emergency service?" Joe asked.

"Who knows. Maybe there's too many other emergencies somewhere," Gus said.

"Now if the septic system would only explode, we'd get priority I bet," the guy on the ladder said cheerfully.

Gus told him to come down.

"I'd say a few of yer solenoids got too damp and just plain shorted," he remarked as he made his way down.

Ray left the flower room and went back along the hallways to the West Mother Pod. He opened the door and there was Damian sitting on one of the tables, bent over with his head in his hands, his palms covering his eyes. There was an inch or so of water on the floor there too. Cassie was dragging a very large soggy pot with a single bushy marijuana plant in it across the floor. Ray went over to help her.

"Thanks," she said, straightening up. She looked over at Damian with obvious disgust before turning back to Ray. "Do you think you can help me put all these back on the table?"

About ten huge pots were on the floor. Trays full of small seedlings currently taking up space on the table would have to be moved to make room. Cassie looked at the trays with obvious exasperation, then she grabbed a couple of them. "Maybe you could just start moving the others to the far end. I'll be back in a sec," she said and headed for the door. Ray started shifting the trays and thought he heard Damian mutter something.

He turned and Damian looked up. Ray wondered if he'd been crying. His eyes were a little red. Mind you his pupils were big too. "What a mess," Damian said. He sat there gazing at nothing. "It just never ends. One effin' disaster after another. Yesterday an infestation. Today this. That crop was due for harvest end of the month. The whole place'll be breeding mold now." He looked at Ray again. "This operation is jinxed, man."

At that point Cassie came marching back into the West Mother Pod. She pointed at the huge pots, and she and Ray proceeded to lift them one at a time onto the low tables. Cassie then pulled out some kind of a probe from her pocket and moved from pot to pot checking the grow media in the pots while Ray began mopping up some of the water on the floor. He looked for a drain but couldn't see one. When Cassie was finished, she motioned to Ray that he could leave the mopping. "It can wait for later," she said. "You'll be needed somewhere else, I'm sure." They both headed out into the hallway again.

"So how are you liking it so far?" Cassie asked. "Some fun, huh?"

"Pretty much," Ray said.

She let out a full-throated laugh then gave Ray a generous smile that he hadn't seen before. "Well around here it's two steps forward and three back. I guess we'll see if we can keep that crop. Plants sure got a soaking. Lucky one of the big flooded rooms was empty."

At that point the three very young men walked by with serious expressions and armfuls of plants with dangling roots still entangled with grow media and dripping liquid. Directly behind them was Cassie's husband, Joe.

"What are they up to?" Cassie asked.

"They're setting up an infirmary in the empty nursery," Joe said.

"What?" Cassie started to laugh again.

"They said the ladies were traumatized." Joe smiled. "Anyway, what harm can it do?"

The three young men had just disappeared down the hall when the door from the air shower exploded open and a tall middle-aged man thundered in. "I can't go away for a week without the place turning into a swamp. This is cannabis cultivation, people, not Everglades reconstruction! What the hell happened here?" he roared.

Ernie, standing across the hallway, caught Ray's eye. "Caldwell," he mouthed.

Ray moved back a step or two even though he was already a few yards away. Cassie and Joe pretty much froze in their tracks. Ernie just smiled at his mop and bucket. Ray took Ernie's lead and focused on his own mop while keeping track of the booming man out of the corner of his eye.

Caldwell's long jacket swung a little as he moved down the hall, and his face was reddish under his russet fedora. Ray wondered if it was from the cold or reflected from his hat or just his natural complexion. He noted the hand-stitched leather man bag too, arty and expensive. And just like Lydia had reminded him of an opera singer, Caldwell reminded Ray of an impresario or a big director, not that he'd actually met any.

"It's a simple question! How did this happen?" Caldwell was staring at Joe and Cassie. Then he spotted Gus coming along the hallway and didn't wait for an answer. "Tell me! Just tell me this isn't another major system fail. The plumbing doesn't all have to be redone, does it?" he yelled.

"No." Gus had walked quickly and it made him breathless. "There's one leak for sure. We think it somehow shorted the fire alarm and set off the sprinkler systems. And then the fertigation went nuts."

"Where the hell's your father?"

"Lyston. He's meeting with his lawyer. Plumber's on his way. So's the fertigation guy and the security company."

"This is ridiculous. How many screw-ups with these alarms now! We should sue them for the lost product. And tell me, if the alarm went off how come the fire department didn't show?"

Gus raised his meaty shoulders and kept them there. "I don't think it went off. I think it just shorted. I don't know."

"Unacceptable! You tell your father he needs to sit on these people until it's fixed. They've been screwing us around for months. And have those chillers come in yet?" Then noticing Ray for the first time, Caldwell said, "And who are you?"

Ray hesitated a second.

"Ray's the new hire for purchasing and general inventory," Gus intervened.

"Good to meet you, sir," Ray said.

"You're the army guy, right?" Caldwell's demeanor changed instantly and he shook Ray's hand, smiling. "Just call me Caldwell. It's good to have you with us. Hope you don't find all this mess discouraging."

"Not at all."

"Hell of a week to start! But this place will be the best of its kind, Ray. When it's all finished and running as planned. You'll see. We'll be making history here."

Chapter 4

"There's just no fuckin' way the state is gonna make me get rid of my plants an' then make me buy from some shit dispensary," Jiggy barked as he plunked himself down at the kitchen table.

"Who said they were doing that?" Gina was peeling potatoes at the kitchen sink.

"Some of the guys down at Chelsea's. They said that's what they tried up in Canada. So there ya go. Just goes with commercialization. Jesus, it just never fuckin' stops!"

"I didn't read anything like—"

"Course not. They like to sneak that kinda shit up on ya."

"But it said if you were registered you could still have your six plants."

"Yeah, for now. But one day when half the people are too stoned to notice they'll take that away."

"Why? Gina stopped peeling and turned to look at Jiggy.

"That's how it always goes. Corporate interests get a hold of anything they're gonna make sure nobody has free access."

"Ah," Gina looked out the window and went back to peeling.

"So they can make a killin' off the rest of us putzes. Shit! They even tried to do that with water in Bolivia. Did ya know that? An' everybody needs water. Not everybody needs weed so this oughta be a slam dunk for the corporate fuckers."

"Well it hasn't happened yet."

"Not yet maybe, but it's in the works."

"Maybe they'll make it free for vets along the way, you know, a good PR move."

"It's not the point, Gina. Every frickin' corporate expansion takes away from the average Joe's access. It's a fact. All the laws now protect the corporations, the multinationals, not you an' me. Every new trade agreement—"

"Jiggy, can we talk about something else?"

"What else could be more important than the fall of civilization an' the rise of greedy pricks?"

"Well," Gina said, "for one thing, I think a couple of the hens aren't doing well."

Jiggy sucked in his cheeks to consider the matter. "Maybe they're broody."

"I don't think so. They're going bald and getting pecked by the others."

"Jesus! That's just like people."

Gina picked up another potato. "I was thinking we should separate them out from the rest of the flock."

"Well that's a good idea. Then they can just finish each other off without disturbin' the more fortunate."

Gina ignored him and continued, "I was thinking we could use one of the old calf pens." The previous owner had built a row of them for calves en route to the butcher. The practice generated prime returns on the dollar for "milk fed."

"Right," Jiggy said, slapping his hand on the table. "Show those baldin' hens what cruel an' unusual conditions really look like. Make 'em appreciate their miserable little existence of chasin' grains an' grubs they've mistaken for freedom!"

Gina rolled her eyes. "The pens are a decent size for a couple of hens at night and the two of them could have the run of the rest of the barn when the others go outside."

Jiggy considered this. It occurred to him there was a very harsh and unpleasant aspect to chickens' lives generally, but it really wasn't his area of politics. He stretched and yawned. "I'll see to it this evenin'." He tapped his prosthetic foot a couple of times on the kitchen floor.

Gina looked down at it. "That bugging you again?"

Jiggy sighed loudly.

Gina stopped her potato peeling, came over to his chair, bent down and put her arms around his shoulders. She kissed him on the side of his forehead, and he looked up and smiled at her.

"Well I guess I could go get those chickens sorted now. Before supper."

Gina patted him on the shoulder and went back to the sink.

"Is Little Cousin joinin' us for supper?" Jiggy asked. "We barely see him. What did he say his new job was?"

"I don't know. It's clerical, some kind of warehouse inventory thing," Gina said. "Outside Lyston somewhere."

"Has he gone to that chiropractor yet? Or the physio lady ya told him about? He's gonna be walkin' around like an old man if he doesn't do somethin' soon."

"One thing at a time," Gina said.

"He couldn't even screw in a light bulb in the barn the other night. Dropped it. I'm still pickin' up glass.

"Give it a rest, Jiggy. He's trying. At least he's not lugging cable anymore and working for a jerk."

#

Gina hadn't planned to go out West the summer she was nineteen. She had a job by then, was taking business courses at night and lived in an apartment with three other young women. Her mother called early one Wednesday morning in June with the dreadful news that Gina's aunt and uncle had been killed in a car accident. Gina was dumbstruck. "Oh," she'd said, and then very quietly again, "Oh." Neither of them could speak. After a minute or so they both hung up together. Gina felt sick to her stomach and she gulped back the first sob. It was a while before she could stop crying. Then in a panic she thought of Ray.

She managed to find him by phone. He was at the neighbor's, almost the first people she called because they had a little boy, Max, and he and Ray played together all the time. When Marion Wilkes picked up the phone and realized it was Gina, she burst into tears. "Terrible what happened! You don't ever think of things like this. Just awful!" Thank God Ray had been at their house when his parents were killed she'd told Gina. Things were a real mess. Her uncle's farm hadn't been doing well. Had she known that? No, Gina hadn't. And her aunt had finally been diagnosed with ovarian cancer. All that back trouble she'd had and those crazy hot flashes. She was way too young to have those. Had Gina known that? No, she hadn't.

"The poor boy! Poor Ray!" Marion blubbered with a fresh round of tears. "Of course he'll stay here, for as long as he needs or wants to!"

And then she told Gina she didn't know what the legal arrangements were, but if Ray wanted, well, he could stay with them. Permanently. They'd be good to him. She could be sure of that. Gina thanked her and was crying again by that point. She asked to talk to Ray.

When Ray came on the phone he didn't sound like Sprout at all. The confusion in his voice and the jumbled answers to her simple questions made Gina decide very quickly to drop everything. She booked off work, packed herself up, got in the car and drove four days straight, sleeping in restaurant parking lots when she couldn't keep her eyes open any longer.

Gina hadn't known much about wills, probates, trusts, farm-leveraged debt, powers of attorney or guardianship. She just knew Ray needed help. Things were happening and they were happening fast. The farm was already up for sale. "Everything's done by the book," Ray's uncle George announced on her arrival. "I want no lawsuits, no trouble down the line." George the accountant had already insisted that it was he who'd told his younger brother to put his books in order the previous month. The insurers were suggesting the accident looked suspiciously like a double suicide. If so, the couple hadn't made any arrangements for Ray.

#

"Well," the big round lady said to Ray, "I know she meant well, but you can't go live with your cousin." The social worker looked up, holding Gina's eyes in a stern and steady gaze. "She's awfully young. She's not all that much older than you. It would be very, very difficult for her."

They were all at the dining room table and Ray was looking over a scattering of colored pencils while making drawings in the sketchbook Gina had bought him.

When Gina nodded, the woman turned her attention back to Ray. "You've got three other sets of relatives much better situated and happy to look after you. Even the Wilkes are willing to adopt you! You're a very popular young man."

"I don't know my Uncle Alvin," Ray said, still focusing intently on his drawing.

"Well maybe it's time to get to know him then."

"My dad talked about him. Sometimes. But I never met him."
Ray was drawing stealth bombers and fighter jets.

"Well how about your Aunt Sissy and Uncle George?"

Ray didn't say anything. He didn't like Aunt Sissy, and his Uncle George never even noticed him when he was there. He worked in an office, wore a suit all the time and he smelled weird. Plus they lived in the city.

The social worker didn't like Sissy and George much either so she didn't press the matter. She considered Marion Wilkes a last resort and also found her emotionally overblown. She thought an eight-year-old boy might have found the same thing. He just might not know what to call it. The grandparents on the father's side had half offered to take him too, but they were elderly and the grandfather was being assessed for dementia.

On the other hand she'd had a long phone conversation with the unknown Uncle Alvin and Aunt Collette, and though Alvin had a very minor blip in his background eons ago, they'd sounded sane, pleasant and had already raised three children who were doing well. "How about this? Your cousin has offered to drive you to your—"

"Why can't Aunt Debbie look after me?"

Gina shook her head and looked down at the table. Aunt Debbie was Gina's mother.

"Because, sweetheart, she's just gotten a divorce and she's not all that well herself right now." The social worker had already told him pretty much the same thing the day before.

"What about later?" Ray asked.

The social worker did not want to have to dwell on the likelihood and aftermath of yet another death. "We have to get you situated for the next school year," she said, "and Aunt Debbie isn't able to look after you right now."

"Okay." He'd moved on to drawing tanks.

"So here's my idea, Ray. Gina drives you all the way to New Jersey to meet your uncle and aunt there. You give it a try. And you know what?"

Ray paused momentarily in his drawing and shook his head. He didn't know what. He didn't know what about anything.

"If it all works out, your cousin Gina can come more often for visits if you stay with your Uncle Alvin." The social worker looked at Gina.

"That's right, Ray. I can come visit on weekends. You can come visit me too."

Ray stopped drawing. He still didn't look at either of them. He was surveying the pencils, deciding on the next color to use. "Okay," he said finally and picked up an emerald-green one.

Gina didn't know much about this Uncle Alvin either. Gina's mother and Ray's mother were sisters. Uncle Alvin was on Ray's father's side. She had only heard his name mentioned a few times and not at all favorably. Uncle Alvin was the oldest brother and the black sheep of the family. Like the social worker though, she'd had a talk with him and his wife and had come to the same conclusion. They sounded real nice. Relaxed. They were so very sorry to hear about the accident and very sad that they hadn't been able come out West for the funeral. But they knew their presence would have been upsetting, particularly for Ray's grandparents. Yes, they'd very much like to meet Ray and make him welcome. Alvin had always missed his little brother. It would be wonderful to be able to do something for his brother's son. Ray could have one of their boys' old bedrooms. They weren't planning on downsizing yet. And there was lots there for a boy to do. Sports? Anything you could want. There were good arts programs too, really good music teachers around. Was Ray musical? Gina wasn't sure.

Gina had a secondhand Honda Civic, a hatchback, so they could pack up all of Ray's things. Gina told him to pick photos and anything he'd like from his parents belongings so he'd remember, so when he looked at the thing, picked it up or used it, he'd remember how they were. Ray thought this was a good idea. He took a whole album of photos his mother had been working on the night before she died. He took his dad's binoculars, his old calculator and his mom's tea mug and a scarf she wore all the time. The mug had botanical illustrations on it and the scarf had a black-and-white geometric pattern.

Other things would be packed away for him, for later, for when he grew up. His Aunt Sissy and Uncle George would store it all. Gina put his clothes and all of his toys in cardboard boxes and big plastic bags. Ray pointed out that some of his toys were babyish. He'd rather leave them for Max's little brother. She watched him as he very carefully sorted out the collection and reduced it by half. Then they'd put the boxes in the car, and Ray's bicycle had barely fit on top of everything. Uncle George had offered to buy roof racks for the bicycle but then they all thought it would be better to have it locked inside the car for the long trip. Finally Ray announced that maybe he should leave that for Max's little brother too. "Mom says it's getting too small for me. She's right you know." Even Uncle George had to take a deep breath.

Gina wanted the trip to be fun and no hurry. A vacation. They would see some of the country. It would be good, educational. And Uncle George, in an uncharacteristic moment of generosity, had handed her a prepaid credit card with three thousand dollars on it. It was to cover hotels ("Do not stay in dumps!") gas, tolls, any car trouble, food ("Make sure he eats really well") and anything else that looked like a good thing to do, except he'd warned her to "steer clear of Vegas." And of course she would buy Ray a new bike when they got there. George was really hoping it would all work out with Alvin — he did not relish the thought of raising another child.

The road trip stayed northerly, but they took some time after Salt Lake City to go south and see some of the parks around Moab. Gina's mom had told her she could miss the crowds at the Grand Canyon and still get her fill of the strange landscapes. In Arches National Park, Gina and Ray took a few of the longer trails, one of them deemed moderately challenging. There wasn't a soul around and they wandered slowly among the bizarre shapes, stopping and turning to discover yet another surprising view. They went early in the morning to Canyonlands, and when they reached Mesa Arch, which gave way to the vast red panorama of chasms, canyons, spindles and mountains in the distance, it brought Gina to tears.

Ray had nodded solemnly. "It looks like Mars. Do you think Mars will be full of crying people one day?" And that had made Gina laugh through her tears.

On their way back from Canyonlands they visited Dead Horse Point. It was challenging to take in so much space and depth. Ray could see straight down to the river from where he stood. "That's a forever long way. Do you think birds come here for vacation and diving?"

"Maybe," Gina laughed.

"I would. I'd be the best diver," Ray said, and he leaned out as far as he could and spread his arms wide.

Gina gasped, grabbed him and pulled him back from the edge. They'd moved away from the crowd where there was a railing for protection. She looked at him bewildered. "Why did you do that?" And then she looked away and started to cry.

"Why does beauty make people so sad?" Ray asked.

After Moab they took the I-70 most of the way until they got to Ohio. After the dramatic landscapes they'd seen in Utah and the trek through the mountains to Denver, Ray found the flat Midwest too long and thought it should be shrunk. Gina pointed out the size of the sky. "You'll never see a bigger one," she said. When they drove through Kansas they sang "If I Only Had a Brain," or at least whatever bits of the scarecrow's song they could remember. They'd also brought a bunch of CDs from the farm. They would sing along to the pop tunes with Ray playing an imaginary guitar. They learned the words to "Livin' la Vida Loca" and they belted out "Born to Be Wild" at the top of their lungs.

Aunt Collette had told them Cincinnati, where she grew up, had a tiny perfect zoo, and if Ray liked animals, it was worth a visit. Since Ray definitely liked animals and big cats and birds in particular, the zoo was on the itinerary. Ray stood for almost twenty minutes watching a leopard try to stare down a lynx. They were in separate enclosures but could look at each other through glass. The enclosures were arranged like a wagon wheel and the cats could all see each other at the hub. Meanwhile the leopard's new mate, a very young female, would come up behind the male and take swipes at his twitching tail. The male would turn and snarl so she'd go bounding off but then sneak back again. It made Ray laugh.

After the zoo, they headed up to the I-80 and it took it straight through to New Jersey. Uncle Alvin and Aunt Collette lived in Hackensack. Gina told Ray that a town called Hackensack couldn't be all bad, and they made up songs and rhymes for it. Ray was looking on the map and found the even funnier Ho-Ho-Kus. So that set them off on another round of rhymes and silliness. It made Gina feel really good that she'd decided to make the trip a vacation. She was starting see her little Sprout come back.

They were a bit giddy when they arrived at Aunt Collette and Uncle Alvin's house. Gina motioned to Ray they had to calm down and be serious. She noted that the house was nice but certainly not huge like some of the places they'd seen on the way there. It was a two-story clapboard and had such a dark stain on the wood it was almost black. The tall windows and trim were all white, and there was an arch over the front door with columns that were white too, but the front door itself was red, like Chinese lacquer. It was all very simple and looked to have been built in a century long past. The front yard had tall mature oaks and maples and there was a huge blue spruce at one side of the house. Gina imagined there might be a big backyard too. There were two small round gardens in the front full of flowering shrubs. Everywhere Gina looked there were trees or grass or flowers. She saw Ray gazing around too. There were no dusty lanes here. No crops and no rows of anything.

They walked up the flagstone path, stood up very straight, and Gina motioned for Ray to press the doorbell. They heard a bark followed by another. Gina poked Ray and whispered like it was the first good news item of many more to come, "They have a dog!" Ray smiled back at her. The old dog at the farm had died two years before and Ray's dad had promised they'd get another, but it never happened in spite of all Ray's pestering.

The door opened and there stood a tall African American woman of slim build with her hair elaborately braided and piled elegantly on the top of her head. The dog, a yellow lab, was still barking. "Shush," she said. "Shush. This is family!" Gina held her hand out for the dog to sniff. It stopped barking. Ray held his hand out too. The dog licked it. Ray had been eating potato chips.

"You must be Gina and Ray!" Collette said, smiling. "Alvin, they're here!" she shouted over her shoulder.

Gina's brain was working very quickly. When Collette had opened the door she didn't know who the woman was and wondered if maybe they had the wrong house. But she soon recognized the voice as the same one she'd heard over the phone. Gina put two and two together and came to a logical conclusion: Ray's California family were just good old-fashioned bigots. That was the problem. That's why Gina virtually never heard anything about Uncle Alvin. And how typical — her own mother had failed to mentioned any of this to her.

For Ray, the lady at the door reminded him of his kindergarten teacher, his all-time favorite teacher ever. He moved in for a hug.

"Well," Collette said. "Aren't you the cuddly one!" And she held him, surprised at his immediate familiarity. She looked quizzically at Gina.

"Hi, Ray! Hi, Gina!" Alvin came into view, leaned forward and immediately offered his hand to Ray. "I'm your Uncle Alvin and I see you've met your Aunt Collette."

Ray released himself from his aunt's embrace and shook his uncle's hand. He was very serious. "I had a dog," Ray said. "He was old and my dad had the vet put him down. He was really sick. What's your dog's name?"

"Portia," said Uncle Alvin, "and she's a girl."

"That's a nice name," said Ray. "Our dog's name was Trotsky."

Uncle Alvin looked startled for a second and then like he wanted to laugh but thought better of it. "Well, that's a really nice name too."

"My dad and me buried him at the end of the almond orchard."

"I remember that," Uncle Alvin said. "There's probably a couple of old dogs buried there. We used to put up headstones."

"They're still there. And we put up one for Trotsky."

"Well that's a really good thing."

"I think so too," Ray said.

Gina stayed in New Jersey with Ray for about a week before heading back to Boston. It had all been planned that way, the hope being that with his favorite cousin around, Ray might settle in better. That Ray was still confused and probably traumatized was fairly apparent. He seemed to accept the death or at least the permanent absence of his father, but when his mother came up in conversation he always spoke of her in the present tense, as if she might even be in the next room. When they'd shown him the school where he could go in the fall if he stayed, he said something about the benches on the lawn where his mother could sit and wait when she came to pick him up. Ray's attention was scattered too. He'd be talking about stars one second and insects the next. He barely looked at his toys and he was ambivalent about a new bicycle. At times he'd go quiet or sullen.

"It's an awful lot for a kid to handle," Collette said to Gina when Ray had ignored a simple question. He just left the room, quietly went upstairs to his bedroom and shut the door. "Even a move with your parents alive and well can be overwhelming," Collette said. "I don't expect for a minute it's all going to be smooth sailing with him."

Before Gina left, Alvin and Collette told her to come often and stay as long as she wanted. They liked having her and she was clearly a lifeline for Ray. So Gina arranged to come back in three weeks for the weekend.

#

Gina was anxious on that drive down. She hadn't heard a word from Ray over those three weeks, only a short email from Alvin saying that Ray was okay and was making a friend or two. She'd left Ray her number but he hadn't called, and every time she called, nobody picked up. She remembered that her hand even shook when she rang the doorbell again in Hackensack. There was a shout and a bark from inside and then the front door burst open.

Ray practically jumped into her arms and started talking a mile a minute. Portia was jumping up and down too. A lot had happened in three weeks. He'd made friends, Derek and Fabio. Derek lived down the block that way. Fabio lived two streets over. They all played ball and Ray was shortstop. It was what he did best. Portia was a fantastic Frisbee player for a dog when she didn't just run off with it. He'd started drum lessons. He had a whole bunch of books out from the library on hawks and owls. Uncle Alvin was helping him build a bench. He and Aunt Collette had found two ripe raspberries already in the bushes in the back. And guess what, Aunt Collette was making spaghetti and they were all going out to a movie that night.

Gina took a deep breath. "Drum lessons?"

Collette smiled. "It's what garages were built for."

They took Portia out for walks and Frisbee in the park. Gina watched Ray play softball with his friends and they got her to be the pitcher. She was very impressed with Ray's ability to make noise on the drums. The garage looked to be soundproofed just like a recording studio. Uncle Alvin had shown him a couple of basic drum beats and patterns and already he could play along with half the stuff on the radio.

She noticed he still talked about his mother in the present though, and his conversations jumped every which way. But it was pretty clear his life was good at Alvin and Collette's house. He was very busy and mostly cheerful. Collette remarked that it had been pretty tough going at first but he seemed to really round a corner about a week earlier.

That Saturday night after they came back from the movie and Ray had gone up to bed, Gina, Alvin and Collette were all sitting on the patio in the backyard enjoying a drink.

"I suppose you got a good earful about us from Ray's folks and his grandparents," Alvin said.

Gina shook her head. "They never said anything much."

Alvin laughed. "Well, there we go. Human tendency to always think you're more important than you actually are."

"It was more like no one was allowed to mention you," Gina said.

"Ah. And then they won't exist."

"It wasn't all because of me," Collette said brightly. "I was just the last straw."

"You want to hear about this?"

"Yes!" Gina hated the whole notion of family secrets.

Alvin scratched his head debating where to start. "So I guess the first thing was I wanted to go to college," Alvin said. "That was maybe okay. But I certainly wasn't interested in agricultural school. That wasn't okay. In fact according to my dad, college was pretty much a waste of time any way you looked at it. But I didn't want to farm. I had no love for it. Or aptitude."

"Neither did George," Collette said. "So that added a little salt to the wound."

"Probably. And then it was 1969, still the Vietnam War. I'd just finished college, had a basic liberal arts degree and I got drafted. I said no way and became a conscientious objector. Well, you'd think I was spying for Ho Chi Minh as far as my father was concerned. Whoever heard of being a conscientious objector unless you were a Quaker or something! So that was my second transgression." Alvin paused, perhaps for effect, and then took a deep breath. "Then I burned the flag. Uh-huh. It was all the rage back then. And I do mean rage."

Collette was watching him and quietly chuckling.

"And because of that, I landed in jail."

"Oh!" said Gina.

"It was a federal offense for a while there. Not an acceptable expression of civil discontent. They could have put me away for a year.

They didn't though. Got six months. Was out after four for good behavior. Not sure how that happened."

Collette started to laugh out loud. "And what about jail?" She was making sure he didn't leave out the best parts.

"Right. A lot — and I mean a lot — of Blacks and Hispanics!"

"It's even worse now," Collette chimed in.

"And being where it was, it also had a high Native American population. Anyway not representative of the crowd you'd normally see on the street everyday." Alvin took another swallow of his gin and tonic. "And there were some very remarkable and impressive inmates at the time. Another education for me really. So I got interested in the Civil Rights movement. Once I got out I was marching and helping organize and writing articles."

"Just a real pain in the ass," Collette said, smiling.

"Big stuff had mostly happened, but there was still lots to do."

"Still is!"

"Anyway, I went for a weekend to Oberlin with this guy who wanted to visit his kid sister. And I met this very beautiful woman with the voice of an angel."

"And he married her," Collette said, holding out her ring finger for Gina to see.

"Uh-huh. And then, well then I took her home to meet the folks." Alvin shook his head at the recollection.

"Your mother looked a little shaken but she was very polite and we had tea with very nice biscuits as I recall — before your dad came in."

"Yeah. I'd say the shouting started about ten minutes later?" Alvin looked at Collette and they both agreed. "He was still furious that I'd refused to go to war," Alvin continued, "and outraged that I'd burned the flag. He said I'd tried to destroy him. He thought I was doing everything to humiliate him. See, he'd been in the army at the end of the Second World War and he'd joined up again for Korea. Oh, I'd never seen him so angry. He even thought I married you just to piss him off. He couldn't understand what I did had nothing to do with him. He just did not want to see the reality of Vietnam. The Pentagon Papers bomb hadn't dropped yet, but we all knew Vietnam was a lie . . ." Alvin stared at his empty glass while he made small circles with it on the table. "So then I told him I didn't care all that much if he was a bloodthirsty mercenary and a racist. Well, he just lost it. He went absolutely nuts."

"I thought he was going to pull that ax off the wall in the living room and take a swing at the both of us. I just jumped up and grabbed Alvin's arm and tried to pull him out the door."

"I got in one last dig though."

"You did."

Alvin looked up. "I called him a thug for hire, a total asshole and suggested he start the Sacramento chapter of the KKK if he wasn't already a card-carrying member. Who was he to be ashamed of me? I was ashamed of him!"

"Your poor mother. She was just crumpled in the corner of the dining room. It was awful. The whole thing was so ugly," Collette said.

"So that was it. I was disowned. Told never to come back. Never to call." Alvin paused and considered this. He rubbed his eye. "I tried over the years, you know. Wrote letters. They'd always come back unopened. Sent cards. Same thing. And you know, Ray's dad was very young. Only about Ray's age when that all that went down. I'm sure he thought I just turned my back on him. But no one would let me speak to him. They thought I'd corrupt him I suppose. And look at me. Hell, I ended up in insurance for God's sake — gift for the numbers — and you can't get more establishment than that. But even when Ray's dad got older he wouldn't talk to me. The only person I've been in contact with all these years is George, and only rarely at that."

"We did get together."

"A couple of times. That's true."

"We rented a big house on the shore one summer. They came for a week. Everybody got on and all the kids sure had a good time."

"Yeah, I thought so," Alvin agreed. "Anyway, I used to call up the neighbors from time to time to see if everything was okay. They were happy to hear from me. But they didn't hesitate to let me know nothing had changed as far as Dad was concerned. And nothing has to this day."

"You'd think they might have at least been interested in their grandchildren. They've never even met the kids," Collette said, squinting at such strangeness. "Course my side of the family wasn't much nicer. But they did come round. Two years and a baby later, we started getting invites to the family gatherings." Collette winked at Gina mischievously. "And some events were more eventful than others."

Alvin and Collette both laughed.

"My brother! He was so outraged I married Alvin."

"Even though he'd introduced us."

"Oh, he said awful things! And he never lets go of a grudge," Collette exclaimed. "Well, last year he sent Alvin a book for his birthday."

"Hard cover too!" Alvin piped up.

"I nearly fell off my chair," Collette said. "Turns out he must have developed a soft spot for Alvin again in spite of himself."

"Your folks were always good with the kids, though."

"Reasonably," said Collette.

Gina had gone to bed that night happier and relieved. She knew she could rest easy because Alvin would take really good care of Ray. He'd do it to make up for all the family he'd lost and so clearly missed, though he'd never admitted to it in so many words.

Chapter 5

Ray sat perfectly still watching a single streak of scarlet shift to orange and then disappear altogether as the cloud layers closed up. There was no other sign of the sun for a few minutes and then it reappeared, a blazing white stream of light coming up over the cloud bank that made Ray squint and shade his eyes. The light sparkled as it caught the wet surfaces from the recent rain. Ray, nostalgic for morning rituals he'd established on the Jersey Shore job, had come to watch the sun rise on his own property before going in to work at the grow facility. He was perched in the old loft where he could see more of the creek and his woods that sloped up the other side of it. Ray wasn't exactly sure how far his land extended up that hill but he doubted the neighboring farmers paid much attention to the property line. The woods were untouched. From his vantage point he could see where he might get across the creek easily. There were rocks close to the marsh that looked big enough he wouldn't get his feet too soaked. Ray decided he'd come back after work and go look at his woods more closely.

When Ray went into work that morning, the first thing he did was check on some orders for Cassie and Joe. As he was doing so, Gus wandered into the room where he was working. Ray still didn't have his own desk or office and he thought it might be a good opportunity to raise the matter with the production manager, but Gus didn't give him a chance.

"What the hell am I gonna do?" Gus sank down heavily on the only other chair in the room. "Things are breaking down again."

"That's no good," Ray said, watching Gus stuff a piece of gum into his mouth.

"Damian wants to torch the place. 'Too many glitches. Too much technology. Floods every other week!' Maybe he's right. Cassie and Joe tell me this shit wouldn't happen in a greenhouse."

Ray didn't know what to say.

"So Greg says you used to work on air conditioners."

"Yeah, in the army I did."

"You think you could take a look at the air handler in the West Mother Pod? Conked out last night just around eight, according to the logs. We got a service contract but the guy can't show 'til Monday. Leaves a whole weekend for the mothers to get fried and moldy."

"I see."

"Yeah. Damian figures we could lose that whole mother pod. He found mildew. Cassie said it was because he put pots on the floor again so they didn't have proper airflow for weeks. I don't know what to believe. I just want it fixed."

So Ray soon found himself teetering on top of a ladder. He looked down at all the mothers below him. The one that had the mold had been shorn of its offending branches and was isolated at the far end of the room. Since the air handler wasn't working, it wasn't making any noise, so Ray wondered what he was hearing. Again there was that humming and pulsing. Even strange clicking. Very faint but still audible. Or maybe not. Fatigue might be setting in. He'd just spent a good two hours getting familiar with the HVAC software. He'd run through the various diagnostics for the West Mother Pod, and a message kept popping up: *Contact Your Emerald-Certified Service Provider*. The software and online manuals, supposedly user friendly and full of diagrams, were not exactly informative and Ray found himself getting frustrated. He needed schematics of the air handler's guts, the controller's guts and the chiller's guts, but such things did not exist. Gus informed him that only the contracted service provider had those kinds of diagrams. Ray wondered if that sort of arrangement was even legal.

Ray hadn't really looked at an air conditioner closely since the army and as he lifted the panel to peer at the inner workings he felt a wave of exhaustion. He persevered though. There wasn't anything he recognized particularly, apart from the obvious fan. What were probably circuits or controllers for the UV zappers and the ion-filter system were all housed in protective casings. He didn't see any loose wires though or evidence of a short anywhere when he opened them. Maybe he'd do better with the chiller.

Gus showed him the access route to the roof. It took Ray a few minutes to make sure he had the right chiller. He took off the panel and stared at the array of tubing, the Schraders and venting valves, and again he couldn't really make immediate sense of anything. Then he saw a couple of things he recognized but couldn't remember what they were called. He had forgotten a lot. This was supposedly groundbreaking technology. Ray certainly hadn't kept up. He felt defeated. And he didn't like the sensation of confusion that enveloped him as he looked at everything. It was as if he was seeing it through a kaleidoscope. And he couldn't find anything obviously wrong. No leaks, nothing loose, nothing looking burned out anywhere.

He suspected the problem was digital, some failure in the control system. Parts would likely need replacing. Maybe the recent flood was just a little too much humidity for these humid-tolerant systems. They'd have to wait for the service guy. He relayed that to Gus. Then he suggested simply leaving the pod door open for the weekend and using portable fans. The HVAC system for the hallways could do double duty. From Ray's perspective all the units looked overbuilt, way bigger than they needed to be anyway. He didn't tell Gus that though. Gus was already looking discouraged.

Ray was glad to leave work that day and get back to his property. He walked down to the creek, to where it widened into a marsh, and he jumped across the rocks without slipping too much on the soggy ones and headed into the woods. He didn't know much about trees except that he liked being around them now and he could identify a few here and there. There were oaks, beech and maples with hemlock lurking underneath. He spotted a hophornbeam — he could tell by the bark that was all peeling and loose. There were spindly birch trees established in small groves too. He kept an eye out for wildlife as he meandered up the hill. He could hear a few birds. He thought if he got some spare time he'd study up to see how he could best manage his little bit of woods.

After a while he came to a level clearing, a small almost triangular-shaped gap. Dead grass from the summer before still rose up in high straw-like tufts while new growth sprouted underneath and around. A few saplings dotted the area. At the far corner of the triangle were some large rocks. Ray wandered over to them and as he got close he spotted a very small lizard basking in the late-afternoon sun. It had stripes and Ray knew what it was right away. His uncle Alvin had given him a field guide to amphibians and reptiles when he was about ten and he'd practically memorized it. This part of the country had only one lizard: a five-lined skink. They wouldn't be very common this far east and north, so he figured he was pretty lucky to see one. It was a still a juvenile with a bright-blue tail. A skink's tail was its ace in the hole. It could relinquish it to a predator. The end of the tail would keep writhing as a distraction while the skink scuttled away newly trimmed. The stub would regenerate a new tail over time. Ray had always been intrigued by the trick.

The lizard must have sensed Ray's approach. It moved about two inches or so very quickly, then stopped for a second. Then it vanished in a bright-blue flash over the edge of the rock. Ray shifted a few dead leaves to see where it went, but the lizard had disappeared. Ray got up from poking around and sat down on the rock himself. He thought about the skink's regenerative capabilities and looked down at his right hand with the missing fingers. The day's events and the confusion he felt looking at the HVAC system bothered him. What if there was more of him missing than the two fingers?

The day Ray had the electrical accident and lost those fingers wasn't all that memorable. Though it did turn out he was lucky he hadn't lost his arm. And given the fingers were on his right hand and he was left-handed, he wasn't all that incapacitated. So they didn't send him home. There was no immediate family to go to anyway. Instead they sent him off for four weeks to the base in Qatar with the lightest duties possible and as many four-day passes as required. Real quality rest and revitalization. Pools. Gyms. Massages. And the pain killers were terrific.

A few months later though, when he was back on regular duty and traveling with a convoy from Balad to Kirkuk, a roadside bomb went off. No one was hurt in the convoy and nothing was damaged, but the boys with the heavy firepower opened up immediately on anything that moved. Old men standing around with livestock, a guy in a car and five or six teenagers, mostly girls. Ray knew enough to stop looking out the back of the truck. And he decided then and there this would never be his kind of war. The convoy continued on. Before they reached Kirkuk though, it met up with a rocket.

He recalled the rocket came screaming in with its own heat and its own voice even before the boom. He stopped breathing. When it hit the vehicle in front, or exploded — difficult to sort out what came first — the truck he was in swerved and crashed, and at some point he was thrown out the back. And he was deafened. As the silence came over him and he was airborne, he watched the explosion unfold before him in slow motion. He noticed a very young soldier, one who'd panicked with such a flurry of bullets a half hour before, come apart in slow motion. In retrospect, he wondered how he could possibly have seen those things so distinctly. The skull splitting, the brains spilling, a leg soaring, the soldier's right hand severed by his own M4. It was a miracle really.

Ray had landed facedown in the dirt in a ditch and dimly wondered if he was dead. He couldn't feel anything for a while and he melted into the silence. Maybe he passed out. But then he noticed it. He could smell the earth. The quiet world of roots and bugs that he'd gotten to know so well as a child. It brought him back to his senses and he realized he was breathing again. He felt the hot sun on his back. He could move one leg, then the other. He pulled his head up, raised himself slowly on one elbow. The stench of the rocket, its aftermath and the leaking diesel fumes brought him to full consciousness. He was oddly clear of the chaos unfolding before him. He felt a sharp pain in his shoulders and his right wrist. His hand was still attached and he noticed he could move his fingers, all the ones that were left, even if it was painful. That was a good thing. He could feel pain.

Then he heard the screams, getting louder as his hearing returned, and he wanted more than anything to be deaf again. A suffocating heaviness came over him, all strength drained from his newly perceived limbs. He wondered if he was doomed from the blast anyway. If it was just a matter of hours or days before his lungs and innards cashed him out. He couldn't get up. It wasn't the first time a bloody aftermath had paralyzed him. He wanted very much to be unconscious but this time he wasn't. He put his head back down.

He smelled the earth again. It took him miles — years — away. He remembered when he was four years old and his mother was showing him the sunflowers that had started growing. "They'll be taller than you, Ray. Taller than me." She picked up a handful of the red-brown Valley soil and held it to her nose then she held it out to Ray. "Smell that, sweetie. That's good soil," she'd said. "Makes 'em grow real high." Ray often thought that memory of his mother somehow protected him. The medic said his survival without a major injury was incredibly lucky. He wouldn't have been surprised if Ray's innards and lungs, along with other parts, had failed. But they didn't. Ray had even hung on to his eardrums.

#

Ray's sleep could be fitful, given his military experiences, but after a fourteen-hour day of cloning at CannRose, Ray fell into a groggy stupor and slept like the dead. In the morning he did not wake up all that well. He did not open his eyes. His skin prickled and tingled. And he was still stuck in the remnants of a dream. He sensed the plants had been at him, slithering, embracing, covering every inch, swirling into him, smothering and finally breathing for him. And they hummed too. They pulsed. They clicked and popped in strange rhythms. "Work, work," Ray mumbled. "Plants, goddamn plants . . . they grow, they grow and they moan. They never stop . . . never shut up . . . they go on and on and on. How long 'til they wipe . . . me . . . out? . . . How many jobs . . . how many, 'til there's one doesn't kill me?" He breathed in deeply and began to remember Gus talking to him the day before.

"We need you. We really need you, Ray. Plus, you're already a pro!"

Ray had helped Jiggy a time or two with a couple of clones and that apparently made him a pro. But CannRose had over a thousand of them to get cut and planted. He and Damian had worked almost to midnight. Such a big push to get it all done in the one day! As Ray woke up a little more it occurred him that pressure on the job should be the dealbreaker. Wasn't that why he'd put his electrician career on hold? He'd have to speak to Greg.

Ray's eyes hurt, when he got around to opening them. Probably from staring so hard to make sure he got the cuts right. Then dipping the stems in that putrid gunk, a jelly laced with rooting hormones. There were chemicals on the product specs he didn't bother trying to pronounce. Weren't they supposed to be going organic? Oh yeah, and

Damian was on about how all the cloned plants would be identical. Same concentrations of THC and CBD in every flower on every plant. But a voice told Ray clear as a bell, *In your dreams, buddy*.

Ray stretched for a few moments, yawned and then sat up. He caught sight of his hands and blinked. He blinked again. His hands were thick, misshapen, his fingers distended like boiled sausages. They were covered in red blotches. So were his arms.

Ray got up and stumbled across the room. As he passed by the full-length mirror he got another shock. His face, chest and legs were covered in blotches too. Everything was swollen. He barely recognized himself. When he got to the bathroom and stood looking down at the toilet, he paused. He had a sinking feeling. He gingerly reached into his boxers and looked down. Jesus, Joseph and Mary! He experienced terror. He couldn't look anymore. From his nose to his toes he was afflicted. Could he even take a piss? It was a very tense moment or two. Sweet Jesus, yes, he could. He sighed with a deeper relief than he'd ever imagined for a morning ritual and luxuriated in the simple ease of it. He debated a little about what he should do next. Not look in the mirror. That was a good idea.

It was Saturday. Ray didn't have to go into work thankfully. But Gina and Jiggy would be home. He figured he'd get dressed, make a bolt for the truck and head out to his property before anyone caught sight of him. He still wasn't fully awake or thinking all that clearly. He cautiously stepped out of the bathroom. Gina, having heard the toilet flush, knew he was up and came out of the kitchen into the hallway.

"Oh my God, Ray!" Gina wasn't sure whether to get a closer look at him or run for cover. She stood mesmerized, intrigued and repulsed at the same time. "Have you seen yourself?"

"I know," Ray said in an agitated whisper.

"What happened?"

"I don't know. I just woke up like this!" Ray was still whispering.

Gina figured Ray must have lost his voice too and this was very alarming. "Are you having trouble breathing? Can you swallow?"

"No, I'm not having trouble breathing and yes I can swallow."

"But you've lost your voice."

"No, I haven't lost my voice," he hissed.

"Then why are you whispering?"

"Don't want to wake up Jiggy." Mostly Ray didn't want Jiggy asking him any questions. He still hadn't told him about the job.

"Jiggy's out. Gone hunting with Harold."

"Good." Ray's voice was back to normal.

"Well at least you sound okay."

"I felt terrible last night."

"Well you kind of looked like hell too for the half minute I saw you. Maybe you've come down with measles?"

At this suggestion Ray brightened, relieved there might be a reasonable name for his condition.

"Are they itchy?" Gina asked.

"What?"

"The spots, the rash. Itchy?"

Ray considered this for a second. "No . . . actually I don't know. My skin just feels really weird."

"It could be hives, but I've never seen them that red or so all over the place. You had chicken pox when you were five. I remember. I was there that summer. So it can't be that."

"Oh," Ray said quietly.

Gina, racked her brain for what symptoms went with what. "You have a headache?"

"I had a headache yesterday."

Gina noticed her cousin's sounding increasingly helpless. She'd just been reading the other day about man-colds and man-flus and how the viruses might actually be giving men a harder time after all. Something to do with testosterone, neural wiring and brain structure. *Poor babies*, she'd thought with a little smile at the time. But Ray's state was kind of alarming. In fact she thought he was being fairly stoic under the circumstances. She continued to stare at him. Finally she said, "There's an afterhours clinic in Lyston. I'm taking you there."

"Couldn't we maybe just call them?" Ray almost whimpered. He didn't fancy creeping out people in a waiting room. He pictured them getting up and leaving as soon as they caught sight of him. Or worse still, taking a snapshot on their phone and posting it with the hashtag #PlagueGuy.

"They won't tell you anything until they see you."

"Money grubbers."

"I thought your job had coverage."

"It does."

"So we'll go. Get some clothes on."

#

"Wow! Hives. Holy mama!" The young doctor was impressed. He wanted to know what allergies Ray had. Ray told him he didn't have any. "Well, something's causing a riot." So then they had discussed what Ray had been eating — not much as it turned out. So what had he come into contact with? Ray hesitated telling the doctor about the medical cannabis job but when he finally relented, the doctor's eyes lit up. "Hemp allergy. Of course!" Hemp allergies were common enough. The doctor beamed triumphantly. "But this case is spectacular!"

Ray then mentioned the other things, the rooting gel and the grow media with all their additives.

"Hmm, could be any one of those things I suppose. There's a cocktail of plant proteins there you've been handling. But this is systemic, like you've breathed it in or eaten it. You didn't eat some did you?" the doctor asked with mock gravity.

"No!"

The doctor peered into Ray's eyes, ears and throat. "Wow. You really got a mess of it. How's your breathing?"

"Yeah. I guess I do feel a little breathless."

"Right. So you got a lot of stress at the job?"

"I guess, maybe. We worked almost 'til midnight."

"Any other symptoms I should know about? Diarrhea? Vomiting?"

"No." Ray hesitated to mention the tinnitus — or the change in it — and that sometimes it went from roaring to pulsing, high-pitched hissing and weird clicking and popping. But nobody ever cared about the nature of the tinnitus, just that you had it or didn't. "Tinnitus," Ray said. "I have it sometimes and it came back worse."

"When did you start getting tinnitus?"

"Iraq."

"Aha!" the doctor said as if that solved yet another mystery. "When were you there?"

"2010 . . . 2011."

"Well how about that! I was there in 2009."

"You army?"

"Yup."

The doctor found out a few more details and he went on to say that the sanitation, inventory and security details sounded okay but Ray should keep clear of handling the plants. In fact it might be a good idea if he could drop a few hours. Maybe just work part time if he could afford it. And slow down a little on the property too and whatever he was building there. Maybe he could just do some fishing instead. He also suggested in a roundabout way that nerves frayed in conflict zones needed a little more care, even if those nerves hadn't experienced the front lines all that much and weren't anticipating combat or calamity every minute. In fact sometimes that was even worse. In the meantime he prescribed some heavy-duty antihistamines and cortisone, and told Ray to go to back to bed because the drugs were going to make him very, very sleepy.

#

Ray pulled his respirator off and looked up at the drive shed. He'd been sweeping, cleaning out the dirt and grime that had been there forty years or more. He'd come outside to take a break from the dust, the smell of old oil and rusting metal. And to get away from the inhabitants. He'd lifted a board that was leaning against the wall and uncovered a nest of bumblebees on the floor beneath. The queen bee likely took the location for an abandoned burrow when she started to build. A bumblebee nest is a haphazard arrangement. He could see many of the chambers were still covered, closed up at the top with eggs gestating inside. Some open chambers had larvae and some were abandoned. The few bees that were visible didn't pay any attention to the disruption. Bumblebees on the whole are a docile bunch, but Ray thought it might take a minute or two for them to realize they were not happy about the dust or the loss of their shelter. He put the board back so the bees could keep their home. They'd be gone in a few months and he'd clean it away then.

He was considering turning the drive shed into his house now rather than building new. It was nestled into the hill just like the barn, but higher up. So if he put windows on the south side he'd have an even better view than he did from the old barn loft. He'd had his heart set on building something from scratch but the more he thought about it, the more it seemed a waste. The drive shed structure was sound and if he gutted the building it would be pretty close to building new and he'd save himself some money. It was a saltbox shape and the upper floor was almost the right size too. He could put in a sleeping loft at the back end of the building under the gable. Keep the garages on the ground floor and turn one of them into his workshop. He didn't need a huge workshop.

Then he'd discovered the disintegrating containers and banned pesticides. There was cupric arsenate, aldrin, chlordane and DDT with lots of oily stuff that had seeped into the wooden floors. Probably wouldn't be good for his health or anybody's health. But the bumblebee queen had clearly survived it, although to be fair she'd built her nest on the far side of the shed away from the contaminants. But he could replace those boards easily enough. There was wood in the barn he could use for that. They'd make beautiful floors too, sanded down and varnished.

Ray sat down on the grass to think more about it all. And then he stretched right out and watched the clouds. Whatever the house would be, he'd want a cistern and he'd have solar panels and maybe even a small windmill. He'd look into geothermal heat too. Maybe he should consider building a bale house. . .

He woke with a start. The lingering image of his mother obliterated everything else. She was working in the kitchen garden as he always remembered her, smiling, young, pretty, humming to herself. Only this time when she turned to him, her face was charred, with bones and muscles showing where the skin had burned off. Her eyes were blistered. "The accident is always with us," she muttered.

As a child Ray had never been told much about the accident. Death had been instantaneous, people said, and they always mentioned his parents hadn't suffered. "Like when they put the old dog to sleep?" he'd asked. Yes, he'd been told, yes, just like the old dog. It was only when he went back to pick up a few things from his Uncle George before he shipped out to Iraq the second time that he found the newspaper clippings. The car had gone out of control, broken through a guardrail and exploded on impact in a fiery crash at the bottom of a gorge.

Ray sat up. He fished in his pocket for his phone to check the time. He'd been sleeping for two hours. Some productive afternoon this had been! He didn't feel like doing anything else now either. He looked around. The old kitchen orchard caught his eye. Ray hadn't done anything about it yet. But he'd noticed some trees were bearing fruit despite the years of neglect. Most of it was buggy and still very green. But one of the trees had pale-yellow apples. They were almost luminescent when the sun fell on them and some even had a rosy blush to them. Ray got up and took a closer look. A few were wormy but most were in surprisingly good shape. Ray picked one. It came away easily and smelled ripe. Ray had been used to summer apples in California when he was a kid, but in the east this was awfully early for a ripe apple. He took a bite. It was juicy. Almost burst in his mouth. A little tart but sweet too and the flesh was white with yellow streaks. Possibly one of the nicest apples he'd tasted in a long time.

He found a bag in his truck and picked enough to fill it. He took it back to Gina and Jiggy and proudly handed them the first produce from his own farm.

Gina picked one and bit into it. "Oh, these are lovely! I wonder if they'd be good for a pie."

"I think," Jiggy said, having bitten into one too, "they're a little too delicate. They'd disintegrate with the cookin'."

"Nice applesauce then maybe."

Chapter 6

Ray's office, now that he finally had one, was without doubt the smallest in the facility. He'd been hoping for a space in the production area but the spare offices there were intermittently used for equipment and building supplies as the area was constantly undergoing construction updates. Plus, as Greg pointed out, having a cubbyhole in the administrative section was probably better for keeping Ray's allergies at bay and for keeping him clear of any construction noise too.

While the administrative section had a large conference room, a fully functioning kitchen and eating area, and rather luxurious washrooms, there were only three traditional offices. One for Lydia, one for Lazlo, and a spare that was reserved for out-of-town executives when they showed up, or for guests or sometimes Caldwell or whoever was temporarily in need of a private space. And a fourth office, if it could be called that, was the great fishbowl reserved for security situated at the far end beside the front entrance. The rest of the admin section was open to the rafters with workspaces set up as niches, often with the help of half-height semi-opaque plexiglass screens that had a faint green tinge to them. And assisting in this regard was the recent addition of large and unexpectedly colored artificial palms, cacti, yuccas and hibiscus.

Real plants weren't permissible because of the disease threat they posed to the CannRose crops, so Caldwell insisted they go bold with the colors. "Make a statement, for Chrissake." And so they did. Possibly a more effective one than anticipated. Lily, the pretty receptionist, had been put in charge of the project and she'd limited the eye-popping spray paints to cobalt blue, cyan, and manganese violet. One of Lydia's assistants did the actual spraying out in the parking lot, and as the last vibrant cactus was decoratively set into place, Lily felt the first of her contractions and had to be driven to hospital. The baby was early.

Not only were the colors in the admin section provoking and clamorous, the acoustics generated by the open design were not helpful for telephone calls. Ray's ordering for CannRose might have been an online activity fifty percent of the time but often it required speaking to an actual person. So the photocopier was moved from one of the storage rooms into a niche in the communal area, and what had originally been its own special room became Ray's space.

Ray was on the phone discussing an order for some bags that CannRose was considering using rather than bottles. But just like the bottles, bags needed childproof fasteners according to the state code, and the effectiveness of the fasteners had been the grand topic of discussion. As Ray put his phone down, Gus, large and lumbering, appeared in the doorway, and beside him was the smaller and far more lithe DOH inspector. They startled Ray. He certainly wasn't expecting any visits, but as he found out later, no one was expecting Ms. Ligner. That was the point. Surprise inspections by the DOH were to become a hallmark of the state effort to sanitize the industry.

The inspector however was startling enough just on her own. As one of Lydia's assistants in administration enthused for days afterward, "She's so fucking hot! She can tie me up and whip me for noncompliance any day she wants. Inspect all precious parts of me! Yeah, baby!" By consensus, he was considered way too over the top on this, and by the end of the day everybody would tell him to just stuff it because as Damian put it, "Ligner's just a little bitch on a power trip and no friend of CannRose." Cassie was in total agreement with Damian for once, though Joe was oddly silent.

After Gus's introduction, the inspector stepped into Ray's diminutive office and sat down in the only available chair, right beside Ray's. Very close in fact. Ray's desk was pushed right up against the wall he'd decorated with a large picture calendar of a forest scene. He'd also set his screen saver to shuffle through photos of woodsy landscapes to help relieve the claustrophobia. But with Ms. Ligner sitting so close, Ray wasn't exactly sure what he'd best be looking at. Her glossy hair, on the reddish side, fell in languid waves to her shoulders. Her pale-gray jacket was open to reveal a rather low-cut black blouse. Her black leather skirt was not particularly fulsome either, whereas her lips, embodying as they did a mesmerizing pout, were. Emphatically so. He could also smell her perfume.

The inspector smiled and Ray smiled back. Her eyes were intense with a steely gray-blue gaze that shot right into his cerebral cortex. But Ray excelled at hiding any awkwardness, attraction and sexual enthusiasm because he was so well-practiced. Over the last six years, the wife of his best friend Gabe had tirelessly tried to interest him in each and every one of her appalling "hottie" girlfriends. Through many unpleasant experiences, Ray learned it was best for him to play dumb and never encourage a woman who looked like this. And besides, there were important matters at hand. Since Ms. Ligner was from the DOH, Ray logically figured she'd be able to help clarify the requirements regarding the childproof packaging. Ray found the state code fairly cryptic.

"Good timing," Ray said brightly. "I was just trying to decipher what the DOH wants in terms of childproof bags if we get them. The sales rep was just telling me a couple of other states are really strict about proof. Formal studies and stuff, not just the usual specs. Do I need to have those too?"

The inspector blinked at his question. He noticed she went a little pink and then seemed to get annoyed. "I believe all the requirements are in the regulations," she said.

"Probably," Ray said, "but half the time I can't really figure out what they mean."

"I'm sorry, but I'm actually here to do an inspection, not help you formulate procedures. Speaking of which, where are your operating procedures?"

Ray sat back. The thought suddenly occurred to him that she wouldn't answer his question because she couldn't. She didn't know. She either didn't know about packaging or didn't know what the code meant. Then again maybe she just had a tight schedule. He went on dutifully to answer her question. "I asked Gus about written procedures myself when I got here, but we don't have any."

"You mean you haven't bothered to write them." She smiled faintly.

"I didn't know they needed to be written."

"Ha!" she exclaimed with a high-pitched exhale. "This was a finding from the *first* inspection." She tilted her head back, revealing the long line of her neck, but her eyes had taken on an imperious squint.

"I didn't know there'd been a first inspection," Ray said.

"Ha!" she exclaimed again and picked up her pen.

That did it. That last little *ha!* with its squeal of disbelief, rebuke and contempt all rolled into one permeated Ray's brain far more intrusively than her gaze could ever hope to. Rather than landing in the central cortex, it had lodged closer to the amygdala then exploded with a burst of unpleasant little echoes. Any attraction Ray felt vanished. And simultaneously before his eyes she turned into a pasty-skinned sack of tissue and bones with irritating movable mouth parts. Her voice had all the charm of gears grating. As she went on with questions and the occasional unmistakably snide observation, Ray came to the conclusion that Ms. Ligner was as much of a jerk as the sergeant he'd had a run-in with his first day in Iraq. And if she thought she'd perfected badgering, Ray had endured grand masters in this regard, so most of what she said he simply ignored. Ray put the inspector in the supreme asshole category, just like the sergeant, and without being aware of it, this showed abundantly on his face.

"You realize I have the authority to close the facility."

Even with his disagreeable assessment of her, the comment still came out of the blue and was completely unrelated to what they'd just been talking about. His filing! Fair enough. He could have kept better files and he'd been promising himself for the last two weeks he was going to sort that out. Mostly he was just procrastinating because it was the least appealing task on his list. But if she was somehow trying to scare him by insinuating that a few poorly organized requisitions, purchase orders and receipts could shut down CannRose, she must be stupid and possibly unhinged too. So he looked at her, this time perplexed, and wondered if perhaps he should just feel sorry for her. And because he'd caught her staring at his hand with the missing fingers and it creeped him out, his face registered a tad of revulsion too. "Shouldn't you be speaking to one of the executives if you're going to shut the place down?" Ray said with all sincerity.

The inspector turned a little pink again, muttered, "Thank you for your time," then got up and left the room.

After a minute or two, Greg showed up at Ray's door. "What did you say to her?"

"What do you mean?"

"What did you say? She just left the place like a hornet on fire. Said she was going to lunch. Looked like she planned on slaughtering it first."

"I didn't say anything." Ray was oblivious. He didn't realize he'd turned Ms. Ligner's customary interaction with men on its head. She wasn't used to seeing faint disdain bordering on pity and dismissal in those she interviewed — that was *her* role. "I don't think she's all that smart you know," Ray said to Greg. And then he remembered the intensity of her eyes and her attention to his missing fingers and added, "Kind of weird too, maybe."

The next day, Caldwell turned the place upside down he was so livid about the inspection. The woman really was going to try to shut CannRose down, only it wasn't because of anything Ray did. Caldwell yelled at practically everybody *but* Ray. Terry, the QA officer, got fired the minute he walked in the door. Gus looked like he was ready to quit. Cassie, Joe and Damian were briefly united in denial about any inadequacies regarding cultivation of the plants. Ernie was keeping his head down and maintaining his cheerfulness even more than usual as he mopped the floors.

Chapter 7

Ray thought a lot about Jiggy. He just couldn't help it — Jiggy could say such crazy stuff and be so ferocious about it. He'd get Ray thinking about something for days. And then if Ray asked him about it, he could just as easily have changed his mind by that time. "Research, Little Cousin. I do my homework." And by homework, he meant hours on the computer. Poor Gina. But like she said, if it weren't for Jiggy's addiction to the internet he'd likely be in jail for punching out a cop or worse. Plus it gave him something to do when he couldn't sleep.

Jiggy also made trips to the city from time to time. "Fact checkin', Little Cousin," Jiggy would say. "Nothin' beats a university engineerin' library." Or like the time when he was trying to find out about the antidepressant he'd been prescribed: "Old medical libraries still hold many secrets, Little Cousin," after which he'd taken his bottle of pills and dumped them in the backyard compost. Jiggy would never say which university libraries he visited. Sometimes he'd go to the state library to check government documents, public archives and so on. "Never believe the official story, Little Cousin. Only rarely is it not fulla shit."

There were two things Ray knew Jiggy never changed his mind about. One, he hated government at just about every level and jurisdiction, and two, he hated big international corporations, especially if they did any business with the military. Corporate tyranny was rampant, and greedy shitheads were everywhere. All you had to do, Jiggy pointed out, was "look at the Wall Street fuckers, not one of 'em in jail." He'd add emphatically, "With their Ivy League degrees an' their gobs all in the pig trough, feedin' off the poverty an' debt of the rest of us." He'd go on to point out how the economic "fashion" was meticulously tailored and how "all the little pricks comin' out of the big business schools were programmed for the same shit. Trickle down my ass." Globalization was just a precursor to slavery. "An' that's only half the problem, Little Cousin. We're just fodder for 'em! Weightless, airborne by the fuckin' whirlwind comin' off that revolvin' door from corporate to government appointments." Jiggy would pause for effect and for that to sink in and in case Ray might have questions that Jiggy'd be more than happy to answer. It would always come down to the same thing. Capitalist economies and their governments were all corrupt, owned by corporate interests, rooted in greed and fueled by fraud, wars and any other crisis, including bad weather. Especially climate change. The debate was never whether it was real or not. Anyone with half a brain had to understand it was real but Jiggy said the bullshit around it was twofold. "Big oil an' its shills suckin' every last penny out of the ground before obsolescence an' the fuckin' military–industrial complex just droolin' at the insurrection comin' down the line from the consequences." And Jiggy would get a little red in the face at this point and maybe pound on the table if he was sitting at one. "The greediest fuckers are all lookin' forward to it. They're all gonna make a killin' one way or another before they destroy the planet."

It could be that anarchy was technically what Jiggy advocated, though he did allow for organizations and committees and some form of loose and benign hierarchy in his vaguely imagined preferences. "After all, somebody has to build the fuckin' roads, Little Cousin." But essentially, Jiggy's ideal world would be made up of all small players. How we'd ever get food into supermarkets or gas in our cars was just part of the problem from Jiggy's perspective. Some things were just plain unnatural, like strawberries in January and supermarkets full of processed poison parading as nourishment. And some things were a plot, like cars needing gasoline in the first place, and then Jiggy would elaborate about "the roomfuls of ve-hicular designs suppressed by the Big Car Makers all in bed with Big Oil." Jiggy's mistrust of anybody or any entity with power was absolute — as in "absolute power corrupts absolutely." This was Jiggy's favorite saying on a sunny day.

It was particularly unwise to get Jiggy started on 9/11 and especially Building 7 or really anything about the Twin Towers. After all as Jiggy pointed out endlessly, while he might have lost a foot, he didn't lose his brains or his fuckin' eyesight. "Any idiot could see from that video . . ." and he'd be on the topic for a good half hour or more. The rant could go in any direction at that point, from the plan of the Powers That Be to the destruction of securities fraud evidence to the Enron bankruptcy and Afghan pipeline connection to the Saudi connection to insurance fraud and — Jiggy's personal favorite — the general thuggery of the military–industrial complex.

Then would come the indignation. Jiggy would sometimes get red in the face, swear a blue streak and then cry about all the people killed in needless wars. Or planned crises. Ray thought if the Powers That Be fed off crises like Jiggy said, then Jiggy himself fed off the indignation about it. When Jiggy eventually exhausted himself, he'd ask if Ray was up for a drink. Then they could talk and Ray could get a word in edgewise over the bourbon or a beer. Mostly they'd talk about family or saving money so Ray could get his house all finished or maybe Ray's lack of a girlfriend.

One day when Ray had pointed out that he must be clueless since he fell for all the wrong women, Jiggy shook his head. "Little Cousin, women might be somethin' of a mystery but I've seen a few of 'em look at ya and there's no mystery there. Jesus, just make a move now an' again." Ray thought about this for a second and wondered if there wasn't a woman or two at CannRose who might inspire him to make a move now and again. But he certainly couldn't discuss it with Jiggy, because four months into his job at CannRose and he still hadn't told Jiggy where he worked. At that moment though, with Jiggy being calm and quite fatherly almost, Ray decided it might be a good time to just brace himself and give Jiggy the good news.

"It's a start-up company," Ray began, "and it's not connected to any big corporate interests that's for sure. More like a family outfit."

Jiggy nodded.

"And it's so close, just ten minutes away, against traffic!"

"You can't beat that."

They both laughed, given Hullbrooke had only just become a three-traffic-light town. Ray went on to explain about having all the various tasks that go with a job when a company is newly formed. He told him about the excitement, about getting in on the ground floor of something and watching it grow. He talked about all the different sorts of people he was meeting. He described just about everything, and then after another round of beer, Ray quietly dropped that he worked for CannRose and was now a shareholder in the medical marijuana business.

Jiggy looked at him, speechless.

"I don't think it's as bad as you think," Ray ventured cautiously, wondering what kind of a tirade he might be in for, hoping Jiggy wouldn't tell him to pack up and leave the house or something. "The people are great, and a few more locals now got jobs because of it, yours truly included." Though Ray didn't know if being so newly transplanted himself, he counted as a local.

Jiggy stared down at his beer.

"Jiggy, I know you don't approve, but it's a good job and I can even give Gina a little more rent 'til I'm out at my own place for good."

Jiggy took in a deep breath and continued staring into his beer. Finally he lifted his head and said to the air in front of him, "I suppose it's not so bad. At least it's not a fuckin' private security firm."

Ray sighed with relief. Jiggy's views on marijuana were no less ardent than on most issues but they were perhaps tempered. Marijuana was one subject especially where Jiggy had never been able to hog the conversation. Half the vets around were using it legally or not, and they always had lots to say about it. It was frequently discussed in the bar. Mostly they wanted better access. And better product. And most were not too happy about the state-sanctioned dispensaries or the way the whole business was shaping up. "There's all these big wigs in it just for the money." Nods all around. "Have you tried it? The stuff's lousy. I get way better shit from my friend in Oregon." More nods. And "Hell, it's still better off the street." There was always the odd dissenting voice that saw some advantage to a state health department getting involved. "Least it's clean. You're not just gonna get high off the pesticides and end up with cancer." All to be countered by, "Who gives a rat's ass? Whatever takes my pain, honey," or "Anything would do, just so I'm not reliving those sunshine moments." And Jiggy could also be relied on to point out that pesticide companies were joined at the hip with Big Pharma, if not part of them, so unless you could grow your own, there was no telling what kind of mind manipulation was going on.

They'd all been hoping a bill would pass so the VA doctors could at least prescribe it and that way they'd likely get it for free. Like they did up in Canada. Still, with the Republicans controlling the Senate . . .

"It's not a partisan issue," somebody would pipe up. Then the conversation would veer off into the publicized stands of various politicians. Or vets who grew their own might start talking about plant pests or lighting. One day the whole to-freeze-or-not-to-freeze question came up, and Jiggy was dead against it, whereas an old air-force mechanic said, "With half a banana, lime juice, the right yogurt and crushed ice, the frozen stuff, raw or cured if you couldn't get fresh, made the best smoothies for a stinking hot day you could ever want."

Chapter 8

Ray rocked gently in the hammock. He was taking his doctor's advice. After another minor flare-up of hives and a change in the noises in his head that seemed to get worse every time he just stuck his nose into a grow room, he'd put in for a four-day week at CannRose. It wasn't so much that he was exhausted. It was more he wondered if he was going a little crazy. He was beginning to think the marijuana was talking to him, or rumbling and percussively sputtering at him, and that the plants didn't have anything particularly nice to say. So maybe the less time he spent at CannRose the better.

Ray had found himself some camping equipment and now that he'd built himself a fine little outhouse not too far from the barn, he could easily live at his farm for the next couple of months until it got too cold. He'd hung his hammock down by the creek with a big bug net suspended over it. There were no plans for the weekend. He was waiting on the delivery of a tank and tiles to install the septic system. The weekend before it had been the well. The old well was good, at least the source was. He just needed to put in a new pit and a pump. There was still a lot to do before he could really start turning the drive shed into his house. Most of it might have to wait until the following year. The various projects had to be timed and budgeted. There were always delays for one reason or another: a broken-down backhoe, another job ahead of his that wasn't finished on time. He was used to it.

Right after he got out of the army, Ray had worked for Gabe, who owned a contracting company with his dad, and delays had been par for the course. After a year or so, Ray couldn't take the constant physical stress of carpentry and the noise of downtown construction sites anymore, so he'd signed up for courses to get his electrician's license. Ray figured being an electrician could be less strenuous and quieter. But one day right after he'd finished all his course work, Gabe called him again.

"Got a big juicy surprise," Gabe shouted, and Ray could hear the sound of nail guns and saws in the background. "There's a new project on the table! You won't be able to resist it! And my man, it absolutely screams location, location, location! Right on the fan-fuckin-tastic Jersey Shore! Waves lapping at your toes and the wind in your lovely head of hair."

The project amounted to the renovation of a 1920s art-deco hotel into luxury condos. Ray wouldn't have to get his hands very dirty at all. He'd be more or less overseeing logistics, basically an assistant running things for Gabe and his dad when neither of them were there. They had bigger projects on the go in Jersey City that were taking up all their time. They needed someone they could trust. And they had awesome digs for Ray.

"Right on the beach, my man! All yours, rent-free and the sound of the ocean to calm your frayed nerves. Not exactly the Taj Mahal of course, but Pa says he'll throw in a club membership. Saunas, circuit, whirlpool."

"Sound's incredible!" Ray said.

"Wouldn't have it any other way. It's the least we can do for one of the brave men and women who donned the uniform for this great country of ours . . ."

"Fuck off." Ray laughed.

"Truth is," his friend said in an amplified falsetto, "you know how we all love to see your pretty, pretty face on a job first thing in the morning."

"You really are a jerk. You know that."

"That's me, sweetheart. You know you love it!"

So Ray had put his electrician career on hold and spent a good year on the Jersey Shore. It had been the perfect job. In fact Ray was feeling better than he'd ever felt since he came out of the army. All that ocean breeze. A good routine with exercise and relaxation. Work that didn't wear his body out and good friends like Gabe to share a laugh with now and again. That was the life he wanted. Needed really.

One day during his work stint on the shore, Ray ran into an old buddy from basic training when he was walking along the beach. Tyler looked a little rough, though he was happy to see Ray. But after about twenty minutes of talking to him over a beer, Ray realized Tyler was an addict. Going for a beer was mostly an attempt to hit Ray up for money or maybe better contacts. Tyler tried to pretend everything was fine at home too then finally admitted his wife had taken off with the two kids six months before. Tyler couldn't sleep, not without a little help; wrenched his back among other things, and now the goddamn VA cut his prescription to practically nothing. Ray figured he was buying opioids off the street, heroin too by the sounds of it.

"Why the fuck doesn't the VA dish out the good stuff in the first place?" That's what Tyler wanted to know. He told Ray he should try it sometime; in fact maybe he'd like to go try it right now.

Tyler had been on night raids and it sounded like that was the stuff he couldn't get out of his head. Things might have been ramping down in Iraq, but Afghanistan? Tyler had been deployed there three times. "You never knew what was hiding in those fuckin' hovels waitin' for you. And then everybody's screamin', dogs barkin'. Wish they learned to shut the fuck up. At least you could shoot the dogs." Tyler saw two children get killed. "Shit, man. They were under a blanket and the way it moved! Anybody woulda done it." He felt sorry for the soldier who did though — he was pretty fucked up about it. One was a little girl, four years old maybe, same age as Tyler's own little girl was now. "Then there was this old guy, barely walking, but probably just screwing with us. He falls down some stairs. Starts having some kind of a fit or something. Guy just lies there with one leg thrashing and jerking around. Fuck! What are you supposed to do with shit like that?"

Ray had seen hints of Tyler's temper in training, but then Tyler told him — and he was laughing when he said it — "Yeah, I've probably gone postal a few times. They should fuckin' lock me up."

Ray figured he might be able to help Tyler out in some way even if it was only to listen to his stories. He suggested they go fishing. Tyler said sure but he never showed up at the docks Saturday morning and Ray never saw him again.

So Ray counted his blessings. He was grateful to the base doctor in Qatar who'd refused to give him a certain prescription. "And don't be getting it off the other guys — it's a death sentence. I don't care what anybody says. Ibuprofen is all you need. Trust me on this one." So Ray hadn't picked up the habit. And he could get a good night's sleep these days without any aids. Sure he had nightmares sometimes, and too much noise wore him down. Or maybe he was just going a little crazy. Who wasn't?

Ray continued to swing in his hammock and listen to the breeze. He could read a book. Or he could do a little fishing. If he felt more industrious, he could go clean up the barn or start seriously gutting the drive shed. Or he could start cleaning up the woods and work on building a woodpile. The purchase of the land had turned out to be wise. Finally a wise decision. There was no place he'd rather be. It was more peaceful than anywhere he'd lived as an adult. With a little effort he could stay here until the snow fell. He could even stay a little longer, set up temporary quarters in the barn if he didn't mind the mixed company.

Ray had discovered an assortment of small animals resided in both his old buildings. He'd set traps. But then he caught a rat and the snap spring hadn't killed it, just caught it right below the gut. The rat was still very much alive, even on the move. The trap was at least three yards away from where Ray had set it the night before. The rat's back legs looked dead as if they'd been severed at the base of the spine but the front ones were lively and strong. The rat had looked him right in the eye, fierce and hanging to life. It had young somewhere too. Ray could see the little teats on its belly. He felt the old nausea starting to rise. He turned and walked away, and the rat started to follow him, pulling itself along on its front legs, dragging the trap behind. Ray could feel the sweat beading on his forehead. He got out of the barn and ran to his truck. The wind on his face took away the nausea. He looked for a hammer. It was the quickest way. He tried to banish the image of the rat's dark shining eyes as he slowly walked back to the barn. When he got there the rat had almost reached the door. He knelt down beside it. It looked at him again. Ray swung the hammer and a little pool of blood seeped out from under the rat's head. Ray stayed kneeling. He couldn't get up. He was frozen. It was like the rat knew him. Knew all about him.

#

Ray got a call from his friends in Boston, a couple he'd met when he was on that job at the shore. Julie and Anna wanted to take a little vacation and it sounded like they'd been bickering about what to do because Julie liked the upscale B&B's, lazy saunters along shores and trendy restaurants, while Anna liked a good hike before setting up camp in the middle of nowhere and fishing for her dinner. So they were looking for a compromise and wondered what accommodations and camp sites were available his way. Ray didn't have a clue really. Told them he was living in a tent himself these days. And since his tent leaked, he'd set it up in the barn. They were welcome to bring their own tent and join him or pick any spot on his forty acres. He also told them about the marsh, that he'd had part of it dug deeper so he had a pond now and noticed more fish in it. About a foot long or so. Probably catfish. They were welcome to come fishing. He hadn't gotten around to catching any himself. He sounded awfully busy, they said. "Not as much as you'd think." He also told them not to forget their bug spray. The bugs were out and as vicious as ever.

A week later Anna and Julie pitched their tent right next to the old kitchen orchard. Anna had brought groceries from Boston. She thought the fish in Ray's pond sounded decidedly unappetizing, a little too much like bottom-feeders, and besides, she didn't want to disturb them. Julie had brought her to-die-for homemade sticky buns for breakfast. They were just staying the one night before moving on to a wilderness park two hours north for a few days then a couple of nights at a hotel on the coast.

The three friends were all sitting around a campfire down by the creek. Anna was abundantly freckled, tattooed, and her skull was shaved up the sides to her temples. The rest of her slightly frizzy dark hair ended at her shoulders. She was leaning against Julie, who was big and bosomy but only rarely big-haired. Her thick curly blonde locks were restrained in a single braid on one side. Occasionally Julie would let the curls loose to favor a sort of retro Dolly Parton look—"Because I can," said she'd once, "and it still pisses off a couple of old drag queens I know, not to mention my great aunt, the most famous dyke in my family."

Ray was seated directly opposite on the other side of the fire and close to the water's edge. They were all feeling pretty good after their barbecue of porgies and clams and they were happy from the wine.

"So do tell. What's it like working at a grow-op, Ray?" Julie raised her left eyebrow, and Ray knew the question would be followed by some teasing remark or a dare or some darkly comic observation that he just might not get.

Anna was already laughing.

"Why is it everybody finds it such a freaking joke?" Ray was squinting across the fire at the bottle of wine between the two of them and it looked almost empty.

Anna sat right up. "Two months ago you told me you applied *as a joke!*"

"Yeah, Ray. What's with that?" Julie then whispered to Anna but loud enough Ray was sure to hear. "Possibly some kind of weed cult happening here and he's undergone a conversion."

Ray sighed. True enough, he had found it ridiculous himself and now he couldn't remember why. "You think it's the stoners? Or the high everybody remembers getting? Or maybe 'cause it's been illegal? Or . . . or what?" Ray looked up and saw a shooting star, then another and another. He pointed to sky and kept looking at it. "It's a meteorite shower! How cool is that?"

The other two looked up and quickly became engrossed in the celestial show as well. Their necks all began to ache so the three of them lay down on their backs to one side of the fire with their heads together and stared up at the sky. After a while Ray said they should sing songs, but the only thing he could think of at the moment was "Livin' la Vida Loca." Then he rambled on about driving across the country with Gina when he was an eight-year-old, right after his parents died. His friends grew quiet. It occurred to him, he was boring the crap out of them like some drunk at Chelsea's, or maybe they'd fallen asleep. The meteorite show was waning. He turned his head and noticed Anna wiping tears away while Julie was up on one elbow staring down at her. Julie caught Ray's eye. "She might talk tough, but she's a baby," and then Julie leaned down and kissed Anna's cheek.

"That is the saddest fucking thing 'cause you don't even think it's sad, Ray" Anna said. "God. Eight years old. I didn't know you were an orphan."

Ray started to laugh. "Technically. But I had fill-ins. No shortage of parents."

"But you lost both of them!" Anna said, sitting up, sniffling. "Don't you miss them?"

"Yeah, Ray. You're . . . uh, remarkably chill," Julie said. "Do you ever think about them?"

Ray sat up himself and shifted around to face his friends again, "Sure. I . . . I think of them."

They looked at him expectantly.

"Um . . . depends on the time of year. What's happening. Sometimes . . ." Ray wasn't sure how much he should divulge. "Sometimes I think of them . . . a lot." He decided not to tell them about the lingering presence of his mother after she died. Nor that she was again starring in his dreams. Or that memories of her often came back when there was some calamity. It might sound . . . pathetic. He'd always found his orphan status cloying. They stopped talking while Ray put more wood on the fire. The night was almost symphonic anyway with frogs croaking, bugs buzzing by, and a bird call Ray couldn't recognize through the crackling of the flames. There was no wind. He opened the last bottle of wine and poured everyone another glass.

"So how long before you start building something here?" Julie asked.

"I've started already." Ray pointed up the hill between the drive shed and the barn.

Julie turned to see the outhouse just barely visible in the dark. "No. I mean how long before the place with heating and running water maybe? That's a little primitive for entertaining."

"It's doing a fine job!"

"Don't insult the biffy, Julie — that's what my dad called them — specially a carefully constructed one. It is quite grand, Ray. A two-holer! I particularly like the ornamental window in the door and the bit of gingerbread at the gable. Nice touch."

"I thought so too. And in the morning you'll see the view is inspiring." Ray smiled.

"Splendid." Julie looked like she was about sneeze and couldn't. "I need better antihistamines." She sighed. "So you really like being here all on your own all the time?"

"Yeah. I see enough people, believe me."

"I'd get lonely. I mean, I like hiking alone." Anna gave Julie a sidelong glance. "I love the quiet then, but I always like to come back to people."

"I just feel better here. I can think."

"How's that work? I'm finding it kind of noisy with all the wildlife. *Hddddrp, Hdddddrp.*" Julie did her best imitation of the local tree frogs.

"I don't know. After getting out of the army, I guess I never felt I could relax. Not really. Not around people."

"You're not relaxed now?" Julie chirped again. "Not even with your best supportive undemanding, no pressure LBFs?"

"Yeah. Kind of, but I'm also a little drunk."

"You ever get assessed for PTSD?"

"Geez, Julie! What's with the friggin' twenty questions tonight!" Anna smacked her on the arm.

"I don't think PTSD's a problem." Ray picked up a pebble and began turning it over in his hand like a worry bead. "I can sleep. I know guys who can't. Or they're addicts. Or they're completely fucked up. Those are the guys who go for assessments. I'm doing excellent." He turned for an instant and threw the pebble, skipping it across the creek.

Anna looked at him and shook her head. The three of them did not speak for a while, just drank their wine and listened to the night. Then Anna had a question. "Do you, uh . . . wash off in the creek?"

"Yes, Ray." Julie finished off her wine. "How *do* you address your personal hygiene at a place like this?

Ray looked at Julie and smiled with some defiance. "Sometimes I jump in the creek. But there're showers at work too."

"I think we should all go skinny-dipping. Drunk dunk in the dark. I'm going."

Here was Julie's dare and Ray did not feel like a dunk in the dark. He half closed his eyes. "You two go right ahead. I'm a morning dipper myself. Don't drown." He got up a little shakily and stood for a few seconds. "I'm going to bed." And then he delivered the line he knew would definitely stop Julie from doing anything stupid. "Watch out for the water snakes. They're kind of nocturnal and busy." He smiled down at his friends, their faces warmly lit by the campfire with Julie visibly wincing from his last remark, and then he turned to go.

"He's had enough of us for one day, Anna!"

Ray waved without looking back and went up the hill to the barn and his tent.

Chapter 9

For Jiggy the world was in such a state of shit, who in their right mind would want to add to the insanity? If you were smart you didn't succumb, you didn't have kids of your own, and if you were really smart you didn't get born in the first place. That this hadn't always sat so well with Gina was beside the point. In Jiggy's mind, Gina had just been naïve and ultimately she'd come round. About ten years earlier, Gina'd tried very hard to get pregnant, especially before Jiggy shipped out to Afghanistan that last time. When Jiggy came back minus a foot she was fairly relieved it hadn't caught. How would she have managed with a young child and a husband who needed special care, at least initially? Not to mention when Jiggy finally came back for good, he was hardly the Jiggy she knew.

In the beginning, Jiggy would have a drink or two and he'd start saying things about how it would have been better if the explosion had gotten all of him instead of just a piece. Even on a good day back then, he'd rant and rage — against the government, wealthy elites, private security firms, higher-ups in the military and inept VA administrators. He was more subdued and agreeable when he just smoked weed, but regardless, he'd state loud and clear how all wars were really only ever about money and oil. "Started by rich fuckin' oligarchs, an' all the rest of the propaganda about freedom an' democracy is shit."

No one would want a child to have to listen to that all the time, would they? Gina reminded herself of this. Who knew what it would lead to and how much they'd blame her for everything when they grew up? Still, her mother had pointed out a child might soften him, make him care about something other than a world full of mayhem. Gina figured a child could just as easily push him right over the edge. He could end up incarcerated or institutionalized. She'd seen it up close and nasty. He was better now, but the memory never left Gina. Deep in her heart there always lurked a whisper of anxiety that a similar incident might occur.

He'd been home about six months and he'd started drinking heavily. He'd polish off a bottle of wine and maybe half a bottle of some kind of liquor almost every night. She'd walked into the kitchen one night and found him sitting on the floor crying. He was bashing his fist into a cupboard door and she figured it might go right through.

"Jiggy," she said. "Sweetheart, you're really drunk. It's time to forget about all that and come to bed."

He'd looked up at her, tears streaming down his face. "You think ya know what this is about?"

"No," Gina said, "but I know it's killing you."

"You fuckin' don't know anything."

"Well you can tell me in the morning. Right now you need your beauty sleep." She'd tried to be funny. She just wanted him to stop drinking. She reached down to give him a hand up. Jiggy slapped it away.

"Jiggy, sweetheart, you can't go on like this. You need to get some help." And she'd squatted down with her hand on his shoulder.

Jiggy looked up from gazing at the floor and at that point Gina saw a rage in his eyes she had never seen before. Then he leaned back a little. He clenched his jaw so tight she could see the little muscles at the back of his cheek bulge. Then he swung at her with a closed fist. She jumped back but not soon enough. He caught her right below her left eye. She stood up in shock and stared at him. He was focused on the floor again. After a minute of standing there numb, Gina began to cry.

Jiggy looked up at her, confused for a second. And then the rage came back in his eyes and he screamed at her, "You fuckin' bitch! You think you're so much better than me you can save me like fuckin' Jesus or somethin'."

Gina had gone weeping to the bedroom, packed a few things in a bag and drove herself to a hotel. The next day she had called Collette and Alvin. Alvin had warned her before she married Jiggy that he was pretty sure Jiggy was involved in more than communications in the army. One time he'd startled Jiggy by accident. He had Alvin pinned so fast — it would have taken some training. Gina drove down and stayed with Alvin and Collette for the rest of that weekend. Her eye grew very black. Jiggy called and she told him she couldn't deal with him anymore. She was done with the marriage.

He sobered up and drove down himself the Sunday afternoon and when he saw her, he started to cry again. He couldn't remember hitting her. He kept saying over and over how sorry he was. After a long talk with Alvin, he left. Gina found out a day or two later he'd checked himself in to a trauma center. He was there every day for two months. Over that time, both Gina and Jiggy got more familiar with PTSD. They got counseling and Jiggy tried a few different trauma therapies that took the edge off his emotional pain. Gina gave him a second chance.

Jiggy hardly ever got drunk now, and if he did, Gina never saw that type of rage again. He often got high but that was okay, it just made him funnier. In spite of everything, he was good to her, and he could still make her laugh even if it came with drugs and a darker worldview. And she did come round to Jiggy's notion about not having children though it wasn't for the reasons he thought she would. In fact she never brought the subject up again and never once asked the doctor why she didn't get pregnant.

So children only ever got mentioned when someone else got pregnant, especially if it was very inconvenient, or someone else's kids were behaving like monsters. It was reassuring. What Jiggy had always forgotten to mention was how he'd had a vasectomy when he was on a little business that took him through Bangkok, right after he'd married Gina. He'd told the urologist he already had three kids and that was enough and he wanted to love his wife unencumbered and so on. The doctor, more than a little world-weary, couldn't have cared less as long the clinic was bringing in US dollars. With a number of tours and more-interesting-than-average assignments in strange places, Jiggy'd decided the planet was no place for the innocent. He'd put up with life but that didn't mean he had to like it or contribute. Nonparticipation was the best revenge.

PART TWO

Gathering

There may be no end to this, at least no easy one. You cannot know what blinds you. You cannot hear what deafens the depth. It's almost never as you planned. Bargained out in the marketplace with pints of penitence, uncorked and lame. You bumble, looking for parts because you must. And this is the just thing in the cycle of all things: that you must search and be mistaken. So acquire rest among the treasures you amass. Learn to sing and store your scraps with patience.

from Cannto IV, *Cannabidadas*

Chapter 10

Larry Muligoff looked Ray up and down while he was shaking his hand. Frances, one of Gina's friends, had arranged the meeting. Ray was there to see if there was something Larry could tell him. Something Larry saw about him that could help. According to Frances, Larry could look at a person and see all sorts of things. Like the alcoholic mother the person hadn't spoken to for twenty years but was still causing trouble anyway. Or the ovarian cancer or the Lyme's disease the doctors hadn't figured out yet. He'd tell you if there were spirits hanging around that weren't doing you any good either and he'd help you get rid of them.

Larry started to laugh. Ray couldn't help smiling himself, though he wasn't at all sure what Larry found so funny. Ray had been doubtful about going to see Larry. He didn't believe in stuff like that. He was doing it more to humor Gina, and in fact Gina had wanted to come along. But the night before, Larry had called Frances and told her only she and Ray should show up.

Ray had brought Larry some pears from his farm. Larry looked at them and abruptly stopped laughing. "Thanks." He put them down on the table. On the drive back, Frances would tell Ray she thought maybe pears were the wrong gift under the circumstances. Maybe they should have asked Jiggy for an ounce of his stash. Ray didn't know. He'd have been happy to pay money, but Larry didn't always take money for what he saw and told about a person. And in this instance he'd told Frances the day before on the phone, "No money."

Larry was an electrician by trade. Ray thought that was a nice coincidence and briefly wondered if he took on apprentices. He might be a better boss than his old boss in Lyston, but it would mean one heck of a commute every day.

"You guys have a nice drive?" Larry asked.

They had. The eighty-mile zigzag north and into the hills with the autumn trees had been dazzling at every turn. It was amazing trees could actually get that color. Like DayGlo.

"See any wildlife in all those trees? Birds? Pheasant? Deer? Anything?"

Ray and Frances looked at each other. They both wondered if Larry was a hunter and if he was curious about the game farther south. But neither of them could remember seeing anything, just that the trees were really bright, especially when the sunlight hit them.

Larry cleared his throat, dismissing the matter. He looked at Ray. "So what do you want me to tell you?"

Ray thought Larry sounded almost confrontational and it startled him a little. "Well. I . . . I don't know if maybe I'm sick or something. That's why I came."

"Doctors diagnosed you with anything?"

"Uh, no . . . well, stress I guess. I had a bad case of hives."

Larry started to snicker.

"And I hear a lot of . . . noise . . . that isn't actually there," Ray added. He didn't want to say anything about the strange sounds that were driving him nuts and sometimes seemed to be coming from the plants. Especially since Larry appeared to be laughing at him already.

"So you got tinnitus maybe?"

"Yeah. That's what the doctors said."

"So that's stress-related?"

"Yeah . . . probably." Ray had thought the guy would be telling him what was wrong, not asking what all the doctors told him. This could turn out to be a total waste of time.

"You don't like your stress?" Larry asked.

"What do you mean?"

"Simple question. Do you like your stress?"

Now Ray thought the questioning was getting stupid. "No! Why would I? Who likes stress?"

"That figures," Larry said and yawned.

"So do you see anything?" Ray tried again. He'd decided to ignore the useless questioning and the tone in Larry's voice.

"Oh I see lots of things."

"Okay . . . like what?"

"Like right here." Larry's fist moved so fast Ray didn't even see it. "Here you got a big hole." The punch landed right below Ray's collarbone and close to his right shoulder. It wasn't a hard punch but it made Ray gasp. Ray's instantaneous response was to punch back but he caught himself. There was a little smile on Larry's face. Like the punch was meant to piss him off. Ray wasn't quite sure what he'd meant by "a big hole" either. Maybe it had to do with the explosion in Iraq. But why there? His shoulder had felt fine for the last four months — until Larry punched it.

"You think too much, man."

Ray hadn't said a word.

"So if you don't fix that hole," Larry continued, "your arm's not gonna be any good at some point. You're gonna have trouble. It'll be arthritis. Or you'll bust your shoulder, wrench your arm. Something like that."

"I already had trouble with my shoulders but they're getting better."

"Maybe you feel better but you still have a hole there. Probably just a matter of time before it gets bad again."

"Okay . . . so you think it was from the explosion I was in?"

"Maybe. People get killed?"

"Yup."

Larry nodded as if that made sense. "Maybe you let somebody take a piece of you."

Ray laughed this time. Larry didn't crack a smile. He just continued to stare at Ray.

"So how do I get rid of it? I mean how do you get rid of a hole?" Ray was still laughing a little and being confrontational himself now.

"You tell me," Larry said. It was difficult to know where to begin. Ray was turning out to be a little dumber than the first impression Larry had of him. But he was also turning out to be kind of interesting. When he got the phone call from Frances, Larry had a sense of Ray right away. He figured it would be pretty simple to help him out. But now that he was here, Larry couldn't really tell Ray very much. He'd never seen anybody quite so surrounded or cluttered up by a bunch of determined spirits, and the immense enveloping entity behind them had pretty much indicated Larry should keep his mouth shut. Ray had to learn for himself. This was their deal and Larry needed to butt out. The spirits were mostly plants. And funny too. Marijuana could be like that. In Ray's case there was a full-blown circus. It was like Ray had shown up with his own private troop of comedians, beggars, priests, lost orphans, freaks and deities that were all vying for his attention. Some were sublime. The more ludicrous were vulgar and outrageous. That's why Larry kept laughing. It occurred to him though to talk about something small and avoid the whole topic of plants. So he focused on the blip in Ray's energy around his shoulder. It wasn't so directly related to the plants and it could serve to give Ray some direction. The punch was also to get the spirits' collective attention for a few seconds, stop their yammering. He'd punched with good intent.

"You got to pay attention to everything," Larry said. "And you got to stop trying to figure things out, man."

"Yeah, well, I know that," Ray said, "that's why I came to see you — because I can't figure things out."

Larry shook his head. "Stop running away. You can't do anything with your brain. With your figuring," he said. "It won't work. You need to listen and watch."

"I do listen and it drives me crazy," Ray stammered, wondering if Larry might actually know something after all.

"That's not what's driving you crazy," Larry said. "You're driving yourself crazy. Because you don't like what you hear. And maybe you don't much like what you see either."

Ray looked at Larry, not hiding his confusion.

"Look, man, the stuff that's bugging you. You made the deal and it's none of my business."

"Deal for what?" Ray asked, incredulous.

"The shit that's bugging you, man."

"Like hives? Like crazy noises nobody else hears?"

"Yeah, that's right."

"And burning hands and feet?" This problem had started the week before.

"Sure."

"That's ridiculous. Why would I do this?"

"Maybe so you can learn to pay attention. Look, man, in another situation I could maybe do something for you. We could even have a little ceremony. Do something creative. I could act on your behalf . . ."

"Okay. So do that. I'll get you whatever you like."

Larry shook his head again. "It's not gonna work like that. This is different. I can't take anything more from you."

Ray did not attempt to hide his disappointment with the way the whole meeting was going.

"Okay. Here's my advice," Larry said, and at this point he was flashed a vision that was both rude and remarkable. He snorted and took a deep breath so he would not laugh again. He was feeling sorry for this dumb guy who was determined to stay split up and stuck. "Go home. Sit down on the ground and listen. Every day, sit down and listen. And sit where it's loudest. Sit by the loudest plants. Whatever they are. They don't have to be marijuana. But pay attention. Okay?" Larry was staring Ray right in the eye.

Ray felt like a child. Actually it reminded him of his first drum lessons with Oscar, his old teacher in New York.

"Don't fight it," Larry continued. "Go with it. Sing with it if you want. I see you got music or something there already. So feel it to your bones. Write it down if you have to. Work it. Stay alert. Okay? Stay really alert."

Ray was speechless and close to tears. This Larry guy was probably a total jerk but this was huge. It meant Ray wasn't crazy. Or if he was, at least he wasn't the only one. Ray hadn't told a soul about the plants. Or that the noises he heard seemed to come from them. But somehow the guy knew. He knew about the music too, but maybe Frances told him something she'd heard from Gina.

"And you need to clean yourself out. Okay? You got so much shit stuck in there it's scary. You do fasting?"

Ray shook his head.

"Well, start learning. Ton of stuff on the internet. Pick something — vegetable fast, fruit fast, water fast, master cleanse. Doesn't matter. Okay?"

Ray shrugged.

"And stay away from the junk food!" Larry added. "Oh yeah. And don't call me for another six months."

Ray didn't know why Larry thought he would call him back. Ray had no intention of ever calling on him again.

Chapter 11

The lookout point was well worn by tourists and vacationers, but at that time of day and especially that time of year, no one was around. Ray sat in his truck with his coffee. He stared at the sea and the clouds. The sky had turned to amethyst and straight ahead was all striated pink with a blast of fuchsia growing on the horizon. Ray had set his alarm for 4:30 a.m. and cleared out of the house before Jiggy or Gina were awake. He'd had to move back to their farmhouse in November when he couldn't take the cold anymore. Nostalgia for the ocean had set in and he needed to get far away. Clear his head. Those two nattered at each other constantly and now Gina was starting to natter at him.

He was going back to New Jersey for a New Year's Eve party at Gabe's, winter driving permitting. Gina kept telling him to go visit Alvin and Collette while he was in the area. "It's Christmas time, Ray. What is the matter with you?" The party was on the Saturday night and Ray was going to be at Gabe's most of the weekend. Gina said the least he could do was stop off on his way back. Ray was angry she was always trying to fix things up like some busybody Pollyanna. Even that whole session with that weird Larry guy was annoying. Always trying to arrange everything and everybody so she could feel more comfortable. It started when he was working on the shore.

Ray had almost no contact with his aunt or uncle after he joined the army. That fall when he was on the job at the shore, Alvin and Collette were going to Portugal on holiday, so Gina suggested that Ray might like to look after Ava, their black lab, while they were away. She set the whole thing up and he could hardly back out of it without looking like even more of a shit than he already felt he was. She knew that. She also knew they could have just called him themselves and he'd have been there in the time it took to drive to Hackensack. But of course they wouldn't call him for a favor, would never impose. Not now. When he did pick up Ava, Aunt Collette was a little hesitant, almost shy. He could see the hurt in her eyes. Uncle Alvin wasn't even there.

The first thing Ava got to know about Ray was he couldn't drive his truck and cry at the same time. He pulled off the road and just sat there staring at the rain with tears oozing out of his eyes. Ava, unable to resist, finally licked his face and that brought him back to the present.

Looking after a dog for two weeks was delightful. Ava loved walks and ball games along the beach and she liked to swim. She'd go barking and splashing after the sandpipers and the gulls, and Ray had to keep lots of treats and an extra ball in his pocket to woo her back to shore when he saw her enthusiasm taking her into deep water. At night he had trouble keeping her off his bed. Eventually he just gave up. He'd wake in the morning sometimes to her snoring in his face. If she'd wolfed down dead things on the beach the day before, her breath would be foul, and if they were well rotted she'd be farting all night too. That did surpass the limits of Ray's tolerance, so he would shut her out of the bedroom and plug his ears so he couldn't hear the whining. Still, she was the best company. It made him want to be established enough to have his own dog.

When he took Ava back, Aunt Collette was relaxed from her holiday and it was as if everything was back to normal between Ray and her. But with his uncle? Things were tense and uncomfortable. Ray saw him for all of five minutes before he dashed off to some meeting. They barely exchanged two words.

It wasn't easy that was for sure, and Gina with her interfering sure as hell wasn't making it any easier. Mostly, Ray felt ashamed. He wished he could take back a lot of what he'd said and done eight years ago. He wished he hadn't left his aunt and uncle out of his life so completely when he was in the army. Gina said, "Well, just write a letter and apologize for heaven's sake. It's not rocket science!" As if it was all so simple. As if you could just erase years of damage with a few words on a piece of paper.

Looking back, Ray figured he'd just been too young and too stupid to realize how hurtful he was. On the night before he'd shipped off to basic training, he and his uncle ended things with another shouting match. And worse. Ray was full of himself, but he was also really pissed at his uncle. Ray didn't want to go to college. He wasn't the academic type. He remembered thinking his uncle was judging him. Maybe he was. But Ray was hardly holding back on high and mighty pronouncements himself. He told Uncle Alvin he was just a ridiculous, self-centered old hippy. Basically useless! All talk no action. A parasite. "What did you ever do for this country?" he'd demanded. Ray had been so angry he'd even taken a swing at him at one point. And Uncle Alvin might be a lot of things but a hypocritical gutless coward was not one of them. Uncle Alvin swung right back and Ray had a bruise on his jaw for a week.

His uncle read a lot. Liked a good book. Liked a good discussion. Ray never tried to match him in a conversation. In fact Uncle Alvin could talk circles around just about anybody, even Jiggy. He'd always manage to have his point understood even if it wasn't accepted. "Debate is good," he'd claim. "Keeps the mind sharp and the spirit honest." His uncle had never meant him any harm. Ray knew that now. Aside from the politics, he didn't want to see Ray get hurt. He and Jiggy had both tried to stop Ray from joining up. They'd taken him out on a weekend fishing trip and Jiggy had set up a visit with an old buddy who was wasting away in a veterans' home. But that part of the plan in particular had backfired.

An older guy, who must have been in the Vietnam War caught Ray's eye while Jiggy and Uncle Alvin were talking with Jiggy's friend. The older guy noticed Ray looking at him and waved him over. The Nam vet was missing half his face, it looked like. He sat in a wheelchair and it was clear one of his arms was paralyzed or gone and the prosthetic wasn't functional. His dead hand was gloved and he wore a mask or maybe it was a bandage that made him look a little like the Phantom of the Opera.

"It's just temporary," the man said, tapping on the bandage with his good hand. "Bad burn. Sometimes it gets all inflamed again and they put this thing on for a while. Course I look like total hell when it's off. Scare the shit right outta ya." He motioned with his head to Jiggy and Uncle Alvin. "Those two clowns with you?"

Ray laughed quietly.

"Takin' you on the tour are they?"

"Yeah," Ray said, nodding.

"And I wonder why they'd be doin' that?"

Ray just smiled. They sat together in silence for a few seconds. Then the man said, "Always a good idea to make up your own mind about things. Uh-huh. That way you only have yourself to blame."

Ray stared down at his own feet, not quite sure what to say. Then he finally came out with it. "You regret being in the military?"

The man guffawed. "Hell. I didn't have a choice. We got drafted."

Ray was more than familiar with the history and he looked back down at the ground.

"Anyway, right now that's like asking do I regret being alive. I've been like this a lot longer than I was all in one piece." The man was silent again for a few seconds. "And I'd have to say, no. No, I don't have regrets. Everybody's got their tragedies," he said. "Besides, you might not guess it by my suave manner, but I was a real punk when I was your age." The man laughed to himself. "I probably would've ended up clobbered one way or another. Everybody does. Divorces, bankruptcies, car accidents. Your kids hate you or your kid gets killed. Dog's the only thing you can love and it dies too! Then you have to start singin' country songs."

Ray put his head down as he tried to suppress a laugh.

"Hell. Everybody's a wreck is how I look at it. Only in my case it just happened all at once." The man leaned over to Ray and lowered his voice like he had a big secret to tell. "And I've had all this time to think about it. And you know what I think?"

Ray shook his head and the man caught his eye again.

"I think the sun still comes out and the rain falls on your skin the same way no matter what shape you're in. You get the experience. It's all the same if you don't judge it. Everybody's dyin' in bits and pieces," he said. "That's the point."

Ray sat back, puzzled.

"Too afraid to die, you never get to live either. And the other thing," the man continued, "I've seen guys in here be stronger than I ever thought a human being could be. And I've seen them weaker than I thought possible." The man leaned back and inhaled audibly, sucking the air through his teeth. "And all that . . . that's made me a lot kinder than I ever thought I'd be." He looked at Ray with a smile. "You shouldn't worry. We didn't all come back crazy as shit, rollin' around in wheelchairs you know. Some guys do just great. Most never get a scratch. You'll do fine."

Jiggy and Uncle Alvin motioned to Ray that it was time to go. Ray got up and shook the man's good hand. "Nice talking to you."

"You're welcome," the man said.

Ray had left the veteran's home smiling to himself. Jiggy and Uncle Alvin had looked at each other wondering what went wrong. The whole weekend they'd plied him with beer, expounded on the corrupt economics of war and so on. But Ray just kept smiling and humoring them. On the last night, Ray overheard Jiggy and Uncle Alvin talking. They were sitting out by the fire pit. Ray was in the cabin and they thought he'd gone to sleep.

"Jesus, Alvin. I blame myself."

"Yeah, you were a little half-cocked."

"But it's not like I ever wanted to join. It was that or the fuckin' sheriff was gonna have me locked up."

Alvin laughed. "Could have been interesting!"

"But then I got to like it, ya know. Shit. I just shouldn't a told Ray about anything."

"Probably not. He thought you were the cat's ass that's for sure. Talked about you for days after. Every time you and Gina came for a visit."

"Jesus. What a fuckup."

"Ah, don't be so hard on yourself. He had my father hovering in the background for the first eight years of his life. Long before he ever met you."

"True enough. Old guys like to reminisce."

"Yup. I'm an old guy."

Jiggy laughed. "Thing about you an' me, Alvin, we don't look back an' erase the shit."

"Or make it heroic."

Jiggy snorted. "Yeah! Fuck that!"

It was all a long time ago. Ray was somebody else then. And unlike the old vet with the face mask, Ray wasn't sure what any of his experiences meant to him yet. He thought about what Larry had told him about being full of shit. No doubt about that. Probably everybody was full of shit, even the old guy with the mask. Gina was full of shit too. Why didn't she just go visit them herself and leave

Ray out of it? And Gina wasn't the only woman trying to arrange his life for him either. A weekend at Gabe's could be challenge enough on its own.

Ray had known Gabe's wife since high school. That's where they'd all met. She was nice back then. When Ray wasn't busy with his music, he was hanging out with them. But ever since she had her first baby she'd been driving Ray nuts — always trying to set him up. "OMG, you'd be such a cute couple! Wouldn't they make a great couple, Gabe?" Gabe would always say something crazy. "Gabe. You're so bad!" she'd say. "Look at Ray. He's so adorable. Why can't you be adorable like Ray, huh?" Why he was her pet project Ray could never figure. And the women she arranged for him were mostly Ray's idea of a nightmare. They went on about clothes, beauty regimens, diets, each other's sex life and how badly the others were behaving on any given occasion. They were invariably "lookers," according to Gabe's dad, but Ray got to the point after a couple of years that he no longer relished spending time with any of these women or even landing in bed with them. Their subsequent expectations for his attention were wearying and their behavior bewildering.

Shortly after he got out of the army, there was one young woman who'd freaked him right out. They'd gone on a date and it hadn't been much fun for either of them, Ray thought. She'd spent most of her time texting and when she did talk to him, she babbled and gushed. Ray figured it was a coping mechanism. He'd dropped her off for the evening but then she followed him home in a cab or found his house somehow.

She was determined to ring way more than his doorbell. But the doorbell didn't work. When no one answered, she climbed in through a window. She heard a shower running and assumed it was Ray. He'd been so tired though, he'd just fallen into bed as soon as he got home and was asleep in seconds.

So she snuck into the empty room beside the shower and arranged herself suggestively on the bed. How could Ray possibly resist her? But it was two of Ray's roommates who were busy in the shower trying new approaches to resurrect their failing relationship. They took a long time and the woman on the bed fell asleep. When they came out and saw her sprawled so enticingly, each thought the other had arranged for this surprise as part of the revitalization effort.

Swapping, threesomes, even plain old cheating had never been part of their bond before, from what Ray gathered, so they each must have been impressed that the other had thought to go to such lengths. They descended upon the young woman. Perhaps too enthusiastically. Ray didn't get all the details. He awoke to screams. When Ray appeared in the doorway, a bottle of moisturizer flew by and narrowly missed his head. Eventually they sorted things out, but Ray had to drive her home again. He asked her very politely if she could please stay put this time. She called him an asshole and slammed his car door.

Invariably the consequences of Gabe's wife playing cupid vastly outweighed any pleasure. They'd tricked her once when Ray was working down on the shore that year and so he'd had a reprieve for a few months. But mostly Ray relied on a kind of stock politeness with the parade of young women. He made an acceptable amount of small talk, persisted in dumb obliviousness to their charms and bade them a good night, a good afternoon or whatever time of day Gabe's wife had picked for the ambush. If he went there for the New Year's weekend, she could really up the ante. There'd be no escape and he'd get drunk and lose all perspective. It's not like he had a whole lot of romantic interests these days. Or friends with benefits. He'd be easy pickings. Maybe he should be praying for a New Year's blizzard. Or he could offer to do security at CannRose over the holiday.

Ray had many things still to think about, but now with the sun fully up, there was nothing particularly dramatic on the horizon to help him with this. He was hungry by then so he left his lookout over the Atlantic and went in search of a diner to get some breakfast. He came across a greasy spoon within fifteen minutes. It was about seven thirty in the morning and the only other vehicle in the parking lot was a little white Toyota Camry. He thought service would be quick, but as he entered the diner and saw who was there, he wondered if it might be wiser to head right back out the door. The only other person in the restaurant and clearly the owner of the little white car was none other than the dreaded DOH inspector. The one with the pouty lips and the voice that landed in his brain with all the appeal of shrapnel. The very same one people at CannRose claimed had a heart made of shit and shards that needed to have a stake put through it.

According to Ernie, who'd been talking to Lazlo, Ms. Ligner really had gone out of her way to have the DOH close down CannRose. Her official report had been excruciatingly detailed and merciless in its condemnation. And yes, even Ray's lousy filing system and lack of written procedures got cited, but they were fairly minor in the mindboggling litany of transgressions and omissions she'd exposed. In addition, she had given over half a dozen hard-hitting arguments to back up her recommendation that the DOH pull the registration.

Still, for all Ms. Ligner's efforts, she hadn't succeeded. Rumor had it, Lydia was a friend of the governor, or her late husband had been. Ernie said that might well be true, but as far as he knew, the law firm brought out their heavy artillery and threatened to sue the state's ass. Ernie couldn't say for how much exactly, but it was in the millions. "I bet it was embarrassing for the bureaucrats scurrying around the DOH," Ernie said, "and given corporate influence these days, I bet the state wouldn't have stood a chance." Ray thought Ernie sounded a lot like Jiggy.

Anyway, there she sat in all her inspector glory, not more that thirty feet away, mandibles in action, chewing on toast and jam. She even had on the same jacket, or no, maybe this one was a little more blue, and she was wearing trousers today. No leggy distraction. Ray slouched and sat himself down in a corner booth. Maybe she hadn't seen him come in. Even if she had, she probably wouldn't remember him. Ray pulled the visor of his baseball cap down a little more and studied the menu carefully. After the waitress took his order, Ray took out his phone to check the latest news. At one point he vaguely registered movement out of the corner of his eye and when he finally looked up after reading the item about a fire at a veterans home, she was gone.

#

Ray planned to get very drunk on New Year's Eve. The weather was going to be ideal, not a blizzard in the forecast anywhere, not even a flurry, and Greg at CannRose had told him to take a few extra days. Gus had looked a little peeved at this and mumbled he'd like to know why Greg couldn't have at least run Ray's holiday by him, so Ray immediately said it would be no trouble at all for him to work extra, even right through the weekend. Gus stood there thinking and Ray stood there enthusiastic and hopeful. Then Gus had smiled, slapped him on the shoulder and agreed it wouldn't be very busy between Christmas and New Year's, and some of the suppliers might be closed anyway. He wished Ray a very happy holiday!

There appeared no way out. Ray could languish in Hullbrooke and be harried — literally to tears — by Gina. Or he could party on in Jersey City and dodge Gabe's wife's latest recruit, then go dutifully pay his respects to his uncle Alvin and aunt Collette. The only unblemished bright spot might be a short visit with Julie and Anna on his way home. They'd be back from wherever they'd been visiting and told him to come for dinner and stay the night.

#

It was around one o'clock in the morning on New Year's Eve when Sibyl came sashaying up to Ray and whispered words he couldn't make out, but her meaning was unmistakable. He was teetering and genuinely feeling woozy. He'd probably eaten more of those mini crab cakes and definitely more squid salad than he should have. As she looked seductively into his eyes, he wavered, then he swiftly turned around as he began to topple. He landed on his knees and straightaway vomited loudly and vigorously into the large potted dieffenbachia, which up to that point had grown undisturbed in the bay window for at least six years.

Gabe, having witnessed the incident and being quite hammered himself, began laughing uncontrollably. He'd never liked the goddamn plant that took up half the light from the window. So he staggered over, and just as Ray started to get on his feet, Gabe gave him a congratulatory slap on the back. This knocked Ray over again and made him spew whatever remnants were left in his stomach all over the windowsill. After that, Ray just stayed on the floor in a crumpled heap and waited for all the excitement to die down.

When he opened his eyes several minutes later, Gabe was hovering over him, grimacing with paper towels in hand and not doing a particularly good job of cleaning up Ray's mess. Gabe's wife was standing in the doorway glaring at the two of them, and Sibyl was nowhere to be seen. Ray woke up on the couch the next morning with a headache he did not believe was even possible. It hurt to move his toes. But all things considered, the evening had been a success.

\#

Gina had of course arranged everything so there was a Christmas present from her and Jiggy to drop off at Alvin and Collette's on his way home. Ava would be there for diversion, thank God. Ray himself was taking his uncle a bottle of single malt scotch that had cost him a small fortune and for his aunt he'd found a particularly exotic amaryllis that should bloom right around her birthday in February. They weren't terribly personal gifts, but Gina was sure they'd appreciate the gesture. At least he was trying.

When he got to the door, Ava was right there barking with jubilation, her tail wagging furiously. His aunt gave him a big hug. His uncle hung back though and merely nodded as Ray made his way from the entrance hall into the living room. A tree decorated with familiar ornaments was in the far corner where they always put one. On seeing it, a decade of happy Christmas memories came flooding back to Ray. Usually there'd been a whole houseful of people, more dogs, often Gina and Jiggy, and as time moved along, his cousins' babies joined the festivities. Ray had not experienced anything like it since he left. He had to look away from the tree quickly.

Conversation during coffee was cordial and innocuous. He delivered the gifts. His uncle was pleased and surprised by the scotch. His aunt cooed over the picture on the box with the amaryllis bulb in it. They had something for him to take back to Gina and Jiggy. They asked Ray about his job and how the building was coming along. After about twenty minutes, his uncle had to excuse himself because he had an appointment. But just before Alvin got up to leave, Collette handed Ray an envelope. In it was cash — a very generous amount. Ray was taken aback.

"We figured building a house, every little bit would help." His aunt smiled and looked up at Alvin who was standing now. "Everybody chipped in," she said. Alvin simply nodded without expression. She turned back to Ray. "The boys are all very impressed you're doing your own building and Gina posted pictures of the property so I could show them. They want progress reports and more photos as you go along."

"Thanks," Ray said in almost a whisper. He could barely speak. It wasn't so much the money but the "Everybody chipped in" part. It was like looking at that Christmas tree. Retrospectives of generosity and goodwill could be searingly painful.

As his uncle left, he turned and smiled faintly at Ray. It was more a perfunctory gesture, as if Alvin had just remembered he should make the effort. And Ray felt the coolness and distance that his uncle was doing his best to hide. Ray tried to smile back but he wasn't any better at it than Alvin.

When his uncle had gone, Aunt Collette asked him how the New Year's Eve party was.

"It must have been pretty good," Ray said. "Yesterday's hangover was the worst I've ever had." And then he told her about Gabe's wife, how she'd been trying to pair him off for the last six years. He relayed the highlights and outcome of her latest attempt.

His aunt laughed. "Evasive maneuvers and sophisticated countermeasures run in your blood now I see. How was the poor dieffenbachia this morning?"

"I forgot to check on it," Ray said. "But Gabe's wife is speaking to me again, so maybe it's okay."

#

"I think we should ask him," Anna said to Julie in almost a whisper, but Ray could hear her as she cuddled up to Julie on the big sprawling couch. "I think now is the best time."

Julie tilted her head and kissed Anna.

Ray was at the couple's apartment and sitting in a big comfy chair himself. He watched this intimacy for a second or two and then looked down at his wine again.

"Ray, we have a favor we'd like to ask you," Anna said. "And we've probably been thinking about it for a long time."

Ray looked up at the two women in their closeness and blinked. "Sure, whatever." He was only a little drunk and about to ask what he could do for them, assuming they were looking for some cheap electrical work maybe or something along those lines but Julie cut him off.

"Ray, Anna and I have been trying to get pregnant."

Ray thought this was another of their jokes and he started to laugh, but when he saw the look on their faces he stopped dead. "Uh, and . . ."

"And it's kind of expensive and we haven't had any luck so far," Anna said, clearly annoyed Ray thought this could be funny.

"I see." Ray nodded slowly and was thinking hard. "So . . . going to clinics and—"

"Yes. Exactly," said Anna. "It's been very disappointing."

"We thought we'd been successful. We've both tried, and Anna finally got pregnant not long after we came to visit at your farm but then she miscarried in November."

Anna's expression swiftly changed and she began to cry softly.

Ray took a deep breath and just stared at them for a few seconds. "I'm sorry," he said in almost a whisper. "Sorry for the loss . . . and for laughing. I-I had no idea."

Anna wiped her eyes. "We haven't talked about it to anybody, apart from doctors and the people at the clinics." She leaned into Julie who hugged her close.

It pained Ray to see them like this. It wasn't ever like them to be this sad. High key, yes, or squabbling and outrageous, but never this. He just sat there feeling awkward. But then after a moment, Julie looked up and smiled at him. Anna did too. He breathed a sigh of relief.

"So Ray," Julie began, "we'd been thinking about asking you but then we just thought it would be easier with a donor from a catalogue, less complication, no expectations, clean-cut transaction, you know. But it hasn't been easy. Not at all. And it's kind of soulless. So we were wondering if maybe *you* might consider . . . assuming there's no genetic disorders in your family . . ."

And at that point a little light came on in Ray's brain and he realized what they were asking. He was so taken aback he didn't actually hear a lot of what Julie was saying. He just stared at them and then shifted his gaze minutely to a poster behind them showing some Hubble view of the cosmos. He began to fly away in his mind. And in the background, bits and pieces registered as Julie went on about how the fathering of their child, if it worked, would not be attached to any expectation, financial or otherwise, or even contact if he didn't want any. And then Anna went on making assurances about legalities and again mentioned finances and they could sign contracts if that would help and they'd cover all the legal fees and he'd be relieved of any . . .

Ray closed his eyes. All this talk made *him* unbearably sad. He thought of the vastness of the cosmos he'd just been reminded of, and then of the silence he'd experienced when the convoy had been hit by the rocket. He thought of his nightmares. And then his farm, sitting abandoned for so long until he showed up. The creek swirling through it, the untouched wildness of its woods, and now in winter, the snow falling, blanketing and swaddling it like a cocoon.

"What if," Ray finally said, cutting them off. "What if I want in on this too? What if I want to be . . . a father to the child?"

"I told you," Anna said as Julie reached for her hand.

Julie looked at Ray. "We talked about this a lot. We trust you, Ray. We love you," she said somewhat fiercely. "That's why we'd like you to be the donor. Any time you'd want to spend with us would be fine. However much you'd want to be involved with the child would be welcome."

"Okay," Ray said quietly, looking back down at his glass. He suddenly felt light-headed. The sadness was gone.

"You mean okay, as in *okay*? Or okay, you just heard the last bit?"

"Um . . ." Ray looked up at them. They were staring at him very intently. "I'm a little drunk . . . but I think *okay*."

"You'll do it?"

"Uh, yes . . . I mean, what exactly would it entail? You know. . . what do you want me to do . . ." — Ray grimaced slightly — "like, for . . . a turkey baster?"

"God, Ray, we're not primitive!" Julie sighed and turned to Anna. "Maybe his future involvement *would* need some curbing."

"It could save a hell of a lot of money." Anna snickered. "But we don't have cryo storage, Ray. And it'd take like, a miracle — you know, an immaculate conception — to get that lucky on one try."

"Don't worry, Ray. It's easy, peasy." Julie smiled. "And it's right on your drive home."

Chapter 12

Gina put three bags of groceries down and pulled out the receipt that was stuck between the coffee beans and the package of walnuts. She examined it carefully while mentally chastising herself for not checking it in the parking lot before she hauled everything home. That would have been the sensible thing to do. But she wasn't always sensible, she supposed. That could be the theme of her life.

Gina slapped the receipt down on the kitchen table. The cow of a cashier had charged her twice for the peanut butter! Gina did a quick mental estimate that included the time it would take to drive into town, the price of the gas there and back, how late dinner would be, and whether or not the sour-faced cashier would even admit to the mistake or if the manager would have to be brought into the discussion. Ultimately Gina concluded a return trip was hardly worth a discount jar of peanut butter. It put her in a foul mood. She stared out the kitchen window and watched as one of the chickens went flapping across the still snowy yard with the young rooster after it. "God, it never stops, does it?" she muttered.

Gina needed to pour herself a glass of wine and get chopping. Alcohol and violence against vegetables could always be relied upon to settle her mood. Jiggy had put together a chicken stew in the slow cooker for dinner. It smelled good. She'd make salad. In fact since she'd picked up some fresh fennel and satisfied herself that she hadn't been overcharged for it, she'd make her mother's old favorite. Jiggy liked it and so did Ray. Fennel, cucumber, celery and apple with walnuts. She'd have to use dried mint, not fresh, for the lemony dressing but it would do.

She glanced out the window again and the chickens, four of them this time, were racing back the other way across the yard. Only it wasn't the inept, love-struck rooster chasing them, it was a little dog Gina hadn't seen before. She put down the bottle of wine she'd just opened, grabbed her coat and scrambled outside. As she did, she picked up one of Jiggy's canes that sat in a bucket by the door. He used them when he felt the need and he'd managed to acquire a substantial collection over the years. She grabbed the knobbly shillelagh.

"Hey!" Gina yelled at the dog as she burst out the door.

"Toby, get back here!" screamed a woman's voice.

Gina repeated "Hey!" several more times as she charged into the fray of little dog, flying snow and scattering chickens. The dog was a brainless-looking fluffy thing, shih tzu probably, mixed with what? Whippet? A sharp bitty face with chicken assassin written all over it. Gina cursed under her breath.

"Toby! Toby!" The voice was increasingly panicked.

Suddenly the little dog stopped to consider the choice of so many chickens running every which way. Gina was holding the shillelagh menacingly aloft.

"Toby! Toby!" The woman was frantic. The dog's skull could be cracked in a split second.

Gina moved quickly, got right up close to Toby, who was so intent on the chickens he barely noticed her, and then she brought the shillelagh down with a loud whack on a rock about six inches away from him.

The woman at the bottom of the driveway screamed as if Gina had brought the cane down on her. Now it was Toby's turn to scatter and he shot off back to his owner, tail between his legs. Outraged, the woman gathered the trembling dog in her arms and began shouting at Gina. Little Toby began to bark.

Gina walked calmly down the driveway, catching her breath. She was still holding on to the cane but using it like a walking stick. The woman, who unfortunately bore a striking resemblance to the peanut butter–swindling cashier, took a few steps back. When Gina got within speaking distance, she said in a steely voice, "You need to put your dog on a leash if you're going for walks around here."

"There was no need for violence. You terrified him!"

"And what do the think he just did to my chickens?"

"He thought it was a game."

"He's a dog. He does what dogs do. Kill chickens if they don't know better."

"He was just playing!"

"Oh yeah? And you had total control I noticed." Gina eyed the woman. She was not a woman used to the country. Who would wear clothes like that for a walk? And the dog, prissily groomed and sporting a fashionable collar, was not a country dog. "Has he ever even seen a chicken before?"

The woman was silent and glared at Gina.

"You know, I'd have been perfectly within my rights to shoot your dog just now."

"Oh for God's sake!" The woman turned her back to Gina and pulled an extendable leash out of her pocket. She put the dog down and fastened the clasp to his collar.

Gina walked back up the driveway shaking her head at the woman's stupidity and entitlement. She did not begrudge the dog its instinct, and in any other situation, she might have asked the woman where she was from and who she was visiting. Likely Gina would find out soon enough. Somebody would drop word her way that a few people now considered Gina a bludgeon-wielding maniac. She'd best be drinking some wine and making her mother's favorite salad. Keeping the hands busy to improve the mood was probably one of those things her mother taught by silent example.

When Gina was thirty, her mother died from liver cancer. Gina figured it was the paints and the fiberglass or maybe just disappointment and grief. Her mother, never traditional about anything, was determined to maintain her artistic interests even while she raised two kids. She filled every garden shed and garage where they lived with strange brightly colored objects that bore no resemblance to anything much. She made space in the outbuildings to do her work and there was the ever-present chemical smell of resins and paint. She was always preoccupied.

Her father was so unlike her mother in every respect, Gina couldn't fathom what had ever brought them together. He was a pastor, a Methodist, even a little on the evangelical side. Their marriage was bizarre in retrospect. Apart from bundling herself and the rest of the family off to church on Sundays, it seemed her mother's only function in relation to her father was to encourage his community involvement as much as possible. He'd immerse himself in the various charitable foundations of the church and even took on secular appointments; he was a town councilor for a while. Gina realized by the age of nine that her mother was enthusiastic about anything her father did as long as it kept him out of the house and didn't involve her mother's time. He would leave early in the morning and often be home late.

Gina remembered her parents speaking only of practicalities and money. A plugged toilet, the need for a new furnace, who was getting A's and B's or D's at school, or who'd grown out of their winter coat and how much the dentist had cost them that year and consequently who should be brushing their teeth better. They seemed to agree on discipline and it was never meted out harshly. Naughty children were given a time-out and as they got older they were grounded for transgressions, or limits were put on their purchasing power. Her parents did not discuss God or the Bible. Ever. At the age of thirteen and going through a very devotional stage, Gina asked her mother about this.

"There's no need for discussion. If you have questions, Gina, ask your father. That's his business. That's what he does and he'd be more than happy to talk with you."

"But what do you think, Mom?"

"It doesn't matter what I think." And her mother had picked up a brush and began dabbing red lacquer onto a rough-shaped slightly furry dodecahedron.

At the time, Gina thought her mother was possibly unliberated. After all, women were speaking out and making the news and taking charge and running for government. The mideighties were about having it all, especially if you were a woman.

"I do have it all, Gina. And it's nicely organized too. Now if you don't mind, I'm going to spray this so you need to get out of the way." And her mother had picked up the spray gun, adjusted the nozzle and started the noisy air compressor, so that was the end of the matter.

Five years later, her parents divorced. Gina saw it as no coincidence that they started proceedings literally the day she moved out of the house. Her brother, who was five years older, had finished college and just joined the air force. While not surprised, Gina had questions. Why did her mother marry her father in the first place? Her mother was no more fulsome with her revelations about that than she had been about religion when Gina was thirteen.

"He was decent. Maybe he was the first guy I thought I could trust."

Ten years after that, when her mother had surrendered to the cancer and was preparing for the end, Gina felt the need to ask her again about the peculiar marriage and the fact that her father was a pastor and yet Christianity or anything to do with religion was barely mentioned between them. Even when her brother was killed in a helicopter accident, they did not discuss these things.

"Gina, we had an agreement. That's all. I told him thirty-five years ago I didn't care about faith or religion one way or the other. I was casually agnostic. And he said he didn't care about art one way or the other. So we decided that was perfect."

"Was it?"

"It was fine. Yes. I could do my sculpture and not have to work at some mind-numbing job. I could raise kids instead. Do my best not to get worn out by it. And you were inspiring, both of you, especially when you were little. Joyful, curious, still full of wonder. It was fun. As far as the art went, I might have been driven but not for success so much. It was more about shape, color, the feel of a thing, nothing controversial. Wasn't like I was going to create or say anything shocking that would get up his nose or his congregation's nose. As long as he didn't try to ram God and religion down my throat, it could be a peaceable marriage."

"So then why get divorced?"

"Sometimes people decide they want more. Or sometimes they always wanted more and never admitted it." Her mother smiled ruefully nodding at her own insight. "You know what he told me right at the end, even ages after your brother was killed? He thought he'd convert me. And he'd thought it right from the day he met me. He thought God had sent him a mission and that his faith could not help but prevail and I would come into the fold. So how honest was that, huh?"

"Maybe it was a simple mistake."

Her mother laughed. "I counted on his faith and religion you know. He wouldn't desert a family like my dad did. I saw safety. So we both played a calculated hand. Except I made the better calculation."

"Yeah. You got to abandon him instead."

"Nobody abandoned anybody and you very well know that. I just wanted a real studio finally. One happened to come up. Plus he was cheating again."

"You didn't even care about his cheating."

"Oh yes I did. It was very useful. I'd raised his kids and he owed me alimony. Nothing like the guilt of a God man. Besides he's much happier. He's got Louisa now. The divorce was embarrassing for him. That's all."

"Did you guys ever love each other? Even a little?"

Her mother had to think about the answer. "Our hormones loved each other for several years. The sex was pretty good."

"That's not what I meant." Gina sighed in disgust.

"Gina, the sixties were lots of drugs and all free love and just another excuse for guys to screw over women. You could look at it that way. You could appreciate that maybe. I'd had enough and your father was a respite of sorts. So I loved him for that. Does that work for you?"

It didn't really. Gina had seen better by that point. It wasn't just Ray who continually drew Gina back to the house in Hackensack. She let herself be adopted by Alvin and Collette right along with him so she could bask in their care and the warmth they showed for each other. She couldn't understand how Ray could ever just walk away from a family that loving and not talk to them for years. And Gina figured her own love life was at least five times better that her mother's. Jiggy had his issues for sure, but even when he'd been nuts, violent from PTSD, she hadn't ever let herself settle for just some soulless agreement to be civil. So Gina surmised it must have been the lure of the strange objects, the making of them and the busyness of the hands that kept her mother on an even keel and blithely stuck in her marriage.

Gina finished putting the salad together just as Jiggy walked in the door.

"That looks good."

"Your stew looks good too. Want a beer?"

"I'll get it." Jiggy noticed the shillelagh lying on the kitchen table. "Did ya have to beat the fennel or somethin'? Is it one of those distressed salads? You know instead of a quick braise?"

So Gina told him all about the city woman and Toby the little would-be chicken killer.

"Jesus, I wish I'd seen that. You in full battle cry, chargin' the field."

"What field?" Ray came into the house at that point, red cheeked and cheery.

"Gina's been terrorizin' little dogs again. It's gonna be all over town tomorrow. Only she'll have been goin' after the little mutt with an ax an' not a shillelagh."

Ray laughed and so Gina repeated the whole story again.

"You guys need to get another dog. Archie wouldn't have let that thing two feet up the driveway."

Gina looked at Jiggy.

"Yeah well, a puppy takes a lot of time to train," Jiggy said.

Gina rolled her eyes and looked at Ray. They both knew Jiggy still wasn't over the loss of Archie, a wise old border collie–shepherd mix. He'd died suddenly from kidney failure two years before and Jiggy had been eerily silent for weeks after.

#

Gina didn't have to wait long to hear back from the neighborhood. It could have been a lot worse. It could have been the lady three properties over who already thought Gina was spare and Jiggy belonged in an institution.

"I understand you met my sister-in-law the other afternoon." Sandy White, a mechanic who lived up the road from Gina and Jiggy was filling up his car at the gas bar, as was Gina. He was smiling and chewing gum.

"Oh that's who she was? We didn't introduce ourselves."

Sandy started to snicker. "I've never liked little dogs myself."

"It wasn't the dog's fault."

"Never liked my sister-in-law much either," Sandy continued, ignoring Gina's observation.

"Why would she let a pampered dog like that run loose in the country? Could have gotten in with cattle or found a porcupine."

Sandy thought for a second and then said, "I think she thinks what's good for her is good for the dog. You'll be relieved to know she's back in Toronto. I'm relieved. We're all relieved."

"Canadian."

"Yup. The wife's brother says they've cornered the luxury-spa market."

Chapter 13

It was early May, about four months after Gus had quit, and Lorne, the latest production manager, still remarkably exhibiting composure in the face of routine CannRose confusion, told Ray he needed to help with the harvest because there was an emergency. They were pulling everybody off their regular shifts. Ray explained he'd be more than happy to lend a hand if he could stay away from the plants. Up until that point Lorne hadn't really noticed that Ray always managed to be absent from the facility on harvest days. Greg had always supported him on this and so had Gus. Ray usually scheduled his day off then, or sometimes there were other things he could do, like odd jobs at the dispensary outlets.

But Caldwell had come in early that morning and made a beeline for Lorne. Ray had been in the production area and witnessed the exchange. "Why aren't we on the Jasmine Star? It should have been harvested yesterday. You need to pick up your learning curve here, Lorne. Where's Damian? Or those other two so-called hort experts?"

Lorne, patiently smiling with perfect teeth, explained for the second time, apparently, that two days before there'd been a skirmish in the potting room between Damian, Cassie and Joe. Fists and a pH probe figured prominently. Actually it was all anyone was talking about: the Hort Wars. Caldwell had been away at the time of the fracas. He was often part of the ongoing conflict himself and always sided with Damian. But this time he was disavowing all association.

"I've got no time for these petty squabbles," Caldwell said, agitated. "It's the plants that matter." And then he went barging into the CannRose lab. "This is just pure negligence," Caldwell said to the dark-haired woman seated on a high stool by the lab bench. "Am I the only one around here who knows when a crop is ready? Trichomes are yellowing for God's sake. You're a plant scientist. Don't you even look at the plants?"

Petra had been alternately peering at spreadsheets on one computer screen and looking at images on another. Her lab tech, Sanjay, stood up and positioned himself between her and Caldwell.

"I think you'll find," Sanjay said, "that research and crop production are very different. In fact we're in the middle of something very important right now." He smiled and then he went on to explain some really complex stuff about correlations and something about cannabinoid profiles, terpene profiles and genome fractions. And then he asked Caldwell if he'd like to see some really clean terpene peaks. Ray didn't understand a half of it. Neither did Caldwell.

"Um . . . no." Caldwell turned around and marched back out the door. Ray saw Petra give Sanjay a thumbs-up. Then they high-fived and brushed past each other very, very closely.

Interesting, Ray thought.

Greg found an easy solution to the harvest crew being shorthanded. He himself would help the crew and hand over the security to Ray. Ray had filled in at security before and thought it would be interesting to watch the harvest unfold on the monitors. There were three large screens and Ray could easily flip to any camera. He could view the feed from one, two, six, twelve or even twenty-four cameras at a time on a single screen. Ray watched the four people who would be doing the cutting make their way through the facility to Flower Room II. They each had shears and bins. They all huddled into the air shower.

As soon as the entry door shut on the air shower, Ray felt a searing pain rip through his head. It almost knocked him off his chair. He took a deep breath and sat for a minute while the screens came back into focus. The four harvesters were opening the door to Flower Room II. Again Ray felt the stab of pain, though not as strong as the first time. But it was like an electric shock, and his limbs, his legs mostly, shook uncontrollably. A metallic sound came with the onslaught. He noticed his knuckles were white as his hands clenched the arms of the chair. His jaw was clenched too, so tight his teeth were hurting. *What the fuck? Now what?*

Ray switched to different camera feeds so he was looking at the driveway and not the cultivation section. Just in time. There was a delivery. He buzzed the truck in and the automatic gate swung open. And right at that moment, as the gate moved slowly and deliberately,

Ray felt something that he would feel for the whole rest of the day as the harvest progressed — regardless of what he was looking at. It was like someone was running a shard of glass up and down his spine. His heart pounded and the muscles in his neck twitched. He heard the metallic noise. It would morph occasionally into a high-pitched whine, almost a scream. It was so excruciating he couldn't think. All that bullshit Larry had told him. "Sit where it's loudest." Well it was fucking deafening where Ray was. But he wasn't about to move into it or flow with it or whatever. How the hell could he? And what if this wasn't anything to do with the plants? Maybe it never had been. Maybe his brain and his whole body were just fucked.

After about an hour, Lily, the receptionist who'd never taken much maternity leave at all and had often talked with Ray over the last several months, noticed he was looking awfully pale in the security office. "Are you okay? You don't look so good, Ray."

"Probably coming down with a migraine or something."

"Oh no. Those are awful. My sister gets them. She's out of commission for a full day sometimes. Used to be two or three. But now she's on marijuana. It really helps."

Ray looked away. *Jesus!* That was the last thing he'd try.

"You should go home. You shouldn't drive either."

Ray shrugged and it turned into a wince as another shard drove up his spine.

"Would you like some water, maybe?"

Ray nodded.

Lily disappeared and returned a minute later with a large bottle of Ash Mountain Springs Natural and a cup. She took the cap off the bottle and poured him some water. "It's easier to drink from a cup. You don't need to be tilting your head back with a migraine," she said.

Ray took a gulp. Suddenly he felt thirstier than he could remember. He swallowed the rest of the water in seconds. Lily poured him another and he drank that down too. He kept drinking water, emptying the cup while she refilled it until the bottle was finished. "I'll go get you a couple more," Lily said. "Maybe you're just dehydrated. That can give you a terrible headache, you know."

"Maybe," Ray said as the screaming in his head seemed to subside a little. Yeah, maybe he was just dehydrated.

#

By four o'clock, Greg was off the harvesting and back at the security office. He took one look at Ray. "Jesus, Ray. Are you sick? You look like hell!"

"Feel like it too." By that time the cutting was finished. The shards had stopped cruising Ray's spine and the screaming in his head seemed to have diminished to a low constant wail.

"I'm thinking you're still pickin' up something through this crappy ventilation here that Lazlo landed us with."

"Maybe."

"You got a bad allergy, Ray. You gotta take care of it."

"Yeah."

"Still can't get you to consider managing security full time for the dispensary outlets?"

"Nah. I don't want the commute. But thanks."

More than that, Ray didn't want to have to see Sammy, the pretty pharmacist who worked at the dispensary in Lyston now. It was worse being around her than it had been initially with Lily. It took Ray about six weeks to realize half the men at CannRose had a thing for Lily, just like he did. Forget that at the time he first met her she was huge and pregnant. She was angelic, cheerful, soft-spoken, even-tempered under stress. And she had a knack for anticipating people's moods and responses. That she was happily married with children did not seem to deter men's affections for her. Maybe being inaccessible was part of it. She was like the girl in school who sat in front of you, and you knew she was way out of your league. But she turned around, asked you about the homework, told you a joke and made you feel like you were important to her at that moment. But Sammy! She jangled parts of him he'd rather save for another life or something. She had a big bruiser of a boyfriend who looked rough enough to be a bouncer at Chelsea's. Ray would likely end up with his teeth down his throat if he ever made a move there. *It's dumb or neurotic or just plain fucked up to fall for the wrong women all the time*, Ray thought yet again. Or was it really just like Jiggy said — "A guy's prick along with his brain stem is always up to covert ops. Best not to analyze too much." Whatever. The answer was no. Ray would never do security for the dispensaries. He preferred the intermittent torture of the marijuana allergy.

When Ray got to back to his property that night, he crept into his tent and collapsed. It was only six thirty. He'd driven to a pharmacy on the way home, loaded up on the strongest antihistamines he could find and taken as many as he could get away with. Ray was worried about hives. But he didn't get hives. He got nightmares. Terrible ones.

It began with a goat and the goat's eye, which swallowed him. Explosions happened everywhere he looked. Body parts and innards were flying. There were mass shootings and mass graves. Crumbling buildings and screaming children. There were men moaning and begging for death. The scenes transformed in front of him with increasing violence and depravity. Torturers inflicting maximum pain and sadistic degradation. Genocide. Whole landscapes destroyed and populations slaughtered. Ray couldn't move because the plants, all the plants, especially the cannabis plants, were wrapped around him holding him fast, making him watch. *This is the human being*, they reminded him. The great fatigue and glorious triumph. This was maximum noise. His species could do all this, and he might want to take a good look at it. Eventually something slit his throat and he woke up in a sweat.

He was very thirsty. Ray checked his phone. It was only eleven thirty. He found a bottle of water he'd taken from work in his knapsack. He drained it. Then he felt a wave of exhaustion coming over him again. It was like when he'd had to stay awake for three days straight during training. And then when he finally got to sleep he was out for ten hours but it wasn't nearly enough.

#

In the morning Ray was achy and groggy. He opened the tent flap and then sank back down onto his bedding from the effort. He lay there for ages watching the clouds through the opening and then he finally dragged himself up and out into the sunshine.

He was washing in the creek, bent over, soaking his head a few seconds at a time, hoping the cold water might help him wake up, when an unfamiliar car came slowly along the driveway. Ray noticed it just as it was coming to a stop. He jumped out of the creek and grabbed his towel that he'd left on a rock. Nothing happened for a minute, as if maybe the driver was lost or had come to Ray's by mistake. Ray just stood there on the creek bank looking up the hill.

At last the car door opened and who should step out but Lily. Ray blinked a few times to make sure he wasn't seeing things. And then as Lily was looking around to see where he might be, Ray picked up his trousers and T-shirt and quickly put them on.

Lily sauntered down the hill finally catching sight of him. "I just wanted to make sure you were okay," she said. "You looked in such bad shape yesterday. I thought I could get you something if you needed it."

Ray smiled. It was really thoughtful of her. But she didn't have to do anything like that for him. "Um . . . I'm fine," he said, his voice a little hoarse from the unpleasant night and possibly from all the antihistamines. "But thanks." And then remembering his manners, "Would you like some coffee? I'm just about to make it."

Lily nodded enthusiastically.

At first he thought she was curious, nosy about his property and how he was living. He couldn't remember if he'd mentioned to her that he was currently sleeping in a tent. It seemed to Ray that Hullbrooke folks were always interested in your details. Gina said it gave them more to talk about.

After a few minutes, during which he'd lit his little camp stove and was boiling the water for coffee, he began to wonder if it actually might be Lily who was not doing very well. She drifted aimlessly along the bank of the creek but stopped every few feet to pick up a stone and then examined it intently before carefully placing it back down again. As she doubled back and passed by Ray, she asked in a very faraway tone, "Do the fish bother you in the morning?" And she didn't wait for an answer. She wandered up the hill to the old kitchen orchard. The blossoms were out, but she didn't look at those. She just climbed up into one of the trees instead and sat there.

He walked over with the cups of coffee and suggested she might like to get an even better view from the barn loft. So they made their way there and sat in between the missing boards — calves and feet dangling out over the edge. They watched the birds flit in and out of the marsh.

"It's calm here," she said in almost a whisper. "The trees down by the creek are happy, aren't they?"

Ray was surprised by this. He thought he was alone in picking up impressions from the plant world. It was encouraging. He might have some company. "Yeah. How do you know that?"

"Oh, that's easy, Ray. They shine. See that one down there beside the big rock?" And she pointed at nothing. There was nothing growing beside the big rock.

"You mean across the creek up in the woods?"

"No, the one right beside the rock. The really tall one. It's all purple. It shines everywhere." She turned her head and looked carefully at him. "It's even reflected in your face, Ray." And then she looked back out toward the creek. "The one beside it is turquoise. Oh, it's so happy."

"Are all the trees shining?" Ray asked, hoping this might clarify things.

"Not like those two. The others maybe glow a little with the sunlight."

Ray didn't know what to say next. He heard things that people would think were pretty crazy. Lily saw things. Maybe there had been trees there or maybe there were going to be trees there. So Ray just left it. He decided to let Lily be and so she continued to wander around his farm all day, making strange comments and occasionally smiling wistfully about something Ray had no clue about. They made scrambled eggs for lunch, and Ray had a muffin left over that they split between them. When she drove away a little before dinner time, he thought she'd finally gone. But she turned up an hour later with all sorts of food from the Hullbrooke deli. Salads, sandwiches, soups, cheese, fruit. It was way more than they could possibly eat in one meal. Ray began to worry. What was she planning? He didn't really know much about her other than she had a husband and kids. And didn't she need to get back to them? She lived in Lyston or maybe on the Lyston Road. Earlier in the day he'd convinced himself she was just giving herself time off. A day in the country, a relax in the spring sunshine with the old fruit trees in bloom and the creek bubbling by. That's all. Now he wondered if maybe he'd been a little too unconcerned.

"Are you planning to eat all this?" Ray asked.

Lily smiled, and it was sweetness itself. She was so pretty. So lovely. Then she slid her arms around him and kissed him very intensely on the mouth. There was no mistaking her plan at that point. And it didn't take much for Ray to acquiesce. Falling under the old beguilement was as easy as falling into bed. Which of course is exactly what they did.

The loving was tender and strange. Otherworldly perhaps. Ray often felt disembodied, and at one point he was sure his spine was glowing. The shards scraping up and down his back the day before during harvest had transmuted into a cohesive force pushing him to bigger perceptions and exquisite sensitivities. Lily was distant, incomprehensible, and yet every touch of her sent waves into the new universe he inhabited. This was not sex as he'd experienced it before. Rather it was an introduction to infinity and a reminder of his own ever tenuous connection to earth. It did not lack for lust but through even the deepest desire it became ethereal, an episode of limitless expanse.

In the morning, Lily wandered the farm again often coming up to Ray at odd moments to hold his hand, to kiss him, to put her arms around him, and he would hold her in turn or they would make love again. He half-heartedly tried to clean the lower part of the barn, but her interruptions were irresistible. The immediacy of her and her lyrical voice took over his being. He was deliriously and deliciously lost in a new world. With what she saw and what he heard, the farm became a hypnotic paradise where everything around them was conscious. Even the stones were alive and making themselves known. She said you had to be careful, said certain ones were stodgy and strict and others were crazy and jealous. The birds were just busy, so busy they'd forget to sing, and she told Ray, he must never forget to sing. And then she sang to the creek with her clear, unadorned voice, and it touched Ray to his core. In the afternoon they sat still under the blossoming fruit trees and Lily said the blossoms were shining too, almost as brightly as the sun, and they were singing a hymn to the sky. Ray believed her because he heard them murmuring himself.

Lily stayed all the next day, and the day and night after that. But Ray noticed on the third evening, cracks were appearing in paradise. She suddenly stopped smiling and wandered away from him. He found her crying in the loft. She couldn't speak. She just cried. He put his arm around her and kissed her. But even as they went hand in hand down to the creek she still wept. They didn't speak, and she couldn't eat.

They made love that night and clung to each other as if their lives depended on it. But everything had changed. The trees were silent and dark the next morning for Lily. Eventually she told him the world was ugly, full of suffering and peopled by demons you wouldn't notice as such. She wept about her children and what they must experience. There were so many things that were supposed to be and weren't. Cruelty was everywhere she looked and it was only getting worse. Why did people insist on living when they suffered so much?

Ray listened.

She wept again and talked about the dreadful botch of all things. The world of botches.

Ray watched the tears drop onto his sleeping bag. How had she become overwhelmed so suddenly and completely by these thoughts? The practicalities of her life before she came to the farm were completely foreign to him. But then everything had been transformed into something else altogether between them. Ray was lost.

At one point he said, "You sound like my cousin's husband. He thinks the world is terrible too. Only, he's mostly angry about it." Then Ray reached for her hand and she let him hold it. "Maybe it's his anger that keeps him safe." Because Lily seemed unsafe now. Fragile, prone to unnamable perils. She was the pretty girl who sat in front, told you the joke and asked about your homework. Only you never noticed the bleakness in her eyes, until now.

"I have to leave, Ray. I can't stay," Lily said.

Ray just nodded. There was unbearable sadness in the faint curve of her lips and it was like a contagion that infected his whole being. For a few moments he inhabited the full extent of it. Somewhere deep in that feeling he knew she could not come back. Would not come to the farm again. She was going to her old life. Maybe the darkness was the threshold she crossed to get there. As he went to the old barn to fetch a new tin of coffee, tears rolled down his cheeks. He heard her car start and then she was gone.

Each day Lily had been there, a gray truck sat at the end of the driveway for an hour or so, half hidden behind the oak trees. Ray had been so immersed he hadn't noticed it. But that afternoon, he saw it pull up and park. After twenty minutes or so the truck came slowly along the driveway. Ray watched as a thin man got out. He didn't know him. His face was angular, gaunt almost, and he wore an old Yankees baseball cap. His clothes hung on him. He walked slowly, taking in the landscape as if he recognized things. Ray extended his hand but the man seemed not to notice.

"Lily say where she was going?" The man's voice had a ring of exhaustion to it.

Ray was startled. And just as it occurred to him that this man was Lily's husband, Ray's back suddenly felt raw again.

The man could see Ray's hesitancy. "I know she was here. I saw her." He bit his lip and nodded to himself. "She didn't say anything about where she was going? Mention anybody?"

Ray shook his head slightly. "Not that I recall." Ray noticed the man looked worse than haggard. He was gutted somehow. "She just . . . said she had to leave."

The man nodded as if he was expecting that response. "One time, she called me from Florida." He smiled a little ruefully, then looked away, down toward the creek. After a few seconds he said, "It's beautiful here."

Ray just stood there not knowing what to say.

The man looked back at him. "I can't get her to stay on her meds all the time, you know. I try, but there's only so much that makes sense to her some days. My mother's looking after the kids but she has to leave tomorrow."

"I'm really sorry. She didn't say where she was going." And just then Ray felt sorry for all sorts of things. There were worlds and then there were worlds — and he might have trouble figuring out which one was viable or caused the least hardship.

The man nodded again. "She's not at work. Called in sick again. Sometimes she stays with her friend in town. Maybe she's there." He said this all more to himself than to Ray. He turned around and walked back to his truck, started it up and backed all the way out the driveway.

Ray went down by the creek and climbed into his hammock. He was aching. His whole body felt as if it had snapped. The physical stress he'd felt during the harvest was making a comeback. The three days with Lily had only been a temporary reprieve, as if a narcotic had been administered by unseen entities now intent on his utmost sobriety. He could not get comfortable. He stopped trying and went into the pain. And that was the key he discovered. That was the necessary thing.

#

A week later, Lily was back at work. Ray had gone in very early, and while he was getting a coffee in the CannRose kitchen, he saw her car drive up. She looked happy as she got out. She smiled at the sight of the facility and then turned to reach back into the car for her bag. She had that same welcoming look she'd had the very first day he'd been introduced to her. She even wore the same color of violet and the same thin scarf around her neck. It took Ray all morning to build up the courage to walk to the front entrance where Lily sat at the reception desk.

He approached hesitantly, his head and heart whirling. He didn't have a clue what would happen next. She looked up and saw him walking toward her and she smiled. For Ray, it was like the sun coming out, but the sun would sear his eyes if he gazed too long at it.

"Ray. How are you?"

"I'm good." Ray could barely look at her. "You?"

"I'm good too."

They were silent and Ray just stood there staring at his feet mostly. Eventually Lily caught his eye. She looked sad but not like he'd seen her at the farm. She put out her hand and touched his arm. "I'm sorry."

"You don't need to be sorry."

"I'm so sorry. It wasn't fair. Sometimes I just . . ."

"You don't be need to be sorry," he said more forcefully. "I'm sorry too then."

"I manage to hurt everybody, Ray. I don't mean to . . ."

Ray nodded and swallowed. He swallowed again.

"Even my children, Ray. And that's the worst."

Ray looked down at his feet again.

"Dennis is really good to me. I . . . I don't even know how he can be like that. What I put him through . . ."

"Yeah." Ray was barely audible.

"He's always been patient. So kind."

"I know." Ray felt drained just recalling his encounter with the man. "He was at the farm. I met him."

"I know you did." Her voice sounded hopeful. Hopeful that Ray might understand, might not be lost to her completely, might not shut her out with finality. But might offer her still some kind regard.

Ray looked at her. "It's okay. Is it?" he asked simply. "It's all okay now?"

"Yes," she said, and she smiled. There was the sound of hope again in her voice, and something new. She was steadfast, determined. "It's all okay, Ray."

Chapter 14

Ray was finally gutting the upper level of the drive shed. If he took the trouble to think about it, the temptation to go at it with a sledgehammer like a madman had been building up for a year. Nothing beats a vigorous wrecking. The water damage in the building was limited to where the crude rooms were, and all of that was coming out. It was junky material anyway. He'd temporarily fixed the leaks above it and the few rafters that needed replacing would be put in with the new roof. Ray had roofers he knew and trusted lined up for August. It was the soonest they could come. So Ray walked through the rooms once again. He donned his respirator, then picked up his hefty crowbar and even heftier sledgehammer and let loose.

It was wonderfully cathartic. After a couple of hours he was standing in wreckage worthy of a war zone. It brought back his army days. In fact everything about the scene brought back his army days. The initial enthusiasm, the speed of the wreckage, the finality of it and the blinding dust. And of course now he had to deal with the aftermath, the rubble and the clearing away. He picked up a load of crumbly, moldy plasterboard pieces and threw them in the dumpster outside and then continued on down to the creek to take a break and make himself a coffee.

Ray's experience in the army hadn't been anything like Jiggy's. He wasn't forced into it by some threat of a worse fate. It was something he'd planned since he was six years old. His Uncle Alvin would have said he was just channeling the dark side of his grandfather. But Ray had never seen it that way. This was him. All him. He couldn't tell anybody why he was so enthusiastic about it, but when he got to basic training something clicked. It was like a gear fell into place and his life made sense. This was what he was meant to be. He made friends right away and he'd been a star, a team player not a shit disturber. There was a group of five of them at Fort Benning and they pulled each other through. They'd laugh about the get-tough screaming sergeants, the food, the exhaustion, the "talks" — but they were all excited about possibilities. After those first ten weeks, they dispersed into different training and different units. Ray kept in touch for the first year until he was deployed.

But Iraq wasn't like he thought it would be, in spite of the preparation. The heat and monotony were excruciating. It was the same thing every day until one day it wasn't. After a routine patrol through one of the city's sections, they were stopped close to a checkpoint by a woman all trussed up with explosives. You couldn't quite tell the explosives were there, given the clothing. Actually you couldn't even be sure it was a woman. She had a goat with her. But she wasn't moving out of the way like she should. She was acting like she was drunk too. This was the cue apparently. They were ordered to shoot so she couldn't get any closer to the soldiers at the checkpoint. She started singing — it was definitely a woman — so Ray shot into the air. He couldn't bring himself to aim for her. SPC Jeffreys, who'd been in the unit and the country six months longer than Ray, shot her in the legs and killed the goat in the process. She fell face forward onto the bleeding goat. Before they could get the engineers or a robot from the base to check for explosives, she blew up and the goat along with her. At the sight and smell of all of this, Ray threw up and then passed out. This was noted.

The next day, it was little boys throwing rocks, and an older one, probably about twelve, threw an IED while they were stopped by a market. It hit the stall in front of them and there was a roar as the whole market corner blew up. Ray happened to be in a Guardian, the priciest of armored security vehicles, so it barely touched them. The twelve-year-old was shot multiple times as he ran across the street. Ray threw up again when he saw the aftermath of the IED. Three more women, some eggplants, cauliflower and countless cucumbers blasted to pieces. And in contrast to SPC Jeffreys, who was jubilant he'd nailed a true insurgent, Ray froze at the sight of the perforated adolescent corpse. He passed out there too. Right in the middle of the street. This was also noted.

Ray's realization that the only grit and guts he could bring to a crisis were his own stomach contents made him doubt many things about himself. The lieutenant said hurling your cookies wasn't a big deal. A stomach could surely toughen up with time and experience. But loss of consciousness, that was problematic. That kind of talent, however you wanted to look at it, was a liability. There wasn't room for diminished capacity. It could get people killed, including Ray. But then Ray knew that didn't he? The lieutenant had liked Ray well enough, but now maybe he wasn't so sure. Fainting was a skill honed by fakers and pussies.

Ray felt the disgust of his peers, even if some of them tried to hide it — after all he'd been one of promising ones. They were buddies. They had each other's backs, except he took holidays now. What was that about? Some flimsy frail underlying part of him. A feeble pathetic core that the sight of a bloodied goat and body parts could topple. What made him so fucking special? Everybody else stayed standing, and some, like Jeffreys, even got high from it. Ray felt he'd betrayed his unit, the army, his family (though probably not Uncle Alvin) and his country. And he'd certainly betrayed everything he'd aspired to. Many nights, as he tossed and turned in his uncomfortable bed, he wished some clever hajji bullet would find him.

His self-recrimination was profound. Doubt and the revulsion he felt for himself changed him. It made him quiet, withdrawn. His spontaneity vanished and he didn't speak his mind anymore. He had to get a little drunk to do that. His humiliation over the transfer to FOB jobs, menial tasks like cleaning toilets and folding towels or maybe a little filing, made him almost as sick to his stomach as the body parts had. The resident doctor at the base took an interest, not because of the dark cloud around Ray — that was common enough on any given tour and he'd seen way worse — no, he had a hunch Ray had a vascular problem. He mentioned his theory to Ray, pointed out that a sudden pressure difference caused even by a small explosion might trigger an equally sudden vascular response in a person with this particular problem and cause that person to faint or freeze. It had nothing to do with being a wuss or delicate. It wouldn't be anything Ray could control. Well no shit Sherlock! That much was clear. It didn't make any difference to Ray though. No amount of science could let him off the hook.

What did finally let him off the hook or at least changed his mood was a drunken brawl with a two-hundred-eighty-pound and not particularly muscular career fobbit. Marcus Bridgeman was a thirty-something communications specialist with a red-and-white-striped belt in judo and he really didn't like what Ray was communicating. Over a series of moves and counter moves, where Ray was mostly on the receiving end and frequently prone, Bridgeman pointed out, "Fobbits do crucial work, moron. You should be proud to be one." He'd picked Ray up by the foot at this and had him on the ground again in an instant. "Testosterone, brute strength and hair-trigger response with oversized weapons do not necessarily make a man." Ray landed with another thump halfway across the room. "Nor do they win wars, at least not since the Middle Ages." And Ray was forcibly summersaulted over the man's outstretched leg. It continued on relentlessly as Ray maintained his belligerence. Nothing quite compares to the stamina wrought of self-loathing. But finally Ray was facedown with Marcus Bridgeman's heavy foot on his shoulder and his arm bent excruciatingly backward and upward. Marcus may have had a pudgy-looking hand, but he had a grip like an orangutan. And it was at that specific moment Ray finally got the point.

After that evening and several bruises that colored deeply over the next few days, Ray slept a lot better and the dark cloud that hovered over him began to disperse. He even ended up on pleasant speaking terms with Marcus Bridgeman. But he still kept his head down. The happy-go-lucky part of him was gone — and he could live without it, he figured. It was okay. Ray had a feeling he'd finally shrunk into himself, into his new role in life.

When Ray shipped back, he applied for more training. He could still be handy. Even a delicate pussy afflicted with the vapors could still pick up a few useful skills. He was back in Iraq before he knew it. The army was starting to vacate the scene but those air conditioners still got debilitating workouts. So did the refrigerators and other electronic conveniences. Wiring in general was often of great interest. And it wasn't monotonous either — air conditioners had their own individual problems, possibly even personalities, and he liked the work. It gave him a modicum of dignity back. Getting around between bases and various posts had really been the only tricky bit. That was the part that finally did him in for good. He could only look back and wonder at his teenage self that brimmed with so much confidence. He hadn't been cocky or a wiseass like Gabe. He'd just been certain he could handle anything with ease. Plain dumb youth likely.

Ray went back up to the wreckage in the drive shed and began cleaning out the pieces. Try as he would, he still couldn't stop reviewing his disappointing army career and coming to the conclusion his own life was like the rubble he was shifting into the dumpster. It occurred to him that the pain up and down his back during harvest a while ago was probably just another manifestation of his spinelessness, only more literal. But not only did he lack bravery in carrying out certain military actions, he could be particularly cowardly on the personal front too. *It's so fucking pathetic*, he thought in disgust, the old self-loathing seeping back into him. He could barely say a word to his uncle, for instance. A word that mattered anyway. And then there was Jiggy. Ray had always been gutless when it came to Jiggy.

After finally telling him about his own job, it took Ray positively ages and a couple of staff turnovers to build up the nerve to tell Jiggy about the constant IT opening at CannRose. Ray was pretty sure Greg would hire Jiggy on the spot once he knew how much experience he had and what a wizard he was with computers.

Ray had mulled over for days how best to broach the subject: *You could get weed at a discount, Jiggy.* Or, *If everybody else is making money, Jiggy, why not you?* And, *Go for the share options. What have you got to lose?* Well maybe not that last bit. Ray knew Jiggy'd find something to lose. "Personal integrity! An' for a body livin' without a foot, Little Cousin, that's important," he'd say, or something along those lines. Or he'd go on about "the rich fucks runnin' the world" and the last thing he wanted to be was "in their frickin' club." In the end, Ray had taken the easier route — and again in his own estimation, the gutless one — of finally telling Gina about it first.

"Wow," she'd said, "that would be something. Our Jiggy runnin' the IT for a marijuana dispensary." Gina laughed. "It would totally piss off my dad too. Jiggy might do it just for that."

Ray hadn't considered that angle. Ray often wondered how Gina had grown up sane at all with an evangelical-minister dad and a free-spirit mom. Anyway, Ray was glad he'd told Gina.

"You should bring it up after he's had a beer and a puff," she said, "and if I'm there I'll put in my two cents too."

So that's what they'd done. Ray and Gina stood in the kitchen and just watched the look on Jiggy's face go from bewilderment to wide-eyed incredulity. He was speechless for the second time in Ray's memory. Jiggy was so flummoxed, he said he needed a walk. Far from being intimidated, Ray found he had trouble keeping a straight face. He and Gina had a good laugh after Jiggy left. So there was the proof, Jiggy's bark could be silenced easier than he'd thought. Gina wasn't afraid of him, why should Ray always feel the need to tiptoe around him?

It was late afternoon by the time Ray finished sweeping up the dust and splinters. Most of the inside of the drive shed was now open. There was one more section to strip down to the joists, but he definitely would be taking care with that one. The inside wall held up that part of the building, and it was where the roof came down low and changed slope a little. The room had clearly been the farm workshop. There was good old wood in the benches and shelving there, which could be useful for all sorts of things, like countertops. Ray decided to turn the room into his kitchen and put in an archway to it from the taller open space.

When he was talking to Ernie one day at CannRose, he found out Ernie was not only a good cook — he'd catered a few CannRose events and Ray thought the food was delicious — but he knew all about kitchens too. Efficiency as well as aesthetics. So Ray invited him out for a look, and Ernie agreed the workshop would make a fine kitchen. Ernie himself lived pretty minimally, so Ray was surprised by all the ideas he had and doubted he could ever afford most of them. Ernie told him to keep an eye out for estate sales and to go visit a certain wrecker outside Lyston, and he gave Ray the names of two secondhand dealers within a hundred mile radius of Hullbrooke. "You'd be surprised what you can do on a shoestring," Ernie said. One idea Ray would implement was to put in a laundry room in the corner end, facing into the hill. Cleanliness would be closest to God there, and Ray certainly didn't want to miss out on that one. He'd take redemption in any form.

When Ray nodded off to sleep that night listening to the low *whuump, whuump* of a bullfrog a few feet away, it occurred to him he could lighten up. *Yeah, lighten up. Maybe I'm a joke anyway!* And so he fell into a dream of deep water with waves as wide as football fields are long and as high as sequoias. Ray was just a speck in his rowboat. And yet he was afloat and the sun was shining. The waves did not coil or break. They were simply huge, and he rode them in his little boat like a flea on a dog. It was a change from the plants — trees, vines, bushes and weeds and all things green and growing, including marijuana — that had recently taken over his dream life. As he came to some lucidity in that scenario, it occurred to him that this was the bigger picture. The great sea was the more important thing. He was just like the plants usually were in his dreams. Busy with doing. Growing, pursuing. But this other part he harbored, the reticent thing that would freeze or faint away, maybe that was like the great sea. It was the thing he had to ride out. And if that was true, well the sea was a truly powerful thing. More powerful than any guts he could ever bring to a situation. More powerful than anybody's guts, really. More vast too and full of other life.

Chapter 15

CannRose owed Ray a proper holiday; he'd been there a year now. And so he decided to take a break from his farm and his renovating and call his New Jersey friend. Gabe was always up for a good time and maybe he could take a break too. If not, Ray could at least inquire about renting one of Gabe's out-of-the-way properties on the shore. He had in mind the slightly rundown apartment he'd stayed in while he was working on the old hotel for Gabe and his dad. Back then it had come with the job. But this was high season. No harm in asking though — if they had anything, they might give him some kind of a deal.

"My man, my man! I'm up to my butt here in condo kitchens. I don't have a minute. But hey, if you need a place, Dad did just buy something on the west side. Delaware Bay. Way south, close to the wildlife refuge. Fortescue, I think. Let me get back to you. It's miles away from us! But then you like desolation." He laughed. "You know you could always stay at our cottage except we're still here!" — meaning kids' noise and Gabe's wife.

Gabe called back within the hour. "You're gonna love it, dude. Water view practically right in the park there! Spacious but no furniture. And you have to keep the windows open. Mold. The place is rotting but the roof won't fall on your head just yet. Still has water and electric — just have to turn them on when you get there. Dad'll delay the demolition for a month. It's all yours."

"How much is the rent?"

"Jesus, dude. It's free for fuck sake."

"I wasn't expecting free rent. I should pay something for the utilities anyway," Ray said.

"Given the condition, it may not be the bargain you think. Haven't even seen a picture of it myself. But seriously man, you know Dad wouldn't take anything. It's not worth the fucking paperwork . . ."

"Cash?"

"Dude, shut up. Just get your ass down here. I'll have the key or whatever for you by the time you arrive. Directions too, so your pretty, pretty little ass won't get lost."

"Jesus, Gabe."

"Do I take care of you or what! And you have to stay a least a couple of nights. Barbecue and beer season, baby!"

"Thanks, Gabe. And tell your dad thanks too."

#

So Ray took off for the spacious cottage slated for demolition. It wasn't completely unfurnished. There were chairs, a table and even a pullout sofa. Peeling paint was everywhere, but apart from that, most people would think the building might just need a few repairs. It did smell though, so Ray opened all the windows when he got there and then the fresh air blew in. The views were terrific.

Ray had managed to rent a kayak so was able to go explore the tidal marshes. He went fishing too. There was no shortage of boats and fishermen to take him out for the day. He walked for hours along the shore past the town, took a little day trip to Dyer Cove and Gandys Beach. The landscape was all so different compared to Ray's farm and there was no work that needed doing everywhere he looked.

But one thing was the same. The plants there yammered too. Or the tinnitus prevailed. Either way, there was no getting away from it. Ray thought maybe he should try to follow that weird Larry guy's advice. Start really paying attention. Start listening. So he did. Every time he went kayaking in the marsh, he'd stop where the reeds grew thick. He sat motionless and closed his eyes. He was a good listener when he wanted to be. He'd had years of training after all. But it was more difficult than he thought. His mind would flit away because the noises were subtle once he tried to pay attention to them and he'd lose focus. And sometimes he had the distinct feeling the plants hushed right up as soon as they knew they were being listened to. But his efforts put him more at peace, and as the holiday grew to a close, he felt rejuvenated and better than he had in years. In fact he was feeling so relaxed he actually wanted to stop in with Uncle Alvin and Aunt Collette on the way back to Hullbrooke.

His aunt was delighted he'd stay for a couple of days and they could get caught up. Uncle Alvin, now involved with even more volunteer work, especially for Amnesty, had gone to a conference in Chicago. He'd be back Monday, the last morning of Ray's visit.

Both Collette and Ava the dog were in the front yard when Ray arrived. Collette was gardening and Ava, who'd been snoozing in the sunshine beside her, woke up and began barking before Ray even made it into the driveway. She bounded over to the truck and Ray could barely get the door open with her leaping.

"How's my girl?" Ray said, along with several more endearments as he extricated himself. Ava's tail wagged wildly along with the rest of her. Eventually she settled down enough to get a hug from him.

His aunt walked over. "Hey there. She's not the only girl 'round here wants a hug." Ray stood up again, his face soggy from Ava's licking. He pulled off his sunglasses, threw them on the truck seat and wiped his cheek with his sleeve. He stepped forward with a smile and threw his arms around his aunt. He was inches taller and she was dwarfed by his embrace. Ava took advantage of the open door and jumped into the truck. She sat down in the passenger seat and looked out the window expectantly.

"Ava!" his aunt chided.

Ray laughed. "See! It's really mostly the truck she misses."

"In addition to cupboard love, we now have a case of truck love?" his aunt asked.

"That's a reasonable love," said Ray.

"You can identify, can you?"

"Yeah."

His aunt shook her head, still looking at Ava. "Alvin makes her sit in the back seat if he takes her anywhere, and I usually manage not to take her! She's becoming a nuisance. Likes to go off now and follow people, teenage girls in particular. I have no idea why. Some days it's like looking after a three-year-old again." She paused and looked at Ray. Then she clasped both his arms. "Oh, Ray, it's great to see you!" She tilted her head to one side, examining him closely. "You're looking good," she said. "More relaxed. Like your old self. Ten days on the shore must have been really good for you."

"It was fantastic. Between the fishing and kayaking, I was out on the water one way or another almost every day."

"Gabe's wife manage to get you a girlfriend?"

"No. She tried her best again though." Ray sighed and then brightened. "You know, one time we turned the tables on her, back when I was working on that hotel, but it didn't last. She figured it out."

"Oh? You'll have to tell me all about that. Let's get your stuff. I was about to make some coffee. You drinking real coffee these days? I can't keep up with all the kids and the various food choices. Ava, get out of that truck."

Ava heaved a sigh and lay down across the driver's seat.

Ray spotted a tennis ball lying in the grass. He ran over, picked it up and tossed it a few times in the air. Ava jumped out of the truck in an instant, and as Ray threw the ball across the yard, she tore after it.

#

"So, you know what I think is up with Gabe's wife?" Aunt Collette said, taking a sip of her coffee and pushing the plate of cookies over to Ray. "Here, I baked your favorite."

Ray picked up a cookie and considered it for a second or two. "These look so good. I've missed them." He took a bite and closed his eyes, savoring the buttery sweetness. "You could stop whole infantries with these cookies!"

"You should tell that to Alvin. He'd like that. Make Cookies Not War."

"I like it too." Ray dunked his cookie in his coffee. "So you have a theory about Gabe's wife?"

"I do. It occurred to me after you told me about the New Year's Eve adventure. I think she wanted you. *You* — not Gabe. And she got Gabe."

"No!" Ray put his coffee mug down and looked at his aunt. "That can't be, Aunt Collette. Isobel was nuts about him all through high school. All she ever talked about was Gabe this, Gabe that."

"Then she married him, had some kids — and then she grew up. How many kids they got now?"

"Three and a half."

"One on the way?"

"Another girl too."

"Oh my. Old Grandpa must be delighted about that."

"I know. But Gabe tells the old man he'll have jobs for all his daughters because he hires lots of women. Drives his grandpa crazy."

Collette laughed. "I see him around town sometimes you know. Run into him at the deli every now and again. Never fails to tell me he's waiting for a great-grandson. Or how sad it is that Gabe's overrun with daughters and a wife who still hasn't learned how to cook."

"Actually she cooks really well."

"Just not Italian probably."

"No. And she doesn't make her own sauces if she does. He hates that. Gabe told me she and his grandad got into a fight once over cheese. She used Havarti instead of mozzarella for something!"

"My God! The nerve."

"Anyway she's into whole foods, you know, veggies, nothing fried, nuts and beans. Mostly vegan."

"Hmm. Gabe doesn't complain?"

"No. Gabe is totally happy. He's the happiest guy I know," Ray said.

"Well maybe Isobel's not. You said you fooled her? What'd you do?" Collette was familiar with Ray's pranks when he was a teenager.

Ray grabbed another cookie from the plate and took a bite. He chewed thoughtfully then swallowed. "So a bunch of us were at the bar one night and one of the carpenters brought along his sister. She's maybe a few years older than me. And she's really big. Like she's an inch taller than I am."

"Wow."

"She's not fat. Just big like a football player but she doesn't look like one. She's pretty much gorgeous or can be when she wants. And she can be hilarious too. She does stand-up comedy. Anyway we started talking."

"Did you fall in love?"

"No, nothing like that. I'm not her type. She's gay. But somehow Isobel came up—"

"And she was sympathetic to your plight."

"Totally." Ray nodded, smiling.

"Hmm. I take it Isobel wasn't there."

"No, she was off with the kids somewhere. But the next night was this barbecue at Gabe's."

"Oh, I can guess. You had your new friend come as your date?"

"Ah . . . yeah, so Julie and her partner, Anna, and me, we came out as a threesome."

"Well, my goodness."

"Yeah. The story was, we were all soul mates. Isobel talks about soul mates every other day. And it was 'new love' and 'love at first sight.' And we wanted to all get married together."

"Did that have the desired effect? Folks in that neck of the woods a little startled?"

"Isobel, yeah. I don't know about everybody else. I had too good a time. Probably drank too much. And Julie was way too funny that night, had me and Anna in stitches. Anyway, as usual, Isobel had somebody all lined up again for me. She's so nuts."

"Yes. Wonder what a therapist would say . . ."

"So, Julie and Anna, as soon as they see Gabe's wife introducing me to this new woman, they come right over and Anna starts talking about how the three of us are going to challenge bigamy laws. You know, because what we had was nothing to do with bigamy since a threesome was a sexual preference. And possibly a new kind of gender issue because Anna identifies as male sometimes."

"Now that's all very progressive. Does Anna like to be addressed as he? I hear that's what happens these days and I know I'd get confused at my age."

"No, she's cool with being addressed as female."

"You still keepin' in touch with either of them?"

"Oh yeah, they're still together. I'm stopping in on the way back."

"That's nice. New friends are always nice." Collette looked across the garden and squinted at the three sparrows and a waxwing fluffing themselves in the bird bath.

"Anyway Isobel never bugged me with a date for the rest of the summer. But just when I finished the job she figured out we weren't a threesome after all."

Collette started to laugh.

"Whenever I want to piss her off I tell her they send their love from Boston. She doesn't like that I go visit with them."

"That's none of her business!"

"I know." Ray smiled. He wasn't going to say anything to his aunt yet, and he hadn't breathed a word of it to anybody else either, but just before he left for holiday, Julie had told him she was finally pregnant. They hadn't wanted to tell him immediately in case there were more problems, but since he'd called about stopping in on the way back and Julie was frequently barfing, she figured he needed warning. She had a few more weeks to get through the first trimester.

"That's all extremely interesting but my theory still stands," Collette said.

"What?"

"That Isobel wanted you all along."

Ray sighed and picked up the remaining cookie on the plate. Ava wandered over, sat down in front of him and put her head on his knee.

"Ava, stop your begging. I didn't bake those for you." Aunt Collette pointed for her to go back and lie down in the garden. And then she squinted hard at the dog. "What has she got hanging out of her mouth?"

Ray looked down and reached under Ava's chin. As he brought up her head so he could see better, she started to chew. Ray grabbed her lower jaw so she had to open her mouth. Her tongue was wildly negotiating a chunky, now mangled bug. Ray reached in and fished the saliva-covered thing out by its wings. It was a cicada. More dead than alive. It just sat in his palm glistening and wet, wings askew, one slightly torn. The beady gray eyes on either side of the bulky head were impassive. One of its legs moved spastically. Ava looked disappointed and made a move for it again. Ray pulled his hand back and Collette got a good view of it.

"Oh good lord! *Those* things! They make such a racket! I thought they were finished for the season. Ray, don't let her have it. She'll eat it and then throw up on the carpet."

"Of course she will," he said, stroking Ava. Then Ray gently dropped the cicada onto the empty cookie plate.

"Ray!"

"People eat cicadas you know. In some places they're considered a delicacy."

"Well, I'm sure as blazes not cookin' that one up for you!"

"Low carb! Gluten free!" Ray reassured his aunt, smiling. "And they're singers too. You should appreciate that, Aunt Collette."

His aunt tried to suppress a laugh and looked away.

Ray looked back at the cicada on the plate. "Not long for this world anyway. Might as well let it die in peace."

Ava pressed her head more firmly onto Ray's knee, and Aunt Collette stared out at the garden and began mentally assessing what needed doing.

"So how's Uncle Alvin?" Ray asked after a while.

"Oh," Aunt Collette said, turning her attention back to him. "Well you know, none of us are getting any younger. In fact we're both the wrong side of seventy. I think in about five or six years things could really start to fall apart." Aunt Collette held up her fingers to show joints slightly deformed by arthritis and began massaging her hand.

"No way!" Ray said.

"Alvin had to get dentures a year ago."

"He did? I didn't notice."

"He keeps pretty quiet about it. I don't think he smiles as much."

"I thought that was just because of me."

"Well you two need to get over all that," his aunt said, giving him a sidelong glance.

"I feel bad about everything you know."

"I know you do. But the way he was with your grandfather — it's like it almost had to happen. Our own boys never challenged him much. Not that way. Oh they'd have fights all right. But nothing about politics much. They were usually in the same camp about those things. Happy to go to university too, do all that stuff. And that track just wasn't for you."

"Yeah, but he'd have been okay if I wanted to be a carpenter or electrician."

"Of course he would. Or a musician."

"It was just all about the military."

"He could not abide the war machine. He still can't. But he was also trying to take care of you."

"I know that. Military changes people."

"Certainly can. You think it changed you?"

"Yeah."

"For the better or for the worse?"

"Bit of both."

"Well, there you go," said Aunt Collette. "Just like life anyway.

Chapter 16

Jiggy was coming out of the barn just as Gina was coming up the drive, back from a day of bookkeeping in town.

"How's your day?"

"Oh, you know, too many bosses. Nobody left to do the work. How about you?"

"Think I'm missin' a calf. Mother's spooked an' bawlin'. No sign of it anywhere."

"Wolves you think? Coyotes?"

"I don't think so. They're not around this year."

"We should go look for it. I'll go get changed."

"Don't want to put your feet up?"

"It can wait."

"Okay. I'll get Bunny," Jiggy said. Bunny was the ATV. Gina had named it and Jiggy just shook his head at the time. That was four years ago.

Gina hopped on behind Jiggy and they headed out to the field where the cattle had been. "Drop me off at the old fencerow," Gina said above the motor.

Jiggy slowed down and stopped when they got close to the corner of the divided pasture. "Watch out. There's wild parsnip." Jiggy pointed to the lacey, yellow-flowered patch of plants along the fence a hundred yards away.

"I see 'em."

"Okay. I'm checkin' the woods. Be back in a bit." Jiggy sped off.

Gina began walking along slowly, listening and keeping her eyes peeled. Years and years ago, the old fencerow had been a solid stone structure. Now it was mostly a long pile of rubble. The land sloped on the same line as the fence and there were gnarled old plum trees, brush piles and gullies that ran alongside the rubble. An energetic calf might just try to get on top of that rubble. Although that was more for goats. Gina wished they had goats, but Jiggy wouldn't have them. Said they were just way too much trouble and Gina'd turn them all into pets. Then he wouldn't be able to do anything with them. It was probably true. Gina made sure she didn't get to know the calves. She didn't know how Jiggy could send them off to market after a year or two and she knew he secretly named them. They didn't have that many breeding cows. Maybe forty. She'd lost count. Anyway Jiggy told her the offspring had a pretty nice life even if it was short and he tried to make sure they just had the one bad day. Unless of course they were little bullocks, and then they had two. "Poor little buggers, but the nuts gotta go."

On her way back along the other side of the fencerow and just up from where the slope was at its lowest point, she heard something. It was almost like the mewl of a cat. There was a deep gulley with water pooled in the bottom, held back by two big stones. The calf was up to its rear in mud. One of its hooves or a leg must have been stuck.

The calf struggled as Gina got close. It wasn't used to people. Gina spoke softly. Its nose and most of the rest of its head were covered in mud. The eyes were big and panicked. She reached out and put her hand on the calf's back. It struggled again and then stopped. It made that peculiar bleating noise. Gina could hear the ATV, still in the woods. Too bad Jiggy wouldn't carry a smartphone.

Gina wondered how deep the mud was and how far she'd sink. She had hiking boots, not rubber boots. The calf was small enough she could probably lift it. She took the plunge with one foot and sank right down, almost up to her knee, but it was solid underneath. She kept her other foot out of the gulley by kneeling on the bank as she bent down with one hand still on the calf's back. She reached along the calf's hind leg closest to her. The mud was above her elbow by the time she got to its hoof. She felt all around it. That one was free. As she pulled her hand out of the mud, it made a sucking noise and a glob fell off her arm. Then she went to the front leg on the same side and did the same thing. That hoof was free too. She repositioned herself a little. The calf complained with another mewling sound as she felt down the other front leg. There it was. The hoof was caught right between a boulder that she could never lift in a million years and something that felt more peculiar. A hunk of metal maybe or wood. It had a sharp edge. Gina wondered if the calf was bleeding. She heard the ATV coming closer.

She pulled her hand out of the mud, stood up as tall as she could and started waving her arms wildly. She didn't know if Jiggy'd be able to see her so she took off her red T-shirt and waved that.

Jiggy saw the flapping bit of red down near the bottom of the slope. He drove the ATV down and stopped on the other side of the fencerow.

"Jesus. Aren't you somethin'! I like the mud look. An' the lingerie effect. Suits ya! Wanna wrestle?"

"Help me, you turkey."

Jiggy made his way down the fence, jumped over the ditch on his side and clambered over the pile of rocks. The calf started to struggle again.

"Don't scare it. I just got it calm."

"So what's the score?" He leaped onto the grass on the other side of the gulley, landing on his good foot.

"The leg's caught. There's a boulder on one side and something kind of sharp on the other."

"Can ya move a bit?"

"Not really. I think you have to help me out."

"Oh, so you're both stuck."

"Jiggy!"

"Here. Grab on." Jiggy braced himself and reached down. He pulled Gina onto the bank and her foot came out of the mud with a squelch. Jiggy looked at her and smiled. Then he looked back down at the calf.

"The poor thing," Gina said. "It's terrified."

"I just hope it doesn't have a broken leg."

Jiggy lay right down along the edge of the gulley and reached his arm down into the mud in front of the calf. He felt the thing with the sharp edge. He could put his hand right around it. He gave it a yank away from the calf. Gina could see the calf trembling.

"I think I moved it a little." Jiggy yanked again. "Maybe if you were down there, maybe you could move its leg sideways."

Gina was back in the gulley in a flash with both feet in the mud this time. She bent down and felt the calf's leg. "Okay. On three. One, two, three . . ."

Jiggy yanked as hard as he could while Gina pulled the leg sideways and got it free. She'd hauled the calf right up against herself in the process. She reached around its rump and below its chest and lifted it straight up out of the mud. Jiggy reached down and pulled it the rest of the way. He straightened up with the calf still in his arms then walked away from the gulley and deposited it on the grass. The calf tottered but stayed standing. Jiggy wiped the mud and took a closer look at the leg. The skin was broken but it would be easy enough to deal with.

"How does it look?" Gina yelled.

"Not bad, I think. Take her home, clean her up then see what her mother thinks of her." He walked back to the gulley. Gina was still standing knee deep in the muck. He wasn't sure if she was stuck again or just tired. She was covered in mud. They both were. He stood on the bank and looked at her. She wiped her forehead and got mud all over that too.

"I gotta say. It's kind of a turn on."

"Will you get me out of here?"

Jiggy just stood and stared. Her red T-shirt was still in a heap on the bank of the gulley. "Jesus!" Jiggy suddenly exclaimed. "Will ya look at that! No wonder they all came down here." Jiggy was pointing about four or five yards away along the bank. "Shit. They got their own private stash!"

And there they were, half eaten of course, a cluster of tall, lacey-looking marijuana plants, gone wild maybe, and all the happier for it.

Gina looked over and started to laugh. "Seriously? You knew this was here!"

"Swear to God. Had no fuckin' idea."

"Well help me out of here then?"

Jiggy took his eyes off the marijuana plants and looked down at Gina again. He cocked his head. He wanted to remember this picture.

"Please!" she said.

"My princess," he said, finally giving her his hand. Jiggy had never called Gina a princess before.

#

"You should have seen the poor little thing, Ray. All trembling and covered in mud."

Jiggy walked into the kitchen.

"I was just telling Ray about the calf," Gina said.

"Oh, I thought you were talkin' about me. You know from when ya had your shirt off."

Gina looked up to the ceiling, sighed and looked at Ray again. But she was smiling. "Turns out the cows were back there for more than a lark. They got quite the stash. Right along the old stone row there. Isn't that right, Jiggy."

"Yeah, real black-market bovines."

"You mean weed?"

"Yeah. It's growin' wild."

Ray started to laugh. "You musta planted it, Jiggy!

"Did not. On my honor. Stack of Bibles." Jiggy sat down at the kitchen table with a thud and smiled at Ray. "So how's Little Cousin doin'? We haven't seen you in ages. How was your holiday?"

"It was great."

"Hear you stopped in with Alvin and Collette. Good man."

"Yeah. That worked out okay. Oh, I got the loft and the stairs built in the drive shed! Finally cleaned up the barn floor too."

Jiggy nodded. Then he cleared his throat. "Hope you're not overdoin' it. Remember what your old army buddy the doctor there said."

"Oh, yeah. The hammock is my home."

"A man after my own heart."

Ray took advantage of Jiggy's cheery mood. "You know, they're still looking for an IT person at CannRose. They want someone experienced to head it all up. They found a kid just out of college again but I don't know that he's gonna last. There was some screwup with the orders to the dispensaries, some glitch in the tracking system, and the surveillance recordings are cutting out again."

"Oh well. Yeah." Jiggy tapped absentmindedly on the table. "I've been thinkin' about it."

Gina glanced at Ray with a lift of her head and a smile.

"I know. You two think ya got me all sorted."

"They'd be okay with just part time probably," Ray said. "I bet you could even do a whole lot of it from home too."

"Well, that's not actually a good idea, given what they do. You want to reduce the chance of a hack, so at least some of it should be dedicated, offline, ya know. The claim that the cloud's safe is mostly shit."

Gina nodded at Ray.

"Like I said . . ." Jiggy stared at Gina. "I'm thinkin' about it. That's all."

At that moment there was a scuffling just outside the kitchen and then in the doorway appeared a fuzzy almost-white puppy.

"Well you woke up!" Gina exclaimed, squatting down with both arms stretched out.

"Great," said Jiggy. "Some watchdog this one's gonna be."

"Come on. She's just a little baby. Aren't you?" The puppy waddled over to Gina, its tail wagging.

"When did you get her?" Ray asked.

"Four days ago. An' our life hasn't been the same," Jiggy said.

Gina picked the puppy up and cradled it.

"Like to see you try that in another six months." Jiggy smiled at the puppy.

"Better make hay while I can then." Gina held the puppy up to Ray. It licked his nose.

"Ever noticed how women's voices go up several pitches when they're talkin' to baby animals?" Jiggy said.

"Probably mine does too, come to think of it," Ray said. "She purebred?"

Gina produced a squeaky toy from her pocket. "Not so much. The breeder said they'd had a slip-up. Likely a little doodle mutt in the Pyrenees there."

Ray watched the puppy wrestle with its toy. "Might be kind of nice."

"That's what we thought and besides they were giving her away."

"Are there any left?"

"Last one, Little Cousin. You're too late."

Ray was both sad and relieved. Training a puppy was fun, but building a house was enough commotion for now. "You got a name for her?"

Jiggy and Gina shook their heads.

"I'm kinda liking Hazel and Mavis . . . or Wilma maybe," said Gina.

"I'm partial to Lucy myself," Jiggy said. "You call her Wilma, she's gonna end up Willie. Hazel, she's gonna be Hazy. Neither of which I think are fittin'."

"How about Ethel? Or Astrid?" Gina said.

"Maybe. Elsie. Bertha."

"Bertha's not bad."

"Talk to us in another month or so, Ray. We might have a name for her then." Jiggy got down on the floor with the puppy. "Took us three months, ya know, to name our first dog."

"Three months to name Fred?" Ray had been about thirteen when they brought a gawky-looking mutt down to Alvin and Collette's one weekend.

"Well it had to suit him," Jiggy said, "an' it took us a while to make sure he really was a Fred. Was touch and go there for a while. Almost ended up Ralph."

"Yeah. We caught a lucky break there."

The puppy rolled around on the floor, going after Jiggy's hands or the squeaky toy in turns.

"So about the wild stuff in the back," Ray ventured. "How much is there?"

"I don't know. What do you think, Jiggy?"

"Maybe twenty, thirty plants. Don't know how much the cows ate already. It's pretty ransacked."

"I was thinking," Gina said, "it might be some old hemp. You know for fiber. Like maybe the farmer here grew it way back."

"Possible." Jiggy nodded.

"You don't think it was planted by a neighbor? Kids maybe?" Ray asked.

"Pretty dumb place to put it. Right in a cattle pasture. Mind ya, the dumbness of people is hard to match." Jiggy tapped the table. "I bet the cattle have known about it since the get-go."

"We just never checked out that fence very carefully down there." Gina said. "At least not that side. Everything's a bit hidden."

"Thing is, the cattle probably finish most of it off before anybody sees it." Jiggy gazed across the room at Gina and smiled.

"Probably never even gets to flower." Gina pretended not to notice Jiggy.

"Well something would have had to seed it. They're not perennials," Ray said.

"Anyway. I've been keepin' the cattle in the front fields, past few weeks. Give it a chance. So that just leaves the deer, rabbits an' whatever else likes it."

"I wonder what's in it they like so much. They're not getting high," Gina said.

"One of the women at work takes the roots home for her compost. She says her dog gets into them every time. Just loves them."

"You could always go back there and check the status," Gina suggested, looking at Ray. "Give us a professional opinion."

"Sure."

Jiggy shook his head. "ATV's all tied up right now."

"That's okay. I want the walk anyway."

Jiggy got up, fetched some work gloves and a utility knife from the mud room and handed them to Ray. "If some of it's lookin' ready, or even almost ready, could you bring us back a few stalks to dry?"

"Sure. Maybe I could take some for Petra too, the scientist at CannRose."

"Oh yeah?"

"If it's some old strain, she'll be really happy."

"Why's that?"

"All the black-market breeding just for the high probably knocked out a lot of the other good stuff, she says."

"Makes sense. People breed everything to the worst possible outcome. Animals, crops, even themselves. Specially themselves."

"Jiggy!"

"Well, take dairy cattle! They bred 'em for higher milk production, didn't pay any attention to the bones or overall health, and now their feet give out! I wouldn't touch the industry with a ten-foot pole."

"So it's okay if I take some for Petra?"

"Why not. Just don't tell that guy at the top ya keep talkin' about."

"Caldwell's easy enough to avoid."

"It's the most off-putting part of a job. There's always a control freak."

Ray headed out the door. It was cool and cloudy. He was thinking that the wild marijuana might be the best thing for him to sit and be with, like Larry had suggested. Since he got back from his holiday, Ray would take his morning coffee and go sit by the trees along the creek. He'd look at them for a long time, trying hard not to think of anything, and then he'd close his eyes and just listen. When all the stuff racing through his mind finally stopped, he'd hear things. Things that had a pattern. Sometimes even a melody, but mostly it was this overlay of murmuring clicks and pops in loose rhythms and timing that were quite alien. And he felt a connection occasionally — just for an instant, he felt an ease and a welcoming. It was always unexpected when it happened but kind of thrilling. Sometimes he'd move his chair farther along to where the bulrushes were. He'd sit and pay attention to them. He'd gotten used to their type of sound when he was exploring the salt marshes. Their music or whatever it was, was completely different. Higher pitched, wispy. Like a brush on a snare drum. And he thought he heard the echo of water flowing through them too. Some more than others. He thought he could almost pick out the individual plants, but then he remembered Larry saying he thought too much. So he just tried to pay closer attention and stay alert. When all the sounds were perceived together, the whole might have a very different message. He wouldn't want to miss it.

Ray thought it was cool to have any skill and this might be the best one yet. He could hear plants by focusing on them. Even if he was hallucinating, it didn't matter really. At least the world around him was starting to get interesting again. Really interesting. He wasn't just grinding through a week anymore, approximating what he imagined to be a normal human being in order to fit in. Before he'd been in the army, he'd never noticed any distance within himself or between himself and the things around him. After he'd been in Iraq that first time, it was as if the world was removed. He was only ever in foreign territory. He had to consciously make up parts of himself just to function. Even when he was at that job on the shore and figured he'd found the answer to his life with some routine exercise, a bearable workload and friends, he was still consciously manufacturing himself. It was just easier to do there. But it was still a chore.

So this new perception, if this was being crazy, then it was fine. That fleeting comfort coming from the plants was his to savor and explore. And he'd finally figured out why Larry told him not to call for six months. Ray realized he didn't have anybody else to talk to about this. If he wanted to talk that is. Maybe he didn't. But Larry might be the only guy who'd understand. He might be the only one interested too. Ray wouldn't dare mention it to Gina or Jiggy. They'd just think he needed therapy or more potent antihistamines. And he certainly wouldn't tell his doctor. Nice as the guy was, Ray might land up in some ward on anti-psychotics. It was like when he used to see his mother for that year or so after she died. She'd come and talk to him, and it was so good to see her but he soon realized nobody else saw her. He heard Uncle Alvin mention to his aunt one night that they might need to get a child psychiatrist because Ray was still hallucinating. Ray didn't like the sound of those words. He asked his friend's brother the next day what they meant. The teenager told a very dark tale indeed: Hallucinating meant you were crazy. They'd lock you up. And a psychiatrist would cook your brain with shock treatments or drugs so you'd never remember anything ever again. So Ray shut up about his mother. And after a while, she stopped coming, but he couldn't remember exactly when that was. In fact he'd forgotten most of what went on those first couple of years after his parents were killed. Odd he was remembering so much now.

Ray came to the two fields with the old stone fence separating them. He went to the far side of the line of rubble and walked along. A rabbit darted out from a gap in the stones and took off across the field. The sun shone for a second and there was a flash of bright-green light. Ray felt something land on his chest. He looked down. There was a large praying mantis clinging to his shirt, staring up at him. Any other time he'd have brushed it off. But he let it be. He kept walking, and after about a minute it flew away.

As Ray came to the slope, he could see down along the stone rubble where all the wild plum trees were. Partially hidden, just past that, he saw where the marijuana was growing. On his way down the slope he found a couple of single plants tucked in close to the fencerow too. They were tall and spindly. Maybe they were old hemp, like Gina suggested. They were certainly nothing much like what grew at CannRose. They never let those plants get very high. They'd start timing the lights so the plants would flower as soon as possible too, keeping the plants short for consistency. The thought occurred to Ray that maybe the CannRose plants weren't so keen on consistency. He hadn't really tried listening to them. He was still wary of hives. And strolling into a grow room to close his eyes and listen would get people wondering. Besides, since the day Percy, the quality assurance officer, started work at CannRose, ages ago really, no one was allowed in the cultivation rooms unless they had work there. Of course Caldwell made himself the exception, and Percy would rail about this. Ray certainly wouldn't want to cause Percy any more grief on that account.

Ray reached the patch of marijuana. Like Jiggy said, the plants were pretty chewed up in places but they were in flower. And you could really see the difference between the males and the females. The males were already far along where they hadn't been chewed up and were releasing clouds of fluffy pollen. The flowers at the top of the female plants were close to harvest and those at the lower nodes were coming along. Ray found a flat stone in the fence rubble and sat down. He watched the marijuana waving in the breeze for a good ten minutes or so and then he felt a strange pressure in his head. He closed his eyes for no more than a second and without any conscious prompting on his part, a praying mantis appeared to him. It was looking at him like the one on his shirt had been but glowing this time as if it were lit up from the inside. He remembered Larry's words again — "Just go with it. Work with it." — So Ray stared back at the mantis.

After a while the mantis beckoned him to follow, so he did. He went with the flow of his vision. His surroundings changed. They got very dark. He was traveling through small, damp, claustrophobic spaces. Ray wasn't sure there was any air. He seemed to be floating, and at one point, lost sight of the mantis completely. Then things opened up. Ray found himself in a cathedral-like structure, the walls sinewy and breathing. Vertical ridges predominated. It was an architecture of roots. Tendrils hung down glistening, and some of them dripped. There was an assortment of bugs and hideous creatures dozing, arranged in rows on the floor, as if they'd fallen asleep after some drunken banquet, snoring, belching and farting. Some were almost as big as Ray.

He looked at one of them very closely. Its mandibles seemed to be made of sabers and saws, and it lazily held out a leg. It wanted to shake Ray's hand, so he obliged, and the creature's mouthparts broke into a crooked vertical smile. Ants appeared. A whole army. They were comparatively small and came up only to Ray's knees. They busily picked up odd scraps from the cathedral floor. As their numbers grew, they converged upon one sleeping bug in particular. Ray thought he heard it scream. They carried it off. There were murmurs from the other creatures. *Too bad*, said the bug that had shaken Ray's hand. Ray heard familiar clicks, pops and hissing coming from above, and then after a while, a deep resonant thumping, like a heartbeat, coming from the structure itself, the earth and ridges or roots. Then he saw the mantis. Again it beckoned him to follow.

The mantis flew straight up. Ray found himself floating in the darkness again. The mantis motioned to look up and when he did Ray saw the sky. In an instant he was flying. He sped up. They soared over vast tracts of barren land and then came to an ocean. He dropped down to the surface. It was the sea he'd dreamed of a while ago. He was there again floating in his tiny rowboat. Only this time the mantis was sitting in the boat opposite him. He noticed the mantis was bigger now. About the size of the new puppy. And very fat. It pointed, indicating for Ray to look down and into the water.

The sea was brilliant green and teeming with tiny plants, seaweed, ribbons of kelp and winding shoots. It shimmered and bubbles rose to the surface creating foam that made the vastness of the huge lumbering waves that much more apparent. When Ray looked up at the mantis again, it had grown even larger and quite imperious. It told him to jump into the sea. *You can swim, can't you?* it queried. And then it peered at Ray as if it wasn't sure he was worth its time.

Ray looked back into the sea and began debating about how he could best get over the side of the boat. Jump? Dive? Lower himself gently? Suddenly he was jolted by a crackly, earsplitting screech. He snapped out of the vision or whatever it was and looked up to see a crow flying away. It must have come quite close to him to have sounded so loud, and Ray thought he felt the slight tingling on his cheek where the feathers might have touched him.

Later Larry would tell him it was a good thing that crow came along. "You know the female mantis can kill her mate," he said. Ray knew that.

Chapter 17

"So Ray, have you heard anything about when Stoyan might have the first oil product ready?" Sammy, the pharmacist, barely said hello and started right in on important matters as Ray came through the Lyston dispensary door. Stoyan was the extraction specialist CannRose had finally hired, and Percy had told Sammy he was very persnickety about his work. Given professionalism was often in short supply at CannRose, Stoyan was indulged in this, though somewhat anxiously.

"Um . . . no, I don't know when the oil will be ready . . . not really," Ray said, looking down at the box he was holding, full of neat calligraphed labels all in their plastic stands. He added, "Percy thinks it may be imminent." *May be imminent . . . Who says that? How stupid is that?* Ray often had trouble looking at Sammy. By all reports she was stunning, and Ray had fantasized about her, though the last few months' events had somewhat curbed his obsession. He looked up at her. The big brown eyes, the sepia skin with copper undertones, and her light-auburn hair struck some kind of color chord in him that usually left him speechless. Today — *Oh my!* — she was wearing a pale-jade blouse that set the colors singing. But for once Ray didn't have the urge to bolt. He had enough presence of mind to just stand and observe. And the first thing he noticed was that the rich brown of her irises became cooler and were almost violet near the pupils. How curious. It reminded him of something but he couldn't put his finger on it. Then all at once he remembered where he'd seen those colors before — her skin, her eyes, her hair, even her blouse. And he remembered why it took his breath away. It was when he was eight years old, standing right next to the cliff edge at Dead Horse Point, and he couldn't believe how far down the drop was to the river, with its edging of pale-green cedars, and how tall the mesas were that towered above it all. And how, more than anything, he'd wanted to be a bird at that very moment, playing and swooping in the air currents because his father was gone forever and the farm was sold and he might never see it again.

"Well," Sammy said. "I sure wish Stoyan would get something out soon. The oils and tinctures are really moving and I'm tired of selling all the other producers' products. Kinda crazy, don't you think?"

Ray just stood there looking at her.

Sammy looked back at him puzzled and then her eyes narrowed. "So do you ever *do any thinking*, Ray?"

Ray, still immobile, was barely breathing as this question filtered through the memories and brought him to the present again. It occurred to him she was teasing. A grin gradually came over his face and then he began to laugh. She was a person after all, not some overwhelming undefinable force. She continued to squint at him with curiosity. He stopped laughing and cleared his throat. "It's probably very hard on my brain. But, yeah. Sometimes I can manage a thought. Sometimes even two."

"At the same time?"

"No. No . . . but maybe very quickly one after the other."

"That's very good!" Her smile was just the tiniest bit crooked but that made it more friendly somehow.

"Where do you want these signs put?"

"Just on top of the display case," she said. "Oh and Ray, there's a light in that display case that seems to keep flickering. Do you think you could take a look at it?"

"Sure." Ray set the box down on the floor. He opened the top of the case, found the problem quickly and went about reconnecting some wires. He'd no sooner finished when she mentioned the toilet in the restroom seemed to be running all the time, so he took a look at that. Repairing it involved a trip to the hardware store for parts and no sooner had he put the lid back on the toilet than Sammy mentioned that the back door lock was sticking. Fixing that involved a walk to his truck for the can of spray lubricant, and he'd had to park several blocks away on his return from the hardware store.

"The lock's fine now," he said, turning the deadbolt back and forth.

Sammy was so pleased with all his repairs but then she sighed. "I'd offer you a coffee, but the machine we just ordered hasn't come in yet." She looked pained by this and purposefully helpless. And then she smiled again, and if Ray was not mistaken, she was batting her eyes at him.

"I see," Ray said, sighing himself this time, noting the slight merriment on her face was as practiced as her indirect request. This was how men, especially handy ones, always ended up doing more work than they'd planned on. And the worst part, he noted sheepishly, was that he was so happy or perhaps just programmed to oblige. "So, I was going to pick up a coffee from that place down the block," Ray said. "How do you take yours?"

"No cream, just one sugar."

#

Ray had ordering to do for the flower rooms. A couple of valves in the fertigation system were malfunctioning. The growers said somebody had used the wrong ones in the first place. Ray figured he'd better take a look. He probably could have asked somebody to take a photo, but this way he'd get to check out the plants. He'd take a chance with the CannRose marijuana. He'd had no physical reaction with the plants in Jiggy's greenhouse or the ones in the cow pasture. Besides he'd be covered from head to toe in a bunny suit, hair net, gloves and even a dust mask. The crop in the first flower room was close to harvest, so he had to gown up accordingly if he wanted to be there.

As Ray grabbed a suit from the box, Petra was on her way out of the air shower.

"Hey, Ray! So I think those plants at your cousin's place might be feral."

"Oh yeah? Is that what you were looking for?"

"Maybe. They're not looking like anything we're growing here and the profile isn't coming up as industrial hemp either. So that's pretty cool."

"So do you want more samples?"

"Can you bring me seeds?"

"I'll try. I'll be there this weekend. They had to let the cows back there again, but I imagine there are some seeds left."

"If it's not too much of a pain. Seeds are easier than getting plant parts into the facility."

"Heard about that. Sorry."

"It's all so ridiculous. But I'm glad you brought flowers — we got to test them right away."

As Petra turned to go, Ray noticed she had a book on the top of her clipboard titled *Endogenous Plant Rhythms*. Was there some science on what he was hearing?

"What's that book about?" he asked.

Petra was surprised by the keen interest. "Um, the internal clocks plants have. Like when they flower or when they drop their leaves, seeds, whatever, they have internal mechanisms that start the processes."

"Oh." The keenness in Ray's voice dropped. But then something occurred to him. "I thought they flowered because of the change in light."

"Some plants, that's exactly what initiates the changes. For others, including some weed like the *ruderalis* strains, they flower in their own time. It's a different trigger."

"So they're even more chill than the stuff we grow here?"

Petra looked at him questioningly.

"The strain you mentioned. They're more relaxed. They just do things in their own time."

"Oh," she said, smiling. She found this charming, but it needed correcting. "Well, everything's been hybridized. A quarter of the stuff in the mother pods already has *ruderalis* somewhere back along the line. They just call them autoflowering."

"I see." Again Ray was disappointed. The rhythms and tendencies in plants that scientists talked about clearly had nothing in common with what he was hearing. He stood in the air shower while the wind whipped off any dust, cobwebs and misconceptions he held about how other people experienced the world.

When Ray opened the door to the flower room, he wished he'd brought sunglasses. It was blinding. He closed his eyes and, even above the noise of the air handlers and the fans, he thought he heard strange harmonics and a pulsing, that if he listened carefully enough, very acutely, contained rhythmic patterns. Ray opened his eyes again so he would not lose himself in the sounds. Better to take in the bright view — notice patterns with his eyes if he must — especially as he was on camera.

The plants all came up to about Ray's nose. The odor was nice enough. They weren't skunky smelling, more like citrus and maybe a little rosemary with new hay thrown in. The crop was frothy and wispy. The hues of green varied from the pale chartreuse of the calyxes and bracts to a deep hunter green in the fan leaves. The flowers, with their stigmas on hairlike styles were cream-colored with only a hint of the light green. A few of them were turned a rich ochre, having given up on reproduction. They were withered, twisted and coiled into fringes. The bracts, the parts that housed the still waiting ovules, were engorged all the more for it. On the small sugar leaves protruding from the flowers and on the flowers themselves, were the trichomes, the tiny resin glands, little jewels that were still clear and glistened in the light. It was like the plants were covered in a frost at dawn.

Ray stood entranced by the rows and rows of these intricate, clustered and untidy bloomings. The visual impact was almost as mesmerizing as the sounds he'd heard.

After a minute or two, he remembered what he'd come to do. He made his way over to the tables with the leaking valves. The cultivation staff had marked them. He took some notes. Then he carefully checked the different valves that were working and took more notes. Before leaving, he stood by the door for maybe half a minute with his eyes closed and his back to the rows of flowering Bambam Lemon. He hadn't been mistaken. They were singing — or whatever that was to them. The harmonics, the pulsing and the intricate rhythms in between soared in his brain and seemed to seep gently into his own cellular structure. He felt lighter when he left the room.

When Ray was about fifteen, he thought he'd be a musician. He was a pretty good drummer back then. He could play any type of music and just about any percussion instrument. He spent four years on Tuesday evenings practicing with a community orchestra on the other side of the county, where the houses were huge and the often young, classically trained talent plentiful. But mostly he liked jazz, funk, rock and Latin. And his Aunt Collette, a singer and devoted teacher, had drilled him in all manner of music history, theory and practice.

At sixteen he had a band and a bunch of musical friends, most of them older and already studying music full time. He even had a girlfriend. Amber played keyboards and they'd necked like crazy and lost their virginity to each other on the couch at her dad's place.

Amber's dad was a keyboard player too and off on some studio gig at the time. Ray imagined her dad would be pissed if he ever found out, so Ray did his best to fade into the background every time he ran into him. The band made a CD and a few demos that didn't get very far. His aunt did gigs in the city from time to time too, so he got familiar with a lot of musicians. His favorite drum teacher was Oscar. Seemed like he'd played with just about everyone from Elton to Wynton. He was definitely the most in-demand studio musician and most demanding teacher Ray had ever studied with. But he was also cool, especially if you worked hard and he liked you.

Ray saw at an early age the music world was a tough one. Commitment and talent still might not be enough to get you to the top of the heap, and a lot of musicians seemed, well, unhappy or something. Besides, when Ray got a little older, he figured there was more to life than just music and he wanted to find out all about it. So he did.

Since he got out of the army, he'd tried a few times to go back to the drums, but it didn't work out, especially once he started on the construction jobs. There were only so many decibels from various sources he could take. Maybe more time with his low-stress job, with sitting and meditating with the plants and taking long naps, might quiet his head more. He could start back slowly. Maybe just a few minutes a day. That might be manageable. He held the thought as a mild hope for the future.

Chapter 18

"Jesus, people are dumb-assed," Jiggy said, looking up from the computer as Gina walked into the kitchen.

"Yeah, and that's news?"

"Thing is they think this turkey's one of 'em. They think he's their boy an' he's gonna get 'em all back to work. Workin' at what? The man's a wreckin' ball an' that's it. Mind ya, I can appreciate the idea of a wreckin' ball."

"You gonna vote for him then? Just to see what happens, like."

"No. You know I don't vote. Not now."

"Oh, yeah, that's real effective!"

"It's a statement! An' yeah, it's effective. Makes my day. Given total irrelevance in the face of the deep state an' the rulin' oligarchy, it's the only fuckin' thing left."

"The definitive protest."

"Look at this." Jiggy landed on another website. "He's been bankrupted more times than most of our friends. Says here he's got the attention span of a six-year-old."

"Attention spans are shrinking," Gina said. "Maybe he's just ahead of the curve."

"Yeah, he's a real trendsetter. Can't stay on topic for more than a few seconds."

"Lotta people like what he says though."

"Slogans and orchestrated fury," Jiggy said. "He's just playin' on desperation. Dumb-asses fall for that when they're scared an' outta work."

"You don't say. And you're not scared or dumb-assed or outta work I take it."

"Well in case ya hadn't noticed, we're farmin'. We're hardly outta work."

"Yeah, well in addition, I work outside the farm. In case you hadn't noticed."

Jiggy cleared his throat. "I noticed your absences. An' my gratitude is deep."

"Solves everything then, doesn't it."

"Listen, at least I don't fall for the obvious shit. An' I'm not livin' in some fuckin' fantasy about the past."

"No," said Gina, "you're just hangin' on by your fingernails to the moment. I know."

"It's not that. It's that the manufacturers are gone!" Jiggy cried. "An' they're not comin' back. Not ever. Not when they can do it cheaper somewhere else. That's how capitalism works. Nature of the beast. Capitalists move where the advantage is. They're opportunists. They hoard money! Capital! Why d'ya think it's called capitalism?

"Maybe you should go be a commie. Make your ma proud."

Jiggy shook his head and sighed. "You're not gettin' it, Gina."

"Maybe I'm too stupid then."

"See it's the globalization thing too. It was only ever for the rich fucks — it was never for you or me or the twelve-year-old workin' in some lousy fuckin' sweatshop in Bangladesh. Countries come an' go. And guess where we're at? We're on the fuckin' way out. The guy playin' the big man there — he's just another rich prick gettin' richer an' I don't know why people don't see that. It's like how everybody loves big-box stores an' cheap crap they can order online. They don't get it. That's the new serfdom starin' back at 'em in those thirty-dollar toaster ovens and hundred-dollar lawn mowers. And they're all happy as pigs in shit they got a deal an' it shipped overnight. Some deal!"

"Some stuff you can only get online."

"But it's the whole fuckin' system. Who needs all this crap from who knows where in the first place! Look at all the shit! Turns to garbage and pollution just movin' from one place to another! It's all wrong. Everything is all wrong. It's fucked everywhere ya look. Nobody stands a fuckin' chance! You know there're villages practically situated on trash heaps in some places. The people there pickin' through all the garbage sent to 'em by us. That's how they make a livin'. There's somethin' to look forward to 'cause that's where we're fuckin' headed too."

"Okay."

"Yeah. Okay," Jiggy said, taking a deep breath. "Time for a puff."

#

Ray had been right about CannRose hiring Jiggy on the spot. Jiggy didn't have much printed material about himself. He liked to hide his tracks rather than itemize them, but he told Greg and Lazlo about the work he used to do when he was enlisted. He told them about half of it anyway. And he explained how he'd kept up with technology. He told them about half of that too. It was for personal interest, he said. It was amazing what people could get up to and get into from a cell phone these days. "Never mind a laptop or even the remote for your garage door." Digital literacy was a necessity.

Jiggy ramped up the interview with technical stories riddled with phrases like "relational database management system," "integrated development environment," "hybrid apps," "scalability" and "object-oriented programming." He liked watching the effect technical language had on people. Of course Gina would have told him to take it somewhere else and that was exactly what he was doing. He had Greg's head spinning within minutes and Lazlo's eyes glazing over. Then Jiggy steered the interview back down to earth and spoke in some detail about how the efficiencies gained from cloud storage needed to be weighed against privacy and security concerns. He turned the tables in the interview and flatteringly asked Greg if he had any opinions regarding the advantages of fragmented systems versus a harmonized single platform, or if he thought the opportunities presented by big data would have any relevance for CannRose or the medical marijuana industry. Finally, Jiggy observed that in his experience "the best solution to a problem could only come with an eyes-wide-open appreciation of the risks."

He'd kept politics and expletives out of it. They wouldn't have known Jiggy held an opinion, let alone a strong one, or that he'd have room for anything else at all, with a gourd so full of technical information. Jiggy was a master at being what he needed to be for a given circumstance. He could bring out a very polished and deliberate politeness when the occasion required. That was part of his charm.

Greg barely understood half of what Jiggy said but he was delighted he'd found such a nerd to help sort them out of their technical morass. They decided on a trial period. Jiggy would work just the mornings.

Jiggy clinched his side of the deal within the first two weeks. The first thing he tackled was the surveillance system that kept cutting out. He had it fixed in the grow facility and both dispensaries by the end of the following week. The executives and Greg in particular were overjoyed. In the month after that, Jiggy addressed the digital inventory, cleaned up the discrepancies, streamlined and customized their interface and set up a dedicated offline library to handle the records and keep them safer. He told Ray that when he was finished, even a chimpanzee would be able to find the most obscure records. But that wasn't all Jiggy did.

"Well Jiggy! Pleasure to meet you." Caldwell's voice boomed. "Good to know we finally have somebody who knows what they're doing! We're changing the face of commercial marijuana production here, Jiggy, and we need IT to keep up."

Ray's accounts of Caldwell's micromanaging and excessive outbursts were suddenly irrelevant. Jiggy took one look at Caldwell and felt an overwhelming and searing dislike hijack his very core. Oh, Caldwell was worse than loathsome. It wasn't just the way the man held himself, his hand-tailored suit, a coiffe that looked straight out of a Dunhill catalogue selling thousand-dollar man bags, and the intoning of his remarks that set Jiggy simmering. And it wasn't because he was a control freak. No, not at all. It was because he was a baying wannabe. A grasping poseur. Jiggy had more respect for the blatantly greedy and revoltingly wealthy than a jerk like this. "The thing about wannabes," Jiggy would say, "is not if they'll sell out, but how much they sell for. And who they drag along to slaughter or maim in the process." From Jiggy's perspective, Caldwell's clear desire to be not merely one of the 1 percent but probably one of the 0.001 percent made him particularly despicable. And if Jiggy could see through him in twenty seconds, some swift mogul from big pharma or big agriculture would see through him in two. Jiggy wondered how long before this man would tremble, drop to his knees and take the Kool-Aid proffered in the gleaming corporate grail.

Jiggy hadn't been on the job for more than two weeks when he overheard Caldwell, fresh from a trip to the Midwest, roaring. He'd set up a meeting with a very important Dr. so-and-so from the international pharmaceutical giant, Pharazom. Caldwell was boasting he'd managed to impress the good doctor and he'd bet within the year major pharmaceuticals would come knocking and put money on the table. *The man's a complete idiot*, Jiggy thought. *Companies like that just eat up the little ones and he doesn't even get it that he'd be first on the menu.*

Maybe it was all the training and talent that hadn't had a viable outlet in years, or maybe it was some particularly corrugated crevice in the highly developed folds of Jiggy's brain, but Jiggy decided at that moment that a course of action was needed. And he was the man to carry it out. He could create a crisis too. Just like Caldwell, only better and more precisely. That's all it ever took. A crisis, well aimed and well timed. He'd sit on it of course. Keep it in reserve. It would be like an insurance plan, like the arms buildup in the Cold War. Only this was way better. His opponent wouldn't even know the war was on. Like Sun Tzu had advised. It was what Jiggy did best and this is how he would do it: He would rig the CannRose facility in the most elegant manner. Ordnance that could go boom in the night with the finest incendiaries. And he would keep that potential and the future glorious blast under his hat, under *his* control and his control only. The notion gave Jiggy a great sense of calm. He smiled at Caldwell. "And how are you today, sir?" he said.

For Jiggy, a "scintillated" or "prepared" instrument — that's how he referred to his projects — was a work of art. A building rigged for destruction with no traces and no potential for collateral damage required true craftmanship and utter selflessness. He didn't see himself to be at all like one of the usual bunch of nihilists, psychopathic pyromaniacs, rabid anarchists, militant libertarians, or right or left extremists of every stripe. They were just mostly miserable little pricks still thinking to send a message, still grinding axes and vying for some kind of hopeless power. Jiggy, on the other hand, felt he was long past that. No, for Jiggy the purpose now was simply to illustrate an unassailable truth: Nothing is permanent.

The best thing was whoever Jiggy knew himself to be seemed to fall away in these instances. It was as if the universe arranged events and there was nothing left but to exercise his skill. Once he got down to work there were no opinions racing through his head, no ideas about anything, just the flow of one thing done after another. It was quiet and methodical. If he stopped for a few seconds, he could hear the sound of his own blood pumping.

As he looked back over the span of his career in demolition and controlled chaos, the things he'd taken out, buildings, vehicles, aircraft and, in one spectacular and surprising case, a Sealift container of rotting turnips, he was philosophical. He saw great beauty in destruction, just as there was in creation, and he firmly believed you could never really have one without the other. The necessity of opposites. The obligation of polarity to create movement. Change. And it was between these opposites, right on the bleeding edge, where Jiggy knew he could dissolve, disappear, and the universe could shift.

#

A week or so after Caldwell bragged about his meeting with the pharmaceutical executive, Jiggy called up his old friend Gord. If Jiggy's talents lay in mastering the rigging of explosives and the languages of computers and technical gizmos, Gordon's talent was for chemistry. He dreamed in it. Formulas were music to him. Materials deconstructed before his very eyes into their chemical structures. He saw the atoms of all the elements coursing through the universe still on their trajectory, surely nostalgic for the original big bang. And he could help them reminisce.

And just like Jiggy, he was very fond of incendiaries. Brilliance in any form was a marvel.

"Nobody comes to see me anymore, Jiggy. Not since I took the early retirement package. Out of the loop now."

"I'd never forget an old friend like you, Gordo."

"So this . . ." — Gord held up a four-inch beige square about an inch thick — "I've been developing this for a whole year now. Patience and love."

"Yeah? I got a little blastin' to do at the farm. So this'll do it?"

"It's stunning. Spectacular. My best work yet. Most chemists don't think this way, you know."

"Looks like nothin'. Block of wood almost."

"Yeah. It's something though. And you know it's completely biodegradable. It's important to be green. The environment is suffering."

"I never knew anybody as talented as you, Gordo."

"Don't leave it buried for more than a day or two though. Microbes love it. It's gone in a flash."

"Um, speakin' of flashes . . ."

"Oh yeah. I've been working on flammables too. Accelerants like nobody ever expected. I'm proud of these, Jiggy, and you know I never like to boast ."

"Jesus. Just looks like splinters and sawdust."

"Yeah. Completely new. Whole different concept of burn. Colorful too."

"You should patent this stuff."

"Nah. Not worth the hassle. Outta the loop, like I said. I just like to quietly do my work. Gives me peace, you know."

"Yeah. I know what ya mean. I like bein' outta the loop myself these days."

Gord lifted up a black lab book. "I got new theories too. I got three more books like this stashed away. My life's work, Jiggy. Maybe someday if anyone's still left, they'll find 'em. Maybe they'll be smarter too. If they used stuff the right way, nobody'd need to pay a cent for energy, you know that?"

"Lotta ifs there, Gordo. But I like the direction."

PART THREE

Coalescence

Of all things, you may want light to vary. It holds the attention to scale. Makes progress nimble. Makes union hale. Some want proofs and limits. Some want only the solid life or maybe sumptuous solitude. Some never know or do not care. Some jump in only for a lark. They want air merged with the moon. Little else. Little bother. But do not stop there. The soul of us is a broader thing, cleaved in flashes and shadows. Its laugh is deeper still.

from Cannto IV, *Cannabidadas*

Chapter 19

It was a foot — one foot — claw-like, segmented and more complex than Ray recalled. It clasped tightly to the stem, but as he looked up and down along the marijuana plant, he could see neither the ground the stem sprouted from nor the leaves at the top. His gaze moved back to the foot. It was attached to a finely haired leg. The spring-loaded arm came into view. It was solid, massive in comparison to the leg. There were barbs, toothy, sword-like and blood-colored. They glinted in the flickering of sunlight that came through the canopy. He noticed a new bud forming on the plant, but then the predatory presence behind it came to him. Ray realized he was staring right into the eye of the mantis. Possibly he was dreaming — the eye seemed bigger than he was. He could not recall if he was even human in that instant, and it occurred to him he could be the bug's dinner. The mantis caught his thought and laughed at him.

You flatter yourself, the mantis said. *Your taste is dreadful.* Ray would wonder what that meant later. *And you're very small*, it added. *Nothing much at all.*

Ray looked down and toward himself and in and around himself, and the mantis was right. There was nothing there.

Insubstantial, said the mantis. *It's your lucky day. These are all my children. See!* The mantis extended its arm with a sweep, and as Ray followed the trajectory, he could see dozens of mantid nymphs tucked among the leaves. They seemed shy at first, wary of predators. Then they all smiled at him in unison. It was just a polite smile. They were killers in training. Well-schooled it appeared, but nonetheless unimpressed or uncertain what to make of this diminished entity before them.

They are amicable, the parent mantis said. *Fear is foolish for you now. You haven't much time and you might miss something, so*

I thought you might find the little ones endearing because of course I do. One is partial to one's own young.

"It's quite a crew you have." Ray did not recognize his voice. It sounded like an old man's, scratchy and hoarse.

Yes, said the mantis. *And they're unspoiled, still innocent. Still sloughing off the skin when it gets too tight. Naiveté is a sin where you live. For us it is irrelevant. The opportunities spring from all directions. Keeping up is the challenge when everyone is edible.*

Ray could see immediately that the nymphs' dinners might arrive from just about anywhere in the canopy. And it occurred to him the nymphs were as clever as they were polite.

The point is, the mantis went on, *the young ones love the ones who love you. We all love them. And the ones who love you love us very much.*

"Okay," said Ray in the old man's voice. He didn't know who *the ones* were. That was fine. Instead he surveyed the nymphs, their arms tucked neatly, waiting. They were still smiling, though not at him. It was more that they were happy in the waiting.

We couldn't be happier, the mantis affirmed. *The art of ambush is a useful one. Especially in pleasant surroundings, don't you agree? And we have patience too, though not so grand or infinite as the ones who love us. The ones we serve.*

All this talk about *the ones.* Who were the ones? "I thought mostly you would serve yourself," Ray said.

The mantis shifted its eye. *Is this impudence?*

"No," said Ray. "I just don't see you serving anyone."

I thought it would be obvious.

"Is it some kind of politics?"

Hardly. That's not what we do.

"But it could be. Theoretically."

No. Why would we ever be interested in "theoretically"? We're about the struggle and the grip. The panic of the prey is irrelevant. You could say that most of them had it coming, given their own dining habits. Is that your kind of politics? Tit for tat?

"I'm not sure. What were we talking about?" And then Ray remembered they had been talking about *the ones.* "What group were they again? Bigger bugs?"

The eye of the mantis expanded. Ray knew immediately it was annoyed. *So appallingly ungrateful and immensely dense!* it shouted.

They've made up the very fabric of you. You're nothing without them. As we can all see. You're the scourge, not us. And yet they still love you. Patience is infinite. Theirs, not mine.

"If they love us all, they must be gods. Sleeping gods, to survive so much love."

Warmer, said the mantis. *It's winter somewhere, and they're dreaming too. Here, I'll show you.*

The images came slowly to Ray in the beginning, and then they came in a series of bursts that pulsed from minutiae to the overarching grace of some grand design. Seas and rolling landscapes turned emerald, chartreuse, indigo and deep forest-green. He could see the tiniest microbes, the cyan colonies and the crusts spewing oxygen, plankton in the sea, algae, forests of kelp — all that harbored thylakoids and the alchemy that brought life from light and the soupy elements. He saw in savannahs, the details of single blades of grass; in great swaths of ground cover, each leaf and leaflet; in flower gardens, the stamens and anthers of every little blossom; in fields of crops, every stalk in every row. And he saw brown scrubland and deserts with cacti and palms; dense low jungles with the curled heads of giant ferns, the infant leaves tucked tight inside; needles and fronds, the leaves on all trees; and the mottled velvet of the tundra. And this in turn led to the instant growth of great sequoias and the storied tropical rain forests, whose architecture dripped and stretched into the clouds. He was shown everything of the plants, their history and their changes through the ages, their self-iterating fabric that enveloped the globe. They formed a massive organism with a deep soul echoing through time. It was ceaseless.

And Ray felt loved by it. A sensation washed over him in a mute sigh, filling him with profound calm. He fused with the wave of it and no longer felt separation from anything. Just warmth and welcome. An infinite caress. It left him in awe for several days.

He'd spent most of his long weekend camping up north in the wilderness park not far from where Larry lived. Ray hadn't eaten anything the whole time; he just drank a lot of water. It had been helpful. The crisp air high up in the hills and the lack of food had cleared his head. Or taken him to some new level of insight. The world was essentially a planet of plants. Life was mostly a matter of vegetation. And animals and people were just specks running around in all the greenery. Newer specks at that.

On the drive over to Larry's, Ray was thinking about his job, how the closeness to the plants was a trip in itself. It was okay. It was just he'd never expected anything like it. Maybe that was the fun of it. Though he still wasn't clear yet: Was the marijuana *for* him? Or *against* him? And he wasn't sure either if they were for their own commercial production or against it. It wasn't like they had mission statements, like CannRose, but they seemed to be pushing for something.

Larry told him production like that was warped, too far from the natural order, and even if the plants in the facility were happy in the short term, there was a spirit underneath that could pull Ray into confusion if things were out of whack. Ray needed to watch himself, Larry warned.

This time Ray figured he knew what Larry was talking about. The plant world was much bigger than people ever were, and Larry pointed out there were all sorts of ways to get overwhelmed and into trouble. "Just look at tobacco. Disrespect it and see what happens. Or sugar. Whether it came from cane, corn or beet — it doesn't matter. There's nothing sweet about that history. Just a long line from slavery to sickness and obesity getting worse every day." Larry said he had to laugh about fossil fuels because he couldn't cry. "People are gonna start to cry soon enough. Some already are. The plants always win in the long run. How could it be anything but a nightmare when you disrespect their dead?"

Larry wasn't sure any of what Ray experienced was about becoming a healer. At least not in the way Larry practiced. Or maybe it was too soon to tell. The dreams and visions weren't showing Ray much about healing. Mostly they seemed to be claiming him, challenging him and showing him how fucked up he was. Or how fucked up the world was maybe. Ray said he already knew enough about that from Jiggy, and that made Larry laugh. "You be careful of Jiggy. I got a sense of him the day you first mentioned his name. He's a nice guy but he's got a bomb on his back."

"Yeah. That's Jiggy. He's always got the most explosive thing in the room to say with the most expletives."

"Yeah, maybe."

Chapter 20

All Ray's old ambitions had changed over the time he'd been with CannRose. He had a growing dissatisfaction with everything he'd done in the past and continued to do in order to earn a living. A few months earlier, Lazlo's daughter had been hired to help with the purchasing and inventory, and when he got back from his holiday it looked like she'd pretty much taken over. Ray couldn't have cared less. He was doing security too now anyway. It was Greg's idea — a way to give him a break "from all the bullshit" — so he'd stick around. With the constant staff turnover, Greg was spending most of his time doing HR.

Greg confided in Ray one day that he really hoped Caldwell, the execs or board members wouldn't send him any more family. "They're mostly useless, inept or crazy." The worst one had apparently been Caldwell's godson. He'd been the production manager before Ray was hired and nobody could stand him. He was cocky, and didn't care a bit that his drug habit was discovered. Caldwell thought of him as a son though and wouldn't hear a bad word about him. Instead he put on put him on "stress leave" and into a pricey rehab program. But that didn't work. Luther, the CEO, finally fired him because his thievery was right there on the video records. Caldwell was still upset about it all.

"Mostly you can't fire 'em and you can't shoot 'em," Greg said, referring to the relatives, although he mentioned Lazlo's daughter was working out pretty well and Gus had lasted about as long as anyone might be expected to in that production manager job.

Doing security, Ray could see all the work pressures and conflicts unfolding on the monitors, like Caldwell gesturing wildly while an employee gave him the finger behind his back, or Luther, who was now roaming the facility more frequently and having grim-faced exchanges with Lazlo. Lazlo was also Caldwell's cousin, and those two could often be seen squabbling. In the cultivation area, various staff would throw down brooms, pails or clippers in frustration. Then there was Percy, the quality officer, looking alternately frazzled and furtive, grabbing a coffee every twenty minutes. And Cassie, the hort specialist, in tears, bent over the plants, figuring she was alone and no one would see her crumble.

And finally there was Guido, the angel investor who'd come on board earlier that spring and taken over the coziest nook in the admin section. He drank copious cappuccinos and often looked to be the only one enjoying himself in the whole facility. Greg said he was even wealthier than Lydia, but Ernie said Guido's presence was "kinda weird" and it was also "kinda creepy that he'd become everybody's favorite father confessor." It looked to be true; Ray watched as various staff members scuttled in and out of Guido's little corner to unload, especially when it was clear they were having a bad day and work was driving them nuts.

The job stress wasn't just at CannRose either. Gina was complaining about what a numbskull her new boss was. She was stuck with twice the work now, though at least she had medical insurance and a pension plan. Not like half her friends who held down two or more low-paying part-time jobs with no benefits.

In fact everywhere Ray looked, he saw people trying to cope. It occurred to him that making one's way in the world was mostly a pain in the neck. How come nobody'd told him that? Or had he just not been paying attention? He talked to Jiggy about it one afternoon at Chelsea's. Jiggy had a good laugh.

"Always wondered when ya might wake up and who'd have to kiss ya!" Jiggy said. "Figured it would probably be a wife an' kids. But there ya go. You figured it out all on your own."

Ray hadn't mentioned a word to Jiggy about his new relationship with plants. Or the praying mantis. Or any of the visions and perplexing sounds and sensations. And he'd never even hinted at the torture session he experienced during harvest.

"Maybe you should learn more about IT an' computers," Jiggy suggested. "Doesn't give ya hives, far as I know." And he pointed out it would tie in nicely with all the electrical experience Ray had. It would give him more independence too. "People leave you alone, Little Cousin. It's always best when they don't know what the fuck you're doin'."

#

One steamy night that August, CannRose had a break-in. The police hadn't bothered to show, in spite of the alarm, but Lazlo arrived at 4:00 a.m. to find some falling-down-drunk teenagers trying to climb through Lydia's office window. They'd gotten as far as breaking most of the glass out of the frame, and in the process, they'd smashed a large crystal egg that had been sitting on the inside window ledge.

Ray felt bad for Lydia when he saw her sitting at her desk the following morning, mascara streaming down her face. She was staring at the shards of crystal.

"They caught the guys," Ray offered. "They won't be trying that again."

Lydia looked up with a faint smile.

"You want some tea?" he asked. "I was going to make myself some."

"Aren't you sweet." Lydia looked down at the pieces again. "It's silly, you know. I think it's the inscription I'm upset about." And she told Ray how the egg had been a gift from her late husband. She'd brought it into the grow facility because it made her feel safe. Jordan had told her it was for luck and prosperity. "Maybe this is a message. Maybe I shouldn't be working here after all. Do you think Jordan could be trying to tell me something?"

"I-I couldn't say." Ray thought it remarkable she had no qualms suggesting the dead were still active in this life. And if this were so, it looked like they were concerned about work and the nature of jobs too.

#

After the break-in, all the executives, along with Caldwell and Guido, decided to have security staffing the facility twenty-four hours a day. It was a rare occasion when everybody agreed on something. Round-the-clock security would also help if equipment failed. Greg had suggested long ago that a guard keeping an eye on the monitors and doing proper rounds every couple of hours would have prevented the big flood and January's frostbitten plants when the generator failed during a winter storm power outage. So Ray had jumped at the chance to be on that night shift. It would suit his new state of mind.

There'd be numerous perks too. He could avoid witnessing arguments, hearing people bitch. And he could avoid gossip. He wouldn't have to answer so many questions or deal with delinquent suppliers or unhappy staff. Or Caldwell. He wouldn't have to feel bad for the people Caldwell berated either. He'd be absent for cloning and harvesting (unless of course they ran late). And last but not least, he'd be absent for the DOH inspections.

Greg was delighted, and even though Ray didn't really want it, Greg talked him into being the security manager too. Mostly it amounted to scheduling and keeping track of reports and records, and the other security staff might call or email him with their concerns, but the job was a piece of cake compared to all the other things he'd done in his life. Ray got all the night shifts he wanted, except for two days a month when he had to show up for meetings. That was the worst part. People bellyached and bickered or they fell asleep. Ray could never see the sense of them.

With his newfound nighttime calm and relative freedom, he decided to take Jiggy's advice and registered at the local college for a couple of computer courses. He'd take his new foray into education at his own pace. Courses were mostly online anyway. Sometimes there wasn't much to do between rounds, and he could finish problem sets and get projects done then. The hardware stuff was easy, just like Jiggy predicted, and since Ray was fairly methodical by nature, had a mind for detail and a lot of patience, the coding came easily too. He wasn't the genius Jiggy was, but he started getting the hang of it and making quick progress. Jiggy could always be relied upon to answer questions. He knew way more than most of the instructors and he started to show Ray a few tricks, like how to clean up code and troubleshoot better by knowing where to look first.

And best of all, at night, Ray could listen to the plants. And he was starting to talk to them too. All in his head, of course. It was a telepathy of sorts.

One night on his rounds he heard the plants clamoring in the North Mother Pod, and it was very different from the things he'd heard when staff had been cloning or harvesting. The room was in its dark period and as he stood outside the door, he asked the mothers,

What's going on? There was silence for a few seconds. Then he got a flash of images. A desert blazing so white and barren he wondered where such a place would be.

He slowly opened the pod door. Along with the clamoring of the plants, he heard a faint mechanical beeping, probably a temperature alarm. The room was way too warm and, apart from the beeping, way too quiet. Must have been another HVAC breakdown. The system must have been off for a good six hours or more while the lights were still on to heat things up so much.

Ray closed the door and made a mental note to the mothers: *On it.* He went back to check the software program that ran the air systems. No alarms. He clicked on the North Mother Pod icon and made his way into the set-up window. Sure enough, the program had lost connection with the air handler. After some fiddling around, he was able to reestablish communication. Then a temperature alarm showed up on the screen.

"Seriously? A little late there, champ," he said to the computer.

Ray went back to check the North Mother Pod, and this time he heard the familiar humming of the fans. As the evening wore on he checked periodically for the temperature to drop and it did. He felt like a hero as he walked back to the office at 5:00 a.m. to make his final report. Being on the plants' wavelength was like having superpowers, and how cool was that?

He closed his eyes for only a second and an image of one of the mantis nymphs eating a blood-bloated mosquito came to him. The nymph looked so proud of itself with the blood all over its complicated mouth parts and dribbling down onto its arms. It was like a baby with an ice-cream cone. Kind of cute. This was also cool! And Ray figured if he was crazy with all these plants and bugs filling up his world, it was at least unsurpassed in entertainment value.

After he got to sleep later that morning in his tent, the familiar mantis, the parent, came to him. It was brilliant green and towering. It smiled, but only briefly. As Ray looked into its intense, inscrutable eyes, it began turning red. A deep and bloody red, a raging red. It lunged and grabbed Ray in its steel-like barbs. He couldn't move or breathe. He could feel wrath simmering through the arms holding him fast. The mantis ripped Ray's head off and began to eat. As the bug's mandibles tore into his brain, he realized he had no thoughts left for it to consume. He woke up at noon with diarrhea.

Chapter 21

Cannabis wasn't like the other plants Ray was getting familiar with, and yet it seemed as if it was in charge of the introductions. A gateway plant. It reeled him in, battled him, punished him for coming too close. It wouldn't let him go. It was invasive too. The noises permeated his body. The dreams and visions often lingered for hours. And in spite of Larry's take on it, Ray still wondered if he was just going nuts.

He would recall and minutely dissect the strange rhythms, sometimes parsing them into something more familiar. Scraps of a few beats remained with him and evolved into full measures and phrases, repeated and layered with variations and sometimes equally strange tonality. He found a pad of blank music sheets in one of his old junk boxes and wrote down what he could. And then there were the metallic knocks he heard on occasion that were accompanied by a physical jolt. They felt like the crack of a whip or some sudden rupture in time and space, as if a rogue bladesmith god, Vulcan himself maybe, was on the loose. These jolts split through any vestiges of familiarity that Ray might hear or try to create. But he'd write them down clumsily anyway, regardless of his grasp of them. His obsession seemed to grow more intense with each experience.

Whatever was going on with Ray and marijuana, it sure wasn't a high. It was more often like torture. Or like when he was out with the wild plants on Jiggy and Gina's farm — it was menacing. And he never used the stuff, and since he got hives, he never even touched it. He'd barely been in the grow rooms at the facility. But it seemed the plants weren't deterred by physical boundaries. They had a broader reach.

Larry told him he could view it as a compliment, maybe, and that might help. The plants had chosen him. "Aren't you the special boy?" Larry was out splitting firewood when Ray dropped in and he just kept working while Ray tried to explain his experiences.

"So what do I do with this?"

"Just what you're doing, I figure." Larry brought down his ax on a piece of log about a foot high and twenty inches in diameter, splitting it almost exactly in two.

"Having nightmares? Listening to clicks and hissing in my head?"

"Yes. And paying attention." Larry lined up one of the halves for another split. "Quit complaining. There's no shortcut, man."

"It doesn't make sense."

Larry began to laugh. Ray broke into a smile himself, but he was discouraged. And he was getting impatient. He wasn't always sure what Larry found so funny about him, but he figured he must be ridiculous on some level. It was hardly the first time Ray felt stupid. Maybe it went along with his old habit of fainting. Maybe stupidity and fainting were just in his nature. He shoved his hands deeper into his pockets and looked up at very gray sky.

Larry stopped laughing and swung his ax, splitting the half into perfect quarters. He looked over at Ray. "Okay, how doesn't it make sense?"

"I don't know. What am I paying attention to? I don't even really care about weed. Working at the place was just a job I picked up. What am I listening for?"

"How should I know what you're listening for? You play drums. What do you listen for with them?"

"That's completely different!"

"How?" Larry shoved the two log quarters off the chopping block with the ax and lined up the second half.

"If I'm playing drums, *I'm* doing the drumming. With the noises from the plants, they're just happening. Sometimes I think they're driving me crazy."

Larry looked over at Ray. "You're telling me you don't like it when you can't make the noise do what you want? You got a few control issues there, Ray. And you got a big opinion about these noises. That's what's not making sense to you. See, if you can't control something—"

"Wait. If I had epilepsy, I couldn't control that, and it would be awful too, but it would make sense to me."

"Because a doctor told you had epilepsy?"

"Yeah."

"You're an easy sell. Epilepsy? That's just a label. But you'd accept that." Larry took a whack at the remaining half log. The split was a little off center this time.

"Yeah. I'd accept that."

"Okay . . . so maybe this is just about acceptance. It's not about making sense or not making sense."

"I'd just like to know what the fuck is going on!"

"You know you could stack those pieces for me." Larry pointed to the very neat pile of chopped wood behind Ray and went off to pick up another log. Ray loaded up his arm with the chopped wood, and as he was stacking them, Larry came back with an even bigger log. It was black and mottled in the middle. He put it down on the chopping block and squinted at it. "So let's say it's not about making sense. Maybe that comes later — when you drop dead. Right now, what if it's just about getting information? These plants are telling you something. Just be curious." Larry looked over at Ray and could see his suggestions weren't having all that much effect. "Let's back up a bit. You play drums."

"Yeah."

Larry picked up the handle but just leaned on the ax like a cane. "You just drum away, right? You got no problem with that?"

"Yeah, that's okay."

"And you don't worry if it makes sense?"

"It makes musical sense. There're patterns. Structure."

"So if the noises in your head had some structure or pattern, it would make sense to you."

"No. Sometimes there's structure and it still doesn't make sense."

Larry shook his head. "See, your mind's a rat's nest. It's got you saying things that just confuse the issue. You got to be more alert, my friend. Start again. When you play the drums, do you worry about whether the act of playing makes sense or not?"

"No."

"No. You just play. And maybe somebody is listening. But maybe you're just playing because it's fun. So let's pretend for a minute, the plants are playing you. You're the drum."

"And they're having fun?"

"You tell me."

"They're pricks, then!"

Larry picked up his ax, and when he swung, it went deep into the wood and stuck there. It didn't split through. "Shit," he said. "Yeah, well nothing says plants have to be polite. Or obliging. Maybe they just really need to get your attention . . ."

"Because nobody listens to them."

"That's right." Larry yanked the ax up and the log came with it. Then he brought them both down with a whack and the ax drove further into the wood but still didn't split the log. "And what's a good way to get your attention?"

"Torture." Ray had not taken his eyes off the recalcitrant log. He began to smile.

"Whatever. See, it's not so hard. You got a story for it. Or you're getting one. You know there's another ax in the shed. You could make yourself useful." He pointed to a second chopping block a few yards away. Ray laughed and started off toward the shed. "Other thing," Larry said, "you still see you're separate. You're not."

"I'm not?" Rays stopped and turned.

"No. Plants stop doing what they do, you're dead, my friend. They stop growing, stop playing with the sunlight, stop breathing, you got no food, you got no oxygen, you die. So you're dependent on them, and they want your attention. They're looking for some exchange, maybe. You too. You just don't get it yet. They like you, man. And you like them."

"Maybe they just found easy prey."

"So? Even that's interesting. You gotta dump all these opinions. What's bad, what's okay. Easy prey: That's not okay; that's stupid. That's what's going on in your head, and you gotta dump that, man."

Ray continued to the shed and found the other ax. On his way back he picked up a log and headed to the other chopping block. He helped Larry split logs and neither of them talked. After about an hour, Larry looked pleased with their progress, so they took a break and went to the house for some tea. Ray was glad because he could feel his shoulder aching again.

"Hey," Larry said, "when the plants help you find your pain, you don't get to think. You get to *feel*. Maybe you even see and hear better. You're hearing already, right? It's a different world they take you to. Maybe nobody in their right mind wants this kind of thing.

But you're it. You gotta do this or they'll drive you crazy. Make you sick one way or another." Larry blew on his cup of tea.

"I bet I could just get better meds and shut the whole thing down."

"Yeah. You could probably do that. And you could go die in a box while you're at it."

Humph.

"If you wanna think about something, think about it from the plants' perspective. Probably what you do to them in that crazy place is as horrible to them as what you think they do to you. It's worse in fact, way worse. They don't kill you . . . yet."

"Jesus."

"Look at it from their point of view, man. You hack off pieces of a live mother! You even call it a mother! You think those clones are completely cut off from that first plant, but they're not. There's communication there, man. They're showing you how they communicate. Then you grow them up. You do everything to make them as sexy as possible and then you slaughter them all before they get a chance to actually have sex and reproduce. What the fuck! I'd be pissed off too. I'd want to torture the son of a bitch who did that to me. So maybe . . . maybe they need you to make some sense to them."

"But I don't cut them up anymore. I don't touch them."

"So tell me, in a room of a thousand plants, can you recognize individual plants? You got a name for each one?"

"No."

"So maybe the plants got the same problem. We're all the same to them too."

Ray was hunched over by this point, rocking back and forth, ignoring his cup of tea.

"You been fasting like I told you?"

"Just that one time," Rays sighed.

"You gotta fast more, man. Telling you, guts are better than a brain with this stuff. You gotta get them cleaned out. Give them a break, so they don't get distracted by all the other shit lands up in there."

#

Ray went on a fast again. It lasted almost two weeks. Every day he went to sit with the plants, any plants — the trees and grass along the creek, the woods at his place or his cousin's. He spent time in the little greenhouse too, with Jiggy's marijuana. And he found some excuses to look in on the plants at work more. He soon realized there was so much chatter going on between plants that if he wavered in his focus and attentiveness, it could be dizzying. Like being privy to all the conversations going on in town at the same time.

And he noticed something else: He was becoming increasingly and acutely aware of the up-and-down of a thing. Or the up-and-down of things in general. Roads he'd driven on possibly hundreds of times suddenly seemed to have more hills and slopes, which would never have crossed his mind unless he'd have to shift gears. Now each took on its own character. He unconsciously strove to catalogue them. A hill in one county would remind him on some profound level of another hill perhaps in the next county or even in another state. Hills he'd negotiated years ago loomed in his memory as if his experience with them had only been moments ago.

I wasn't just hills either. He could be in an elevator, walking up or down stairs, or staring down from his airy loft. He could only imagine what being in a plane might do to him. Depth and height: They became the preeminent polarities in his awareness. There was an urgency to them that he couldn't imagine living without, and yet this was all new. It was as if a spatial library, lovingly dedicated to the vertical, had opened itself up to him. Awareness of his positioning between high and low, that extended from the celestial to the bowels of the earth, became instilled in him.

And so with these new parts opening in him, and all the new information swirling about him, he finally bought himself a sweet set of drums to go with it. He found somebody on Craigslist who was selling a quality kit for next to nothing. Ray had to drive a hundred and fifty miles to get them. He could have driven an extra fifty and just picked up his old set at Alvin and Collette's for nothing, but he didn't want anybody knowing he was trying to play again. When he got the drums home, he set them up in their own secondhand tent in the barn.

Chapter 22

"Fuck that," said Jiggy. "Who comes up with this crap?"

Ray reached for his coffee. The latest memo from the executives was pure Lydia or something cooked up by one of her assistants. It was another rambling missive requesting all employees, now referred to as the "CannRose family" to take a moment in their busy day to consider what CannRose-Medi meant to them and to share those thoughts and feelings with the next person they saw. Then they were to come up with a single word to describe how they felt about CannRose-Medi and submit that word to Sandra in Communications. The memo went on about the need for shared values and the neural effects of smiling and that if each member of the CannRose family smiled at one more person that day and for every day thereafter, the family would be more amazing than it already was. It ended with the new slogan: CannRose-Medi . . . We Care About What's Best — For Now, For Tomorrow and For Always. The *For Tomorrow and For Always* part had recently been added to show the company was visionary. It didn't have all that much effect on the employees.

"Jesus! Next they'll have us genuflectin' or makin' peace signs at the security cameras to leave twinkle-dingdong vibes for posterity," Jiggy said.

Ray leaned back in his chair knowing Jiggy wouldn't let things rest until he'd exhausted the subject. Staff often sat in the security office when Ray came in for his sole daytime shift every couple of weeks. They could vent their discontent and knew it wouldn't go any further, though none were as vehement as Jiggy.

"People in charge here are fuckin' assholes." Jiggy was fidgeting with a pen. "Especially Caldwell, I don't think he's operated anything other than a con his whole life."

Ray agreed but he understood it — as Greg had explained, "The guy selling the show has to have that kind of charm, and sometimes a knack for skirting the law just comes with it."

"Yeah well, I think he's about to get truly buggered." Jiggy smashed the pen into the table. He sat back in his chair and looked closely at the bent end of the ballpoint. "I mean who in his right mind partners up with a guy named Guido *from the old country*, in a black Mercedes SUV? An' where is Greg in all this?" Jiggy said, shaking his head. "That's what I'd like to know. Isn't he supposed to check this shit out?"

That Jiggy was now obsessing about possible underworld criminality rather than corporate and institutional corruption was interesting, Ray thought. "Greg did check out Guido," His story was all true. The only thing that took his wife's pain away was weed. He said it added years to her life too. Guido's a believer."

"He's a multimillionaire," said Jiggy.

"So he's wealthy, so what?"

"How'd his family make the money?"

"Shoes?"

"Bullshit. Since when were cobblers ever known for their wealth?"

"Maybe they made shoes for the pope! Maybe they had big investments . . . mergers and acquisitions."

"Right." Jiggy bent the pen back on itself. "Fuckin' Bank of the Vatican. That's stellar that is! He even carries a violin case. A fuckin' violin case! He's kiddin' us, right?" Rumors about the Vatican's financial operations had taken up a good month of Jiggy's sleuthing on the internet a year or so before. Each day he would regale Gina and Ray with some new juicy tidbit, a suspected criminal connection, evidence of money laundering or an assassination with too few degrees of separation from the Mafia to ignore.

Ray handed Jiggy another pen. "Guido's okay. He really does play the violin. He played at the barbecue at Lydia's. You should have come. There were fireworks and everything. It was real nice. He collects art too, you know — he's cultured."

"Cultured, my ass. He's right outta Sicily, I'm tellin' ya. In no time we'll all be sayin', *I know nothin' about this*, or we'll end up dead in a car trunk."

Ray didn't want to lie to Jiggy, but he didn't want to give him anything more to go on either. And he'd promised Greg he'd forget the conversation the two of them had a couple of days before about Guido's loose connections.

"Jason's a goddamn biker thug. Did ya know that?"

"No," Ray admitted, "but I guess it doesn't surprise me all that much if he is." Jason was Guido's assistant, and a lot of people at the facility were suspicious of him, with those tattoos up his neck. And he barely spoke to anyone except Guido. Most of the time he was on his phone.

"Well he fuckin' well is." Jiggy tapped the new pen on the table. "Got an old buddy up in Canada there — well connected with the federal forces — says our Jason was real star around Montreal."

"Huh! Really?"

"Beat a bunch of charges, includin' manslaughter. A few well-planted technicalities . . . police there not necessarily bein' all that impartial as it were."

"Seriously." Ray was leaning back in the chair, cradling his coffee.

"Very seriously, Little Cousin, very seriously. That whole fuckin' merger with the new angel friends? Fuckin' Hell's Angels more like it. You keep your eyes an' ears open, Little Cousin, an' watch your back."

"I don't know. First it's the Mafia. Now it's Hell's Angels. Can't keep up to you, Jiggy." Ray was purposely sounding as nonchalant as he could.

"It's not me ya have to keep up to. Mark my words, Little Cousin, those two are plannin' on takin' over!"

Ray smiled. Some days Jiggy's theories were entertaining. But Ray was starting to call Jiggy on them when he felt irritated, like he did now. "You know, Jiggy, the state is all over our asses. First little sign of diversion, they shut us down in a heartbeat. If you're a criminal, why would you risk it? Why even get involved in the industry?"

Jiggy looked at Ray like he had a screw loose. "Why wouldn't ya get involved in the industry? From the criminal perspective, this is fuckin' perfect. You control everything from the seed to the finished product an' you can cook the books any way ya want. Poached to roasted on a spit."

"Yeah, but you gotta have a big profit item to begin with, right? With the prices going down so fast, after a while maybe it would be like having a black market for chewing gum. Who would bother?"

"Look, if nothin' else, with the state all over the industry, it's a terrific place to hide in plain sight. You know, you keep your friends close, keep your enemies closer. Look where Bin Laden hid! A block away from an army base."

"Yeah, I know and he probably had inside help from the Pakistani military and the CIA."

Jiggy was nodding.

Ray sighed. Jiggy's mind was a hive. Ray knew one thing for sure: The military had fucked Jiggy up more than it had messed with Ray.

But there was a good side. Jiggy had this job now. He'd found other things to rage about and he could get weed at a discount. In spite of all the craziness of a start-up company and Jiggy's own craziness, or maybe because of the variety of crazies, there were pluses. Ray noticed that in spite of everything, Jiggy smiled more often.

About two hours later, Caldwell showed up at the facility. Ray buzzed him in but Caldwell didn't open the door. He just stood in the fishbowl lobby looking dazed, as if he couldn't remember why he was there. Ray buzzed him in again and this time he did come through and headed in the direction of the conference room. About three minutes later, Caldwell appeared again, coffee in hand. He looked to be just strolling the hallway and then he wandered right into the security office.

"It's quite the day, isn't it? All this sunshine." And he sat down right where Jiggy had been sitting, but he didn't face Ray. He was talking to the air. "It's strange how a beautiful day can have so much trouble." And then he turned to Ray, but still distracted, said, "Do you think your generation is particularly troubled?"

"I couldn't say, though I do know a few people having a hard time."

"It's so difficult to know, you see. You young people have more choices than I ever had. I-I'm sure of it. Maybe it's just probability that you'd make that many more bad choices? Do you think so?" Caldwell was looking at Ray now as if Ray really could answer for his generation.

"Um . . . I'm not sure," Ray said, biting his lip. Caldwell had never asked him anything much more than how he was doing on any given day.

"My godson just overdosed." Caldwell turned away and was talking to the air again. "They don't know if he'll make it."

"That's terrible," Ray said.

"It is, isn't it. He didn't have to do that. I've always helped him. He's a bright kid. A good kid really. At heart." Caldwell turned back to Ray with a faint smile. "He'd have made the majors, you know. Baseball."

"I didn't know he ever played."

"He was brilliant. A rookie at seventeen," and Caldwell went on to tell Ray how the godson had shown such talent, advancing in the minors until that dreadful day — another sunny one — when he got in a bad car accident."

"When was that?"

"He was just twenty. In a lot of pain you know. I don't know what drugs they gave him at the time. I wasn't paying attention to things like that then." Caldwell spoke slowly, softly even, and tears were in his eyes. It was a side of Caldwell that Ray had certainly never seen.

Chapter 23

Ray settled into the routine of nighttime security work. It was so peaceful. Even the plants seemed quieter, especially if they were in the dark cycle. More friendly. Maybe because they weren't so busy chomping light and CO_2 and guzzling nutrients. Maybe the gulp, gulp, gulp was kind of nutty for them. Like being on speed or something. Darkness would surely be a reprieve.

Sometimes Ray thought he heard the plants breathing at night, just like animals and people. He knew that was ridiculous of course. Though night was when plants were most like animals and people — just respiring — so maybe this perception was his way or their way of providing him some comfort. It was just getting so tricky to sort out what was him and what was the plants. He decided to not worry about it. Boundaries were an illusion anyway, according to Sri Gupta Benhi Bingo. He was a comedian who'd seen the light — maybe just like the plants! And Larry had said pretty much the same thing. Anyway Benhi Bingo was hot these days among self-proclaimed gurus. His new book, *Losing Self at the Convenience Store* was creeping up the bestseller list.

One night, Petra's assistant, Sanjay, who often came in late to check on some analyses, saw him reading it. "Any good?" he asked.

"I don't know if it's good or not. It's funny."

"Is he imparting *great wisdom*?" Sanjay came into the office, grabbed a chair, sat down and looked at Ray with exaggerated solemnity.

"Hard to say . . ." Ray smiled. Sanjay liked to tease and Ray never took it seriously or was put off like some people at CannRose.

"You know mostly he's considered an idiot in India." Sanjay chuckled. "They say he should have stuck with Bollywood. He's got way too much competition. No real lineage."

"How's that?"

"Well if you're from a long line that leads back to a revered guru, it gives you more clout."

"Like pedigree."

"Exactly! Unless you can produce little miracles. You know, water into wine, ashes into petals." Sanjay raised his hands as imaginary objects were produced between his thumbs and fingers. "Rings too — preferably expensive ones." He smiled. "That's street cred for the guru."

"Yeah, I don't think this guy does that."

"No. But the Brits loved him," Sanjay said. "I read an article about him a few years back and even my mum said he was all the rage."

"And now he's conquering America!" Ray held the book aloft.

"Well somebody has to conquer America now, I guess."

"Might as well be a comedian."

"It could be a promising turn of events." Sanjay nodded thoughtfully.

"Wouldn't it!" As Ray said this, a flash of lightning lit up the window. The lights in the office flickered for a moment and then came a great crack of thunder.

"Oh my God!" Sanjay exclaimed and they both began laughing. Within seconds rain was pelting against the window. Sanjay got up out of his chair and all mirth vanished. "Damn!" he said, wide-eyed, "That power blip probably just screwed up my run!" He glanced at the window before rushing out the door. "Holy mother! It's coming down in sheets."

Ray was sad to hear that Sanjay was leaving CannRose to do a PhD, and a little surprised to hear that he was getting married too. After his own observations and a few snarky revelations from Percy, it was clear Sanjay had something going on with Petra. On top of that, Sanjay flirted mercilessly with some people, especially Percy. Aside from the "hotties" Gabe's wife sent his way, Ray usually found flirty people quite funny, especially when they didn't take themselves seriously. Sanjay seemed to have perfected this, but the important thing about him was that he knew so much and he was open to all sorts of views and ideas. Ray could talk to him about anything. In fact Ray often found Sanjay just as helpful as Larry when he was wondering about his own sanity from time to time, though unlike Larry, Sanjay had few opinions. He just seemed curious, and sometimes he would tell Ray about someone he knew who'd had similar experiences. Or he'd talk about how something like that might be viewed in certain Hindu traditions.

Sanjay told Ray it was a pity he couldn't recommend a good teacher for him. A real guru who could take Ray where he needed to go. Ray replied that he didn't really want to be taken anywhere by anybody. The experiences he was having were quite enough, thank you. Sanjay was thoughtful for a minute and then said, "Yes, come to think of it, that makes more sense. You already have the guru. Maybe we all do, and what's fifty thousand lifetimes in the face of eternity anyway?"

Ray wasn't sure about the reincarnation bit — but it sounded like a good idea. And if Sanjay was right about the fifty thousand lives, well, that could be really interesting. Think of all the things he'd learn. And surely some of those lives would have to be spent as a plant. Then he'd get to see what was what. Imagine three thousand years on the side of a cliff. Some trees were even older. He'd seen them as a boy in California — his father had pointed them out. What a life. Terrible weather of course, but a great view, and he'd be there for everything changing. He'd probably think it all went by in a flash too. A sedentary life would surely do that. The knowledge collected though would make him fearless.

#

The very night that Ray and Sanjay talked about the comedian's book, something terrible happened. It's possible that it even happened the very moment lightning ripped through the sky and created a boom so loud it startled them both to laughter. It was certainly something no one anticipated. Some people even had trouble believing it when they heard.

Three inches of rain fell in six hours that night. The old Lusteadt Sideroad that Ernie waxed on about because of the wealth of wild food along it — blackberries, chicory, wild grapes, hawthorn berries, and hickory nuts — was completely washed out. But that was hardly the worst of it. Not by a long shot. The worst of it was Caldwell. Of all the crazy things in a crazy world of deluge and bad timing, Caldwell was on that sideroad that night. And in the morning, his body was found floating facedown in the ditch beside it.

It was hard to understand why Caldwell had been there, but then Ray heard it was a shortcut. He'd flown in from Colorado and was expected at a dinner party at Guido's place but he never showed up. Damian told Ray that everybody just assumed he'd missed his flight again and forgotten to charge his phone, or maybe he decided to stay in Colorado for some reason and he forgot all about the dinner party. Caldwell was like that.

The shock of his death produced immediate confusion as well as grief at CannRose. Rumors swirled among the staff and got grislier by the minute: "Luther finally snapped and murdered him." "Gus and Lorne took their revenge." "Guido ordered a hit." "The Guardians of Jude and Ezekiel finally embraced true violence." But very quickly the police determined it had just been a very sad accident. Caldwell's car had broken down. He'd started to walk in the dark, and it would have been so easy to slip and fall right into that ditch.

As time went on, more details were discovered. And these bothered Ray. Apparently Caldwell had tried to phone the facility that night, probably right about when he and Sanjay were joking. Ray had been only twenty minutes away and could have easily driven over to help him. Sanjay said another person's trajectory through life was always mystifying. You couldn't change things. Beating yourself up about it was futile, not to mention unkind. And this did make Ray feel a little better.

The grief expanded around Ray and manifested in different ways, especially at the funeral. Greg and Lazlo were pale and looked exhausted. Luther was distracted, then clearly annoyed by his bungling of the few words he spoke at the service. Lydia and Damian just looked lost. Lily was teary but smiling, and she and Ray gave each other a long hug. People Ray would have never expected broke down in tears, like Percy, the QA officer. Petra kept handing him tissues. Guido played the sarabande from the first Bach Partita. It could set anyone weeping. Cassie's eyes were soon red. She and Joe held hands and Ray caught a glimpse of the three young lads hiding behind their hair, sniffling. But Guido and Jason seemed quite invigorated. Of course that only prompted Jiggy — whose eyes had watered up too, Ray noticed — to speculate vehemently about the drug world's underbelly.

Unfortunately Jiggy's suspicions were somewhat prescient. A week later the police showed up because the official autopsy report had a few surprises in it that the police hadn't been aware of and now they did think there could have been foul play. That set CannRose buzzing. All the theories and paranoia resurfaced. Even Greg, who was planning on retiring anyway, seemed spooked. He moved his departure date up by a couple of months and claimed it was all because of his wife's health. Or Ray figured maybe he was leaving because Guido took over and started changing everything, especially the staff. Greg had never liked issuing pink slips.

#

Several weeks after Caldwell's funeral, Ray noticed that Lydia was often staying late. And she wasn't herself. She didn't look healthy, Ray thought. Then he realized she just wasn't wearing makeup. Still, she didn't move the way he remembered. She seemed to shuffle a little and her shoulders were hunched, as if she was harboring a wound or protecting a sick pet. He watched on the monitors one evening as she went into the production area, found herself some visitor scrubs and went into Flower Room II. The crop there was about halfway through the grow cycle, all the plants around fifteen inches high. There was always a table area left clear in the cultivation rooms for tools and whatnot, but Lydia used it as a bench and just sat there like Ray had been tempted to do himself several times.

Ray took his time doing the first round of the evening. He didn't usually go into the flower rooms or nursery unless he saw a problem, so he hesitated outside Flower Room II before opening the door. Lydia was still there, sitting, staring at the plants. She turned her head as she heard the door close behind him and then put her hand up in greeting.

"I thought it might be nice to just be with the plants for a while."

"I like to do that too," Ray said.

"You sit with the plants?"

"Not here. Not at work. Although I have spent some time with the mothers, I guess." Ray almost went on to say that they made way more complex and interesting sounds, but he stopped himself and sat down on the table a few feet away from her.

"I'll have to try one of the mother pods next time. Maybe tomorrow," she said. "Older and bigger plants. Some of them can get very old, I hear."

"Yeah, Cassie said she'd heard of mother plants that people had kept going for fifteen years. More even."

"My goodness. I wonder if CannRose will be around that long."

Ray could hear the grief still in her voice. At least he thought it must be grief. Ernie had told him Lydia and Caldwell had once been a couple, before CannRose was even started. Not only was Caldwell gone now, people were leaving every day it seemed.

The two of them sat there not saying a word, and Ray listened to the yammer from the plants mingled with the white noise from the air handlers. He'd never felt at liberty to do this before at CannRose, just sit and not have to be busy with anything else while he was in view of the surveillance cameras. He was very happy that the president of the company — even if she didn't actually run things — had taken the lead.

#

Life and death seemed to figure prominently that autumn. Ray had received an invitation to Sanjay's wedding and he could bring guests! Ray had casually mentioned to Sanjay something about the renovations he was making to his house to accommodate his soon to be part-time family with Julie and Anna. Sanjay thought the domestic arrangement was brilliant and even confessed to Ray he wished he'd maybe thought of something like that himself a while ago. "Never mind," he said, "I'm bound for great love to a great beauty. She's way more charming than I could ever be. Plus she cooks. My mother never did, on principle I think." He smiled. "But I must meet your two friends. You have to bring them."

So Ray did. The wedding was in Boston anyway and it was two-and-a-half-day affair. Sanjay told him, in India, weddings often lasted five to seven days but this was going to be something of a fusion. Modest by Indian standards. His bride, who really was coming from India, wanted it to be as Western as possible. In fact she suggested what amounted to an elopement by Indian standards since neither of their immediate families were very wealthy. But Sanjay's uncle was and he insisted there be basic festivities.

Julie was long past barfing by then. Ray was able to put his ear to her stomach and hear the baby's tiny heartbeat. He also thought he could maybe feel it kicking when he put his hand there. Julie said she sure could, and she was determined to spend an afternoon at a spa and insisted on dragging Ray along. She said if they'd been on the bride's side they'd probably be spending the time getting their hands decorated with henna. It was a time meant for beauty. Anna wasn't going. She had a commercial to finish editing, and with luck she'd have it done before they left for the first evening's celebrations. So Ray went along somewhat hesitantly and got his first facial and pedicure. The woman told him his feet were a mess and he should soak them more often. But he really did like the whirlpool.

After pampering at the spa came the dressing up and preening. Julie being so tall and large, barely showed even at six months but she opted for the empire-waist dress anyway. Sea-green velvet. "Color is important," she said, "and bling too." Her mass of blonde hair had been trimmed and styled into a cascade of beach waves, not so much Dolly as Hollywood. Anna also wore velvet, but slim-leg teal paisley pants with a silk shirt and spike heels. She piled her dark swath of hair into a chignon exposing the intricate maze-like patterns on the buzzed sides of her head. They both wore big necklaces with matching earrings. Anna's were turquoise and lapis, and Julie was ablaze with Austrian crystal. Ray felt quite subdued in his blue-gray suit, but Anna and Julie had bought him an arty silk tie à la Mondrian. They all took a cab to the hotel and the driver seemed not to be able to take his eyes off them in the rearview mirror.

"Oh my God. You're all so gorgeous," Sanjay said, backing up to take in the full view of the three of them. He'd never seen Ray in a suit, of course. When he introduced them all to Dhatri, his fiancée, who really was stunning in her blingy sari, she smiled, shook their hands and said with a British accent that she was "most pleased" to meet them. She looked at Ray and squinted slightly, the way Larry did sometimes, and then she gave him a big smile and whispered something in Sanjay's ear. Sanjay was about to say something to Ray, but a tall man who looked like he might be a relative suddenly appeared and swept the couple along to some elderly ladies who were standing a few yards away. That was almost all the contact the three of them had with Sanjay and his fiancée. There must have been over four hundred people. "The diaspora is great and very connected," Sanjay had told him, "and you really must invite everybody you possibly can."

The two subsequent days were packed with even fancier clothes, ceremonies, tons of food from all corners of the earth it seemed, music, dancing, well-acted and entertaining confrontations, the appearance of a huge motorcycle that Sanjay rode at one point, and shoe stealing. What Ray really enjoyed most was the small classical dance troupe that performed the second night, and in particular their musicians caught his attention. The rhythms reminded him a little of what he was hearing from the plants.

The biggest surprise for Ray was that Percy was there with his husband. There was so much going on, Ray barely spoke to him, but he seemed to be having a wonderful time, always smiling or laughing. Ray thought this was very strange given the often snide and well, just plain bitchy remarks he'd made about Sanjay at CannRose. When he told Julie and Anna about it later, they just looked at him and shook their heads. Julie turned to Anna and sighed. "Our Ray is sometimes so emotionally naïve, I worry for our offspring."

Chapter 24

It was late November and Ray's drive-shed house was starting to shape up. It sat pristine on the hill in its white polyethylene wrap with the big print on a diagonal. "Advertisin' corporate interests," Jiggy said. "Jesus, Ray! You gonna leave it like that all winter?" Yes. Siding and a few other things would have to wait for spring. Ray had big plans for finishing the roof with solar panels and putting some on the barn roof as well. The house still wasn't exactly habitable. There was the matter of the interior insulation and wiring, not to mention the drywall. And the water wasn't hooked up. The brand new heat pump was there but not running because there was no electricity.

Ray found he was often annoyed with himself. He procrastinated. And because he had so much wiring in his work history it was the thing he procrastinated about the most. He tried a game with himself several mornings. He'd lie in his sleeping bag in the tent in the barn, stare up through the netting at the old rafters and announce to the pigeons, "Today I'm going start wiring my house. It will be the best wiring I've ever done." Or he'd mumble to himself, "Ray, what is it with you and the wiring? Just do it. What could be easier?" And then he'd get up and invariably find some distraction. He'd notice some little issue with a window or a doorframe, some caulking somewhere that needed perfecting, screws that got missed and needed sinking. Alternatively, he might grab a coffee and spend half the morning looking through a tool catalogue. Or sometimes he'd go for a walk and just get lost in all the noise in the woods and not make it back until noon. Then of course it would be too late to get started. Now that he was back at his drums again and taking computer courses, he had even more distractions.

He talked to Larry about it. "The drums are good for you," Larry said. "But man, you are making this crazy place out of something old where nobody can be home 'cause you got no lights. Just think about it."

Ray asked Larry if he thought ditching the apprenticeship for his electrician license was stupid too, and Larry told him it didn't matter what he did. "You learn stuff anyway. You like it? Great. You don't? Maybe that's great too! You go look for something else. Or maybe you stick with it and it kills you. That's your life. Not for me to say."

"So I might as well do what I like."

"Why not, if it's gonna make you happier. You're gonna need that."

"So does electrical work make you happy?" Ray asked.

"No. Electrical stuff was just easy for me. And the pay is good. The other stuff? I didn't have a choice is how I see it. It's not anything anybody would want to do. At least I don't think so. You can get overloaded by all the crazy stuff around people. Not to mention discouraged and depressed. Sometimes better not to know — like you wanting to shut that part of yourself down with better meds. But it's everything I learned from my grandfather and my aunt and it's the only way I know how to be. Why else would I see what I see and hear what I hear? In another time maybe, I'm not an electrician. Wouldn't have to do that. Wouldn't have to be picky who I help either. Just looking after my life, having one foot here and helping whoever wanted my help would be enough." Larry looked a little wistful at this point. "You know these people . . . they come up here to see me. They're driving fancy cars. They got nice clothes, nice houses, nice kids. Only they know they're gonna die and that bothers them. So they want me to postpone it. They tried everything else and now it's down to me." He shook his head. "They heard something. Just like you a year ago. Only with them, I can't do anything. Even if I did something for them, they're gonna be sick again in no time. They don't have a connection. All they got is their view. It's like they're all memory foam."

Ray had seen Larry do some interesting work. A local teenage girl had come to him with an ankle injury. Larry had massaged the ankle and according to the girl, took all the pain away in just a few seconds. Ray had sat with them afterward, talking about this and that, with Larry's wife joining in the conversation. Ray looked down at the girl's ankle and saw the swelling was all gone too. He asked Larry how he managed to do that. Larry just shrugged. "Sometimes I see things, really tiny. And I move into the trouble spot. Sometimes it has a color to it. Mostly though I don't think about it or see anything, I just go with it. It's about the connection. I'm just a conductor. A lot of resistors can show up in the body. Yeah."

#

As Ray got more comfortable with the world opening up around him in strange new ways, he found he was sensitive to all sorts of things. Of course light figured prominently no matter where he was. Light could be even more complex than verticality. It felt like he was archiving these perceptions in some grand way, too, that made use of the trillions of cells in his own body. The maximum brightness of a noon hour seemed to seep right into his bones. And he felt the minute differences in light from day to day as the earth made its elliptical progress about the sun.

He was acutely aware of moonlight too. It wasn't so much about the incoming waves, the brightness or the intensity, it was more like the pull and push of fear, anger, sadness, aversion and desire. He'd have preferred less of this. What could that kind of sensitivity do for him anyway, other than distract and engulf? How could anybody negotiate it without drowning in it?

And the vibes in a room. In an instant he could pick up the least little discomfort. Especially when people were smiling in spite of themselves, feigning all manner of goodwill when they were ready to explode. Or convincing the world they were fine while their lives were falling apart. Or holding on to grudges, unconsciously sabotaging everyone, including themselves. He could see the distress so easily in someone's eyes now, or the rage looming behind them. And he could hear the unhappiness in a voice too. People held a lot of emotional refuse. Shit really, just like Larry said, and it sat stinking and steaming right below the surface.

Moving out of his tent and spending yet another winter with Jiggy and Gina was going to be a challenge. He'd postpone it until the snow was actually flying and he couldn't bear the thought of winter camping anymore. Initially he thought more beer or bourbon would work but that just made him sick now. His stomach and liver had gained sensitivity along with the rest of him. A reprieve would come though in February.

One late afternoon right before the first flurries were forecast, Ray took a few things over from his farm to theirs, namely his drums that he put in the attic he last occupied when he lived there. He found Gina and Jiggy out by the lean shed for the cattle filling the hay feeder. Jiggy'd just dropped the bale in with the lift and Gina was slicing it open. They were both excited but still squabbling somehow. They'd booked a two-week vacation in Cuba. Jiggy said it was necessary "if only for fuckin' historical purposes." It was an all-inclusive and they'd gone through a Montreal travel agency because it was just easier going from Canada.

"Cuba's gonna be real interesting, Ray." Gina was right in the feeder pulling the wrap off the bail.

"Looks like they got a lot of old American cars there." Ray had seen the brochure sitting on the kitchen counter.

"Russian Ladas too." Jiggy said, walking back from the tractor.

"Like steppin' back into the 1950s I hear." Gina was working her way around the other side of the bale.

"Except they do actually have universal health care," Jiggy announced.

"So would we, Jiggy, if our doctors only made fifteen bucks an hour."

"It's not just our doctors, Gina. Even with the whole new system the asshole in the Whitehouse now is gonna try' to dismantle, you still got insurers, hospitals, clinics and fuckin' big pharma bilkin' everybody and anybody. It's still just one big greedy corrupt industry. They got most of the people in this country over a fuckin' barrel."

"You think it's so different in Cuba, Jiggy?" Gina yanked out the last bit of covering that was stuck partially under the bale.

"Well, it sure doesn't look like here. Did you notice in the brochure, Ray, people in the pictures aren't so fat there."

"Maybe it's the food." Gina began folding the plastic bale wrap into a bundle.

"Yeah, no junk food, Ray!"

"Maybe they don't eat much, Jiggy. The travel agent said food likely wouldn't be stellar at the resort."

"You know, Ray, I don't know why anyone feels the fuckin' need to terrorize America. We're terrorizin' ourselves everyday anyway. Fuckin' killin' ourselves with the overpackaged processed shit we eat.

All full of sugar an' fats, pesticides an' antibiotics, fuckin' GMOs. You know I'm amazed supermarket ham doesn't just get up outta the cooler an' work the cash."

"The agent did say it was healthy food in Cuba. There's kind of a forced organic farming there, Ray. 'Cause of all the embargos." Gina was scrunching the bundle of bale wrap into a ball.

"Tellin' ya! Better see Havana before the corporations get there. They'll wreck everything. They'll have golden arches and fast food on every fuckin' corner in no time."

Gina ducked through the bars of the feeder and handed the ball of wrap to Jiggy without looking at him. "I hear it's quiet too, Ray. I want a lot of sleep. They say take a book. I'm taking three!"

"Wonder if the lads in Guantanamo think it's quiet." Jiggy snorted.

Gina rolled her eyes. "Well, maybe you should go visit, Jiggy. You can ask 'em yourself."

"It's on the other side of the island."

"Well that's lucky then, isn't it? Bertha, sweetie, would you like your dinner?" Bertha — they'd finally named the dog — had come bounding up to them from behind the shed where she'd been busy with something. Jiggy said probably a groundhog. There was a burrow under the shed.

"Dinner? Yes? You would? You'd like your dinner!" Gina said more loudly and Bertha barked and started making a beeline for the house. She sure knew what the word dinner meant.

Ray envied the dog's crystal-clear focus in the complicated and cluttered atmosphere around the cattle feeder.

Chapter 25

Not long after Ray had moved back in with Jiggy and Gina, he had to deal with even more couple dynamics. Only this time it was at work unfolding on the monitors right in front of him. The biggest source of gossip at the grow facility had surely been the rift between Damian, the master grower, and the horticultural specialists, Cassie and Joe. It had ended in a brawl and physical damage that Ray noted produced a shocking level of mirth among his co-workers. The three involved were fired and the pH probe repaired. There were rumors about various lawsuits but then Cassie and Damian were hired back. There was no sense to any of it that Ray could see.

There appeared to be some kind of truce between the two, perhaps because their jobs had changed. Damian was no longer the master grower but had some executive role, Strategic Product Planner or something like that — people's job titles changed every week now — and Cassie was in charge of the cultivation. Regardless, there was no mistaking the ongoing tension, and it appeared to Ray that Cassie held herself in check while Damian casually baited.

Damian periodically wandered through the production section, and every time Ray happened to see this on the monitors, it was like Damian was seeking out some new confrontation. It could well have been harassment since Ray never heard what was said but he admired the way Cassie resisted. She would usually smile politely and vacate the area quickly, but as she went through a door or into a hallway she might shake her head, flip the finger or demonstrate her displeasure in some other way, but only when she was well out of Damian's sight.

On this particular occasion Cassie had stayed very late preparing for the following day's harvest. Damian was in the facility too. On the monitors, Ray saw Damian look around in the cultivation area and then eventually make his way to one of the drying chambers where Cassie was sanitizing racks. Ray didn't like the looks of what was transpiring. Damian put on a bunny suit to enter the drying chamber, and Ray anticipated he might need to dash to the scene to break up another fight. Cassie or Damian could start hurling those racks around. That's what they'd done before. They'd turned cultivation tools into weapons. Ray would have to exercise his authority, especially as head of security — violence would not be tolerated at CannRose.

Ray enlarged the camera feed from the drying chamber to fill the monitor screen. They appeared to be talking peaceably enough. Then he saw Cassie suddenly grab for the rack she was working on, but it looked more as if she was steadying herself with it. Ray couldn't see Damian's face. And then as the rack was rolled aside, Cassie lurched forward and Damian caught her. Ray held his breath. One more suspicious move and he'd be on his way. But Damian just held her. Had she passed out or done that on purpose or what? And then of all things, Damian kissed her! Or they kissed each other. It certainly went on for quite a while and there wasn't any struggling. On the contrary, she had both hands locked around his head and was getting more passionate by the second. Then Cassie, who was still more or less facing the camera, opened her eyes and seemed to look right at Ray. It was at that point the shock came over her face, no doubt about it. The two separated and Cassie left the drying chamber while Damian just stood there with his ponytail of blond dreadlocks facing the camera.

The next time Ray saw the two of them was when he came in the following Monday for the monthly meeting. Cassie and Damian just sat at opposite ends of the conference room, staring into their coffee mugs. Afterward, Cassie followed Ray to the security office like she had something to say to him but when she got to the door she suddenly looked preoccupied, turned around and walked away.

It was Damian who actually came in and spoke to him a few minutes later. "Hey, man. How's it goin'?" And then he proceeded to hum and haw and it was clear he had something to say. "So . . . like . . . the other night . . . Thursday . . . did you uh like see . . ."

"Yeah . . . I saw." Ray put him out of him misery.

"Yeah, man . . . so like do you need to preserve that footage . . . like . . ."

"You know what?" Ray said. "Nobody cares. Nobody looks at those records except the DOH. And they only care if there's product in the room."

Damian stood for a second staring at Ray. Then he shifted his gaze and looked out the window, his perpetually enlarged pupils shrinking somewhat with the blast of sunshine coming at him.

"Yeah, man. You don't usually think about that," he said. "You know, you just think *surveillance*. But yeah. A lot of stuff is irrelevant, man. Lotta information . . . maybe . . . yeah . . ." And Damian walked out of the security office looking just as preoccupied as Cassie had.

Ray wondered if Cassie and Damian had finally come to any deeper understanding of each other or at least a more steadfast tolerance. Or was it just the case that something had to give? Maybe they were both just crazy, and even with plant noises ringing in his ears and a mantis that showed up sometimes bigger than a horse, he was saner than they were.

Chapter 26

Julie called Ray to tell him about a weekend prenatal course they were going to in the new year. The midwife running the course told them they could bring in a third person, if Ray was interested. Ray said that would be fantastic. He was working over the holidays this year and would take a few days off after that. He was pretty excited and felt honored they would invite him to take part in the birthing. He began preparing, reading up on the things to expect.

When the three of them headed out to the course on Saturday morning, he was all smiles. But by Saturday afternoon Ray was feeling a little nauseous. The pictures, the descriptions and one little film in particular brought back memories of body parts, blown-up markets and roadside bombs. He went very pale and had to get out of the room. Julie and Anna didn't get the connection and he didn't mention it. But Anna sympathized. She'd had the same reaction when she saw her first film of a live birth. She'd gotten over it. She had to. But she said it was nice to know she wasn't alone in the revulsion. Ray wasn't quite so sure he'd get over it. Julie and Anna found his reticence about attending the Sunday session hilarious. And in their company Ray began to find it funny too. He mustered his courage and went along. It wasn't as bad. But he told them afterward, he wasn't sure he'd be very helpful on the big day. That was okay, Julie told him. She understood and she didn't mind. He'd been pretty brave already.

\#

"Ray, come on, it's just for an old folks home. Not some scout for a record deal."

"They don't make deals much like that anyway these days, Aunt Collette."

"Show your aunt a little compassion. Please."

"I'd really like to but you know I haven't played anything in six years."

"Rubbish. Gina told me you were sounding great."

"Gina's not a drummer."

Ray really wished Gina would mind her own business. Sure he was doing okay again now. Having a little fun on his own. Often he was improvising on the strange rhythms he was hearing from the plants. But he sure as hell didn't feel like performing for anybody.

As a kid Ray had played with any kind of grip: matched, traditional, French. And he'd messed around with the sticks as if they were batons. When he left the army behind, along with the two fingers on his right hand, he tried all sorts of grips until he found the ones he could modify and make work — like a traditional grip, but with the stick resting between the first and second fingers rather the second and third. He dropped the stick a lot at first and he figured he'd probably never get any real speed back, but after a while he wasn't doing too badly. The main thing was not to tighten up anywhere. When Ray began working in construction though, the drums aggravated his tinnitus so much he couldn't even look at them. He took his kit back to Alvin and Collette's.

"It's just a few standards," Collette said. "Just the snare. You could play them in your sleep when you were fourteen."

"Yeah but I wasn't minus two fingers. In case you hadn't noticed."

"Oh, I noticed all right, Ray. They're not expecting Art Blakey."

Ray felt the tinge of annoyance in his aunt's voice. "Why can't Uncle Alvin do it?"

"He's busy with Amnesty tomorrow."

"What's wrong with your guy again?"

"Randy? He's got the flu. Ray, please. Otherwise it's just me and a guitar. It's not the same."

"You should get a drum machine!"

"Your kit's in the garage. Alvin set it up. You could practice a little this afternoon. Tomorrow you'd probably be better than Randy." His aunt's tone was no longer pleading. There was an anger behind it he'd rarely heard.

Ray knew he'd probably upset his aunt when he joined the army. She'd berated him at the time. She talked about her students who'd scrape, scavenge and go deep into debt to be in a good music program and here was Ray turning down a full scholarship to one of the best schools in the country. Now Ray realized she was furious with him. Had been all along maybe. He could feel it right in his spine with all that newfound sensitivity. She reminded him of the mantis in his dream just before it ripped his head off.

Ray got up and disappeared into the garage. After a few minutes of sitting staring at his drums, he picked up his old sticks. He practiced the rudiments, taking little breaks every ten minutes or so. It all felt fine. By his own estimation, his speed still sucked and he dropped his stick once on some paradiddles. But with each little block of time he practiced, he felt better and better. It made him joyful. It dawned on Ray that he must have a peculiar relationship with memory. He often forgot about how good this felt. He started playing for longer stretches and even though he was supposedly polishing up his chops to oblige his aunt, he couldn't help improvising on a few more rhythms he'd picked up from the plants.

He got up after an hour or so to get a glass of water. Collette was standing by the sink and Alvin had his arm around her shoulder. Tears were pouring down her face. Alvin glared at him. The kitchen was very chilly. Ray turned around and went to the bathroom to get his water.

He looked at himself in the mirror above the sink. Now what? Was it something he'd done or was it just bad timing for a visit? He did not want to piss off his uncle. Ray just found out Alvin had been diagnosed with Parkinson's. And he did not want to create or add to Collette's frustration or misery right now. Seemed there was enough of that already. One of his cousins had just divorced, and Collette said the new girlfriend was "just horrible and his children are going to bear the brunt of it." She was also upset that Alvin had put the house on the market before they knew where they were moving. Ray could leave, but that might upset his aunt even more. He stood staring at his reflection. He didn't have a clue how to make this better. He went back to the garage and played for another hour. Light stuff. Easy stuff. Brushes. Like what he'd play with his aunt the next day.

Aunt Collette finally calmed down in the kitchen. She'd had one of her rare meltdowns. And yes, it was Ray's practicing that brought it on, and yes, this did piss off Uncle Alvin. Collette had never been able to really voice her own anger at Ray's enlistment. She said Alvin and Jiggy had hogged all the oppositional thunder and she didn't want to alienate Ray even more.

She'd opened the kitchen window after a while to hear how he was doing out in the garage. When she heard Ray's practicing and there was that immediate elegance, precision and nuance she remembered, brilliant even for a ten-fingered drummer, she lost it. What a waste of a gift. Couldn't Ray see that? He could have even joined the army as a musician. But no. He chose a hopeless war. Then he had to lose two fingers. And then he had to get blown up. It nearly killed him. And that nearly killed her. Now he was a security guard at a damn pot factory. She'd wanted to wring his neck. And the more Ray played and the more complex and strange the rhythms became, especially when he'd hit the zone for a moment or two there, the more Collette let loose her emotions. "Where did all that come from, Ray? You could have made music your life."

#

Ray played the old folks home the next day. As always, Aunt Collette mesmerized the audience. When Ray complimented her on this, she kissed him on the cheek. "With all the drugs some of them are on, it's not too difficult."

"I think they just know when the angels are getting close," Ray said. "They're paying attention."

His aunt stared at him. "Almost reminds me of Alvin's first line. But in your case, you could be talking from experience."

Ray laughed.

"You've been awfully secretive," she said. "Gina spilled the beans ages ago, you know. Were you ever going to tell us you're about to be a father?"

"I was going to tell you. And Uncle Alvin. I was just waiting for the right time. Sometimes it's still a little tense."

"So when's Julie due?"

"Another six weeks."

"You going to be there?"

"I went to classes with them, in fact, just this weekend on my way down here."

"Good for you!"

"Yeah. There were films . . . Honestly, Aunt Collette, I'm not good with that stuff."

His aunt nodded. "Is it a boy or a girl?"

"It's a boy."

"You moving to Boston?"

"No. I need to be in the country. And really I'm just a friend. Lots of visits planned though."

"So it's going to be a laid-back arrangement."

"Yeah." Ray smiled. "I'm already arranging the house. Holidays you know."

"How's the house coming?"

"Oh . . . it's slow still. Not habitable yet obviously. And now I'm back at Jiggy and Gina's, I'm not getting much done."

"I'm sure you'll be in by next winter."

"I sure hope so, Aunt Colette." Ray thought of the wiring and sighed.

Chapter 27

Jiggy was in Cuba sitting on a beach with Gina. They were staring at the waves and watching the pelicans hunt.

"They look like senators or somethin'."

"The pelicans?"

"Yeah. Look at 'em with their heads tucked back like that. Flyin' around with all that authority. Great bobbly pouches under their beaks."

"Like they own the sea."

"They do. Lethal to some unsuspectin' little fish. Look at that!" There were about half a dozen pelicans circling around and one of them had just swooped into a small wave and emerged with a catch.

"Nice life though."

"I'm thinkin' it's dog-eat-dog everywhere, Gina. Or fish-eat-fish. Or bird-eat-fish in this case."

"So you don't think Cuba ever got it right either?"

"I never thought it did. I was just curious is all. There's nothin' but the same shit everywhere, looks like. People are shitty. That's the problem. Or they're desperate. An' they're forever screwin' each other over somethin'."

"That's it? Apathy then? Isn't that what you say the real criminals of this world bank on."

"Yeah, well, it's true enough. That an' exhaustion."

"Maybe we should go visit Iceland next holiday."

"Yeah, let's do that. They got volcanoes. All sorts of crazy stuff. Hot springs. Divin' in ice lakes."

Jiggy was suddenly startled by two pelicans that collided and then scrapped over a fish that ultimately fell back into the ocean. It made his brain shift. The mid-air scuffle combined with the week of relaxation gave him an insight. Or maybe it was just an idea. It was about greed.

When Caldwell had died and the new CEO arrived, way more suits started showing up at CannRose for meetings. Jiggy'd been asked to join a couple of them so the new people could get his boots-on-the-ground input. They wanted numbers for the planned expansions. As he sat in the room, with the jargon and buzzwords flying every which way, a nausea rose in him. These men only ever talked about money. They were antsy about banking and insurance; tricky business when the feds still put the kybosh on weed. And oh yeah, they had touchy-feely concerns too: consumer health, education, scientific advances and even the eventuality of "adult use" — the term of euphemistic optimism picked up from a recently passed act in California. But that was all bullshit.

"It's only ever about the fuckin' money," Jiggy'd told Gina at the time. And their global ambitions, their reverse takeovers and international mergers were only about getting listed on public stock exchanges. They could have been in the business of anything, from diamonds to garbage collection. Everything was built on shifting money. "An' fuckin' hype. Bringing home the next smooth financial move."

Jiggy figured this did not bode well for the marijuana business. Sure there were big players in some places where company profits soared and in some countries there were shares that had gone through the roof. But what was any of it really based on? CannRose was still in debt with money draining out the door. The pricks in suits were in a trance. The scale of the place wasn't competitive yet they'd say. Jiggy thought maybe it was just one elaborate fuckin' Ponzi scheme. Everybody waitin' for the rapture in green to make it all better. The suits around the gamblin' table just figurin' how to keep the dice rollin' until the divine deliverance. They'll keep doin' the same shit, only bigger. The promised land obliterates reality.

Jiggy was surprised any of this surprised him. But there it was: Greed made people stupid. While he'd wasted energy on paranoia about corporate interests curbing his rights — and maybe that was inevitable — the root of the problem was actually the trance. The greedy fuckin' bozos were lost in a trance.

So Jiggy decided to extricate himself. His efforts had been misdirected. Setting the scene for one of Gordo's science experiments, no matter how brilliant and dazzling, was a waste of time. It wouldn't affect the trance. He'd just been nostalgic probably. And if he really was focused on the inevitability of collapse, he could harness more destructive forces with a quiet little cyber hack. He'd unrig the grow facility, de-scintillate it, remove Gordo's astonishing explosives and clean up the software on the isolated system. Probably updates to the security software were not integrating too well with his buried bits of code. It was the first thing he'd do when he got back. And Jiggy figured he'd never need to blow up the building. The company would blow up all on its own soon enough.

Besides, there was the flap-eared malevolent dwarf in the justice department to consider. That guy would use a firestorm at a marijuana facility to further his own twisted, purposely ignorant and fucked-up agenda. The rest of the folks — the majorly dumb-assed, too stupid and complacent to look any further than the shit that puts them to sleep in the first place — would never wake up either. No matter how big the bang. They'd just keep pointing fingers at the easiest scapegoats. The trance was strong everywhere. It was all too bad but he had to admit divesting himself took a weight off his shoulders.

As the sun started to set, Jiggy removed his prosthetic foot and rested it on the blanket. The end of his severed ankle felt good in the warm sand. He'd had a couple of Cuba libres and two capsules of high-THC marijuana oil — they looked like vitamin A. As he told Gina —without of course mentioning the reason why he should suddenly think of this — "Even if some fuckin' corporate interest is just waitin' to make another money-grubbin' move, the people who work there still depend on that place. An' they might not have very long." Layoffs and firings, as Jiggy saw them, being the most skilled handiwork of a new crop of executives.

"Say what?" Gina was examining a shell she'd found.

"The workers at CannRose. They care about stuff. Right? Their kids, their house. They hardly ever see what's goin' on. They almost never get it right. But still."

"Yeah, I think most of 'em are busy with their lives."

"They try. They try real hard. You gotta hand 'em that."

"We try hard too, Jiggy."

"I guess we do with the farm an' everything."

"And Ray's gotten a lot better working there. Don't you think? I think it's great he's back with the drums again."

"Yeah, Little Cousin's gettin' a bit of life back to him. I noticed that too. Helps he's only workin' half time. I think he's spendin' the other half in the woods!"

"He's havin' a kid too. Don't forget that!"

"How could I? You keep remindin' me."

"I think it'll be fun."

"You might be right. We get to watch. Don't have to pay the bills or change the diapers." And at that moment, Jiggy had another insight. He realized he cared about tangible things. More than just Gina and the farm. These other associations and his recognition of them made his world surprisingly a little bigger and a little brighter.

Chapter 28

Ray was tired from his graveyard shift at CannRose and was looking forward to having his breakfast back at the farm. Bertha would beg of course and he would give in. When Gina and Jiggy came back from Cuba they'd give him hell for sharing his meals with the dog. But she was too entertaining around food. You could put a small piece of buttered toast on her nose. She would sit and slightly cross her eyes as she looked at it, and then with a swift roll of her head she'd tumble it off, catch it in her mouth and usually swallow it whole. Unless Ray put a gob of peanut butter on it. In which case her mouth would keep going for a minute or two. Ray had videoed her doing this and gotten right up close as she negotiated the peanut butter.

Thinking about food, even if it was for the dog, made Ray hungrier. So when Guido rather than Alex, who was scheduled for the day shift, showed up at the facility at 5:45 a.m. and came straight into the security office, Ray was a little annoyed. He'd begun to see Jiggy's point about Guido. He was up to something, except it was all perfectly legal as far as Ray could see.

"The truly outstandin' criminals often own the operations they pilfer," Jiggy had said. "Take bankers, for instance."

Even though Ray couldn't say what kind of pilfering might be going on, he did see that the "streamlining and efficiency" efforts were causing a lot of heartache. Guido's old-world charm was wearing thin. Ray wondered if he was coming in early to fire him so they could bring in a cheaper head of security.

"Ray. How are you this fine frosty morning? It's invigorating for an old man you know. Getting up in the dark. Gets the blood pumping."

"I'm good, thanks."

"Ray, I have a favor to ask. Well, it's not a favor exactly. The job, I think, falls best to you as head of security." He smiled benevolently and let his hands fall open to express his helplessness in the face of facts. "Yes. Anyway. The Lyston dispensary is in need of camera work. One has bad image quality, and according to the last inspection, the position of another is not right. Big blind spot, something like that. Sammy is worried because the unpleasant inspector is due for a follow-up visit. Soon, Sammy says."

"Okay. I'm pretty sure I can look after that."

"Sammy will be very happy. I know. When can I let her know you're coming?"

Ray found this a little odd. He could just phone her himself. Guido was as much of a micro-manager as Caldwell had been. Ray sighed. "I can probably make it there this afternoon once I get some sleep."

"Wonderful, Ray. I'll let her know. She's still sleeping." And Guido smiled as if he were picturing this.

Ray was somewhat taken aback by the remark. He was pretty obsessed with Sammy for a while but recent interactions had been easy, like he was with his friends in Jersey. It was a good thing because he often saw her now that she was the director of sales in charge of both dispensary outlets. Alice, the previous director, had just resigned. Everybody said it was because of the recall, but Ray also couldn't help wondering if she'd been forced out by Guido and the new CEO.

Guido was full of surprises, but this remark about Sammy was creepy. Maybe Guido was getting senile or this was his attempt at a bonding-over-lechery moment. If it was, Ray didn't bite. "Fine. I should be there by two o'clock."

"I will let her know over her eggs benedict. We are celebrating this morning. Three-month anniversary." And by then Guido was smiling like a Cheshire cat.

Ray stood up and nearly fell over his own chair as he made way for Alex, who'd just walked in the door. Alex eyed Guido warily.

"Ah, good morning, Alex." And the old man patted his own chest. Ray wondered if he was encouraging his heart to keep up the good work. "I should be going," Guido announced and smiled again broadly at the two of them. Then he turned and headed out the door. "Ciao," he called out.

"Bye," Ray said and stared after Guido. Ray felt like he'd just been smacked over the head with a flounder. He wondered who else knew Guido and Sammy were "celebrating." He'd have to talk to Ernie about this one. *And wait 'til Jiggy finds out.*

"What was that all about?" Alex looked worried.

"Your job is safe, my man. There goes a contented old bugger." Ray shook his head. What did she see in him? Money, money and money? Power? *Or maybe she just likes violin sonatas*, he thought.

#

There were only four cameras in the Lyston dispensary. From the back room, Ray began to run through the security feeds to see which camera was the problem. After a moment he could see the bad one was in the front, right over where Sammy was standing with a customer. Easy enough to replace as soon as they got out of the way. Ray wasn't sure which one needed repositioning. He tried to see things through the eyes of an inspector but he couldn't find any space omitted or blocked views. Whichever camera it was, he hoped moving it wouldn't entail ripping out a chunk of ceiling. He found a ladder by the back door and met Sammy as he came into the front section. He pointed to the camera he was going to replace.

"Yeah, that's the bad one," she said. "And the inspector didn't like the other one over there because somebody could crawl along that wall and then go into the back."

"Then the cameras in the back would catch them."

"I know. That's what I said. She wouldn't budge."

"What a nutcase."

"That's nothing. Time before she demanded to see every record in the place. Even confidential stuff. Said the code was amended again. Threatened me with closure."

"Was it amended?"

"No. Alice sent in an official complaint about her."

"Did it go anywhere?"

"Doubt it. The DOH is inaccessible at the best of times. They haven't even apologized for making us do that recall we never needed to do."

"Is that why Alice left? The recall?"

"It sure didn't help. But I think she just got tired of everything. Though she did say the state oversight of cannabis was way more trouble than anything the FDA had ever sent her way. And that would include the recall and our favorite DOH inspector."

"I wonder if that inspector is as much of a jerk with the other companies."

"She isn't!" Sammy exclaimed. "I have a good friend in the capital. He's with Medcan. He says she's not always cheery, but she's okay. And quite reasonable."

"Interesting. And speaking of good friends, congratulations on your three-month anniversary. How were the eggs benedict?"

Sammy caught the sauciness in Ray's question. "Don't you judge me, little boy!"

"Wouldn't dream of it."

"He's a gentleman, Ray. And he's got genuine style."

"Plays a mean violin."

"That too. He's very refined."

"I see." Ray grinned as he stared down at her hand, which now sported an expensive ring with a brilliant blue stone surrounded by what were undoubtedly diamonds. "Looks a little intense for aquamarine, not dark enough for sapphire."

"Paraiba tourmaline."

"Very nice! Rare?"

"Yes indeed." She smiled and Ray noted the Cheshire-like expression, similar to the one Guido had. "He knows how to treat a woman, Ray. Something you could learn I bet."

Ray laughed. "Maybe I'll hit him up for some pointers."

"My ex sure could have taken a few pointers from him."

It dawned on Ray, given the way Sammy just referred to her ex, that Guido might have been an escape out of something that was unpleasant. Her ex was the meanest-looking mountain of a man Ray had ever seen. Like he could take out the world heavyweight champion with one arm before breakfast. Ray imagined he'd have scared just about anybody. But maybe not Guido. Guido had Jason. *And if Jiggy's even half right, God knows who else*, Ray thought.

Ray spent the next two hours replacing the bad camera and then re-angling the other one so he didn't have to get into the ceiling and shift the wiring. It was finicky work and he had to keep referring back to the computer monitor so that he didn't lose the field of view too much the other way.

"That should keep the inspector quiet," Ray said, coming out of the back room, having checked the screen one last time.

"I swear she thinks we all spend our time figuring out how to get away with something."

Ray laughed. "Yup. She's pretty convinced we're up to no good. Mind you there was that business about Greg. "

"You really think it was true?"

"He retired in a hurry. I doubt the DEA just shows up on a whim every day."

"They never showed their faces here."

"Well if it is true, he was running the operation on the side. And he'd shut it all down. That's what Ernie said. Had nothing to do with this company."

"Guido thinks Greg might have murdered Caldwell."

"No way! Ernie says Greg just got nervous when the police decided it probably wasn't an accident."

"Greg thought he might be next?"

"Yup." Ray nodded. "You know, Ernie told me that Greg was worried Guido had maybe ordered a hit."

They both started laughing. In retrospect, the next day, Ray considered their laughter a mite sinister. Poor Caldwell. Ray bet he wouldn't be too happy with the way things were going at CannRose now. Everything was changing. Herbert, the new CEO, was a real cold fish of a bean counter nobody liked. Lazlo had been fired. And they brought in just one guy, Jeremy, to replace him and Greg — "After they'd fobbed as much work off on the underlings as they could," Jiggy noted.

Before Ray headed off home to Hullbrooke and his best girl, Bertha, he stopped at a little café on the edge of Lyston to pick up a coffee for the road. As he walked to the counter he did a double take. There ahead of him, already collecting her items for purchase and chatting with the barista, was that DOH inspector. She sure did keep turning up like a bad rash. People at CannRose shuddered at the very sight of her. Her being in town like this could really mean only one thing. The CannRose inspections would start the next day.

Ms. Ligner hadn't seen him. And unless she was going to sit down she'd be out the door again before he got his coffee ordered. He'd get on the phone and send out the alarm as soon as he got back in the truck. Sixteen hours notice was better than no notice. Unless of course she was traveling from somewhere else. He looked a little more closely at her. She was in casual attire. Those were hiking boots, not stilettos. Come to think of it she looked like she'd been mountain climbing or running some cross-country marathon. He watched her pay for a big, meaty-looking sandwich, coffee, two bottles of water and two nutbars. The nutbars didn't surprise him.

When Ray got back in his truck he sent out a few warning messages. He had that night off and the next two as well, so he'd miss the immediate fallout. The gods must have been on his side this month.

Chapter 29

Three days later, Ray showed up at the CannRose security office just after 5:30 p.m. One of the guards was sick, so everybody on security was doing twelve-hour shifts. Connie, who'd been on security all day, had texted him that afternoon about a problem with one of the cameras. It was very high up on an outside pole and a bird's nest was drooping over it. The nest, long vacated, was falling apart and blocking the view of most of the back of the building and the roof. Ray didn't relish climbing up ladders in the winter, but Connie could spot him.

"Anything earth shattering today?"

"Nope. Just the bird nest. Everybody's still reeling from the inspection. And more layoffs." Connie grimaced.

"Heard the inspection was a real honey," Ray said.

"Yeah. Percy told me to thank you for the heads-up, by the way. Cassie too. Didn't do much for security though. That witch sure has it in for us. Ligner and her assistant spent over five hours going through videos."

"You can't say she's not diligent."

"They didn't like the blips."

"Heard about that too."

"Rest of the time they spent on inventory and the waste facility. I bet they think we're selling it on the street."

Ray started to laugh. "We don't produce enough to put in the dispensaries!"

"I know. Cassie was all upset again 'cause someone screwed up the fertilizer and now they have toxic levels of something. Plants in the nursery rooms are all goin' brown around the edges. You gotta wonder what's next. More firings probably."

"Maybe plants don't like growing indoors all that much. Weakens their spirit. Or maybe they just don't like the people growing them."

"It's crazy. That's for sure. You know what Petra started today?"

"What?"

"She's playing classical music in the mother pods." Connie pointed to the little black box showing on the screen for the South Mother Pod. It was a good old ghetto blaster.

"What's she got them listening to? Mozart, Beethoven?"

"I don't know. I listen to country!"

Ray nodded. This was interesting. He never thought Petra, being a scientist, would consider something like that. Maybe the job was finally flipping her out, or she was hearing things too and thought the music would amuse the plants. "Let's get this bird's nest out of the way shall we?"

Ray collected the ladder and Connie put on her boots and parka. As they were walking out to the back of the building Connie said, "I know you said I could spot you, but can I go up the ladder instead?"

"Sure. You don't mind heights?"

"No. And if I slip you'll break my fall a lot better than I could break yours."

Connie was skinny and couldn't have been more than five two. She scaled the extension ladder to the top of the pole with ease and had the nest pulled down in seconds. When she got back down she said, "That's a really cool view up there. Maybe I'm paranoid, but I coulda swore I saw somebody in the woods up on the hill with binoculars checking out the grow facility and me in particular."

"Well, there're a lot of birders around here."

"Oh yeah?"

"Mostly they're out early. But you taking out a nest at sunset might not sit all that well with some of 'em."

Ray waited until everyone was gone before starting his first rounds for the evening. Since Sanjay quit and Caldwell couldn't make snap decisions about harvests and clonings from the grave, the place was always deserted after seven or eight o'clock. Just the way he liked it.

He went to check on the mother pods first. He was curious about Petra's music choices. The playlists for the North and West Mother Pods were loaded onto the touchscreen pads that sat in a rack outside each room. Ray was impressed she was using wireless speakers. The North Mother had various atonal and arrhythmic delights from twentieth-century heavies like Stockhausen and Berio and — WTF!

Jimmie Death Brother's Heaviest Heavy Metal Hits? Petra must be losing it. The West Mother playlist included Stravinsky, Prokofiev, Piazzolla and a few other modern melody-and-rhythm-conscious notables.

Ray stood outside the mother pods for a few minutes, closed his eyes and listened carefully. The plants were still eating light, but the noises coming from the South and West Pods, seemed a little more animated than usual. Ray stuck his head in the West Pod. *The Rite of Spring* was just wrapping up so there was rhythmic complexity, not to mention spring *was* just around the corner. And then he poked his head into the South Pod to hear what was on the ghetto blaster — a Vivaldi trumpet concerto. It made him smile and he got the distinct impression the plants were kind of crazy about it in a good way. The East Mother Pod had nothing, just the constant hum from the fans and the HVAC. Hmm. No jazz, rock, R & B, hip hop. No pop. Also interesting. When he opened the door to the North Mother Pod, the screeching Stockhausen piece nearly knocked him over. And the mothers weren't responding to it at all. They ignored it. *Wow*, Ray thought, *it would be so cool to just completely block out the stuff you don't like.*

#

Ray had been noticing blips in the security videos for weeks before the last inspection. The screens would sputter for a couple of seconds, as if the cameras had suddenly lost track of what they were doing, particularly when Ray switched the screen from one camera to another. He figured it might be the software, and he'd mentioned it to Jiggy just before Jiggy and Gina took off for Cuba. Jiggy told Ray he'd look into it when he got back. "Yeah, might be somethin' to do with the update, Little Cousin, no big deal."

But Ray decided to take a look at the software himself. It was mostly out of curiosity. He was learning Java and Python in his courses, but the surveillance software was C++. He knew there were similarities, but C++ was older, always compiled, and didn't get rid of its own garbage or something like that. More room for error probably. At one point he'd gotten himself a reference book but had trouble wading through it without a course deadline hanging over his head. But the blips in the security system gave him an idea. He could pretend he was a program himself, like *diff* or *FileMerge*. Formidably tedious but he'd get familiar with the coding that way and maybe he'd even come across something that could help Jiggy out.

When he eventually found backups on a cloud account, he was surprised. He thought Jiggy would have stored them away in the remote archives — a server in the little building in Hullbrooke that Lazlo owned and CannRose still rented. That's where all the video footage files were. There was a periodic hook-up to the other computer in security for those backup downloads, so maybe the stuff just landed on the cloud from that computer. Anyway it was something to ask about.

Ray spent a few hours every night working on his little excursion into C++, but he couldn't really see anything that was out of place and he got slightly confused with all the files. When Jiggy had customized and streamlined the security software, he told Ray there was an art to breaking up the C++ so it would be easier to implement upgrades. Also he just liked to have his programming the way he liked it. But seriously, there could be some tiny corruption anywhere — the libraries, the assembler, the compiler. Who knew? Ray thought he should double-check the isolated system though. See what was actually running. So far he'd just been comparing backups. He might as well be thorough.

After an hour or so and about fifty lines in on one of the subroutines, Ray saw something, a couple of lines of code that didn't match the backup file. They looked a little like, well, they looked like some kind of call but they didn't look like Jiggy's work. This was the update? Or could it be some kind of hack or spyware that hooked a ride in with it. Except Jiggy surely would have caught something like that, wouldn't he, even if the anti-malware missed it? Then again what kind of an idiot goes randomly combing through lines and lines of C++?

Ray had debated whether he should do something about it. That was a few days ago. Now because of the inspection, Jiggy would have to attend to the blipping-camera problem immediately. Maybe do overtime, depending how extensive it was, and get exhausted again right after his holiday. Ray thought he might as well go ahead and clean it up. He could always go back to the saved program if he did something wrong. And anyway, it might not have any effect one way or the other — could be just garbage.

When Ray got back to the security office after his first round for the evening, he pulled up the software on the isolated system again. He copied and saved. He edited and checked and edited and checked again, and then he checked it all two more times. And after his third security round of the night, he compiled it. And then he let it run. There was a major flicker in all the open camera screens and then things seemed to settle. Ray shifted from one block of cameras to another. No blip. He tried again. No blip. He let it run for a couple of hours then checked the video records. It was looking good. Maybe he'd fixed it! What were the odds? Crazy, that's for sure. Maybe it was spyware. There would likely be more of it lurking around in the other files or somewhere on the computer. Jiggy would probably blame the NSA.

As Ray was finishing off his fifth round of the evening and making his way back to the security office, he felt a sharp pain go up his spine. It was excruciating, just like when he'd been there for harvesting. Ray heard the screeching in his head again too. Maybe it was the Stockhausen! He hesitated. Ray's hand was on the door into the administration section. The screeching in his head got so loud it hurt. The plants were screaming. Demanding immediate attention. He'd missed something. He needed to go back to the cultivation rooms. He turned and took a step toward the horticulture section.

First there was a rumble. Then a flash and a roar.

A shudder made its way along every nerve and vibrated up to his head. It was almost familiar. He couldn't place it exactly though. It was as if each cell of his body had become a point of awareness. Everything slowed. He waited. There was more. The flash moved into him and the roar scooped him into what. Infinity? He soared with it. There were new lengths and odd spaces — a phantasmagoria of colors, vibrant and audacious, and so many tones in fractions whistling above a deep and lush pulse. A sonorous contentment. There was astonishing joy too. Was this it?

An answer boomed richly. Yes. This was it. Ray was done. Ray was done with this life. Then there came the juncture where he was grateful. For everything. It was familiar too. He basked in this. Perhaps it was his own eternity, his own personal absolute before the great dissolve. And yet . . . and yet there was this little thing, a nagging thing, a tiny wondering . . . *What of the plants?* It was a question barely murmured. Barely conceived. A wisp of a notion. But as the notion occurred there was a glowing. And out of the glow a towering obelisk appeared. Green and iridescent. It floated. The edges softened by the glow. Did it perhaps smell a little like skunk? He couldn't tell for sure. He was barely himself anymore, whatever that was.

The obelisk shimmered and began to dissolve, flowing into him like a neon river. The flowing was welcoming, warm, and Ray felt again loved and engulfed with patience and a deep resolution to prevail. It was better than all the happy accidents and excruciating surprises in a life.

Chapter 30

Ray came to and saw a very pretty dark-haired woman hovering above him. He watched as a thin lock of her hair fell from her shoulder toward him.

"Hello there! You're with us. Maybe a bit more this time." And then the woman walked a few steps away and he heard her call out, "David, he's awake again."

Ray was conscious of swallowing. His throat was raw, as if scraped by razors. The air entering his nose felt corrosive. He was aware of nausea too. He vaguely remembered a fireman and being in an ambulance with an oxygen mask covering his face. There was still one covering his face. A flashing recollection of people in scrubs racing him on a gurney through doors, and talking to people, but he couldn't remember what about. And then he recalled the roar. The blaze of light that seemed to come down the hallway from the IT room and then the *boom* to the right as the wall beside lifted off its bearings and seemed to fly away. Except he wasn't really in that part of the building when everything happened. He remembered that much as well. He'd been on the other side of the door and he'd turned around and was walking back. So how could he remember events like that if he hadn't seen them? It was curious and yet it was so vivid.

Ray closed his eyes. In an instant he was floating again. His mind was quiet, empty. And he sensed again a vast and ineffable freedom. It was a deep recognition in him. As if he were speeding into so many dimensions, and all time was shrunk to the head of a pin. Ray again met a multiverse of infinite particulars. An expansion dissipating to the void. All analysis defied. He was the paradox and the miracle. This sensation did not last. It was just a momentary flicker, like the other recollections from the previous night. He would never speak about this but he would long for it.

And he knew it had changed him. The dying. That's how he would think of it: The Dying. And as he came back to this world, he thought perhaps his brain was scrambled now for good in his dim and rough occupation of a body. He wondered if any more parts of him were missing. His right leg squealed unpleasantly. Something was off there for sure.

"Hello!"

The man's voice gave Ray a jolt and he opened his eyes again. The woman reached around and lifted Ray's head a little and took the mask off Ray's face.

"How you feelin'?"

"Crappy." It came out as a whisper.

"Yeah, I bet. So I'm David . . . the emerge doc. And this is your very competent and kindly nurse, Janet. She's been with you since you came in. We knocked you out once we saw you could breathe. You were in a lot of pain. You're a fortunate man. Much longer in that building and you wouldn't have made it."

"Yeah." Ray could still only whisper.

"So. Can you tell me your name?"

"Ray."

"Ray, that's good.

"You know what day it is, Ray?

"Valentine's Day."

"It is! And how are old are you?"

"Twenty-eight, going on luck."

"Great, we got wit here!" David smiled.

Ray heard a faint whirring noise and the bed lifted him into a more upright position. Janet put a pillow behind his back and he felt a very uncomfortable twinge. He looked down at his leg. It was still there. A point for wholeness.

"Got a headache?" David asked.

"I don't think so."

They ran through some simple tests. And then the doctor told him to squeeze Janet's fingers. He did so first with his left hand and then when she offered her fingers to his right hand he grabbed them and kissed her thumb. She laughed.

"He's a Romeo too! Love helps the healing," David noted.

Ray looked up.

"Overall you're looking pretty good, Ray. Your CT's good too. Mostly it's the carbon monoxide that worries us and whatever else was in that smoke. So we want to keep you here for a few days. Any sudden dizziness, visual problems, breathing problems, vomiting . . ."

Ray was nodding like he'd heard it all before, which he had from the medic in Iraq.

David wrote a few things down. "Somebody at your work's been trying to get in touch with your relatives. Gina and—"

"They shouldn't bother them," Ray said with some urgency. "They're on holiday!"

"Okay. We can pass that along," the doctor said and then turning to Janet, "I love what this sedative brings out in people. Ray here's almost killed and he's still making sure his sister or whoever gets a nice holiday. I like that."

"There . . . are animals at the farm," Ray whispered with the same urgency.

"Yup. I think somebody's got that too. Somebody called Ernie? Sound right?"

Ray nodded.

Another woman came into the room.

"Ah. Perfect timing. This is Dr. Jandra, and she'll take it from here."

"Am I in Lyston?"

"Yup. Hullbrooke only does the corpses." He winked at Ray as he left the room and handed the file to Dr. Jandra.

Dr. Jandra was carrying a portable touchscreen and set it up for him to look at the x-ray images of his leg.

"You're lucky, Ray. The paramedic told us they found you half under a collapsed wall. You've got three broken ribs, and here you can see the shin is badly fractured just below the knee . . . the tibia is going to need a nail." The doctor continued but Ray didn't hear much of what she was saying. He was looking at her eyes. At the slight amber fleck in her iris, just to the right of the pupil in her left eye. He thought it must signify something; this tiny imperfection sprouting up in the rich earthy color around it. Was it the point of an infinity too? The imperfections and the blips always took him there and it was always more than he could grasp. Greater even than the warm concern that seemed to be emanating from her.

"So we need you to sign a couple of forms here. Just a local anesthetic we'll be using."

Ray began to pay attention to the words again and awkwardly took the pen. He tried to read what was on the page. It didn't make all that much sense but he didn't see the word *amputate* anywhere, so he signed.

"You're going to be on crutches for quite a few weeks. You'll get good at hopping." She smiled.

Ray smiled back. Were other women that pretty and he just hadn't noticed? He had never seen such beautiful eyes. And he wanted to laugh.

#

Jiggy was in a daze. He had been ever since he and Gina drove up the driveway after their holiday and met Ernie coming out of the barn with a bucket in his hand. Gina had burst into tears at the news that Ray had been hurt. "God! You could have been there too, Jiggy. You both could have been killed!" Once she calmed down, she got in her car and drove straight to Lyston to be with Ray. Jiggy stayed back to finish the chores. He was exhausted. The highways up north had been icy on the way back from Montreal. He'd driven white-knuckled and teeth clenched for several hours. His absent foot was bitching again. Once Ernie was gone and the chores finished, all Jiggy wanted was to smoke himself into a stupor. It wasn't a thing he usually did. Right then he just couldn't face the whole situation. The next morning after Gina left for work, his brain moved into overdrive.

That explosion should never have happened. The whole program was buried, encrypted. There were a series of actions and linked coding only Jiggy knew about and virtually all of them on the isolated system. And there were no back doors! Jiggy'd made sure of that. A hacker would have to make it his life's work just to get into that system in the first place, never mind find his cascade of programs or even recognize them as a sequence. It didn't run completely. That was clear. But it shouldn't have run at all. And certainly not with anyone in the building. What the fuck happened?

Jiggy figured he must have become so screwed up or old he'd lost his touch. That someone had been there when the place started to blow made Jiggy sick to his stomach. That it was Ray was unbearable. It took Jiggy three days before he could face a visit with Ray. Gina figured it was just he hated hospitals and any reminder of his own experiences. At least that was the excuse she made for him.

Ray was happy to see Jiggy when he finally showed up. He'd been wanting to tell him about how he'd been getting familiar with C++ and found this weird coding on the isolated system in the security software. He'd gotten rid of it and it had stopped the blips. At least for a short time. A fat lot of good that had done though. All the equipment in the security office was fried now. The IT room gone too!

Jiggy almost threw up hearing all this.

Ray went on to tell Jiggy about his theory that maybe the last update was corrupted in some way, maybe even planned so the saboteurs could sneak in undetected. Timing. Whoever tried to blow the place up, maybe it was all about timing. Anyway he was really glad the plants were all still fine. Wasn't that lucky? And now everybody was waiting for Jiggy to sort out the backups.

They sat in silence for a few moments.

"Ray, you're like my little brother. You know that."

Ray thought he saw tears in Jiggy's eyes. Maybe the painkillers were tricking his perception.

"I'm so sorry," Jiggy said.

"Wasn't your fault," Ray replied.

Jiggy wasn't looking at Ray anymore. He was staring at the flowers and the basket of fruit on the table. A notion occurred to Ray. Just for an instant. But Ray put that notion right out of his mind. He'd had too many talks over beer and bourbon where Jiggy would end up apologizing indiscriminately.

"It's okay, Jiggy. Wasn't that bad. Just a little smoke inhalation, busted rib or two and my leg is gonna be fine. I'll probably be outta here by tomorrow or the day after."

Jiggy nodded, still staring at the table.

"I'll be bugging the crap outta you and Gina again in no time."

"Jesus, Ray! You've never bugged the crap out of us. What the fuck are you talkin' about?"

Ray laughed. Some things you could count on. Touchy old Jiggy.

"You're easier to live with than I am," Jiggy said.

"No shit!"

"Gina'd vouch for that in a heartbeat!"

"Gina'd vouch for that in a heartbeat!" Ray mimicked and started to laugh again even though it hurt. He was aware, in spite of all the pain killers, it was high time he moved out of his cousin's relationship. Totally and forever. Even if it meant camping in a blizzard. Ray started to feel really sleepy. He yawned. Jiggy noticed.

"Gina's gonna come see you before she goes to work tomorrow. I'll come later in the morning."

"Okay,' said Ray, smiling.

"You need anything, Little Cousin?"

"No, I'm more than well taken care of here."

"I can see that. CannRose's medical plan is better than I thought."

"No. It's Lydia. She insisted on the private room and everything. She's been here every day. She's even set up a fund for my physio. It's really nice of her."

The information made a bigger knot in Jiggy's stomach. Had he ever considered Lydia anything other than a brainless rich ho?

Ray yawned. "You know, I think she misses the way CannRose used to be. I think she really misses Caldwell." Ray was smiling to himself and remembering the times he and Lydia just sat in the grow rooms looking at the plants. He'd never mentioned what he was hearing from them because it seemed to him she might already know.

"What's this?" Jiggy asked, looking at a thin, beat-up book with a corduroy cover lying on the bed.

"Old poems by marijuana plants." Ray began to laugh at the coincidence and happy nuttiness of his situation, but it gave him such a twinge of pain he gasped. "Damian wanted me to have it because I've borrowed it a few times. One time I forgot to take it back and I think he was pissed. Did you know he's quitting?"

"No."

"He says nobody could pay him enough money to stay after the fire."

"Can't say I blame him."

"He thinks the place was jinxed from start . . . But I don't think so . . ." And Ray was smiling to himself again.

"Ray, there's gotta be something I can get ya. Magazines? DVDs? Junk food?"

"You don't have to fuss, Jiggy."

"I fuckin' well do too. So you're just gonna have to get used to it."

"Well in that case, I wouldn't mind a couple of congas to round out my percussion collection."

"Done," said Jiggy.

"I'm only kidding."

"No. Too late now. You're gettin' 'em. Sleep tight, Little Cousin."

"Night, Jiggy."

Jiggy climbed into his truck in the hospital parking lot. He sat there for a minute and without a sound or even a breath, tears started pouring down his cheeks. Had anyone been passing by they would have seen a face so contorted they might have thought Jiggy was having a heart attack. But how could anyone help? Jiggy had nearly killed the best kid he knew. The kid Gina loved like he was her own son. How could he live with that? That, along with the other shit he'd seen and done. Or been helpless to do anything about.

The memories came crashing in. The times he had to "confer" with toadies of the "recognized and rightful regime" or some warlord, where he couldn't miss the screams from down the hallway or the gaunt dead faces staring at him from behind bars as he left. Idiots from his own unit making deadly mistakes and covering their asses by throwing the guy least likely to fight back under the bus. Collateral damage profuse and unending, staring back from fields and street corners. Everywhere he looked, ordinary people's lives maimed and destroyed for no other reason than living in the wrong fucking country.

Jiggy caught his breath in a moan but he couldn't stop. He wept until the sun went down. Until he was empty. Numb. He sat in his truck and watched the stars come out. He noticed his own breathing. It calmed him while he took in the spread of the night sky. The billions of galaxies stared back, unblinking and unmoved by his personal sorrows. The stars in them spun with their tiny planets, the revolutions and their speed of retreat accelerating in the universal expansion. He was nothing and becoming even less with every second. Thank God.

#

Two weeks after the fire, people who usually worked in the administrative section began operating out of a couple of jobsite trailers. Jiggy was working in one of them himself. And that morning, Jason, who had never said more than half a dozen words to Jiggy, raised his chin like he had something important to say. And he did. "They nabbed her."

"Nabbed who?" Jiggy said.

"The piece of work. That inspector from the DOH. She's under arrest." Jason shoved his hands deeper into his pockets, closing the front of his leather jacket as if he were cold.

"I can believe that." Jiggy stared at the gold chain hanging around the man's neck and wondered how much it weighed. "Hardly surprising a government employee is corrupt."

"Yeah. First they don't even want to show up because it's 'a state problem.' Now they're pissing their pants congratulating each other. They had to 'make sure she wasn't some part of a terrorist cell.' Give me a break."

"Wait, what? Who's they?"

"That little shmuck. Idiot from the ATF. He called Guido an hour ago. Guido's out buying champagne now."

"The ATF." Jiggy's voiced dropped at this mention. It produced an almost altered state in him. He'd always thought it ludicrous the Department of Alcohol, Tobacco, Firearms and Explosives, left off the E — the most important letter of all. And right now the ATF seemed so very close. So very intimate, and surely a meeting with them was in his near future. That's what Jiggy had supposed . . .

"FBI still has a file on her whole family. The shmuck didn't elaborate."

At the mention of the FBI, Jiggy began to return to the moment and realize the significance of what had just been said. "So . . . so they think she's connected with . . . that?" He pointed out the window to the wreckage.

"*Ben oui.*" Jason sniffed. "They said she's not mentally stable."

"Seriously? They really think she had somethin' to do with it?" Jiggy stared out the window, incredulous.

"Not just something. She did it! How she did it with only one drone, they don't know yet."

"A drone!" Jiggy looked at Jason. "She had a fuckin' drone?"

"They found some pieces."

"Was it armed?"

"*Je sais pas.*" Jason shrugged. "The shmuck says she was staking us out for weeks. Planned everything. *Câlisse!* Look what blew up. The admin section — maybe a message for the execs. Guido says maybe she's got shares with some big producer. Could be industry sabotage."

"She had a fuckin' drone." Jiggy shook his head. "That's crazy."

"*Mets-en!* She pays cash for it, then dumps the remote, dumps all the other evidence, but she's already registered online for the warranty." Jason laughed. "*C'est fucké!*"

Never having seen Jason smile before, let alone laugh, Jiggy took a deep breath. Then he looked straight up at the trailer ceiling and mentally counted to five. It was a game he'd always played with himself when the insurgency reports came in. It allowed him to tuck away memories in a particularly deep fold of his brain so that by the time he got to five, any remorse could join the other memories in a cerebral safe house. "A fuckin' drone," he said, shaking his head, and he turned around and walked out the trailer door, closer to being himself again.

By that afternoon, the news was all over the facility. People were looking relieved but also indulging in extreme Schadenfreude. The wicked bitch from the DOH had gotten her comeuppance. And they were loving every minute of it.

Jiggy ran into Ernie who was exceptionally cheerful. "Hey Jiggy, you know the sheep farmer at the back of this place?"

"Ollie, yeah."

"He's the one called it in! Told me all about it. He was picking up a load of hay and on his way back sees her little white car just sitting on the side of the road, nobody in it."

"Oh."

"He notes the license plate because it's a thing with him. Then he's out in the barn with one of the ewes at three in the morning when the explosion goes off. He comes out to look and what does he see but her car racing by like a bat outta hell. Fucking crazy man!"

"Yeah, fucking crazy all right."

"Lucky the fire department got there when they did. How's Ray now? How's he doing?"

Jiggy felt his knees flutter again. A part of him was fading at the mention of his Little Cousin. "Oh, pretty well. He's outta the hospital now, back with us. Gina's takin' good care of him."

Lily had just stepped into the trailer where they were all talking and heard the tail end of the conversation. "Hope he liked the gift basket from all of us."

"Yeah, he sure did. I'm sorry, I keep forgettin' to bring in the thank-you card. Sittin' right by the door too."

"Hey, I think everybody's a bit discombobulated these days. We're just so glad Ray's okay."

"Me too," Jiggy said.

#

Jiggy had planned what he might say when agents showed up at his door. He thought giving them a piece of his mind about the rising police state, the thugs running the show and the state of democracy in America generally would be a no-brainer, since he'd be toast. Maybe a lawyer could plead insanity. He'd still be toast. And deep down part of him wanted to be toast. He deserved it because of Ray. But they never showed. And now he was thinking they probably never would. They'd only questioned him like they'd questioned everyone else. And they even brought up Ray's theory about some spyware on the security system that might be involved in a stakeout. They asked him what he thought about it. Jiggy didn't lie. He said checking the isolated system had been the first thing on his To Do list. They didn't press the issue.

When Jiggy went to remove his explosives, he found no evidence his work had been touched. No one had bothered to check the innards of the security system or the wiring in the rest of building, or if they did, they didn't have a clue what they were looking for. He suspected the former. No one had pulled apart the ceilings or checked the walls in the production area. Nor had they checked all the other little crevices and corners around the surveillance system where the stupendous and creative material sat waiting for instructions. It was all undisturbed. Undisturbed for months and months and collecting dust.

So Jiggy methodically went through the building and removed everything that remained. He even combed through the wreckage once the ATF had finished with it. He told the lads on security he was looking for any components that might have escaped damage, batteries and parts with heavy metals that shouldn't end up in a landfill. Nobody questioned it and nobody paid any attention to what he was doing. And in the wreckage he found a couple of Gordo's specially made, biodegradable explosives, and plenty of the incendiary splinters too. Clearly the ATF didn't know what they were looking for either. The only place where everything detonated was the conference room. Maybe Gordo's inventions had an expiry date.

There was certainly something very peculiar about the pattern of damage to the administration section. When Ray had accidentally set off the destructive cascade it didn't follow the route Jiggy had set for it. But Jiggy had been too depressed about Ray to dwell on that at the time. Jiggy took two days to disarm everything in the production area and four days to get it all out of the facility. Smuggling the materials out of CannRose was easier than smuggling them in had been.

Back at the farm, Jiggy dug a ten-foot-long ditch in the still partly frozen soil. It was in the back field as far away from everything as it could be. The microbes wouldn't wake up for a while. Jiggy figured it would be April before it was really gone. "A couple of weeks," Gordo said, "and all the little soil bugs and fungus will turn it into black earth."

A day after Jiggy got the news, another investigator showed up at the facility and pulled apart the ceiling in one of the very smoke-damaged washrooms. Jiggy certainly hadn't bothered with anything there. The agent also scoured the wreckage again and the loading dock. When Jiggy found out about the bugging, and that some extra wireless system had been surreptitiously installed, a few things fell into place. Actually one in particular: Interference! Cameras and the window alarms in the front of the building were wireless. Jiggy'd been extremely careful setting up channels but obviously not careful enough. And who knows, maybe she had planted a bomb of her own and dropped off a packet or two of traditional accelerants with her drone.

Chaos is not for deciphering. It's very useful that way. Jiggy counted to five one more time and really was almost back to being himself again.

Chapter 31

Larry came to visit the day after Ray got out of the hospital. "I stopped by your place on the way down. We have work to do."

Ray brightened up. He might end up owing a lot of favors but if Larry was offering to help finish the wiring and anything else, he'd be really grateful. Right now Larry was staring at the leg with the nails in it.

"You want me to do something for that?"

"Sure."

"You got some injury here too, right?" Larry was pointing at Ray's broken ribs.

"Yup."

Larry put his hand on Ray's chest. His hand was warm, almost hot, and Ray felt kind of a buzzing coming from it. Then Larry put his hands over Ray's calf where the bone was broken and he felt the same sensation there.

"Ribs should heal up pretty quick. You still got trouble breathing?"

"No. Hurts when I cough though. Or laugh."

Larry nodded. "You got a problem at your place you know."

"I know," Ray said. "I just got bogged down. Kept finding other things to do."

"That's not what I mean. You got a different kind of problem."

"Like . . ."

"We need to really clean your place up. Dark spirits, my friend."

"Dark spirits?" Ray almost laughed.

Larry shook his head. "This isn't a joke."

"Seriously?"

"Yeah. It's not live and not dead either."

"Sounds like zombies."

"Don't laugh. It hurts, remember."

"How do you know it's dark spirits?"

"I walked right into it, man. Made me sick."

"At my place."

"Yeah. It's sucking energy out of your land. Out of you too probably. You can't get work done, right?"

"That's just because I'm lazy."

"Maybe. But that thing isn't helping."

"So how does that work?"

"Like I said. It's not live and not dead either. You know somebody like that?"

Ray smiled and shook his head.

"It's . . . almost malevolent, you know," Larry said. "Yeah, malevolent. That's a good word for it. Definitely not happy. Angry probably. Darker than your shoes."

"Maybe that inspector who blew CannRose up?"

Larry closed his eyes for a minute then shook his head. "I don't think so. This is very old stuff. You got a bit of its imprint."

"I do?"

"Look at what just happened to you! You need to pay attention to what this is telling you."

Ray was suddenly very tired.

Larry sighed. "So you don't know anybody? Maybe they're senile? Maybe in a coma?"

"Oh!"

"You do know."

"Maybe. The guy who used to own the property. He's in a coma or something. In some nursing home somewhere."

"Yeah. That would fit!"

"He came back like that. Nobody knew what happened to him."

"I bet he knows. We need a ceremony, my friend. I'm calling my cousin."

"Really?"

"Not so much my area of expertise. Could be difficult. We need more people. More energy. Critical energy, like critical mass maybe."

"So . . . this is like possession or something?" Ray was mildly uneasy at the thought.

"No. But maybe someone's done something to him. Feels like ropes. Ropes of energy tying the person up. Like a bug builds a cocoon. Only you'd never do that to yourself. And some little part, maybe mad as hell, has gotten away. That's what's sitting on your property. Maybe even feeding the other part."

"Creepy."

"It is."

"So when do we do this ceremony?"

"Soon," Larry said. "Once we get rid of it, we'll finish the wiring."

Three weeks later Ray, Larry, his cousin Alma and her friend, an older woman called Ruth, all met in the early evening at Ray's place. Larry told him to watch what he ate. In fact it might be a good idea to fast that day and the day before.

They built a fire and found stones and put them in circles. They'd also brought their own objects and herbs. The two women went down to the river and brought back more stones, a bird skull and lots of old bulrushes from the season before. The women told Larry and Ray that the reason the man was stuck in that awful place was poison. Plant or maybe animal poison had caught him and also the things he'd done caught him. They thought he had blood on his hands. It's how the ropes held him fast. It could be someone with dark arts helped put him there, bound him up with his own misdeeds and malice, but whoever that was had a lot of help from spirits and the ancestors. It was very powerful. Not anything the women liked to engage with. They would limit their focus to Ray's property. The rest was out of their hands.

Larry brought two drums: One was goblet shaped and ornate with what looked like bone inlays. The skin on top was secured with a metal band and screws for tightening, very much like a conga. The other drum was flat, more like a large tambourine, and there were some rings that jingled very subtly. Larry handed the goblet-shaped one to Ray. "Keep it simple, okay? It's just to get you there. So pay attention." So that's what Ray did. He followed Larry's lead, and after a while he had to put the drum down. He could barely focus on what he was doing. The ceremony went on all night. Ruth and Alma seemed to go into trances periodically. They brought more water up from the river. They kept the fire and the smoke and steam going and drank some herbal concoction. Larry told Ray the marijuana was on his side. It had saved his life. Ray could use it now. He was sure it wouldn't hurt him. And it might help the ceremony. Larry had brought some and told him he should eat a little of it first. So Ray did. Ray asked Larry if he and the women were eating some as well or making tea with it and Larry said no, it wasn't their plant. They had other plants that were closer to them that they used for healing.

About a half hour after Ray ate the marijuana, he started seeing everything in slow motion. He looked at the two women. Alma was drumming now. Ruth was inhaling smoke and then spitting it out with force. Larry was sitting cross-legged nearby with his eyes closed, and Ray saw a form loom up out of Larry's shoulders. When he looked closer at the women, he could see something shifted a little out of their bodies too. The three of them were suspending this dark, amorphous, almost sputtering mist between them. Ray didn't know what he should do, if anything. He realized at that point there was always a mantis that took him to the new places and taught him, especially when he was around cannabis. He didn't see one anywhere and then he remembered to close his eyes. Gradually a familiar head came into view. The antennae waved casually.

So, it said, *you want to play in the big time!*

"I don't know."

That's wise. Keep that.

"What can be done?"

They are doing it.

"Can I help?"

The one who loves us can help.

"How?"

Smoke.

"Like Ruth?"

Better underneath.

Larry's bag of dried marijuana was beside Ray. He took a few buds out of the bag and put them on a flat rock. They were very dry, and after he lit them, he moved the rock between the three of them. He'd lost sight of the dark energy by that point, but then he felt it hovering. He was too close and almost fainted from the wave of nausea that overtook him. He leaned away quickly. Then he slid himself back along the ground and stayed at a distance. He closed his eyes again.

You weren't paying enough attention, the mantis said.

"I know."

But you're getting better.

"I am."

Travel with the smoke. It's less treacherous.

So Ray opened his eyes. He saw the smoke coming from the buds on the rock. He stared at it. Then he closed his eyes again and without any thought he became the smoke. He felt the darkness of the aberrant energy but he could slip within it. He could move through it. He could circle it. He kept moving through and around it until he felt a change in it. It was becoming softer, lighter, more like smoke itself.

Very good! The mantis came into view.

Ray felt exhilarated.

The mantis vanished right into the middle of his forehead and he heard it throwing things around in there. Then it reappeared holding a small dark and very flat pebble. The mantis chortled and Ray followed it down to the river where it threw the pebble so it skipped across the water surface and then sank.

Ray opened his eyes. Larry, Ruth and Alma were still in the same formation, singing quietly though without words, and in some mode that had microtones and the strangest harmonies Ray had ever heard. The intensity of the singing and drumming began to increase and gradually rose to a fever pitch. They were wailing. Until they stopped suddenly. Everything went silent and for several moments they were motionless. Then they looked at each other and began laughing; there was such relief. It was a while before they could stop. When they quieted down again, Ruth closed the night's work and thanked all the helping spirits, the earth and the elements, and each person turned to face one of the four directions; Ray was looking south. Then they all trooped up to the old loft to watch the sun come up. And Ray made coffee for everybody.

#

Over the next few weeks Ray felt a new lightness everywhere he looked on his farm. The snow was thawing. The pussy willows were starting to show and when he checked some of the planting and trimming he'd done in the fall, he realized the land was transforming itself with only just a little help from him. As if all it ever needed was some appreciation and understanding. Ray knew the more he paid attention and acted on his perceptions the better the place would grow. He'd gleaned, for example, that if he wanted a vegetable garden, he shouldn't put it where the old one had been. It should be on the flat area, farther down the slope, halfway between the old barn and the creek. And he should mulch it with the dead and dried grasses and cattails from the marsh. And if he wanted roses, he should plant climbing ones on the west side of the house. And he could rebalance and strengthen his patch of woodland by removing just a few particular trees here and there. If he listened well enough, there were instructions from all the plants. His farm was going to be paradise. It was determined to be a paradise. All he had to do was pay attention.

Ray thought he was a changed man. Overnight it seemed he was encouraged by life. While he was in the hospital, Julie had given birth. She swore that hearing about Ray's accident was what sent her into labor. Then they were so busy with the new baby, all they could manage were a few phone calls and one Skype session. Anna and Julie finally came to visit Ray when they felt confident enough to travel. They stayed at Gina and Jiggy's farm.

The weekend had been a revelation. Even just holding the baby gave Ray a surge of energy. And of course when the baby grabbed his fingers he melted like most new dads. Gina had a delightful time. She said it was even more fun than their holiday had been. Ray saw a tender side of Jiggy he'd never expected. Jiggy was so careful handling the baby and laying it down for a nap. He said he figured Ray had worked out the smartest way to have a kid. He wouldn't have to lose nearly as much sleep as most fathers do. Ray figured he'd still probably lose a lot of sleep. Already he couldn't believe how protective he felt.

After Julie and Anna left, Ray was feeling so good he decided to call up his old drum teacher, Oscar. Ray hadn't talked to him since before he'd joined the army. Oscar had been surprised to hear from him but said sure, Ray could come for a visit. They arranged for the Tuesday after the following weekend. Ray was going to New Jersey for Gabe's birthday party and of course he would spend a couple of days with Julie and Anna on the way back.

#

Oscar lived on Canal Street over an old photocopy shop that was now closed and boarded up. The ancient sign on the window said Nick's Noodle House Coming Soon. Ray had gone there for lessons from the time he was thirteen.

"Well! How you doin'? Jesus, I barely recognize you!"

"I guess I changed a bit. You're looking good! Little bit grayer maybe." And Ray stroked his own chin to indicate Oscar's beard.

"You're lookin' gimpy! I thought you finished with that army shit a few years ago."

"This was a different explosion."

"Jeez, you remind me of that knight in Monty Python. C'mon in. You want a coffee or somethin' stronger? You drinkin' stronger things these days?"

"Coffee would be great." Oscar motioned to the chairs at the table and padded off into the kitchenette. Ray sat down and put his crutch under his chair. He could see Oscar pouring cups of coffee from an ancient coffee maker.

"Place still looks the same."

"Yeah." Oscar came in with the coffees, then went back to get the sugar and a small carton of cream.

"You been at Collette's today?" he said as he sat down.

"Thanks." Ray held up his coffee. "I was there overnight."

"Haven't talked to her in a month or so. How's she doin'? How's Alvin?"

"She's fine. Worried. He's starting to show a few more symptoms."

"Terrible. Hey, I hear weed helps with Parkinson's. Imagine he's only too happy to get himself a prescription."

"He's having fun with it. Teases Aunt Collette."

"Ha! I'll bet."

They fell silent. Just sat and drank their coffee. Finally Oscar said, "So what brings you here to my little place, Ray?"

"Well . . . I wanted to say hi. I haven't seen you in ages."

"No you haven't seen me in ages. So how come you're knockin' on my door now?"

"Well—"

"You know, why not when you were on leave, maybe, or five years ago when you got out of the army?"

Oscar's question caught Ray off guard. From the phone call he'd had no indication Oscar might be upset with him. "Well, I-I've started doing some practicing again. You know getting back into playing a little, however that works." He looked at his hands, especially his right hand, rather than at Oscar.

Oscar tilted his head back and squinted at Ray. "Oh you been practicing a little? I been practicing for the last fifty years, motha fucka! You tell me why I should even take you seriously for a second?"

"Well, I know it looks peculiar but I'm managing to compensate and—"

"I mean I get it that you didn't want that scholarship. Lots of opportunities here in the city. Less academic. And God knows Collette shoved more than enough theory, history, ear straining and sight screaming down your throat. I still remember you doing that solfège and your voice was starting to break. You were hilarious, man. But you broke my heart, Ray. You know that, you little prick? I put a lot of my time and my best efforts your way. And you just fucked off without a word."

Ray sat there silent. He shouldn't have come.

"I didn't know what to expect when you called," Oscar continued. "Figured maybe you might be comin' to apologize. Take me for a drink. We shoot the breeze. Talk about everything but drums. Know what I'm sayin'?"

"I'd love to buy you a drink, Oscar, and . . . I-I am sorry. I'm—"

"I don't have time for you. Look at you. You're crippled. That leg ever gonna work again? You're minus fingers. Don't insult my intelligence, man."

"But . . ." Ray looked up at Oscar.

"Get outta here, man!"

Ray sat paralyzed for a second. He felt all his strength drain away. The universe was still happy to crash in on him. But he invited it at every turn, didn't he? He forced a smile. He couldn't make eye contact with Oscar. He picked up his crutch and limped his way over to the door. He wanted to say goodbye at least, but nothing came out when he opened his mouth.

Oscar moved quickly. He put his hand on the doorknob before Ray got to it. "Jesus. You are a pathetic sorry-assed mess. Like my ex, the drama queen. You even travel with your own fucking props!" He tapped Ray's crutch. Ray still couldn't look him in the eye. Oscar tapped Ray's crutch again. Ray finally looked up and Oscar saw the resignation and defeat. There were tears in Ray's eyes.

"Ha," Oscar said. "Thought so." He stood with his hand still on the doorknob so Ray had to stand there too. Oscar heaved a sigh. "Against my better judgment," he said. He nodded at the studio in the back of the apartment. "Show me what you got. You have fifteen minutes. Play for ten, I'll talk for five."

It took Ray a second or two to register that Oscar was, for all intents and purposes, auditioning him. "Thanks ... Thanks, Oscar," he said.

Oscar shook his head, amused at his own susceptibility to Ray's beat-up state. "Don't flatter yourself. Don't get carried away. I just want to see how a left-handed drummer plays with only a thumb and two fingers on his right hand and gimpy right leg."

So Ray played. Ten minutes almost exactly.

Oscar was silent for a while and then rubbed his chin. "Well. It's a little spooky what you're doin' with that right hand. But I guess it's working for you in some way. And it's not like you lost your timing or anything."

Ray was hanging on to these words.

"Yeah." Oscar was chuckling softly. But then he stopped as if it occurred to him all over again. "You fucking broke my heart! You broke Collette's heart too."

"I know."

"You broke Amber's heart. You remember Amber? She married a real asshole of a trumpet player about a year ago."

"That's not my fault!" Ray was beginning to feel the limits of his contrition.

"You sure didn't help."

"We broke up fair and square. It was a mutual agreement!"

"Yeah 'cause you fucked off!"

"C'mon, Oscar. Gimme a—"

"Give you a break?"

"What was I supposed to do? You think you should have married your first girlfriend or something?"

"Hell no!" And Oscar started to chuckle again.

Ray wasn't laughing. He was still feeling chastised. "You know if it's any consolation," Ray said, "I broke my own heart."

"Oh, I can see that!"

Ray hoped Oscar was finished with the reprimand. And Oscar was, pretty much, but he would never miss the chance in the future to just seemingly out of nowhere remind Ray what a jerk he'd been at eighteen.

"But realistically Ray, you're going to have limitations."

"I know."

"But I mean, hell, you could play with some rock band or blues band. You could still maybe be a half decent jazz drummer. Then again you might have been a great drummer. But we won't dwell on that."

"I want to write," Ray said. "I got some ideas. Do some arranging too. I'm taking computer courses. There's a whole area I can work with in there."

"That sounds good, I guess." Oscar paused. "So why put a lot of effort into this? You play well enough, if that's where you're headed."

"I don't know. I just want to get as good as I can."

"Feelin' a little guilty? Rightly so. You little shit!" Oscar started laughing and Ray laughed too.

"Okay. Here's the deal. You come once a month for six months. Get your chops back up to where you hit the actual wall. And you're gonna hit a wall. Believe me. You have to pay big bucks for the lessons though. You afford that?"

"Probably not, but I'll make it somehow."

"Samples from your workplace maybe!"

"Doesn't go like that."

"Still such a good boy. Apart from bein' a little shit. That's the army talkin' isn't it?"

"I don't know."

"You done much arranging? Composition? I can't remember."

"Enough."

"Okay. Interesting. Maybe some time you show me what you come up with."

\#

Ray sat on the bench admiring the Victorian architecture. He'd never been interested in conservatories — greenhouses that is — but since he was in the city, he thought he'd check out the Botanical Gardens. He wanted to know what he might hear in such a place. He knew they had a little tropical rain forest all under a glass roof. All sorts of exotic plants. He wondered if being tropical, such plants might shed more light on the guy who used to own Ray's property. That guy sure was in a bleak place. Ray was feeling adventurous. He wanted to know more. He also wondered if the mantis would show up again. He hadn't talked to it since that night of the ceremony.

It was a Tuesday afternoon and it wasn't busy in that part of the conservatory. He almost had the place all to himself. He closed his eyes and breathed the humid air. He relaxed and the sounds came to him. The strange rhythms. He thought he could even hear odd scraps of melody. With his eyes still closed, Ray turned his head from side to side and rolled it a little to give his neck a stretch. When he straightened back up, he realized he was staring into the eyes of the mantis again.

You've come to your senses, I see.

"Maybe," Ray hesitated at the notion.

Keep that doubt. It's good for you, the mantis said. *That man you worry about?*

"Yes?"

Don't.

"Why not?"

Not your business. And this! This, just this is so much more important. And the mantis cast its gaze around the gallery.

"Plants."

Always. The mantis raised its spiked front leg as if it were about to conduct an orchestra.

"I've missed you."

Now you're teasing me.

"It's all I have."

Yes. You're coming to your senses. The mantis paused. *Would you like to hear more of them?* And it pointed to the winding vines and leaves dripping down overhead.

"Of course."

You'll like this.

And then Ray heard a faint whistling that verged on a singing voice. It was the most humanlike noise he'd heard a plant make yet. And it soared above the clicks and all the other noises and bore the fragments of a strange melody. And then he heard a slightly different voice with its own beat and peculiar scale. These two wove together and then a third joined in, and a fourth. More and more voices kept emerging and adding to the complexity. Then he heard a rumble, a deep but gentle boom like a heartbeat. In no particular time at all, Ray was surrounded by the most astounding symphony he'd ever heard.

It's even better in the real forest, the mantis said.

Ray felt breathless. "I can imagine."

You'd like the old temperate rain forests too. Maybe even more your style.

"I should go there."

You have too much to do. Maybe later. You're going to be busy. Very, very busy. And I'd like you to meet a friend. The mantis moved aside and Ray saw before him an orchid. It was white and magenta with delicate stripes. Its petals flared out past the speckled orb that protruded from its center. Then it moved. Ray saw the head of it and the legs and the barbed arms that had looked like petals. Its eyes were vertically oriented. It was another mantis. For a bug it was amazingly unbuglike.

"That is stunning camouflage."

Thank you, the new mantis said. *And I'm glad you like the music. It's worth the immersion. A lovely soft focus to the ensemble. Puts all the pieces in view. And then there's nothing but surrender to the sway of it all.*

See. She's not just a pretty face, said the familiar green mantis.

"Well you certainly are striking." Ray looked at the orchid mantis and noticed how the color in its arms and legs was more startling than any magenta or purple he'd ever seen.

More beautiful than you can possibly imagine, the green mantis said, and then the mantises both looked briefly at each other and began laughing uproariously at Ray. He smiled. He was getting used to this. Whatever the joke was it was all fine with him even if he was the butt of it. The sounds of their laughter reverberated in the gallery and then melted into the symphony from the plants. The two vanished.

Ray tilted his head down, stretching the back of his neck again. They were still gone. He opened his eyes. The orchid that the new mantis resembled must be somewhere in the gallery. He'd like to know the name of it. He noticed he liked to know the names of plants now. But then he remembered something. The thing about the orchid mantis was that it didn't actually mimic any particular orchid. It was its own version of a flower, its own artful invention. And it worked. It was another of nature's clever knacks for surviving in the vast world of plants and predators.

Acknowledgements

This book is the second one extracted from a much larger project that began in 2015. Again I am very grateful to Beth, who was the project's original midwife.

The following beta readers kindly gave helpful feedback on parts that still managed to appear in this book: Anne, Virginia, Frances, Sonja, Iris, Brian, Sandra, Michelle, Ann, Michele, Barb, Dave, Teresa and Cynthia.

A very special thanks to Larry, Peter and Mike, who provided expertise on military matters, computing and HVACs, respectively. Any errors or omissions in these subject areas are overwhelmingly mine.

A special thanks again to Maureen, who edited some parts of the first project.

Most of all, I'm grateful to the people at Iguana Books for their editing, proofreading and production expertise, which brought this book to its finished form.

BCD

www.ingramcontent.com/pod-product-compliance
Lightning Source LLC
Chambersburg PA
CBHW031942010726
47493CB00007B/2034